The Finding
MACHINE

LUCY LYONS

TWIST HOUSE
B O O K S

Published in the UK in 2023 by Twist House Books
Copyright © Lucy Lyons 2023
Cover Art by Spiffing Covers

www.lucylyonswrites.com

This is a work of fiction. The characters contained within its pages are wholly imaginary. Any resemblance to actual persons, living or dead, is entirely coincidental. The Hertfordshire and Suffolk towns, although loosely based on real places, have been re-imagined to suit the convenience of the story. The opinions expressed are those of the characters and should not be confused with the author's own.

Paperback ISBN: 978-1-7393079-0-5
eBook ISBN: 978-1-7393079-1-2

"For there is nothing lost, that may be found, if sought."
Edmund Spenser, The Faerie Queene

1

— • —

FEBRUARY 1998, HERTFORDSHIRE

Our postman has two bad habits. Number one is calling first thing. Number two is pressing the bell repeatedly like we're a couple of OAPs who forgot to put our hearing aids in.

'You getting that, Alex? Alex?' my housemate yells from the bathroom across the hall. Antony loves a long, hot shower first thing. He also hates missing deliveries.

'I'm on it!' I yell back.

The bell shrills on. God, I regret giving the postman that fiver for Christmas.

Shivering in my pyjamas, I fumble round in the dark for the hall light-switch, wondering why I'm making the effort for what will probably turn out to be a pension pack or load of religious bumf from Mum.

I thump down the stairs, risking my neck in loose slippers that shoot from my feet and cartwheel ahead of me. From the bottom step, I leap across the cold floorboards to the front door mat, grab the latch and fling the door open.

The postman takes his finger from the bell, leaving my ears ringing. He's holding a brown paper parcel the size of a shoebox under one arm. It looks interesting, which means it won't be for me. I guess it's some tech thing for Antony.

Beyond the postman's pluming breath, orange streetlights shine in the dark. It doesn't look much like morning. Across the road, a woman bundled up in scarf, hat and long puffy coat walks her dog. Even the dog's wearing a coat.

'Parcel for Miss Alexandra Martin.' The postman sounds chirpy.

'For me?' Maybe, just maybe, it's something good.

'Sign here, please.' He hands me a Royal Mail card and a pen.

I scribble my name and swap the card for the parcel, which is surprisingly heavy for its size. Intrigued, I nudge the door closed with my hip, push my feet back into my slippers and read the label.

As soon as I see the *Priority Aerphost* sticker and *Eire* on the stamps, my spirit plummets. The address is written in my mother's hand. She writes elegantly, despite her penchant for using Bic biros. The cheap pen is one of her trademark cost-cutting measures - the result of an upbringing in rural Ireland. My mum was one of twelve, born slap-bang in the middle, sharing three to a bed until she was in her teens. She had to wait until the eldest boys left for the army or the church to get a bed to herself.

I hope the package isn't another Bible or prayer book. My mother has become fond of sending me religious literature. She seems to think if she cannot be here in person to guide me to spiritual salvation, she can do it by post.

I carry the parcel into the kitchen and plonk it down on the table. It can wait. I need a cup of coffee and some hot porridge to warm me up.

My housemate appears in the doorway as I'm filling the kettle, his short afro glistening from the shower. He's wearing posh, stripy pyjama bottoms with a towel slung round his dark shoulders. Most women and probably plenty of men would give Antony's muscular physique a long appraisal, but I ignore it on a daily basis. He likes what he sees in the mirror a bit too much for my liking.

We met through a Loot ad for a house share, after we'd both graduated - I scraped a 2.2 in Fine Art from Central Saint Martins while Antony got a first in web design from UCL. Neither of us could afford to stay in London, so we followed the train lines north until we stumbled upon Ware, a commuter town a short hop from London, nestled on the banks of the river Lea.

We rub along well. He's like an annoying older brother, and as I already have one of those, that's one too many. Still, we don't have any issues like dirty cups in the sink or toilet roll running out - things you normally get in a houseshare. If anything, he's the one who ticks me off for leaving grease on the hob or forgetting to clean the bathroom when it's my turn.

Antony pours boiling water into two mugs. Coffee for me, a ghastly chamomile teabag for him. When he's not prancing around with cups of herbal tea and quinoa salad bowls, he likes to try out the new fusion restaurants popping up all over the place. Antony is an interesting fusion himself - a sophisticated nerd with a Hackney edge.

'That idiot put me right on edge.' Antony squeezes the teabag. 'Did he superglue his finger to the bell or what?'

'I know! Why does he have to call so early?'

'Eight o'clock is hardly early. Just because we're a couple of lazy sods doesn't mean everyone else is.'

I suppose he has a point, but then neither of us commutes to work. Our offices are straight up the stairs and over to the desks in our bedrooms.

Antony tips his head towards the package before going over and examining it. 'Feels heavy. What do you think it is?'

'It's from my mother,' I break the news. 'So don't get your hopes up.'

'You should open it.' Antony passes me my coffee. 'I'll get the scissors.'

As a guy who likes everything just so - mouse central to its mat, fridge space with Tupperware boxes ordered like a spaceship cargo bay - not opening a package immediately upon receipt goes against the grain.

'No scissors.' I stand firm. 'I'll do it later.'

Gold star to Mum, though, for putting the correct amount of postage on. A first for her. Sometimes I wonder if she makes up an amount she thinks is sufficient, depending on what stamps are available in her stationery drawer. Usually, I have to pay Royal Mail for the privilege of opening stuff that turns out to be both useless and worthless. The last thing she sent was a religious calendar from the Knights of St Columba. That cost two pounds and forty pence to collect. I opened it outside in the street, then chucked it in the nearest bin.

The only interesting thing I've received by post within the last year is a Bob Ross art set which I won from a competition in the local paper. The set must have been sitting on a shelf somewhere since the eighties as half the paints had dried up. They were as out-of-date as Bob's perm, so I chucked them in the bin as well.

Antony comes alongside me and nudges me with his shoulder.

'Aren't you even a bit curious?'

I try and nudge him back, but he won't budge.

'Not in the slightest.'

Antony leans closer. 'Could be an inheritance from a long-lost aunt.'

'I don't have any long-lost aunts.'

'Could be a bag of gold.' His eyes, behind his rectangular designer glasses, widen in anticipation. 'It's heavy enough.'

'When has anyone received a bag of gold in the post?' I'm laughing now.

'You have to find out. Come on. Open it.'

'What if I don't want to?' I give him a friendly shove, ineffective, but satisfying. 'If you don't shut up about it, I might go and chuck it in the bin.'

'You can't do that.'

'I can. And I might.'

Antony turns away. 'Shoot me for being curious.'

'Look, it's probably a load of prayer books. I'll give you one to read. Then you'll understand why you don't see me jumping for joy when I get a parcel from Mum.'

'Sure, whatever.' My warning zips over his head.

While Antony prepares our bowls of microwave porridge, I go to the back door and stare into the barren garden.

The sky has lightened to the colour of lead. Leftover leaves from autumn spin in vortexes on the wet path. If I could, I would hibernate like a bear until the end of March, but reality means I must work and think of my future. I am one year away from the big three-o when the magazines say all your systems start going into decline. I must take better care of myself which means cutting out junk food and exercising throughout the colder months, no matter how much I loathe the idea.

Antony is baffled how I remain a size ten with all the rubbish I eat. I must have inherited the slim gene from Dad's side of the family, as Mum's always been a bit tubby. Although I've been lucky with my metabolism so far, it can't last forever. My internal organs could already be slathered with visceral fat.

I'm considering a long run to reverse my bad habits, when a blast of wind sends the laurel bushes at the back of the garden into a wild tussle. A high-pitched shriek forces its way into the kitchen through gaps in the back door.

Antony draws air in through his teeth as the cold reaches him. He throws his towel round his head and swishes the ends round his shoulders. The tasselled ends drape across his chest. He looks like a Berber prince. Or a model ready for a desert shoot. He would look good in rags and he knows it.

'I'm thinking of going for a run,' I say bravely. 'Do you want to come with me? You could think of it as a bracing constitutional.'

'No thanks.' Antony does an exaggerated stretch, casually displaying his six-pack. Actually, it's more of a twelve pack, with the extra talons of muscle coming round from the sides. 'How about *you* come to the gym with *me* instead? It's warmer.'

I tut and avert my eyes from his body. I make it a rule never to boost his ego.

Antony grimaces and turns away from the window.

'On second thoughts, I'm staying in. It's brutal out there. You go and enjoy your run.'

The microwave pings. He grabs a tea towel and removes our porridge.

'Better get on,' he says. 'I'm slammed with work.'

'See you on the other side,' I call after him as he heads for the stairs, taking his breakfast with him.

2

I finish my porridge and wash my bowl before returning upstairs with the parcel.

On the landing, disturbing noises come from behind Antony's door. Dull booms of gunfire accompany tortured groans and the sound of dripping water. It sounds like he's got a second job working for Satan. So much for his deadlines. He's having a sneaky play on one of his grim shooter games with the volume way up. Thankfully, the neighbours have already left for work.

I flinch as a malevolent roar vibrates through the floorboards. We've had discussions over his refusal to wear headphones. Antony says he likes to stay alert and keep an ear out, not that he would be able to hear anything over this din. It's a remnant of his upbringing in Hackney.

Despite repeatedly pointing out Ware is not as lively as Hackney and the only intruders we are likely to get are straying cats, he won't budge.

My room is at the far end of the hall. Although it is smaller than Antony's, the window is bigger and south-facing. My drawing-board is set at right-angles to the window to catch the light. My latest work in progress is propped up alongside my easy-clean enamel palette. I'm working from a photo I took at Athelhampton House last spring. It shows sunlight streaming through the fresh leaves of a pleached lime. Magical patterns of luminescence give it an abstract feel.

Casting a critical eye over my progress, I don't think I'm doing it justice. This is the problem with painting. Turning an idea in your head into an expression on canvas is a tricky business; something gets lost on the way.

My favourite painting hangs beside the door. I completed it for my degree exhibition, when I was optimistic about following my dreams of being an artist. Every time I look at it, I feel a little thrill. The long, panoramic canvas follows the twisting roots of an ancient sycamore tree. Lichen, toadstools and exotic fungi flourish where the light hits the forest floor.

Sometimes, I feel quite low about my art. Life after graduation hasn't turned out the way I hoped. I expected commissions to flood in once I started lugging my portfolio round to art directors across London, but I swiftly discovered it wasn't the golden field of opportunity I'd envisioned. Commissions were hard to get and editorial budgets were pathetic. This wasn't going to be a viable way to earn a living.

Fallback employment for struggling artists is restaurant and bar work, closely followed by temping. Eight years later and I am still temping. So much for the benefit of a degree.

The touch-typing I learnt at secondary school is my most useful and profitable skill. I don't have a formal qualification and yet it is the method by which I support myself. I suppose I'm the '90s equivalent of a '50s pool typist. The agency I work for, *Write On!* sends me typing projects by fax and audiotape, things like conferences that need transcribing, novels and lengthy musings by people who don't want to face their own handwriting. These include the reminiscences of the elderly, keen to pass on their life stories before they die. It's sad, but I guess these things often end up in the hands of grandchildren who never read them.

My workload has dropped off since Christmas but I'm sure it will pick up again in spring, the time for new projects and new beginnings. Things could be worse - I may never be wealthy and there is no career progression, but the deadlines aren't set in stone, and I can take time off as and when I need it.

7

The package makes a dull *thunk* as I put it on my desk.

I am saving up for a replacement car, so paid work takes priority over everything. My run will have to wait until later. So will my painting.

My plan is to get some work done, then head down to the river with my Kodak. The camera's got about ten shots left and I've been waiting for an excuse to finish the film roll. There haven't been many photo-worthy moments since Christmas in Ireland with my mum and extended family.

Once I've showered and layered up in thermals, jeans, jumper and a tartan snood, I tear open Mum's package. It's the work of seconds to rip the brown paper apart, revealing a *Scholl Shoes* box.

Mum's stuck her letter to the lid with sticky tape, no expense spared. She's used a single sheet of near-translucent airmail paper instead of a nice piece of Basildon Bond. Typical for her to try and save a few pennies. As soon as I start reading, I hear her soft Irish lilt.

'Dear Alexandra, can you believe it, I've only just finished unpacking your dad's bits and bobs. It's taken five years for everything to be done and dusted. Where has the time gone?

I found this in an old suitcase up in the loft. I think your dad is having the last laugh as I haven't a clue what it is. Himself up there has a great sense of humour.

I think he would have liked you to have it. You were always more technically-minded than your brother. I recall your dad making it a long while back from bits left over after he'd finished building the TV. You wouldn't remember the TV, as you were only four or five at the time, but I've photos in an album somewhere.

There's a lovely one of you and Matthew kneeling inside the empty set before he fitted the screen, you with your Sooty glove puppet and him with Sweep, pretending you're both on TV.

I hope you're keeping well and working hard. Remember, if you fall on hard times you can come home. There is always a place for you here. Love, Mammy x.'

A warm glow runs through me. I clutch the letter to my jumper, missing my mum despite her annoying ways. In her heart she wants the best for me. Best of all, she's sent me something that isn't religious!

It's something from my father.

I never expected to receive anything from him so long after his death. He fell while clearing leaves from the garden at the age of seventy-four, having been fit as a fiddle his whole life. Fatal epileptic seizure, the coroner said. It had come out of nowhere and there was nothing anyone could have done.

Dad didn't act or look his age. I never thought much about him being an older dad, as he was always so vigorous. Mum is fifteen years his junior; with the pair of them always on the go, age was never a factor. All I know is he went too soon.

Mum told me later, there was some history of epilepsy in the family. Dad's uncle, Stanley, suffered from it, so I suppose there could be a genetic connection, but when I asked for more details, she couldn't tell me any more. Stanley moved up north a very long time ago and Dad lost contact. No-one's left to shed light on the matter - both grandparents on my father's side are long gone. Vera died in 1971 from heart trouble, and Jack from pneumonia fifteen years later.

I have lots of photos of Dad in my albums, but my favourite sits on permanent display in a shell frame on my desk. It dates back to the '80s when I was in my teens. Dad's in the garden tinkering with something and Mum has surprised him with the camera. He has a handsome grin on his face and some natty sideburns. There's a twinkle in his eye.

He's wearing an awful orange cardigan with huge brown buttons that look like leather but were probably plastic. He wore that cardigan every day he worked outside, unless it was high summer.

I have my father's smile - my brother Matthew takes more after Mum, with redder hair and rounder features. I've got Dad's blue eyes and generous eyebrows

- more Brooke Shields than Frida Kahlo I like to think. My hair is lighter than Dad's, more chestnut.

Whenever I feel sad he's gone, I remind myself he had a good life. He followed his passion for technical stuff in his job as an electronics engineer and at home with ambitious projects constructed in the workshop at the bottom of our garden. He made a scale model of the Flying Scotsman, authentic in every detail. I never worked out how he managed to paint perfect circles around the boiler.

Another project was a miniature steam engine which he drove up and down the garden path at one mile an hour, with me and Matthew on his lap, screaming with delight and begging him to go faster. He was also a radio ham, in regular contact with the rest of the world at a time when few people travelled outside the UK.

Building the TV was a natural progression. Mum thinks I'm too young to remember, but Dad's creation was like Big Ben or the Taj Mahal - once seen, never forgotten. While our neighbours watched Happy Days on little plastic sets, our TV was raised high inside an enormous teak cabinet with shutter doors. It was good enough for royalty. The set sported five buttons when there were still only three channels. My dad knew about future-proofing way back in the '70s.

The buttons were a problem. Through some glitch in design, every time you changed channel you got a mild, electrical shock. In addition, if you got too close to the screen your hair would stand up on your head. You could smell an invisible fuzzy forcefield clinging to the screen, which crackled when you touched your nose to it. One thing's for sure, Dad's TV would never be allowed now for health and safety reasons.

Returning my attention to the package, I lift the lid off the shoebox.

A black, wedge-shaped block sits inside. It looks like a big doorstop, thick at one end and thin at the other. The exterior is made from cold, black plastic.

Lifting it out, I'm surprised at its weight. Maybe it's lead-lined or made from that substance that's supposed to be the densest in the world. I wasn't much good at Physics, but I remember an illustration in my 'O'-Level textbook, showing a balanced seesaw with a block of this stuff at one end and an elephant on the other.

It's strange, the way the machine retains its chill, like it's been stored in a cellar or an ice cave. I run my fingers over a ventilation slit on the right-hand side, where the cold is more intense.

On the plus side, it's not religious.

The thickest part of the wedge forms the top of the machine. My old LCD calculator is a similar shape. Dad's machine has another similarity to my calculator - a long display strip running across the top.

An on/off switch sits above the ventilation slit. I flick it up and down a couple of times, but nothing happens.

Below the display, where you would expect to find number buttons on a calculator, is a large, transparent square of plastic. An astonishing array of circuitry and electronics sit behind it - a smorgasbord of transistors, capacitors and other components. These must be the remnants from the TV. I wonder if they're the reason for the weight, being so densely packed inside.

Back in the '70s, they were extremely keen on colour-coding: the components are a decorative mass, like a pick-and-mix of exotic stripy sweets stuck together. If I were a child, I would be tempted to lick them. I suppose it's the reason Dad put the screen in. To stop my silly urges.

Below the electronics, near the bottom of the wedge, is a rectangular panel with an arrow moulded into it, pointing down. The same panel is on the back of my calculator and TV remote control. I use my thumbs to apply pressure to the arrow and the panel slides off, revealing an empty slot for batteries. Two sets of padded connectors have wires running into the machine. I recognise the connector type – they fit a square, 9-volt battery.

The last feature stumps me. A long slot runs along the top of the machine, above the display strip. Two strips of hard material sit inside. I gingerly take hold of one, making sure I don't force anything. The surface of the strip feels different to the body of the machine, like it's coated with fine felt.

The two strips fold up and out of the slot like windscreen wipers. They lock vertically in place, one on the left-hand side and one on the right. Each one ends in a plastic crocodile clip. Clearly, something's meant to go in there. It needs to be thin, as the clips only open a few millimetres. The distance between the clips is about ten centimetres.

I examine Dad's invention from all angles, including underneath. Apart from the on/off switch, there's no other way to operate it.

I have a rummage through my stationery drawer for a 9-volt battery, but all I can find are AAs and a couple of those coin ones.

For now, it will have to stay in its box.

3

The morning is slipping away. It's nearly ten o'clock and I haven't done any work.

After switching on my transcription machine, I boot up my PC and open Word. Once my headset's on, I put my foot on the pedal that fast-forwards and rewinds the audio tapes, and start typing. The conference I'm transcribing concerns the deteriorating state of the Department of Transport's main building. Bad concrete, apparently. The job should get an award for being the most boring conference in the history of conferences. It has turned into a brutal test of my ability to persevere, and I cannot imagine anyone else who would willingly face it.

I get paid per hundred words, so I put down everything, including hesitations and repetition. It's sneaky, but it builds up my word count, and at the moment I need every penny I can get. Scanning over the last few paragraphs, the discussion's stuck on whether the concrete is too rotten to save.

I press the pedal.

'... *the computer servers are located. You'll know if you've been down there how dark it is! [faint laughter] The storerooms were built after the second world war in response to anticipated threats from Russia. They were...they were, as I mentioned built to be bomb proof and even nuclear proof. Er...I...this will add immeasurably to the cost of demolition along with hidden asbestos. I will be moving onto hidden asbestos with a report from Mr. Harper following our break for lunch...*'

Joy of joys. I can't wait for Mr. Harper to get back from lunch.

········

A fter working solidly for two hours, I take my foot off the pedal, then leap from my chair.

I'm free! I stretch out my back and take a quick peek out the window, feeling a frisson of excitement as a shard of sunlight momentarily breaks through the clouds. A dramatic band of lead-grey sky in the distance threatens rain, so I make a snap decision to postpone my run and drive into town. I can always make up for it tomorrow with a longer run.

I head downstairs for a quick lunch of reheated fried chicken and some BBQ beans, hoping Antony's not there. Everything he eats is so healthy, it's awkward when I gorge on takeaway leftovers while he's sitting opposite, sipping a glass of wheatgrass juice or whatever the latest fad is from LA.

Unfortunately, he's in the kitchen, eating a ricecake with Marmite on it.

'Yo,' he greets me, heading for his cupboard to put the jar back, label facing out.

'I heard you playing your game earlier,' I say. 'I thought you had deadlines.'

'I confess. I'm addicted.' His eyes twinkle. 'It's not all bad, though. After half an hour of Quake, I'm so stoked that I burn through my work like fire across petrol.'

He draws his arm in an arc, describing imaginary flames blazing into the distance.

'Maybe I should borrow it.' I tell him about the concrete tapes. 'I need something to get me through this job. It's so dull, and I've got another three tapes to get through.'

'If it's so boring, you should try something else.' Antony washes his hands at the sink. 'With a bit of training, you could get into web design, back or front end, it's all good.'

'A bit of training?' I roll my eyes. 'You've got a degree in that stuff. I spend most of my day rewinding a microcassette back and forth. It's nothing like creating websites from scratch and writing in LISP or ACORN or whatever you guys use.'

'It doesn't work like that, now.' As he leans towards me, I catch a whiff of his expensive aftershave mingled with Marmite. It's an unusual, but not unpleasant combination. 'I'll let you into a little secret. We don't do the programming ourselves these days. We use pre-written chunks of code to build the sites. Things are changing, it's more design than programming, and I know you're good at that. Making things look artistic.'

I keep my mouth shut. I can't do his job. What is he thinking?

'You should at least become your own boss,' Antony adds. 'Loads of companies outsource admin these days. It shouldn't be hard to get the work, and then you can keep the agency commission for yourself. What does your agency take? Twenty percent?'

It is actually thirty. Although it's a lot, I think it's worth it for peace of mind and consistent work. *Write On!* never misses a payment, and they have a tried and tested system to get reluctant clients to pay up via their legal team. I wouldn't want the stress.

'I'm not like you,' I tell Antony, zapping my lunch in the microwave. 'I don't want the hassle of self-promotion, having to think of things I should do to make myself 'a presence.' I want to be able to stop at the end of the day and say I'm done.'

'Here's an idea. Why don't you do both?' Antony goes on to suggest I could do both my agency work and self-generated stuff side-by-side until I find my feet. 'You can start low-tech. Put a card up in the newsagents on the high street. Could bag you a decent income stream.'

He's making perfect sense, but what he's suggesting involves effort and change, when I like things the way they are.

'What about your paintings? Have you taken anything round to galleries, yet?'

'I'm thinking about it.'

'Why wait?' He flicks through his leather Filofax to a section with sleeves full of business cards, and pulls one out.

The Gallery, St Albans, is typeset in an elegant silver font on a slate grey background.

'I popped in last week, forgot to give this to you. They've got local artists on display. Your landscapes would fit in well there. I had a chat with the manager. She's more than happy to take a look at your work.'

'Thanks.' I make a suitable noise of agreement, tuck the card into my sleeve. The amount of effort he's gone to is shaming.

'I'll try and go this week.' I change the subject before he can give me any more wonderful business ideas. 'I don't suppose you've got any nine-volt batteries, do you? Those square ones?'

He shrugs. 'I'll have a look. What's it for? Has your vibrator packed up?'

A gasp escapes me. 'That's outrageous! What is wrong with you?'

A tickling sensation rushes up my collarbone. My cheeks are burning. I seem to be ridiculously sensitive to Antony's teasings, especially when it's anything to do with sex.

'I don't hav... it's not for anything like that!' I look away, wanting to fan my face or stick my head out of the window.

'Cool. It's just that one of my girlfriends had one, and it took nine volts. She threw it in the bin once we were an item. That's a fact.'

I cover my ears. 'La la la la!'

'You are so easy to tease.' He steps in and tries to lift my chin, tipping my head up to meet his eyes. He thinks he's got me, but I'm on my guard and swiftly duck out of the way. If he catches me, he'll only give me a head-noogie or put me inside a cupboard.

'In actual fact, the battery is for the thing my mum sent me,' I explain. 'You know, the package I got this morning?'

'You went and opened it already?' Antony sounds disappointed. 'What is it?'

'If I knew, don't you think I'd tell you?'

Antony shoots me a sceptical look. 'You must have *some* idea.'

'All I know is, my dad made it back in the 1970s. It looks a bit like a calculator, but it isn't. It's something else.'

'Thanks for clearing that up.'

'You're welcome to take a look. I haven't a clue. It could be a signal box for his old train set for all I know, or a transmitter for talking to aliens. I need one of those batteries to get it working.'

'OK, I'm Mr Intrigued.' Stirring his tea, he leans forward. 'Let's get this thing working.'

Just then, I hear a trilling upstairs. Antony turns on his heel. 'That's my phone. Hold that thought. Gotta go.'

· · • •• • • · ·

W ith Antony safely upstairs, I have my lunch and a cup of tea, grab my coat, scarf and camera and head for the great outdoors. I need to get my mojo back.

Even though I'm braced for the cold, I can't help cringing on the front step as gusts of arctic air scour my face. My breath plumes from my nose like dragon snorts as I run to my ancient, mustard-yellow Mini and throw myself into the driver's seat. The springs give little squeals as I bounce around, finding the ignition, pulling out the choke, getting the engine to rattle into life. The windscreen is misted on the inside - a wipe with my gloved hand leaves watery smears.

I turn the dials to maximum and get a blast of cold air in the face. My blind optimism that the interior will quickly get hot is dashed as I sit there in the cold. Gritting my teeth, I wind down my window to help clear the windscreen, shuddering. This never-ending winter can't last into March, it just can't.

My Mini is also suffering. I picked it up two years ago at a car auction because no-one else would bid on it and I felt sorry for it. My mechanic took one look and told me I'm the one I should feel sorry for, as the car's subframe is on its way out. Unless I want to find myself on the M25 holding a steering wheel with my legs paddling tarmac like The Flintstones, I'd better sell it on sharpish.

My shivers merge with the shuddering of the car. However much I hate the cold, I am trying to accept it. It is a new kind of thinking for me since Christmas. It is called mindfulness. From what I have read, I must accept where I am, knowing it will pass.

I stare at Antony's black Audi TT through the clearing windscreen. His car looks like something from the future with its sleek lines and body-coloured bumpers. When Antony bought it, he showed me the crumple zones and air bags, the multi-stacking CD player and full leather.

Not for the first time, I wonder why a guy like him is living with someone like me on the outskirts of a river town packed with retired people and young families, when he could be in a sleek London apartment, overlooking the Thames. I worry he will eventually move onto better things, and I will have to share the house with a stranger. I couldn't bear it. I don't want things to change. I like living with Antony.

I take a deep breath, close my eyes and find my Zen space.

The future should not concern me. Or the past. Only now.

4

— • —

An elderly gentleman comes up to me in the library carpark as I'm clambering out of the Mini. He informs me one of my brake lights is not working.

'I wouldn't sit on it if I were you,' he advises. 'In the dark, people will think you're a bicycle!'

He walks away, throwing his hand up over his head like a rear-flung salute. His observation prompts me to walk round my car with a critical eye. It really is on its last legs. The rear light in question blows every six months, and the front lamps are cloudy with age. Bubbling rust is advancing on the yellow paintwork from all directions.

I make a mental note to pop into Halfords on my way back for a replacement bulb - a good intention instantly forgotten as soon as I head down the River Lea with my camera strap wrapped round my wrist.

Pulling my hood up to shield my face from the stinging cold, I set off at a brisk pace, swinging my arms to warm up. I look for swelling buds or blossom to show spring is on its way, but the trees are barren frameworks, stark against the sky. Yet, despite the absence of greenery, there is beauty. White Victorian gazebos overlook the river, reflected in the still, dark water. Swans glide towards toddlers pushed in buggies with bread-bags slung on the handles.

The canal boats are moored for winter. If I were to commandeer one and follow the river south, I would eventually arrive in London. A commemorative plaque beside the bank celebrates Ware's former status as the malting capital of the world. The town used to send boatloads of brown porter to London, even during the Plague, and boasted the highest number of pubs per head in England. Quite an achievement for such a small place.

After half a mile, my breathing begins to labour. My weekend was spent lounging around binging on junk food and TV. The only exercise I got was second-hand – watching Sean Bean as Lieutenant Sharpe, hacking and slashing the French to pieces. I cheered him on as he rose through the ranks, all the while eating fried chicken and slurping red wine. Now, I feel the weight of my choices.

I pick my way around puddles, heading towards Hertford. The open canopy of oak trees frames the far bank. In summer, wildflowers and grasses flank both sides of the river, but all I see now are brown, withered stalks.

Town falls behind me as I keep up the pace, passing dog-walkers at a fair clip. Half a mile further, I step aside to let a group of middle-aged women of all shapes and sizes jog past, gobbets of mud flying from their trainers.

'Thank you!' one of the joggers calls back.

'No, thank you,' I mutter, realising they've splashed my coat.

They're yards ahead by now. Some of them looked well over fifty. Even the larger ladies were pretty fit. A wave of guilt hits me - I should have come out for a run after all, instead of driving.

Should have. Could have. I need to stop making excuses. Otherwise, where will I be in five years? Will I be like one of those joggers, fit and full of vigour? Or will I still be in my room in 2003, eating another takeaway and watching another boxset? God forbid I'm back round to watching Sharpe. I'd have to kill myself.

I stomp through a corridor of trees, following a long curve leading into marshland. The area looks as bleak and desolate as my mood.

The A10 bridge crosses the river ahead. Its legs are concrete monoliths covered in graffiti. As I head into the shadows, the sound of cars passing overhead is amplified into a continuous roar. I call this place The Noisy Bridge.

Above my head, vehicles cross the expansion gap in a rhythmic series of low judders and bumps.

My attention is drawn to the graffiti covering the supporting columns. Antony showed me an amazing book with loads of wildstyle pieces by artists like Seen and Cope. Since then, I've gained a deep respect for spray can art with its fluid lettering, incredible reflections, drips and highlights. Compared to the LA and New York masters, what I am seeing is a pale imitation, but then again this is Ware, not the Bronx.

Unclipping the lens cover from my Kodak, I photograph the best of the spray art and tags, carefully cropping out the teenage scrawl you see on bus shelters and bridges everywhere - *Sandra's a slag. Callum woz 'ere. I love Pete W. 4evA.*

Standing under the giant legs of the overpass, I take in the isolation of the spot as cars and lorries continue to pass above me, unaware I exist. It's a strange feeling: isolating, but oddly thrilling.

I'm not alone. Across from me, a small herd of fuzzy brown cows munch on a bale of hay. They make a soft visual contrast against the hard concrete and garish graffiti. I set the camera's aperture to F-8, my go-to for landscapes.

Click. Click.

I come into the light, moving so that I get the block form of the bypass against the natural landscape. It should make a dramatic shot. One of the cattle turns and observes me, its large eyes kind and docile. I crouch and get a shot of its head.

The sky darkens, threatening rain. I walk a bit further to the lock-keeper's cottage and the derelict house opposite. I take a picture, even though a van parked by the garage spoils the effect. Hopefully, one of these photos will be a cracker, the inspiration for my next painting. Photos often show up surprises, things you hadn't noticed when you took them.

At the next turn in the path, the view opens out to a sole oak tree atop a crest in the distance. Its skeletal branches are cringing from the wind, the trunk is bent and shattered down one side. I raise my camera and as the shutter clicks, I hear the distinctive whir of the film reeling back to the start.

The first drops of rain hit my coat.

. . . .

I head back to town, coming off the river path opposite The Saracen's Head. The pub sign's been painted really badly – it's obviously Sylvester Stallone in a turban. The pub sits at the end of an ugly 1960s block, matching the row of shops across the road leading to the train station.

By the time I reach the high street, the rain starts falling in earnest and makes loud spatters against my hood. I take a right past the old Maltings where barley used to be stored a century ago, now converted into luxury apartments.

Whatever the weather, the bustling Victorian high street always cheers me up. Shoppers hurry past, bundled up in winter coats and puffer jackets. The children are red-cheeked and zipped-up in snow-suits and wellies.

An old-fashioned bell rings as I open the door to Boots. I drop off my reel of film and request the 24-hour service. It's not cheap, but I want to see the photos I've just taken along with the rest on the roll. I buy a multi-pack of 9-volt batteries. Dad's machine is waiting for my return.

The rain intensifies as I hurry back to the car. By the time I get home, it's raining stair-rods.

The kerbs are lined with cars and vans, bumper to bumper. We're lucky to have a driveway; a lot of the Victorian terraces have barely enough space for the bins. Water cascades from our overflowing gutter like a makeshift water feature - one Alan Titchmarsh wouldn't approve of.

Splashing up the concrete path, I almost fall through the door in my haste to escape the filthy weather. After pulling off my boots, I hurry upstairs. Antony's room is silent for a change, which means he's either out or working.

Inside my bedroom, I tip the batteries out of the Boots bag. I get my dad's machine and slot one of the square batteries into the compartment, pressing the connectors on.

I flick the on/off switch.

Immediately, the LCD display lights up.

.

A green dot on a black background. Waiting for something.

After the initial thrill of success, I stare at it blankly, realising that's all I can do with it.

There are no buttons to press unless I want to switch it off again. I try walking the device round the room, lifting it higher and bringing it to the window but the display doesn't change. Back at my desk, I raise the two clip holders at the back and examine how they connect to the body of the device.

It is an oddity of a machine, with all its insides on display, especially when I compare it to my tower computer with its components hidden within a sleek, silver box.

What is this thing my dad made? Is it a sensor of some kind, like a Geiger counter? Maybe it's something completely of its time: a 1970s machine that counts the swirls in your carpet and tells you if you haven't got enough.

I look at the clip holders. Something must go there. I think about tubes of mercury or neon. Maybe something like that would run an electric charge across the gap and illuminate the fluid. I rummage through my drawers and eventually find an old mercury thermometer my mum bought me when I moved out. Other girls might get a bottle of fizz to celebrate their independence, but I got a medical kit and an article on resuscitation cut out of The Mail on Sunday.

I pinch the clips open and put the thermometer between them. It just about fits in there. I check the display.

.

No change.

I switch it on and off again.

Just a single, green dot.

How I wish Dad had demonstrated this machine to me when he built it. But I was only five at the time. If I'd asked, '*What does this do, Daddy?*' how would he have replied?

'*That's where the pixies live, Alexandra. They jump about inside the machine and, hey presto, you've got logarithmic functions!*'

I sigh and sit back on the bed. I have to find out what it does, or it's going to bug me forever.

5

It takes a lot for me to phone Mum. Usually I prefer to email her, as talking inevitably leads to probing questions about my religious life, or lack of it. Plus, the cost of calling the Republic of Ireland will eat up a lot of my wine money.

But in this case, the situation calls for it.

'Alexandra! Is that you?' Mum hollers at the other end, making me jump in my chair. I move the receiver away from my ear. 'Well, isn't it lovely to hear from you? Are you keeping well and being good?'

The insinuation is that I'd better be doing both. Not only has her accent become stronger in the three years since she moved back to her hometown on the wild Atlantic coast, but also her beliefs. And they were pretty strong to begin with.

Following Dad's death, she moved to Ireland to be with her family. The decision was easy. A huge gap in her life needed filling and with both myself and my brother out of the nest, moving back was the logical step.

I tell her I'm well and insanely busy with work. This is insurance, in case she annoys me so much I need an excuse to hang up.

'I got your package.' I get straight down to it. 'How come you only just found it?'

'Oh, you mean, Dad's thingamajig? When I moved back to Ireland, your Uncle Fintan put all the suitcases in the loft and I forgot about them. That's where I found it, you see, in an old suitcase. One of those ones you had to carry before they invented wheelie suitcases. Your aunt Camilla came over from the States last year with one that weighed three kilograms. Imagine that, three kilograms!'

'Mum,' I prompt, but she's lost to herself.

'Mind you, the romance has gone out of airports now. When your father and I were courting, he used to take me to Luton to watch the planes take off, and a fine day out it was too.'

To pass the time, I make grotesque faces into the reflection of my computer screen, which has gone to sleep. I don't blame it. As Mum gabbles on, I think about wormholes in time and space and how much easier it would be to step into Mum's lounge in Ireland, find the stuff I need and get back without her knowing I'd been.

'Mum. Look I need -'

'I'm getting there, Alexandra. So, I was giving the old suitcase a little clean before dropping it round to the Red Cross when I found your dad's thingamy. It was in a zip-up compartment, wrapped in brown paper. It was that heavy I thought it was a breeze block. And it was cold from the loft. Truth be told, I was pleased to get it out of the house. I thought I'd send it to you rather than throw it out.'

Thanks a lot, Mum. You thought it was rubbish and it gave you the creeps, so you sent it to me.

'So, what is it, then?' she asks. 'It looked like an odd kind of calculator to me.'

'I was hoping you could tell me!'

'Ah, I never paid any attention to what your father was doing in the shed with that soldering iron. He could have been making a load of bombs for all I knew! After he'd finished making the TV, he used some of the left-over bits and bobs to make other things. Nothing as good as the TV, though.'

Dad followed weekly plans from some Radio Nerd magazine - forty weeks to build your own colour set.

'It was marvellous to see what colour jumpers Val Doonican was wearing,' Mum goes on. 'It made a welcome change from accompanying your father down to Radio Rentals, I can tell you. He'd have stayed there all day annoying the salesmen with his questions. Given half the chance, he'd have taken the TVs apart in the shop.'

'Mum, do you remember the magazine Dad used to build the TV?'

'I've no idea, sorry.'

'I don't suppose you've kept any of his technical papers?'

'No, they were thrown out long ago.'

'What about any other plans for electronic stuff. Books. Folders. Drawings?'

'No, but I'm sure you'll figure it out, Alexandra.'

'Please can you have a last look? See if there's anything you've missed. He must have built this machine from plans. Would you double-check for me?'

'I'll have a look, but don't hold your breath.'

'Thanks Mum, I appreciate it.'

'You know, I was meaning to mention...our church has a wonderful group of young people. They're called Youth for Mary,' Mum segues into one of her favourite subjects. 'They go on coach trips and fund-raise and have get-togethers. Now, they're the type of boys you should be meeting, Alexandra.'

And here we go...

Mum's pet subject is my single status. Nothing would give her more pleasure than to see me hooked up with a nice Catholic boy who wants oodles of children.

'Does your church have a group like that?'

My church? What church? It's a worthy cause but a dreadful idea and the start of a spiral of lies I don't want to get drawn into. I've let Mum believe I'm a practicing Catholic for so long, I can no longer get out of it.

I think of my fellow students at art college. The dope-smokers, the tarot-readers, the ouija-board players, the Wiccans, the atheists. I doubt they went home for the Easter break and dutifully resumed going to church for confession followed by the Stations of the Cross, followed by the big Easter Mass. Yet, I did and have done nothing to let Mum know I no longer practice. So now, I am in a hell of my own making.

'Afraid not.' I say. 'There's no youth group at all.'

'Well, you should start one!'

'I'm already busy.' I swallow hard. 'Fundraising.'

'Who are you fundraising for?'

'The...Christian...breadmakers of Jerusalem.'

'Breadmakers in Jerusalem? I've never heard of them.'

Neither have I, but it was the best I could come up with.

'They sound a bit far from home, Alexandra. What you should do is start your own youth group. The Legion of Youth, you could call it. Just go up after Sunday Mass and do a little presentation. You never know, you might catch some nice young man's eye. You're never going to meet anyone the way you're going.'

I snort at her presumption.

'I'm meeting loads of people here, Mum. Don't worry about me.'

But the truth is, Ware is not the place to find romance. Not unless you're into pensioners or builders wolf-whistling out of vans. The good-looking guys are usually one of two things: either gay, or househusbands carrying their kids around in slings.

'I'm only trying to help.'

'Don't!' I feel a sudden flare of indignation at the idea. 'Look Mum, I didn't call you to talk about church and I'm on a bit of a timer.'

'Well, I hope you're not too busy to come and see me. My spare room is always ready. They have some cheap flights over to Knock.'

There's no point telling her I can't afford to take time off. She's on transmit, not receive, so I make a sound which I hope gives the impression of deep consideration.

Ireland is a place where nothing changes. While it's nice to get a warm welcome, I'd much rather spend a week in Sicily, soaking up the sun and eating pasta.

'When will you be coming over?' Mum demands.

'I'll have to check my calendar. I'll let you know.'

I stifle a sigh. I saw her for a week before Christmas, but in her mind that's ancient history. In fact, if I scuttled back and forth on the ferry from Holyhead to Dún Laoghaire once a week, it still wouldn't be enough.

'I'm really sorry but I have to go. Let me know if you find anything to do with Dad's machine.'

'All right. But don't leave it so long next time.'

'I won't, Mum, I've really got to go. Bye.'

And finally, *finally,* I put the phone down.

Mum and I are such opposites. She thrives in company and struggles to be alone whereas I love my own company and struggle in crowds. I'm much more like Dad. He was happy in his own space.

Every time I speak to Mum, I realise how much I loved his quiet solace, his aura of calm. He never made demands or expected things from others, he always took me as I was and let me follow my path. He never judged me.

I press my lips together to stop them trembling.

I miss him.

6

'Antony, have you got a minute?' I call through the door.

'Yo,' he replies.

I walk into a room that's so on-trend, it should be in a different building. Antony's tubular-frame bed is neatly made up with all-white bedding. The combination of rattan rugs arranged over the floorboards, linen curtains draped artfully across the window and dragon fern in the corner is very feng shui. His L-shaped workstation sports not one, but three monitors. A 3-D screensaver swirls across his PC screen. Both Mac monitors display webpages under construction, page layouts in Quark and DOS boxes full of computer code. It looks impressive; I wonder if his web job is just a front while behind the scenes he doubles as an intelligence agent for MI5.

Antony swings round in his black leather chair, lines of code reflecting across the surface of his glasses. I feel like I've stepped into a Bond film and met the technical mastermind.

'Not chainsawing pink mutants to death?' I ask.

'I wish. Got my work, then I get my play. This job's a good one, gonna make me some big bucks.' He rubs his hands together. 'I'm going to treat myself to a new iMac once I get paid, in Bondi Blue.'

I slip inside the room, my dad's device in my hands. 'This is the box of tricks my mum sent me.'

'Oh, yeah!' Antony's eyes light up. 'Your old man made it, didn't he?'

I nod. 'I wish he'd left some instructions. I've hit a dead end. I put the 9-volt battery in and switched it on, but there's only this dot on the display. Nothing else.' I point out the two clip holders. 'I don't know what goes in there or what they are for. I've tried a thermometer.'

'What did you do that for?' He shakes his head. 'I worry about you sometimes, Alex. Perhaps it's time to call the men in white coats.'

'It was worth a try!' I shoot him a glare, one hand on my hip. 'Have you got any better ideas?'

Antony takes the device from my hands.

'Jeez, it's heavy. And why is it so cold? Have you had this in the freezer, or something?'

'I know it's weird. It's been like that since I got it.'

Antony holds it out at arm's length and gives me a stern look.

'There better not be anything nuclear in here. If I lose my hair or my balls drop off, I'm going to dig your dad up!'

'He wouldn't have left it lying around if it was unsafe,' I say with more confidence than I feel. 'Besides, I've touched it loads and I'm all right.'

'So far.' Frowning, he puts the machine down on his desk and rubs his hands on his jeans, before examining it from all angles. He points to a series of small glass tubes amidst the mass of electronics. 'What are those things?'

'They're valves, I think.'

'Valves!' Antony's expression transforms from suspicion to wide-eyed delight. His look of wonder is what you'd expect from a child who's just spotted a fairy skipping across the garden. 'They're so tiny! Look at their mini rubber sleeves! Are they to keep them safe? And look at this soldering. Beyond precision!'

He scrabbles round in a drawer and pulls out a magnifying glass to examine the electronics.

'Wow! I am in awe of your old man.'

31

'Do you know anything about circuits?' I ask. 'You're the technical one. Can you tell by looking at them what they do?'

'I can't help you. This is seriously dated. You've got old school transistors, resistors. There's not a microchip in sight. And these black things, God knows what they are.' He runs his fingers lightly over the two straight bits sticking up from the top of the machine. 'I wonder what they're made from. They feel a bit...velvety.'

'Like antlers.'

'Used to feeling antlers, are you?'

'No...it's just how I imagine they feel.'

Antony returns his attention to the machine. 'I was thinking coated metal, like a powder coating.' He scrutinises the internal components. 'This thing may not be modern, but it is electronic. My guess is we need to find something it can read electronically.'

Now we're getting somewhere.

Antony plays around with the clip holders. 'These don't open very wide. There's only one thing I can think of thin enough to fit inside.' He rummages on his desk and comes up with a CD case, which he levers open. 'You may be a cassette kinda girl, but this is properly digital, designed to be read by laser.'

He holds the disk up to me. It catches the light, shining with a myriad of colours.

I feel my heart pick up pace. Perhaps he's really onto something.

'Are you saying my dad's machine's got lasers in it?'

'Won't know 'till we try.' He takes a moment to ponder the problem. 'You've made a good point, though. There's a pretty massive technology gap going on here. When your dad built this thing, computers were using reel-to-reel tapes for storage.'

'Maybe Dad was ahead of his time. Like that scientist who was in the middle of the electricity revolution. Tesla.'

'Nikola Tesla?' Antony pushes back in his chair. 'I've got massive respect for the guy. He invented all kinds of stuff, predicted mobile phones and TV way back in the twenties. He even drew plans for robots and laser guns. There's stuff he invented, people still don't know how it works.'

He goes to insert the CD into the device.

'Hold on.' I grab his hand.

'Chill, Alex, it's Public Enemy. I don't think it'll fry the system.' He points to the sleeve inside the jewel case. 'Way better than that rubbish you play in your room.'

'I like what I like. There's nothing wrong with Simple Minds.'

'Simple Minds?' Antony throws himself back in his chair and a great smile breaks out on his face. 'They got that right!'

'Not everyone wants to listen to your jungle garage, Antony.'

'What are you on? Public Enemy is hip hop! What's Simple Minds, anyway? No disrespect to your dad, but if it plays your stuff, he's going down one peg in my estimation.'

'Just stick the disc in and let's go.' I give him a glare. 'And stop being mean.'

Antony slides the CD between the square holders. It fits snugly.

We peer at the display as he flips the switch from Off to On. The display remains a resolute dot, even when he moves the CD around within the holders and pushes it down as far as it can go.

'Suppose that's not it,' Antony says.

'Or maybe Dad's machine doesn't like Flavor Flav.' I give him a smug look. 'Can we try mine now?'

We try a succession of CDs, both his and mine and then move onto DVDs, but nothing happens.

'I was right about the technology gap,' Antony says. 'We're going to have to go old school.' He swivels back to his desk and starts hammering instructions into his PC. His modem squeals and growls in the background as he connects to the internet. 'Give me a second.'

He flicks through a few search screens, checks there's paper in the printer.

'I'm printing off some Strauss,' he says. 'You like Strauss?'

'I'm sure I do. I just can't remember anything particularly.'

'My sister Trianne got to Grade 8 on the piano, she knows all this old stuff. The closest I get to classical is Star Wars. Or maybe Jaws. But she loved this piece, The Blue Danube. That's the only reason I know it's Strauss.'

'I'm going to tell your mates you like Strauss,' I tease him, as the laser printer whirrs into action.

'What happened to, 'don't be mean?'' Antony teases, as he whips the score of The Blue Danube from the printer and passes it to me.

As soon as I attach the clips to the bottom of the paper, the sheet folds over. I can't make out the score. It doesn't look promising.

Antony watches as I switch the device on.

Nothing, just the little point of light.

'It was a longshot.' I swallow back my disappointment.

'Perhaps your dad's machine never worked. Maybe he made it as an experiment. Or a prototype.'

'You mean, like those Top Trumps with electric cars, or the jet packs we're all going to use to get to work in 2025?'

'Something like that.' I expected a laugh, but Antony appears distracted. He pulls his jumper over his hands and carefully picks up the machine. He carries it to the window and holds it up to the light, turning it this way and that.

'Hang on a minute,' he says, peering closely at the machine's left hand side.

'What is it?'

Antony brings the machine back to his desk and works at the blank panel on the left hand side, pushing it this way and that. After a moment, I hear a *click*.

'Open Sesame.' Antony slides off the panel, revealing a dark recess.

I put my hand over my mouth, stifling a gasp. 'How on earth did you know about that?'

'I sensed something was off with the case,' Antony says. 'Your dad was so precise with everything else, it didn't make sense for the panel not to fit perfectly.'

'Is there anything in there?' I move forwards to the desk.

Antony puts a hand up to ward me away. He rummages around in his drawer and comes out with a pair of eyebrow tweezers.

'Let's play it safe until we know what we're dealing with.'

He inserts the tweezers into the dark cavity and explores the space. After a moment, he withdraws his hand. Within the grip of the tweezers is a small white envelope, yellowed with age.

'For you, Madam.' He proffers the envelope, lets it drop into my outstretched hands.

My fingers tremble as I touch the envelope. Residual cold from the machine seeps through the paper.

I open the flap. Inside, are four black and white photographs.

'Alex.' Antony gives me an intense look. 'Are you thinking what I'm thinking?'

7

— • —

Four old photos, hidden inside my dad's machine since the 1970s.

'Give me a moment.' My legs have gone weak. I flump down on Antony's bed and stare at the sepia discolouration creeping round the edges of the photos.

A weird feeling comes over me as I look through them, like a door is opening somewhere far away.

The first photo shows a lounge with a cast iron fireplace. An enormous wooden-cased contraption with metal swirly bits dominates one wall. It boasts switches and a centre console with a massive dial. I reckon it's a wireless. Jack worked in the RAF as an engineer during WW1, and Dad inherited his love for tinkering.

I recognise my grandmother Vera in a fitted check dress, her hair set in shiny curls. She's standing behind a little boy aged around three or four. It's got to be Dad. She holds his arms up with a fixed smile on her face, encouraging him to face the camera.

Dad's wearing shorts and a tanktop, proudly displaying a toy bus in one hand and a bi-plane in the other. I wonder if Vera always looked immaculate and wore her best at home, or if her slippers are hiding just out of shot. Dad's arms are a bit blurry. He looks a typical boy, full of boundless energy, unable to keep still as the shot was taken.

I do a calculation in my head - this would have been the 1920s at their home in Sudbury. I never knew my paternal grandmother, Vera. She died when I was young from a heart condition. Congestion, they used to call it.

The second photo shows my grandfather Jack, smoking his pipe in the garden. It's wonderful to see him young and strong. My last memory of him dates back twelve years, when he was in hospital. He contracted pneumonia following a hip replacement operation and died three days later.

Jack was very much a man of his time. Routine was essential, from set meal-times including elevenses, to his treasured pint down the pub before Sunday lunch. I got the impression he saved his best conversation for work colleagues and friends rather than family. Whenever we visited, he rarely addressed me unless it was to request something or state his views. However, he was affectionate to Matthew. He would ruffle his hair and chat at length to him and Dad about trains, new technologies and the state of the nation.

Vera's in this photo, too. She stands next to Jack with a broad, honest smile, holding a baby in her arms. The baby's dressed in a white woollen bonnet and long dress, Victorian in style. I can't see the baby's face as Vera is carrying him or her pressed against her shoulder.

Could this be Dad as a baby? It seems odd he's wearing a dress. Then again, I remember seeing Victorian portraiture photos in an old library book. There were several boys wearing what looked like dresses for their christening. Perhaps this is the same. Dad is wearing his christening gown.

Looking closer, though, I notice frills and ribbons round the neck and a large bow at the back. The dress isn't white, as you'd expect, but a mid-tone. So, if it's not a christening gown, the baby could be a girl.

But Vera didn't have a daughter. Dad didn't have brothers or sisters. He was an only child.

I turn the photo over. On the back is written: 'L x'

Of all four photos, it's the only one with writing on it.

Could Vera be holding someone else's child? A child with a name beginning with L? Perhaps she was holding the child of whoever took the photo. But if that was the case, it wouldn't be a treasured picture. Dad kept these photos safe for a reason.

I push my questions to the back of my mind. The next photo is sharper than the first two, and the whites are brighter. It's an outdoor celebration with lots of people smoking, flying streamers and Union Jacks. It must be VE Day. The flags are enormous. Vera and Jack are centre-front with their arms round each other. Jack's wearing a rare smile. The relief once the war ended must have been enormous.

Vera's other arm is round a short, stout woman with shoulder-length dark hair. She's grinning broadly, but the camera's caught her with her eyes closed. There's something familiar about her, but I can't put my finger on it. Behind the group is a long table set in the middle of the street, with a mass of kids sitting round it. I spy a few sneaky hands reaching for slices of cake as women patrol the table in housecoats and floral dresses.

The mattress sinks as Antony sits next to me.

'Mind if I take a look?'

I give him the first three pictures, pointing out who I know. The last one shows Dad, aged about seven or eight with a bag of sweets in his hand, outside a grocery store. An advert for Cadbury's Drinking Chocolate is stencilled on one window. Behind the glass are perfect towers of packets and tins. Racks of fresh produce are arranged outside the front.

Above the door, a sign reads: '*S. V. Martin. Tea Dealers and Provisions.*'

'Who's that guy?' Antony points to a face behind the door, staring out. Obscured by the glass, the man's features are impossible to make out except for two dark spots marking his eyes. Something about the intensity of his stare creeps me out.

'It must be Dad's uncle's shop.' I pass the last photo over. 'His name's Stanley Martin, but that's about all I know.' I put my hand up to my forehead and rub at my brow. 'This is a lot to take in. I've got brain-freeze.'

I give an apologetic laugh, rubbing my hands together to warm them.

Antony puts his arm round my shoulders and gives me a quick squeeze. 'You OK?'

'I wasn't expecting this.' I look at Dad's black-cased machine on the desk. 'It's not just an old keepsake, is it? It's got to mean more than that.'

'Are you up for trying this, then?' He brandishes a photo at me. 'Shall we go for it?'

'I suppose so.' My stomach gives a little flip. 'You do it.'

Antony places the photo of Vera, Jack and Dad in the machine and flicks the switch.

.

Just the dot.

Antony's forehead creases in puzzlement.

'I was convinced this would work. Mind if I try the others?'

'Be my guest.' I put my hand out.

One by one, he tests out the remaining three photos.

.

Nothing. From any of them.

8

I cannot bear to ring Mum again. Instead, once Antony's replaced the side-panel on Dad's machine, I take everything back to my room. After scanning the photographs into my computer, I draft an email to my mum, explaining what we found.

'*Do you remember these photos?*' I ask. '*Is this Uncle Stanley's shop? Who is the little girl? I think her name begins with 'L.' Let me know anything you can remember a.s.a.p.*'

I email them over. To be precise, I email them to her brother Fintan with instructions to print everything out for her.

My mind's buzzing. I'm so restless, I have to get out.

I jog into town, setting a surprisingly fast pace which I put down to nerves. Once I reach the high street, I stop at Boots and pick up my photos. By the time I return home, the exercise and breathing space has given me a much-needed sense of calm. I resolve to go jogging regularly, especially as I read somewhere that running in the cold builds character.

Back home, after showering, I take a look through the photos. The early ones are from my recent trip to Ireland. Mum looks happy in the bosom of her family. Each shot seems to have been taken in a different kitchen or living room. I will scan a few of the best ones and email them over.

My river shots have come out well, although the ones under the Noisy Bridge are a bit dark. The contrast I was aiming for, wild cattle against the modern graffiti, has worked. The image will be the basis of my next painting, but I don't want to simply copy the photo, I want to add my story to it. The portrait of the shaggy cow, with strands of hay and goop sticking out of the side of its mouth, would make a fabulous canvas print.

I flick through shots of friends I met up with before Christmas. The remainder are from Ware's Christmas Fair, including one of a fat sheep on a lead surrounded by a swarm of people. That one would look better in black and white.

Tucking the photos away, I get to work. The fax has been busy in my absence. Almost an entire roll of paper is spooled across the carpet. I pick up the first page and read below the *Write On!* header.

The job is a hand-written manuscript from an aspiring author who goes by the pseudonym Gerald W. Plucket. He has confidence galore in his book, *Where the Blood is Thickest*. He wants the cover letter, synopsis and first three chapters done as soon as possible. The rest of his novel is a priority, in case his phone starts ringing off the hook from publishers desperate for his signature on the contract for immediate publication.

After reading the first few pages, I suspect his publishing journey may be bumpier than he's anticipated. For a start, he appears to have created a brand-new multi-genre - a romantic comedy war horror.

'You will laugh, you will cry, at this timeless classic that's got it all: Nazis, werewolves, vampires, love and pirate treasure! It's the classic tale of hopeless love: she a beautiful countess, he a travelling jeweller, trapped in a Bavarian Schloss as the SS war machine closes in on them. Gasp as the shadows come alive! Scream as centuries-old vampires arise once more from the crypt. They want bodies, they want souls, they want to bite WHERE THE BLOOD IS THICKEST.'

I wonder if he's shown this to anyone other than his mum. Or maybe there's something I'm missing. It could be a work of genius and I just can't see it. Still, I feel a little skip of excitement. This is my favourite type of job and it certainly beats a bit of concrete.

I tear off the end sheet from the fax machine and fold the whole lot back and forth until I have a neat, concertina pile. Before I start work, I fax my agency an acceptance form.

The fax machine squeals as it makes the connection. As I'm waiting for the form to go through, my eyes go to Dad's mysterious device.

The two black holders stand up, their clips empty. The machine might not work, but something needs to go in there. Then it occurs to me - the machine would be a more fitting picture holder for Dad's photo, than the old shell frame.

Trickles of sawdust fall out as I prise the back from the frame and extract the photo. Dad smiles at me. I hold him in my hands for a moment, feeling close to him.

Even if it never worked, you should be close to what you created.

The clips hold his picture like a sandwich held within tongs, and without really giving it any further thought I chuck the shell frame in the bin. I shall be a slave to cheap tat no more!

And then, just for the hell of it, I switch the thing on.

52.039419 00.725435

I stare at the display with my jaw dropping.

Underneath, where the row of five LEDs was formerly blank and dead, the leftmost one is now flashing.

I must have shouted something out in shock, because a moment later Antony explodes into the room with his fists clenched, as if expecting to find a knife-wielding nutter at my throat.

'It's OK, I'm good,' I tell him. I keep forgetting about his triggers. You can take the boy out of Hackney and all that...

'Everything's fine,' I reassure him. 'It's just...I got Dad's machine working!'

Antony's stance softens as he looks at the machine on my lap. 'How did you do it?' he asks, his breathing still heavy.

'All I did was put in Dad's photo.'

'That all?' He frowns at the machine. 'That's what I did with those black and white photos, and nothing happened.'

'I don't understand what the difference is.' I shrug. 'But it's working. That's the main thing.'

Antony crouches next to me, peering at Dad's photograph held between the clips. 'Jeez. That's one hefty cardigan your dad's got on.' He touches his forefinger to his lips, staring at the read-out on the display.

'Those numbers, I'm sure I've seen them somewhere before. They're a code for something, but I can't think what. Mean anything to you?'

I shrug, my mind a blank. I'm struggling with the fact my dad made this thing so cryptic, but I suppose he had to work with what was available at the time. With only a limited LCD display, he's had to use numbers as a form of electronic shorthand. But a shorthand for what?

'I've got an idea.' Antony's hand starts tapping his leg. 'Do you trust me with this thing?'

'It depends on what you want to do with it.' I look back at him with growing alarm. A terrible thought pops into my head - the next time I see him, he'll have pulled out all its workings or electrocuted himself.

'I'm not going to mess with it,' he reassures me, pulling his sleeves over his hands before picking it up. 'I've got a contact over in the States. She's a coder, a serious nerd who lives life by numbers and strings. She's into multi-tier architecture and all that kind of stuff. I've got a hunch she can help.'

After a long pause, I give him the nod.

'Trust me, Alex,' Antony says on the way out. 'If anyone can find out what this thing does, it's her.'

· · · · ● · ● · · ·

Hi Matthew, hello from sunny Ware! I say sunny, but there's freezing fog outside the window, and when I went out earlier, I couldn't see down to the end of the road. I suppose the weather over in Seattle is way colder than here, seeing as you're so close to Canada.

I don't know if Mum told you, but she recently went through the last of Dad's stuff and found something he made back in the 1970s. It's really hard to describe and I forgot to take a photo of it before I got my film developed, so here's the next best thing - a drawing of it instead!

Basically, Dad made the machine from electronic bits and pieces left-over from when he finished building the TV. Do you remember anything about it?

This sounds crazy, but when I stuck a photo of Dad in his machine, it came to life! A load of numbers appeared on the screen. Antony's trying to find out what they mean, but if you can shed light on it, please be my guest.

We found four old photos hidden INSIDE the machine. I've enclosed jpegs. Do you recognise anyone, especially the little girl? Does she jog your memory? I was four or five when Dad made this machine, but you would have been nine or ten. Did you see him making it? Anything you remember, absolutely anything at all would be really helpful.

I love that I'm finding out new things about Dad. I never expected to, so long after he died. I mean, he was an incredible Dad, the best ever and he was so clever, but this machine is like a mystery he's left behind for us. I wonder if he planned it that way?

Love to Kate and to little Oscar. Let me know what he would like for his birthday and tell me all your news!

Love, Alex x

After I've sent the email to my brother, I force myself back to work, but it's a struggle. I'm distracted by Dad's machine and Antony's plans to decipher the numbers. I keep wondering what his American contact is going to say.

After numerous stops and starts, I manage to get into the zone, churning out page after page. Even when I stumble on Mr Plucket's sentence structure and questionable grammar, I put it all in. The only thing I alter is spelling mistakes.

Even this can be a minefield, as some writers prefer American English for a broader market reach. I leave words like *center* and *behavior* and change old favourites like *rhythm* and a mixture of *motes* and *moats*.

When Antony knocks on my door, I'm so absorbed in my work that it takes me a moment to respond.

The door cracks open.

'Can I come in?' Antony's buzzing, up on his toes. My dad's gizmo is in his arms, wrapped in a towel. 'My contact's come up trumps! You are going to love me for this. This is serious stuff and you need to sit down for it.'

'I am sitting down.'

'So you are.' He grabs my little coffee table and sits on the edge which is only a foot off the floor and makes him look ridiculous, like a dad seated in his child's primary school chair on parent's evening. I swivel round to face him and have the joy of looking down on him, a rare occurrence.

'So, what you've got here is a really weird type of GPS receiver.'

I give him a blank look.

'GPS stands for Global Positioning System. It's American, owned and managed by the US government.'

I open my mouth to ask what on earth this has got to do with my dad, but Antony puts his finger up to silence me. 'Just hear me out, OK? So, back in the 1970s, the United States started launching satellites. They started off with three or four and now twenty-four of them are watching over us. The US military use them to monitor all their planes and tanks and stuff, but you can basically find anything on the planet that's visible above ground going by altitude, latitude and longitude. All you need is the right software. America allows other countries access to these satellites so they can use GPS. We're one of them.'

Antony holds up my dad's device. 'The thing is, this isn't an authorised receiver from the States.' He holds up the device and turns it this way and that. 'My contact was very clear on that. Did your dad ever do any work over there?'

'God, I don't know. I suppose it's possible he worked abroad when I was younger, but I don't remember him doing it.'

'As far as you know.'

'Sure, as far as I know.'

I wonder if my dad picked up a set of technical plans somewhere, like the ones he followed in his weekly magazine to build the TV. Maybe there was another set of instructions for building this machine, along the lines of - *GPS weekly: Build your own Satellite Receiver in twenty-four easy instalments. The US don't mind!*

Antony's leaning forwards with the device held between us.

'I'm only asking because my contact told me the US Military can get seriously twitchy about unauthorised devices hacking into their satellite signals.'

I try to get my head round this.

'Are you saying the CIA are going to come after me?'

'Not the CIA. More likely, the National Security Agency. They're the ones who advise the President about security breaches, military threats and so on.' He sees my look of horror and puts out a hand. 'Hey, don't worry, you're only receiving the data. As far as we know, you're not trying to transmit anything. It's just we don't know how much the Americans are picking up.'

I'm starting to feel freaked out. The story Antony's telling is one of wide-reaching surveillance over a world-wide population, with one of the greatest superpowers behind the controls.

'Don't worry, Alex.' Antony puts a hand on my arm. 'They're not going to put out a kill authorisation against us or anything, it's just that 'coz we're not spies, we don't know if they know what we know. You get me?'

I have no idea what he's on about, and now all I can think about is kill authorisations. It triggers thoughts of men in black smashing my door down in the middle of the night, and rushing in to point their silenced pistols at my head.

'Forget I said that.' Antony puts the machine down on my desk and kneels in front of me, taking both my hands in his. 'Nothing's going to happen. Please, calm down. Your eyes are jumping around all over the place.'

I take several deep breaths. He is right. I am overreacting.

'Just tell me how it works.'

Antony gives my hands a squeeze before releasing them.

'In a nutshell, your dad's receiver picks up radio signals from the satellites. It needs signals from at least four satellites to work out where you are, or where other people are, plus the time delay. I don't know how he's done it, but his box of tricks can do all this from a single photograph. That's what these digits mean. They show the location of whatever's in the picture. Somehow, this photo of your dad has generated a location.'

'So, tell me, then. What's the location?'

'Well, I would hazard a guess it's this one.' He hands me a Post-it note.

I take the note and focus on it. My eyes start to go bleary the instant I read it.

St Gregory's Church, Sudbury, CO10 2AS

9

— ◆ —

'How did you get this?' I blurt. The corners of my mouth tug downwards.

'Hey, hey.' Antony puts an arm round my shoulder as my breathing starts to judder. 'I didn't mean to upset you. Just trying to show you it works. This is where your dad's buried, isn't it?'

I nod, as I don't trust myself to speak without blubbering. A weird feeling settles over me – was it intuition that prompted me to try Dad's photo in his machine?

'You OK?' Antony gives me a moment to get myself together.

I wipe my eyes and try to get a grip.

'It just caught me by surprise.' I give Antony a small smile. 'I guess if we can find my dad, we can use his machine to find other people.'

'As long as you can find your own way of decoding the co-ordinates,' Antony says. 'My contact used a classified tracking system to get this address for you. I called in a seriously big favour to get it, and now she's out.'

I grab a tissue from my desk and wipe my eyes.

'I don't understand why we can't use whatever program she's using?'

'It's classified, Alex.' Antony's look softens. 'And the computer she used is probably as big as this room. I'm not too hot on the technology, but she told me these two readings are latitude and longitude. It's a bit more complicated than that, but her mega-computer's positioning is accurate to about ten feet in any direction. Good enough to locate anyone, unless there's a load of people together, like in a mass grave or something.' He pulls up short and puts his hand on my shoulder. 'Sorry, I don't know why I said that.'

He looks down at my carpet, takes his glasses off and pretends to clean them. 'It's all right. Let's just get to the bottom of this,' I say. Even though I'm bewildered by the technology, I refuse to believe Antony's contact is the only one who can decipher the numbers. 'There must be another way of taking the readout and turning it into an address.'

'Maybe, but first of all we need to check it wasn't a fluke,' Antony says. 'We should test it with another photo, like a comparison test, and see if the numbers change. I'm thinking the black and white pictures we tried were too old to work.'

'Or...maybe they didn't work because they had more than one person in them.'

'That makes sense.' Antony nods. 'Let's test that theory.'

I reach for the Boots envelope and start going through my photos while he paces round the room.

'Could be your dad just built this thing for himself and it gives out the churchyard reading and nothing else. I hope that's not the case, but we won't know until we try.'

I flick through my pictures, stopping at the portrait of the cow by the Noisy Bridge.

Antony raises an eyebrow. 'You're joking, right? You know that's a cow, not a person?'

'All my other pictures have got more than one person in them.' I sniff, managing a small smile. 'It's because I'm so popular.'

'You're one crazy girl.' Antony gives me the eye. 'I suppose it's worth a try.'

Removing my dad's photo from his machine feels like betrayal and I'm worried his device will never work again. But I force myself to set him aside and insert the new photo in its place.

After toggling the On/off switch, we both peer at the screen.

51.779547 0.005487

'That's two different numbers!' Antony checks the post-it note to be sure. 'It must be a different location.'

'You're saying that's where the cow is?' I stare at the numbers, grab a pen and write them down. 'Antony, please can you ask your contact to help you again? Just ask really, really nicely.'

'I told you, she already broke the rules helping us,' Antony informs me. 'I kinda know where she's coming from. We could be feeding her co-ordinates to a militarily sensitive site.'

'What on earth does she think we get up to in our spare time?'

'Look, she doesn't want to end up losing her job or getting sued because of us. She's a definite no. We're going to have to do this ourselves.'

'Isn't there anyone else in your computer field? Someone who's good with codes?'

'I'm a graphic designer, not a NASA scientist. This is military grade. You're talking about complex, top secret technology combined with world mapping. I can't think of anyone.' He draws in a sharp breath. 'Hang on, Alex. I saw one of the numbers change, I swear it. The last number changed!'

He double-checks the last number with the one I wrote down. They are different.

'This is extreme.' Antony's pointing at the machine, as if I'm in any doubt where the drama is coming from. 'It's doing it in real time! It's tracking that cow!'

I've never seen him so rattled.

'This is way over my head. I mean, how is it following the location from a photo? Where is the data coming from? It's just a photo!' He gets up and resumes pacing, hands linked behind his head. 'Unless your old man was working for MI5 and they found some way of implanting invisible trackers inside all our photos. But then they'd have to put receivers inside of us, without anyone knowing, like something from Bladerunner.' He looks at me in shock.

'What if we've all got tiny microchips implanted inside our bodies, sending out permanent beacons to all those satellites in outer space?'

He looks at me, waiting for my reaction.

'I've never seen Bladerunner.'

'Seriously?' Antony's tone is full of disbelief. 'But it's one of *the* all-time classics! No ifs, no buts, Alex, we're going to watch it together. You can't go around with these gaps in your cultural education. Just take it as fact - that film was way ahead of its time, like your dad's machine.'

He runs his hands over his tight-cropped hair.

'Maybe I'm wrong about implanted micro-chips and scanners, but I do know the US, Russia or any government would love to get their hands on this. Think about it. You could get a hit on enemies of the state anywhere in the world with just a photo. We need to be careful what we do with it.'

Antony's line on conspiracy theories sounds so far out, I can't get my head round it. I look at the photo of the cow, thinking of an old propaganda poster from World War II – *'loose lips sink ships'*. But it is just a photo of a cow, and unless we get a fix on its position we can't prove the machine works with any photo.

'I don't think the Russians are after a cow,' I point out. 'We should be safe with it.'

But Antony's still tied up in conspiracies.

'The market for this thing, it's out of this world,' he whispers. 'You could make millions if you handle it right, but if you do it wrong you could end up...' He shakes his head. 'Let's not go there.'

I put my hand out to calm him before he transfers his jitters onto me.

'Don't you think you're jumping the gun a bit? To date, we've got the location of the graveyard where my dad's buried, and the possible location of a local cow. And the cow's just a hypothesis at this stage, by the way. We don't have a way to find it.'

'I'm just saying, we need to be careful. Let's keep this strictly between you and me, OK?'

'All right, but you've got to stop with the conspiracy theories.' I push away from the desk, chewing the end of my pencil. 'Let's prove it works, first. Then, we decide what to do with it.'

At the moment, that might be any number of things, from putting it inside a display case on my desk, laying it to rest alongside my father, or blowing it up.

Until I find a way of translating the latitude and longitude co-ordinates into a physical location, I may as well stick it back in my drawer.

10

—— ◆ ——

The next day, I have a deadline to complete the first chunk of Gerald W. Plucket's Nazi-Vampire masterpiece. I work on it all morning and end the session by proof-reading my transcription and emailing it to the agency. After a quick lunch of a cheese and crisp sandwich with a banana, I get stuck into the next round of chapters. All the time, I'm painfully aware I'm throwing myself into work to distract myself from the elephant in the room. I can't offload on Antony because he's locked himself away in his room, preparing for a trade exhibition at the NEC in Birmingham in two weeks' time. He's booked a stand at considerable expense in a bid to expand his business.

I have more than enough to keep me busy and we do not run into each other all day. By late afternoon, I've had enough. My eyes are blurry from hours spent staring at a computer screen and I've got lower back-ache from sitting for so long.

I grab my coat and bag and take the Mini into town for a change of scenery. Under the fading light, a number of cars have their headlights on. Through the windscreen, the glare from passing vehicles reflects in standing water on the road.

The lights on the pedestrian crossing outside Tesco turn from amber to red. The driver in front stops, keeping her foot on the brake. The array of brilliant red lights remind me - I never got round to fixing the brake light on my Mini. Hertford police station is just round the corner, and patrol cars regularly drive down the high street. If they stop me, I'll get a fine.

There's no time like the present. I turn right off the next roundabout, heading for the Halfords autostore on the industrial estate at the edge of town.

The store is quiet so late in the day, with only a handful of customers browsing the shelves. A familiar smell of engine oil mixed with rubber hits me as soon as I enter. I quite like it, but I wonder if it's good for me. Hip-hop music plays a little too loudly on the far side of the store. I spy a couple of store assistants walking about – waiting to pounce.

I slip down the windscreen wiper aisle to avoid them, the music masking the squeak of my trainers on the shiny floor.

The parts directory is at the far end of the aisle. It's the Halfords Bible of automotive parts, listing items for every car sold in the UK since the 1960s. It's thick as five Yellow Pages stacked together, attached to a metal shelf by a heavy-duty chain threaded through its spine. This security measure seems over the top - why anyone would want to run off with it is beyond me. Even if you had a valid reason for wanting to steal your own Halfords directory and had the foresight to bring a bolt-cutter to get through the chain, you'd still need to be a professional weightlifter to lug it out the door.

I find the right part for my Mini somewhere in the middle of the catalogue, page seven hundred or thereabouts. As the bulbs on my car fail regularly, I've learnt how to fit them myself. I decide to buy a couple in case the other brake light goes, although I'm not sure which will go first – the bulb or the car.

On my way to the till, the thumping music catches my attention, and I take a diversion towards the in-car entertainment section. After ogling the set-up in Antony's Audi, I'm determined to get something similar for my next car. Besides, no-one's around to stop me dreaming.

The hip-hop booming from Sennheiser speakers is raucous in content as well as volume. I'm pretty sure the manager must be absent, with the f-word thundering from the subwoofer at a volume that makes my jaw vibrate when I put my hand on it.

A console sits in front of the bank of stereos. You can press various buttons to play the music through various set-ups. My mind boggles at the price of a Blaupunkt six-speaker set up, but I can't deny the sound quality is amazing. I press buttons one after another and am having so much fun, I don't notice the sales assistant sidling up alongside me.

'Can I help you, madam?'

His label reads: *I'm Brad. We Go the Extra Mile.* With his fresh-faced smile, he looks not a day over sixteen. Once I've established I'm just browsing and my current car is worth twenty pence, the spark fades from his eyes. Feeling guilty for wasting his time, I tell him my housemate is thinking of upgrading the stereo in his Audi TT.

Brad perks up again, pointing to a Sony scrolling multi-coloured text across its display.

'This is a great unit. It comes with a six-CD multichanger unit that goes in your boot. It's all set up for Digital Radio.' He points at a symbol on the display: DAB. 'With DAB, you get a clearer sound than your analogue FM signal. You won't get any static. And you'll see the name of the radio station scrolling across the display. Even the song that's playing. You'll be able to pick up indie channels, so there's something for everyone. What kind of music does your housemate like?'

'Oh, he loves Simple Minds.' I smirk at the small victory. As the assistant drones on, his stream of tech talk gets me thinking.

'Hey, Brad, do any of these units have GPS? I hear that's a new thing coming over from the US.'

Brad looks perplexed. 'GPS? I don't know anything about it.' His brows lift slightly as something occurs to him. 'But I know someone who can help. Tim. I'll go get him.'

At my encouraging nod he heads off and comes back after a few minutes with a beanpole of a guy about my age, with a receding hairline and a lanyard round his neck which reads – *I'm Gus. Ask me about In-Car Entertainment!*

'Hi...Gus,' I say cautiously, remembering the name Brad called him. 'Or should I call you Tim?'

Gus gives me a short laugh. 'T.I.M.'s an acronym. It started off as a joke but now I'm stuck with it. It stands for The Ice Man. You know, I.C.E.?'

I stare at him blankly.

'In Car Entertainment,' he explains.

'ICE. Yeah, Now I get it.' I fight the urge to roll my eyes. 'Brad tells me you're an expert in all the latest tech. I need someone to explain GPS to me. Can you do that?'

His smile widens and he rubs his hands together.

'How long have you got?'

········

I return home with a spring in my step. My Mini's sporting a new brake light and I've got a diary full of notes. Gus knew stuff far beyond his usual remit of car stereos. He flooded my mind with bewildering terms: differential GPS, reverse geocoding, geographic information systems and geospatial data; an encyclopedic amount.

In the end, I wound up with brain freeze and begged him to start again from the beginning.

As I couldn't take Gus home with me, I resorted to scribbling everything down in simple terms Homer Simpson would understand, so I could make sense of it later. We went back and forth a few times, but eventually we got there regarding longitude and latitude.

Gus told me GPS receiver kits for the general public were new, even in the States, and prohibitively expensive. Satelite Navigation Systems for cars were available in limited options, called Satnav for short. Well, beam me up Scotty! Gus told me you could get one for your car and program in a location that would change in real time as you travelled towards it.

All those times I'd been lost down a B-road with the red light flashing on my petrol gauge would be history. There was just one problem. At the moment, there were only a handful of cars available with Satnav, and I wasn't going to be importing an American left-hand-drive Toyota for $40,000 just to get hold of one. Not that it would be any use to me anyway, as there's no UK coverage. Major drawback, USA maps only.

Back home, I re-read my notes before booting up my PC. As the computer grinds away, I get my dad's machine from its drawer, reinsert the picture of the cow and switch it on. I make a careful note of the digits.

I click on the modem icon to connect to the internet. After a distinctive string of clicks, warbles and electronic shrieks, the Alta Vista search engine comes up. I scan my scrawled notes for the website Gus gave me, then enter the address into the search bar.

www.geospatialdata.co.uk

I keep my fingers crossed while I'm waiting, hoping and praying this will be the answer to my prayers.

After a few moments, the webpage loads. I clap my hands in delight.

Following Gus's instructions, I choose Decimal Degrees, click the tick box and enter the co-ordinates of the photo. Then, I hit the button labelled *Find My Location*.

It's beautiful and simple. Within thirty seconds, a map appears in fractured stages to show the River Lea close by the Noisy Bridge where I originally saw the cow, just a bit nearer Hertford. A pointer in the shape of a white, gloved hand points to an expanse of green at the top of my screen. The hand is so large it obscures part of the map, but I've got the result I wanted.

Zooming in, a tag appears, *Hertford Marshes*.

I double-check the finding machine to ensure the numbers haven't changed since I last looked. The last digit of latitude flickers. I input the new co-ordinates but the pointer stays where it is. The minor change in location is probably beyond the sensitivity of the software, but it's awesome to be able to watch the cow move in real time. It is like being a spy, without any risk.

I shut down my PC and jump back in my car, gunning the Mini down the hill and back to the riverside car park. It takes twenty minutes of fast walking to get to the Noisy Bridge. There are no cattle here and no signs of any fodder.

Adrenaline makes my heart pound as I hurry under the bridge and continue to the green expanse I saw on my computer. The ground is dull and brown rather than green, but pied wagtails and robins flit along the verges of the towpath. In the distance is a group of shaggy cattle, chewing on bales of hay.

I hop up and down and laugh to myself. I can't help it.

I'm buzzing. At long last, the machine is revealing its mysteries to me. It works! I can't be one hundred percent sure if it is the exact cow I am looking at, as there are several grazing together, but I am going to assume it has done the business.

What on earth were you up to, Dad? This is amazing!

Tingles of excitement zing through me. Deep down, my nerves are frazzled at the unknown path I'm treading. The journey back to my car passes in a haze – as though I'm being carried along the path by my new discovery. What a gift for my dad to have left me. I wonder if he used it while he was alive, if he had a secret agency finding lost people. There must be more to the story, and if only my mother hadn't turfed all his papers out, I might know exactly how it came about and what he used it for.

My dad's dead, but his machine found him. The cow's alive, and was also found. I can't get my head round this. Is it possible this machine can locate *any* animal or person, alive or dead, from a single photo?

Thinking through questions that remain unanswered, I nearly walk into a mum with a toddler as I take a direct line to my car. After apologising profusely, I sink into the driver's seat and attempt to calm down.

It's ten minutes before my hands stop shaking on the wheel.

11

⸻ ◆ ⸻

The following Saturday morning, the weather finally takes a turn for the better with the advent of March. I have been taking regular runs down the river, which are more bearable now spring has arrived. One big plus - I'm getting fitter.

I jog home through residential streets, ducking under cherry trees heavy with pink blossom. Buds are swelling on every tree and hedge, and sparrows chirp in the hedges. Sunshine transforms the scene and warms my face, promising an end to a long, hard winter. I pick up my pace for the last leg as finches and robins flit across my path in search of nesting materials.

I run past Victorian terraced houses with ornate, tiled porches and stained-glass panels. As I slow to cross the road, looking carefully for speeding drivers, something catches my eye.

A poster is taped to a lamppost on Bowling Road. I stop to read it.

MISSING. House cat – Sebastian. Bengal with leopard spots and white tip to his tail. Not used to being outside. Missing since 26th February. Please check your gardens, garages and outhouses. £100 reward.
Nina 01632 965221.

I study the large photo above the description. Sebastian is one of those gorgeous, designer breeds that are so popular these days. With his spectacular markings and large amber eyes, he looks like a miniature leopard. Where has he got to?

I stare at the poster, chewing the inside of my cheek. Nina must be worried. After a quick look over my shoulder to check no-one about, I peel away the tape and take the poster home.

Something's come over me and I don't know whether to give in or resist it. Back at my desk, I consider what I am about to do. I go back and forth between calling Nina and doing nothing until I've driven myself mad. Finally, I make a decision.

The phone rings a few times before it's picked up.

'Hi, is that Nina?'

'Who is this?' The female voice on the other end sounds confident, young.

I tell her I have seen her poster.

'Oh, have you found him? Have you found Sebastian?'

Quickly, I admit I haven't, but I wanted to know if she was still looking.

'He's not back, if that's what you mean. I've heard nothing.' Desperation tinges her voice. 'I think someone could have taken him. He's a house cat, but I left the back door open when I was putting the bins out and he made a run for it. It was pitch dark, so there was no chance of finding him. Someone told me to put his litter tray outside as cats can smell it from over a mile away. I've done it all week.

'Even if the worst has happened, I just want to know. I've heard the same story three times now about cats coming back a month after running off, but Sebastian doesn't have any road sense or knowledge of the area. If he's lost, he won't know where home is.'

She tells me where she's living, a few streets away.

'I'll keep my eye out for him.' I add that I'll make sure I check my shed and tell our neighbours. Nina mumbles a farewell, and after I've put the phone down, I take my scissors and cut out the picture of Sebastian. The photo's too large for the finding machine, so I scan it into my PC at the highest resolution available and resize it to 6 by 4 inches, a standard photo size.

I insert a sheet of photo paper into my printer and, after five minutes, have a useable image. In the time it takes for the ink to dry, I get a cup of tea and go online. I insert the photo into the finding machine with shaking hands and switch it on.

51.808535 -0.016277

The figures take my breath away. I pace round the perimeter of my room, my nerves shooting. Staring out of the window helps bring my heartrate down. Once I've mastered my nerves, I look at the readout again.

I wish I had a clue what geographical area the numbers represented. As it is, I'm helpless without referring to the geospatial website. Sebastian could be next door or in Inverness. I resolve to make a list of the latitude and longitude coordinates for key places round Ware so I have a frame of reference for locations when the numbers come up on the display.

Beneath the digits, two of the five LED lights are solid red. I don't know what that means, but I hope it's a function my dad put in to help the user, and not a sign some parts have packed up or are in error mode.

The geospatial website takes so long to load, I end up swearing at my computer. I'm going to need anger management therapy if I have to go through this palaver every time I need to find anything.

Once the menu screen's loaded, I type in the co-ordinates and wait for the website to do its work.

If the location's miles away, I'll know Sebastian either hitched a ride in a car or was catnapped. I can't help Nina if that's the case because how can I explain what I know – unless I say I'm working undercover for the RSPCA? But in my experience, lying always comes back to bite you on the bum.

Why does it have to be so complicated? I haven't even found her cat yet!

I peer forward as the page comes up. The image fractures as it zooms in.

A sudden breath escapes me. It's local. In fact, it's a green space less than a mile from me, where the edge of town meets the countryside. A white finger points to the place on the map.

Zooming in, I see Sebastian is in the top righthand corner of the green space. I put my hand to my neck and feel the vein pounding.

I stare at the finger on the map for so long, I can see it behind my eyelids when I blink. I rub my eyes, take another look at the display on the finding machine. The digits haven't changed.

Sebastian is not moving. Not a good sign.

What if he's dead?

I have to know.

I print out the map, tuck the finding machine into my rucksack and head for the door.

12

A brutal gust hits me the moment I open the front door. Winter's back, which means reinforcement clothes. Swiftly, I dash back to my room to change into full thermals with a jumper and a padded coat on top, topped off by my tartan snood.

Suitably kitted out, I head down the road with a determined step. Before I reach the corner that turns into Little Widbury Lane, I turn my back on the wind to tug the bottom of my snood over my nose and mouth. My face is warmer, but my breathing becomes muggy and uncomfortable. A balaclava would be more suitable for this weather, but I don't want to look like a terrorist or a bank robber. It's such a shame that something so well designed is so un-PC. Perhaps I could knit one in pink and see how that goes.

Past the rows of 1960s semis, Little Widbury Lane narrows into a one-way street. Large, detached houses overlook a steep drop across the woods on the right-hand side. The view is epic, but all I can think of is Sebastian.

At the end of the lane, the B1004 crosses the junction. The road rises into the countryside to my left, and disappears over a tree-flanked crest. A lonely looking Total petrol station sits across the road. I can't imagine it gets much business in this no-man's land between town and country.

A rough track, half-hidden behind a leaning oak, leads off to the left of the petrol station. I've never noticed the track before.

A few cars come flying down the hill into town. Once it's safe, I dash across the road. The geospatial map showed the track leads to a large green area where, hopefully, I will find Sebastian.

A display board with a hinged, glass frame stands in the grass verge. The wood is weathered and flaking and looks like it has been in situ for years. **Green Lane Allotment Society** is inscribed into a wooden panel at the top. Various notices hang within the case, most of them yellowed and illegible.

There's not much to see past the display board except a chain-link fence tangled with grass and dead briars. A side-gate sits a little way down the track, bolted and locked with a combination padlock. I don't fancy clambering over it if it turns out there's another, easier way in further down.

At first glance, the allotments look barren and neglected. But there are signs of life around the perimeter - trees limned green with emerging leaves.

As I walk down the deserted track, the sound of traffic is replaced by the lively chatter of birdsong. I wonder if bird activity tempted Sebastian here. The promise of a warm, feathered body in his jaws, after a year or so of chasing feathers on sticks, must have been impossible to resist.

Muddy trenches in the track bear tyre-impressions. If vehicles are coming down here, there must be another way in.

With no-one around, I slip the rucksack from my shoulder and unwrap the finding machine from a thick bath towel, feeling its innate cold penetrate my gloves.

Flicking the switch, the location hasn't changed. But now, three solid red lights are showing, the fourth is flashing and the fifth is still off. If the lights are proximity locators, I must be going the right way.

I press on, glancing down at the display from time to time while splashing through mud.

The allotments cover a huge area. From a rough calculation, there must be hundreds of plots covering the site. I carefully peer through the fence as I walk along, wary of being spotted by solitary, old men tending their plots with their

64

radios on and their caps pulled low. But the old men are nowhere to be seen; instead, a trio of middle-aged women in wellies chat as they work the soil. Further down, a mum battles the weeds while her toddler puts stones in small piles. In the distance, a group of teenagers wearing thick, green fleeces gather round an older instructor who points to the earth with his trowel.

Finally, the road opens out into a rough, parking area with several mud-spattered vehicles parked alongside the trees. Opposite is a metal five-bar gate pushed back to the post. A sign tied to it with string states: *Trespassers will be Prosecuted.*

A pick-up truck sits inside the gate, emblazoned with the logo of Hertfordshire County Council - a stag on a green background. Beyond the truck, a large Swiss chalet-style hut dominates the clearing. A second noticeboard planted outside the door displays crisply printed notices. I have found Green Lane Allotment Society HQ.

Two men wearing fluorescent yellow tabards bearing the council logo drink tea beneath the porch and chat to a tall, balding man inside.

None of them are looking my way, and I slip inside the gate unobserved. The plots at this end of the site are the best maintained I've seen so far. Each one is fenced-off with posts strung with rabbit-proof wire, containing weed free, neatly tilled rows. Early vegetables sit in the soil, waiting to be harvested. I recognise leeks and cabbages amongst the leafy greens. Everyone knows a cabbage.

My route takes me past a large metal water tank with hosepipe snaking from its tap. Several balls float on the top of the water. The perimeter fence is visible beyond the last two rows of plots.

A quick check of the finding machine shows four red lights and the last one is now flashing at the same speed as my heart.

Re-wrapping the machine, I tuck it safely into my rucksack and wade through wild grass and knee-high, dead bracken to a well-worn path ending at a rickety gate. A large metal shed stands in an overgrown plot. Brambles and nettles advance from all sides. Whoever owns this hasn't done anything with it for a long time.

The shed is at least twelve feet long and eight feet wide, with a single, dirty window. Looking through, I can't see anything except a fence panel leaning against the glass from the inside.

The slats of the shed are coated in red oxide primer, and the lower section has started to corrode. In contrast to the overgrown surroundings, a well-trodden path leads to a matching red door with a traditional keyhole. I try the handle, but it's locked.

I pick my way round the shed, looking for any gaps and holes. Halfway down one side, rust has eaten through the bottom edge, and it's split from the frame. Crouching down, I wonder if I can enlarge the gap, which is currently far too small for a cat. I put my mouth close to the darkness.

'Sebastian?' Damp grass chills my knees as I kneel. 'Seb-as-ti-an?'

I hear a whimper. Could it be him? The sound is too faint to be sure. I repeat my call, louder this time, and am rewarded by a definite meow. The sound is low and forlorn, and my heart picks up in response.

Getting right down, I push my hand inside the hole and feel for any give within the rot. Brown rust flakes shower down as I root around. I'm glad I'm wearing gloves; the last thing I want is a tetanus shot.

'Hang on, Sebastian, I'm coming.'

'What do you think you're doing?'

A gruff voice behind me makes me start.

Looking round, I recognise the tall balding guy from the Swiss shed. He stands over me, wisps of grey hair waving around his forehead in the wind. He's stuck a pencil behind one ear and wears an unhappy grin, exposing teeth like yellow tombstones that have suffered serious subsidence.

I clamber to my feet, brushing down my muddy knees.

'I'm really sorry. My cat is stuck in there. Actually, Sebastian's not mine, he's my friend Nina's. Sebastian's the cat. Sorry.'

'I saw you try and creep past earlier.' His eyes narrow. 'I'm the club secretary. I know everybody here and I've never seen you. You're not an allotment holder, are you?'

'No.'

'Then you're trespassing. We don't allow people in here unless they own a plot or they're accompanied by someone who does. It says clearly - No Trespassers - on the sign you ignored.'

'I'm after my friend's cat. That's all.' I try to appeal to his better nature. 'He's been missing a long time. I didn't mean any harm.'

'No harm, you say?' he goes on. 'You're breaking into a shed. We get tools stolen round here. And our crops damaged. We don't take kindly to people poking around uninvited.'

'I'm not stealing tools and I can assure you I'm not here to damage your crops. Look at me. Do I look like a vandal?'

'What's in your rucksack, then?'

'Sorry?'

'What have you got in there?'

'I don't see how that's got anything to do with it.'

'I'm not the one acting suspiciously.'

'Look, I've got a bottle of water and a tin of tuna for Sebastian. That's it.'

'That's as may be, young lady. But you're still trespassing. I'm going to have to escort you off the premises.'

I stand there with both arms out, showing him I'm no threat to anyone, no trouble at all.

'Look, can we just reset here? I heard the cat in there before you came. I tried the door but it was locked. Put your ear to the door and you'll hear him.'

'What's the matter, Geoff?' While we've been talking, the two council workers have strolled over, still drinking their tea. One of them sports a thick, dark beard, bringing to mind Captain Haddock from Tintin. His comrade has a belly on him, and red points on his wind-bitten cheeks.

'Found this girl sneaking around,' Geoff gives them the low down. 'She says her cat's in there.'

'Please guys, can you just help me?' I gesture behind me. 'He's been trapped inside for days.'

Sebastian obliges with a large meow.

'I heard that.' The bearded worker points his mug towards the shed door. 'Listen.'

Meow! This time, everyone hears him.

And then, I catch movement from the hole. A white paw.

'Look! That's him!' I yell. 'It's Sebastian!'

13

— • —

'**R**ight, who's got the key, Geoff?' asks the chubby worker.

'That would be Terry. He's been here since the year dot.' Geoff eyes the shed. 'This was the society's original HQ before we built the new one. Terry took it over years ago.'

That explains why the shed is so large, but not the neglect.

'Hi, couldn't help noticing the commotion,' comes a voice from behind. The mum with the toddler I saw earlier has joined us. She looks a horsey type with a sturdy build and tousled blonde hair cut in a practical, short style. Her little boy is wearing Power Rangers wellingtons and clings to her hand, a plastic bucket and spade held tight in his other fist.

She eyes me up and down. 'Is your name down for this plot?'

I put my hands up. 'No way. I've no interest in gardening whatsoever. Or allotments.'

The mum confronts Geoff, hands on her hips.

'Can I have it, then? It's three times the size of mine, and no-one's even using it. I mean, look at it!' She throws an arm in the direction of the weeds. 'If you have an allotment, you should turn up and grow something, or let someone else have it. From the state of the place, it looks like Terry's kicked the bucket.'

'Spade!' her son calls out, holding up his plastic spade.

Geoff rocks back on his heels.

'I'm afraid we're full. Someone has to leave before we can offer their plot.'

'But Terry's doing sod all.'

'That's as maybe, but he is one of our founding members. This plot was a perk for all the years of hard work he put in.' He grins. 'Long before you showed up.'

'I see.' The woman wears a tight smile. 'This is cronyism, pure and simple. That's why the waiting list is such a joke. I've got friends who've been on it for over a year. What chance have they got, if that's your attitude?'

'We never had this level of interest before. You can thank Alan Titchmarsh for that.'

The mum rolls her eyes. 'I don't think your Terry has ever watched Alan Titchmarsh.'

'Look, I only know the bloke in passing,' Geoff defends himself. He looks round the plot as if seeing it for the first time. 'Maybe I will have a word with him.'

'Excuse me?' I shift from one foot to the other behind them, fingers and toes going numb from the cold. 'Terry must have been here recently, or Sebastian wouldn't be stuck inside. I've been looking at this path. Someone's been up and down here a lot.'

'Who's Sebastian?' the mum asks.

'My cat. Nina's cat. Please, can someone just get Terry or the key before he dies in there?'

'I'll have to dig out his phone number back at HQ,' Geoff says, seizing the chance to leave. 'You wait here. I'll see if I can give him a shout.'

As he heads back to the Swiss cabin, I crouch by the hole in the shed.

Sebastian puts his paw through. I touch it, but he pulls it back.

The little boy squeals, pointing his spade at the hole. He drops down on his knees beside me and stares at the hole, wating for the cat to reappear.

'Careful, Timbo.' The mum steps closer. 'Cats scratch.'

The boy maintains his vigil.

With Geoff gone, I look up at the council workers. The bearded one seems the more approachable of the two, so I direct my question to him.

'Is there a way of widening this hole?'

'Nah, best wait for Geoff,' his chubby colleague butts in, pulling a battered Golden Virginia tin from his pocket. He opens it and removes a roll-up. 'We don't get involved in non-contractual work.'

'Have you got anything to put the cat in?' Beardy asks.

I never thought about that.

'We've got a dog crate in the back of the van you can use.' Beardy tips his head to his colleague. 'Go and get it for the lady.'

The chubby worker taps his roll-up against the side of the tin. 'I'm on my break.'

'Just get it.'

After a lengthy pause, Chubby slowly wanders back to the van, puffing as he goes.

Beardy steps forward and rattles the handle on the shed.

'I've got a power cutter I could use on the lock. There's no power down here, but I could run out an extension cable from HQ.'

The thought of power tools on a metal drum like that makes me shudder.

'The noise of that would kill him. If Geoff can't get in, we should call the RSPCA,' I say.

'Good idea,' says the mum.

'What can the RSPCA do that we can't?' Beardy crouches by the door and examines the rusty hole.

'Out of the way, son,' he warns the boy and, with his thick workmen's gloves, grabs the lower edge of the panel and gives it a yank.

The metal shifts with a sharp snap. A shower of rust covers his sleeve.

He tries to push his hand up inside the gap, winces.

'It's all sharp edges.' He blinks rust particles from his eyes and retracts his hand. Blood trickles down his exposed forearm, above his heavy-duty glove.

'You want to get that looked at,' the mum advises, as Geoff trots over.

I'm almost pleased to see him.

'I couldn't get hold of Terry.' Geoff wheezes. 'Tried the number. Phone just kept ringing. I found a set of spares from when it was the old HQ, hiding at the back of the drawer.'

He holds up a keyring with three keys on it. He tries the first key in the lock. It rattles around in the keyhole.

'With these old locks, there's going to be a knack,' Geoff comments.

Everyone hears a satisfying *click* as the second key turns in the lock.

'Well, that was easy,' Geoff says in surprise. 'Turned like new.'

'Careful,' I say. 'I don't want Sebastian to rush out. Can you open it just enough to let me in?'

Geoff edges the door open. It's well-oiled hinges make no sound as I slip through the gap.

As my eyes grow accustomed to the low light inside, I spot two shining circles low down on the floor. My heart jumps.

Sebastian's staring from the far corner.

'Hey, Geoff,' I call back. 'Open it a bit more?'

More light enters. I crouch down and make encouraging noises. Sebastian walks over, yowling to meet me. He headbutts my knee, and I pull off my gloves to stroke him.

'Sebastian, it's all right now.' I can barely draw breath with elation. I pick him up easily and he climbs onto my shoulder, rubbing his wet nose on my ear. I manage to stop myself from giving him a big squeeze.

My God, it actually works! The finding machine works!

'You're safe now,' I mumble into his fur. 'I've got you.'

'Good timing,' I hear Geoff say outside, just before the smoking council worker comes in with the dog carrier. 'You got him then?'

Sebastian's deep, booming purr is so loud, I can feel the vibrations coming through my coat. I ease him off my shoulder, into the dog carrier. He gives a large meow in protest as I close the door on him.

'You missed the light switch,' Beardy says, flicking it on.

The fluorescent strip buzzes and blinks three times before it comes fully on.

Blink

TVs on a table.

Blink

Stacks of cardboard boxes.

Blink

A row of filing cabinets.

'What the...?' Beardy says, just as the boy runs past me.

'Mummy, look!' he shouts out. 'Videos!'

14

---•---

I have never wanted to leave anywhere so quickly. After mumbling something to Geoff about the cat needing food and water, I grab the dog crate with Sebastian inside, promising the council workers I will return it tomorrow. Beardy and Chubby are deep in discussion with Geoff over the contents of Terry's shed and whether to contact the police, and don't notice me leave.

Sebastian weighs a ton, and the enormous plastic carrier bangs against my legs with every step. I grit my teeth and hobble towards the main gates, willing to put my back out if it means putting distance between me and the shed.

The joy I felt at my success has been replaced by a ball of anxiety. Even the finding machine feels heavier on my back.

Sebastian meows through the top-hatch on the long-haul home. Nina lives a few streets away from me, but I'm so out of puff by the time I get to my front door, I squeeze the carrier in the back of the Mini and drive him round.

Nina's place is close-by, and thankfully, there's a parking space outside.

After setting the carrier down on the doorstep, I take a deep breath and ring the bell, hoping my explanation regarding Sebastian will hold up.

I prepare a smile.

The woman who answers the door is younger than me, in her early-twenties, professional looking with Indian heritage – tawny skin and sleek, black hair. She looks at me, then at the carrier. Her eyes widen in shock and she drops to her knees with one hand over her mouth. Tears swiftly follow.

Nina is, quite simply, over the moon. Her overwhelming reaction lifts my spirits - my fake smile turns genuine. She stoops down to grab the carrier and invites me inside. The sight of Sebastian being cuddled and kissed a hundred times, lapping up cat milk and chomping down a bowl of ocean fish pushes the shock of Terry's shed to the back of my mind. It probably won't stay there, but it's good enough for now.

'I know it sounds ridiculous, but he's like my baby,' Nina says, her voice ragged. 'I'm supposed to be taking my mortgage broker exams. But the stress with Sebastian has ruined my studies. I'm probably going to fail.'

She leans down to tickle him behind the ears.

'Silly boy, getting yourself locked inside a shed,' she sniffs. 'I'm not letting you out of the house again.' She turns her attention to me. 'I can't thank you enough for getting the allotment society to check inside all their sheds. If it hadn't been for you, he'd still be stuck in there.'

It's a white lie, one that sounded good when I came up with it on the long trudge home. Nina doesn't question it. She's so loved up getting Sebastian back, she doesn't care about the details.

'You've made my day.' Her eyes shine. No, you've made my year! What's your email address? I want to draft a proper thank you!'

I'm happy for her, but all I want to do is go home, have a hot bath, and climb into bed.

'Are you OK to take the dog carrier back to Green Lane Allotments tomorrow?' I ask. 'You can leave it by the HQ.' I describe the Swiss chalet just inside the main gates.

Straightaway, she agrees, and a weight lifts from my shoulders.

On the doorstep, she pushes an envelope into my hand.

I give it a blank look.

'Your reward. For finding Sebastian. A hundred pounds.' She gives me a hug. 'But really, for what you did, I would have given you a thousand.'

‘What's the matter with you?’ Antony finds me slumped at the kitchen table in the dark, a mug of tea going cold in my hands. ‘You look like you dropped a tenner and found a quid.’

‘I'm just knackered, that's all.’

I look up and try to lighten my expression, but all I manage is a weak smile.

‘Come on, I can see there's something wrong.’ He puts the light on and takes a seat beside me.

‘I'm all right.’

‘You're not. Tell me.’

As soon as I start talking, I feel a desperate need to offload everything. I describe Sebastian's rescue in every detail, including the moment I saw inside Terry's shed. I give him the bare minimum regarding what I saw in there. I don't want to relive it.

‘No wonder you're shaken,’ Antony says, taking a seat opposite me. ‘Look, you did brilliantly. You've got to take the pluses away from this.’

He counts them out on his fingers. ‘Your dad's machine actually works. You went out and rescued a missing cat and reunited him with his owner. You got a cash reward. Plus, you're a hero. The fact Sebastian was in an awful place is plain bad luck and it's upset you. I totally get it.’

When I don't react, he scrapes his chair back and comes round to me. Putting his arms round me, he pulls me close and gives my shoulders a squeeze.

‘I'll be better in a bit.’ I give him a gentle bump with my head without taking my hands from the mug. ‘Just need some time.’

Antony releases me. ‘If you think about it, finding the shed was good luck, not bad. You've uncovered an evil, old git. You've stopped a lot of kids getting hurt, too. What did the police say?’

‘They didn't.’

‘What?’

'I left before they got there. Geoff can handle it. It's his allotment, his problem.'

'So, you're not on their radar.'

'They don't even know my name.'

Antony leans back in his chair, a smile growing on his lips. 'You know what, you remind me of one of those silent hero types who goes in and does the business but never takes the credit.' He gives me a conspiratorial wink. 'Peter Parker would be proud of you.'

My shoulders slump. 'I don't feel like much of a hero. I bungled everything. I got caught by some old duffer trespassing on his allotment. I didn't think to bring a box to put the cat in because I didn't think I'd find him. All I brought was a tin of tuna and a tin opener. I was hardly going to prise Sebastian out of a locked shed with that, was I? Finding the cat was the easy bit. And that wasn't even me. It was Dad's machine.'

'You are way hard on yourself.'

'You're right.' I let out a sigh. 'The machine was amazing, but I can't get over the other stuff it found. That's not something I want to go through again.'

15

— ◆ —

*H*i Alex, cheers for your email. I'm struggling to get my head round it.
Your description of Dad's machine was pretty nuts. So was your drawing. Here are my thoughts for what they're worth. First, if his machine was in any way important, why didn't Dad show it to us before? I don't want to put a downer on you, but it sounds like an experiment – especially if he put it together from leftover parts. I remember quite a few unfinished projects sitting on a shelf somewhere.

Anyway, I'm glad Mum has gone through the last of his belongings. I think it will help her move on.

One thing I'm pleased about - you got the machine, not me. The house is already jam-packed with Oscar's Lego, Transformers, bike, roller blades and hockey gear. The last thing I need is more stuff. I can't wait for you to have kids, Alex. The last time I had a lie-in was sometime back in 1990.

I looked at the black and white photos. Obviously, I recognise Dad, Grandpa Jack and Granny Vera. Isn't that Dad outside Uncle Stanley's shop? Dad used to spend his pocket money there every Saturday on sweets - a quarter of rhubarb and custards, or toffee you had to break with a hammer. Dad said the toffee took some of his milk teeth out. I don't know what happened to Stanley. His shop was in Sudbury town centre, but I doubt it would be there now.

That's Margaret in the VE-Day picture. She was best friends with Vera, and they were neighbours, too. I remember meeting her at Dad's funeral – obviously,

78

she's a lot older but her smile is the same. I can't remember her surname, but she was awfully fond of us. I think she still lives in Sudbury. Mum might know.

I have no idea who the baby is. I agree, it does look like a girl. It reminded me of something Dad used to say. He'd have these heavy chats about how lucky I was to have a sister. He really drummed it into me to treasure you, as if a brother's ever going to do that!

But it made me wonder – did Mum have a miscarriage or something? Or did they nearly lose you when you were born? There has to be a rational explanation. I wouldn't get too hung up on it, sis. It was a long time ago.

In other news – Oscar's a real grump. He's a few years off being a teenager, but you wouldn't know it by the attitude. I'm looking forward to another decade of teen-angst.

Whenever you want to come over, the spare room's yours. You're small enough to squeeze past the junk to find the bed. If you came for a couple of weeks, we could do some island hopping across the Puget Sound, maybe cross the border to Vancouver.

Matt

If my brother knew the finding machine worked, it would blow his mind. He'd have to see it with his own eyes, though, as he's pretty sceptical. The truth can keep for now.

Matthew's insights into the family photos intrigue me. I'm Mr Intrigued, as Antony would say.

Looking through the photos again, I find the one of Margaret. I should have recognised her. We had a really good chat at the wake following Dad's funeral. She was pretty old compared to the hearty looking woman in the picture, but her mind was sharp as a pin.

Margaret and Vera lived next-door to each other for years. When I was a child, whenever I visited Granny Vera I used to pop across to Margaret's house. She always had something nice for us to do together.

If she's still living in Sudbury, I can make arrangements to go and see her.

Staring at the photos, an idea occurs to me. All four have more than one person in them, and I think that's why I couldn't get a reading before.

My remedy for that involves my PC, a scanner and a bit of rejigging. I scan in the pictures, then crop the faces from each photo and save them as separate images. Starting with the baby, I isolate the back of its head and enlarge it as much as possible. By the end, I have eleven individual images. Vera appears three times, as does Jack, with Dad twice. In addition, I have the baby, Margaret with her eyes closed and Stanley behind his shop door.

Even though the photographs are in black and white, I print them in full colour to ensure I capture every detail. Thankfully, my cartridges have enough ink for the job. Once I've chosen the best printout of each person, carefully cut to size, I switch on the finding machine.

.

Dad's Dot appears.

The first picture I try is Dad as a boy.

52.039419 00.725435

The reading's the same as before. St Gregory's Church in Sudbury.

The next photo I try is my grandfather, Jack Martin.

52.039418 00.725434

An almost identical location. They are buried in the same plot, as is Vera.

52.039418 00.725437

It's what I expected. Nonetheless, my heart clenches at the machine's power. My grief and sympathy is heartfelt but impractical, whereas the numbers are a tangible connection to my loved ones. It is precise and final. A single row of digits represents actual, human lives.

How can a cold block of capacitors and fuses make me feel emotional? It's like the machine will not allow my family to be forgotten. It will not allow *anyone* to be forgotten.

The succession of readings leaves me a little maudlin as I insert the print-out Margaret.

51.991548 0.836854

The similar numbers make me think she's somewhere near Sudbury. I open another window on my computer and put the figures into my geomapping website. After a wait, the map comes up with the pointer in the middle of a road called Wrights Way. It's in Leavenheath, about eight miles from Sudbury town centre.

I'd prefer to call her before I turn up on her doorstep.

Next up is the man presumed to be Uncle Stanley. His enlarged face, obscured by glass, has not come out well. It's nothing more than a pale blur with dark blotches for eyes.

.

Hardly a surprise. If I go and see Margaret, I could show her the photographs and see what she thinks.

The final image to try - the faceless baby. I pick it up.

Hoping and praying, I insert the heavily cropped and enlarged image into the finding machine.

16

— • —

Over the next few days, I put the finding machine on the back burner and concentrate on agency work. My hands fly across the keyboard, as restless as the sparrows outside my window.

After I've completed Gerald W. Plucket's novel and emailed it back to my agency, I find myself in the unusual position of having no work. I might have to pick up the phone and chase some down. That'd be a first.

With time on my hands, I pick up the photo of the baby, its little face turned away from me. The finding machine failed to generate a location for it. I hadn't held out much hope it would. Dad's machine needs a face to do its thing.

Mum still hasn't emailed me back regarding the photo of 'L' and Uncle Stanley. I know she's got Margaret's surname and phone number in Dad's old address book.

Should I ring her? I'm in two minds over it. Maybe Matthew's right. I should let the past go.

To put it off, I paint. I capture dappled sunlight hitting the lime trees' leaves. The vivid greens on my canvas match the colour of the leaves unfurling outside my window. By the end of the week, I've completed my best work in years.

Success spurs me to get my next canvas ready. I scan in the photo of the cattle by the bridge and enlarge it to fit the canvas. After priming it, I transpose the outlines of each element directly onto the canvas by tracing over A4 sheets of carbon paper tacked together. At this rate, I'll have ten paintings to show to the art gallery in St Albans by summer, as long as I paint at least four times a week.

The old photo distracts me. I find myself staring at it, imagining the baby's face. Granny Vera holds the child with a familiarity that shouts 'here's my girl!' Her husband, Jack, was a traditionalist. If the baby wasn't a member of the family, it wouldn't have been in the family album.

Why would Dad keep it, if it wasn't significant?

Desperate for distraction from my circling thoughts, I bust in on Antony, who graciously lets me play Quake on his PC. The ultra-violent first person shooter is a perfect way to forget my troubles. Level One opens on a US military base and swiftly progresses to other hellish dimensions, though I doubt I'll get to see them as my skills are so poor.

I cannot seem to master the keyboard with my left hand, mouse in my right.

'I thought you'd be a demon on Quake with your typing skills.' Antony shakes his head as I die for the umpteenth time, his initial sensei patience turning to ridicule.

'If you want to improve, you need to *relax*. Every time a bad guy comes at you, you tense up. Your shoulders rise to your ears! Shake your arms out.'

He scoots his chair behind me. I feel him hovering, his warmth radiating across my back. He gathers my hair together at the base of my neck and starts twisting it in a hank. He tucks it over my shoulder, out of the way.

'What are you doing?' I protest.

'Relax, I said.' He places his hands on my shoulders.

'Is that necessary?' I protest, and try to shrug him off, my go-to response whenever Antony touches me. Our history is one of him pulling stuff from my hands and running gleefully away with it, pushing me onto the sofa or preventing me from moving by pinning my arms to my sides.

'Go with it.'

He presses his thumbs into the muscles round the base of my neck and starts working on the kinks. It feels so good, I stifle a groan at the sensation. I close my eyes and relish every second as he releases the tension in my shoulders with a deft touch a professional masseuse would be proud of. The pressure he applies is firm but not too firm, although I wince a few times as areas crunch beneath his rolling thumbs.

'Ouch. You're carrying bags of stones in there,' Antony remarks. 'Must be all the typing.'

'This is actually nice,' I say, my voice sounding a bit woozy as my breathing slows. 'I might give you a gold star, as long as you don't prank me. You're not going to put an icecube down my back or anything like that?'

'I will if you don't relax.' He moves away and I instantly miss his touch. 'There, did you feel that? Your shoulders dropped. Go again.'

I look round for more, but he steps back with folded arms.

With a preparatory breath, I unpause the game. A blobby, pink monster in full armour comes at me with a chainsaw. I sidestep and fire at the same time, blasting the creature to smithereens. Who knew so much pleasure was to be had in blasting monsters to kingdom come?

'That's more like it.' Antony's rare praise sends a glow through me. He catches my eye, grinning.

'Not just for boys, is it?'

'I love it. I shouldn't. It's so grim!' I hit the pause button, swivel round on the chair. 'What about Josie, does she play Quake?' Josie is his current girlfriend. Antony met her before Christmas, but hasn't invited her back recently. She has flaming red-hair and Irish smiling eyes and a loud, generous laugh. With her big personality, she's the perfect fit for him.

'I wouldn't know.' Antony removes his glasses and buffs them with a cloth.

'Why wouldn't you know?' I frown in puzzlement. 'Do you mean to say you're over? I thought you got on really well.'

'Yeah we did, at the beginning.' Antony replaces his glasses. 'She's got the looks, personality, great style. But after New Year, I knew it wasn't there so I told her. I don't keep them hanging on if it's not going anywhere.'

'That's generous of you,' I say primly. 'I don't suppose you've ever been at the other end of this process, yourself?'

'Sure I have.' He shrugs. 'No-one likes getting dumped. But when you look at it logically, it's a numbers game. You have to be in it to win it, Alex.'

His gaze bores into me.

'Are you talking about me?'

Antony gives a shrug. 'There's more to life than Ware, you know. You could try speed dating or something.'

'Give me a break!'

I've heard stories about speed dating, and although it's easy to laugh hearing them second-hand, the idea of meeting drunk blokes dragged in by their mates, with half the women equally inebriated and shrieking is my idea of hell.

'Kathy from aerobics told me prostitutes do the rounds at these places, mopping up disappointed blokes.'

'And you believed her?' Antony asks, laughing.

'Whatever. I want things to happen naturally.'

'You mean, by doing nothing and staying in?' Antony talks over my half-hearted protest. 'If that's how you want it, fine. But you're going to be twiddling your thumbs while I'm at the NEC.'

It completely slipped my mind Antony is going away. The web design exhibition in Birmingham is a massive deal for him. With everything that's been going on, I never made a note in my diary.

'When is that, again?'

'Sunday afternoon until Wednesday.'

'You'll ring me if you get any job offers, won't you?' Although my tone's light, inwardly I can't stop running through the possible consequences of his trip.

'Course I'll tell you. But nothing's guaranteed, Alex. The best of the best are there. We're all competing for the same jobs, trying to be noticed.'

'I've seen your work. You are the best.'

Antonys eyes me from his desk, digital pen hovering above his Wacom tablet.

'Are you doing the next level, or what?'

Shaking my head, I stand and stretch out my back.

'It'll have to wait. I've got to go and ring Mum.' I give him a military salute. 'Ranger, signing out.'

'Fall out, Commando.' Antony returns the gesture. 'Now, get your butt out of here.'

17

— • —

'Alexandra, is that you?' This time round, I keep the phone well away from my ear. Once we've established it is indeed me, my mum takes off like it's the start of the Formula One.

'I was thinking about you this morning when the rain let off and the sun came through. I thought, Alexandra would like that now, she always likes a bit of sun on her face. Well, I'm here with your uncle Fintan, say hello Fintan. You should ring more often, so you should. Wait there, I'll put your uncle on.'

As Mum talks over my uncle in the background, I glance at my kitchen timer which is steadily counting up the seconds. As far as BT are concerned, calling Ireland costs the same as the Solomon Islands.

'Well, hello to you from Leitrim!' the warm voice of my favourite uncle rumbles down the line. 'We're sitting together at the old computer. Your mum's learning how to send an email. She's typing one as we speak.'

'That's great!' I reckon my luck is in, as Fintan is technically minded and Mum listens to him.

'She's getting there with the old technology, aren't you, Brigid?'

'I worry I'll press the wrong button and destroy the computer,' she calls out. 'I went to make a cup of tea earlier, and when I came back the screen was black. I thought I'd killed it.'

'It only went to sleep,' Fintan reassures her. 'It's not a nuclear power station. There's no red button or anything like that.'

'I don't want to be held responsible for breaking the world wide web.'

'Uncle Fintan, please tell Mum she can't break the internet.' I raise my voice, hoping he'll hear me over Mum's constant babble. 'You're doing a great job helping her.'

'The Irish Times says the Russians are spying on us through the interweb.' Mum drowns out his reply. 'We have to take care.'

For once, Mum's thinking along the same lines as Antony. Over breakfast this morning, he mentioned something he'd read in one of his technology journals. The US, together with Russia, are conspiring to surveil us. He told me to be careful using the finding machine. He thinks foreign, sinister technologies might be behind the dark feeling I get when I handle it, and why it's so cold. Russian cold.

I shrug off these negative thoughts as Fintan encourages Mum.

'Keep going Brigid, and you'll have the world at your fingertips.'

'That's easy for you to say, Fintan. You're already a computer whizz. But it's hard for me. I'm supposed to be enjoying retirement, not running an international computer bureau.'

I cut in. 'Mum, once you've got the hang of it, you can email photos to me and Matthew as often as you like. And it's free. No more international postage.'

'You take care now, Alex,' Fintan says. 'I'll let you two enjoy your conversation.'

I hear a clunk as he passes over the phone.

'Mum, did you get those black and white photos I emailed to you?'

'What? Oh, those old ones.' Her voice drops. 'Vaguely. I mean, I've so many photos of everybody I didn't look too hard at them.'

'Do you remember the one of Granny Vera holding a baby? In the old lounge in Sudbury. Do you remember that one? And the shop. Was that Uncle Stanley's shop?'

'If you say it's your uncle's shop, it must be. You know as much about him as I do.'

'Not my uncle. Dad's uncle. Didn't Dad ever talk about him?'

'About Stanley? Not really. All I know is what I told you. He moved up north when your dad was a boy. I doubt he'd still be with us, Alexandra.'

'What about the baby? I'd really like to know who it was. Did Dad have a sister?'

There's a pause. 'A sister? No. Richard was an only child.'

'It's just, I've got a feeling about her.'

Another pause, longer this time.

'You have to remember the time,' Mum says. 'When was that, the 1920s? People were in and out of each other's houses all the time. It was probably someone else's child.'

She has a point. Things were different back then. People didn't lock their doors the way they do now. Neighbours knew each other. They shared a community spirit that everyone says is missing these days.

'Maybe it was Margaret's baby,' Mum suggests. 'She's in that VD day photo.'

'You mean VE day, Mum.'

'That's what I said. Anyway, Margaret used to live next door to your Granny Vera in the old house. They spent a lot of time together once the babies came. It'll be something like that, for sure. You probably don't remember, but you used to think of her as a second Gran. Whenever we used to go round and see Vera, you'd pop next door to see Margaret.

Now that Mum mentions it, I remember Margaret having a soft spot for me. I used to love helping her decorate the Christmas tree or pick strawberries from the garden.

Mum rambles on. 'Margaret's husband Bernard, poor fellow, was never the same after his stroke. When their sons grew up and moved out, she was ever so lonely.'

I was a child when Bernard had his stroke. He would sit and watch whatever we were doing, unable to speak but always wearing the hint of a smile. The stroke had robbed him of the capacity to talk clearly and move about. Caring for him must have been exhausting, but Margaret never complained.

Something else hits me.

'Mum, you mentioned Margaret's sons. Did she have any daughters?'

'No, just the boys. I don't remember their names. They would be about my age now.'

'Then that baby in the picture can't be Margaret's. It's definitely a girl.' I'm reluctant to say what's on my mind. But if I want answers, I have to push for them. 'Could Vera have had a daughter who died?'

Silence.

'There's *something* about this picture, Mum.'

'Now, come to think of it...' the following pause goes on so long I think Mum's gone off to make a cup of tea. 'There was a sister. I heard Richard mention it once or twice.'

'A sister?' I straighten, pulling at the cord. 'Why didn't you say so?'

'I'm sorry, Alexandra, I didn't want to mention it. It's sad, isn't it, and we don't need that kind of sadness in our lives.'

'So, let me get this straight. The girl in Granny Vera's arms is my aunt? Dad's sister?'

'I suppose so, if she was around. But you were right about one thing. She died.'

She died? I struggle to process what she's saying. I lean forward, the headset pressed to my ear.

'How did she die?'

'No-one knows. She was only a child. Richard wouldn't talk about it.' Mum pauses. 'Remember, I didn't meet Richard until I was in my twenties. His past was neither here nor there to me.'

My mum has never been one for nostalgia.

'What was her name, Mum?'

'Lilian, I think.'

'Do you have any photos of her? Anything I can look at and keep? I really want to know what she looked like? Did she look like Dad?'

'I haven't a clue. As I keep saying, I've been through everything. I didn't bring any memorabilia like that to Ireland with me.' After another long pause where my mind's whirling and I'm struggling to find a comeback, Mum goes on. 'Best not to dwell on it. You have to remember there were all kinds of cruel things back then waiting to get you. That's why my lot had such big families. Our healthy Irish stock must have helped us, as we're all still here!'

So you're all right, then. I can't help feeling bitter at her jolly tone.

'Mum, please can you have one last look for any photos? You said you were going to check.'

'I chucked most of them out when I had my big spring clean.'

I grind my teeth to stop myself having a go. How could she throw those precious memories away? And why didn't she tell me this earlier, instead of ignoring me?

'I doubt there was anything,' Mum goes on. 'God knows, the photos I threw out from my side of the family weren't much to write home about. My father used to line the twelve of us along the wall outside like we were waiting for a firing squad, with the sun directly in our eyes. All of us squinting and looking in pain, but there you are. It was a right old rigmarole.'

I decide to abandon this line of questioning as it is going nowhere. There is someone who can possibly shed light on this mystery, who might be able to give me answers.

'What's Margaret's surname?'

'Long. Margaret Long. She was very good, she never forgot your father's birthday and she always sent us a card at Christmas. Nothing at Easter, but then, she was C of E. That's all you can expect, a big nothing at the most important time of year.'

'And do you send Margaret a card every Easter?' I can't help goading, even though I know I'll regret it.

'My list for Easter cards is already long enough. And she was always partial to your father, not so much to me.'

'I need Margaret's phone number. It'll be in Dad's address book. Can you email it right now, as you're sitting at the computer? It'll be good practice.'

'I'll have to look for it.'

'You didn't throw his address book away as well, did you?'

Another long pause. Mum's blazé attitude leaves me fuming. If she chucked Dad's address book, there goes any hope of chasing up his old friends who might know the story behind the photo of Lilian. Without Margaret's number, I'll have no option but to turn up at her house unannounced.

'If you've been sending Margaret Christmas cards for years, you must have her phone number,' I point out. 'I need it today.'

Silence.

'By the way,' Mum says, just as I'm about to put the phone down. 'I'm emailing you the flyer the Youth for Mary handed out at Mass on Sunday. You can see they have all kinds of interesting things going on. If I was forty years younger, I'd be there in a flash! I thought you could use it to get ideas for your own group.'

'Mmm.' I thought this was something that had gone away. How foolish of me.

Why am I still pretending at the age of twenty-nine everything is just as she imagines, that I am a Member Of The Parish? It's ridiculous, the way I adapt my responses to please her, just like when I was a child, even though I'm full grown with a hundred miles of Irish Sea between us. This has to stop. I can't keep lying.

'When you send the flyer, make sure you include Margaret's phone number with it.'

How many times can I ask the same question?

By the time the phone is back in its cradle, I'm horrified to see thirty-five minutes on the timer.

That's probably thirty-five quid. For nothing.

18

L ife goes on as usual until Sunday afternoon. Antony has left for Birmingham, leaving me at a loose end. I sit at my desk checking for emails, wrapped up warm and toasty while the wind blows a hooley outside the window. My in-tray's empty for the first time in months, perhaps years. I should give the agency a call first thing Monday morning and find out what's going on.

Just as my mind wanders to what I fancy for dinner, a new message pings in my Inbox.

It's from Nina, Sebastian the cat's owner.

Hi Alex! How are you? I have to keep removing Sebastian from my keyboard to type this, so if you see any strange words, that's him, naughty boy! He is such a pest but I am so grateful that you found him. I have been telling everyone how clever and resourceful you are!

I chew the inside of my mouth, unsure how I feel about that, before reading on.

I popped down to the allotments to return the dog carrier. I wanted to see where you found Sebastian, but I couldn't get past Geoff. The place was cordoned off and the police were there. It looks like a crime scene. Do you know anything about it, Alex?

I feel an uncomfortable twinge as I think about Terry's shed.

Anyway, that's not the reason I'm emailing you.

'Thank God!' I exclaim at the screen.

My mother's best friend Maisie just lost her dog. He's only a puppy, a Labradoodle called Sputnik. She was doing some training with him at Hertford Rec. when he ran off towards the car park. She chased after him, but when she got there he was nowhere to be seen.

She noticed a pick-up truck speeding out of the main gates. It was white and had lettering down the side and an image - something like a trowel or a spade. She didn't have time to make a note of the number plate or see who was in the cab. All she remembers is that the back bumper was really smashed in. She thinks her puppy's been nabbed.

Would you put the word out about Sputnik, like you did for Sebastian? Maisie's desperate, I thought there couldn't be any harm in asking you. I've attached the poster she's put up in the Rec. It's got all the details on it. I could print some more if you want. We've already spent a morning giving them out round Hertford and sticking them to lampposts.

I feel really guilty because I've got Sebastian back. Anything you can do would be fab!

Nina xx

I click on the attachment with my mind whirring. The poster includes Maisie's phone number, Sputnik's details and a reward of £350. The photo shows the cutest dog I've ever seen. Sputnik's head sports a golden mop of fur with his shiny black nose poking through. Button eyes glint below expressive brows. My heart clenches. I always wanted a dog, but we never had any pets when we were younger, not even a hamster. Mum didn't like the idea of pawmarks on the lino or hoovering up fur.

If the people in the van took Sputnik, they must be crooks. Who picks up a dog that's not theirs and drives off with it? He could be in the process of being sold on. Pedigree dogs are a lucrative business.

For a long time, I stare at Nina's email, biting my lower lip. Do I really want to head out into the unknown again, after the trouble I got into with Sebastian? It means dragging the finding machine out from its hidey-hole.

I have a cup of tea and wander round the garden, and come up with a plan. First off, It can't do any harm to test the photo. The search for Sputnik will be the finding machine's final, sign-off test.

I resize the image of Sputnik to 6 x 4 inches and print it out on photo paper. While the ink's drying, I unwrap the finding machine from its towel, keeping the extra layer between its base and my lap. Even so, cold seeps through.

Did Dad ever test the machine like this, I wonder?

I insert the photo into the machine and switch it on.

52.042269 -0.052431

Over the next hour, I repeatedly check the coordinates. A flicker of movement to the last digits suggests Sputnik is moving only a short distance. Or being moved.

Inputting the co-ordinates into the geospatial website brings up a map showing the outskirts of Royston. The white finger points to a tiny place called Reed End, just under twenty miles from Ware. The exact location is down a road called Silver Lane, out in the sticks. Only two roads pass through vast swathes of woodland and fields.

Now I know where Sputnik is, I could simply tell Maisie the address and leave the rest to her. But what possible explanation can I give her? How can I explain how I found him so quickly?

Perhaps I should ask Gerald W. Plucket for help. He doesn't seem to have any problem tackling unbelievable scenarios.

Finding things is turning out to be the easy bit. So far, Dad's machine has worked every time. It's the rest – the retrieving and explaining – that's proving far more difficult.

95

Above all, I want to discuss my plans with Antony. He won't be keen on me setting off into the wilds of Hertfordshire on my own. But he's away until Wednesday, and Sputnik doesn't have the luxury of time.

If my experience finding Sebastian taught me something, it's to expect problems. The first one is the distance. Once I'm on the road, I won't be able to recheck Sputnik's position. For that, I need access to my PC and the world wide web to look at the geospatial website. If the puppy moves location while I am on the road, my trip will be for nothing.

Antony left me the phone number of his hotel. I seriously consider ringing him. As he's at a web conference, there'll be no shortage of computers connected to the internet. But then, the last thing he wants is me bleating down the phone, distracting him from his one big chance to further his career.

Problem number two is more serious.

I don't think I can get Sputnik back. I doubt he'll be unsupervised. Which means I have no way of retrieving him.

I wish Nina had never emailed.

Finally, I drop Maisie an email, introducing myself. I tell her I'm putting the word out regarding her puppy, and ask her to list his distinguishing features. Labradoodles are popular around Ware and if I find him, I need to prove he's the one and only Sputnik.

Maisie emails me back after dinner. Sputnik has a white chin, and his tail has a kink in it. She tells me these quirks meant he cost less than a top pedigree dog. He answers to his name and has three pale spots on his tongue. Attached is a low-res video of him yipping and running in wild circles, crazy with happiness. The video ends with him rolling onto his back, a hand coming into view to give him a belly tickle. He's adorable, a real fur baby. I can see the temptation for an opportunist thief. Who wouldn't want a dog like that?

My plan is to find and photograph Sputnik, but only if the opportunity presents itself.

I won't take any risks.

My camera's loaded with a fresh roll of film. If I get shots of Sputnik, I'll have to use the one hour express service to get them developed. I should really look into getting a digital camera, as I'm single-handedly propping up Boots' developing department these days.

My plan is to send the prints to Maisie. She can call the RSPCA or go down there herself. Then, my job will be done.

I write out the route to the farm on an A4 sheet of paper in large block letters, so I can check my directions easily while I am driving. The weather outside is blustery, but it's supposed to be sunny tomorrow with clear skies.

Time to grasp the nettle.

19

— ◆ —

I leave on Monday morning after rush hour, feeling a mixture of nerves and excitement at the prospect of a flight into the unknown. My Mini putters away from Ware, skirting the market town of Hertford before diving into the countryside. The trees lining the thoroughfares are sprouting leaves, as the last of the blossom falls to the ground. In the verges and hedgerows, hawthorn is coming into bud alongside swathes of sunny daffodils.

The view is more pleasant than the bone-jarring ride. Sleeping policemen are high enough to kiss the undercarriage, so I steer between them wherever possible. Potholes are another hazard – with my rotten subframe, one good jolt could tear the car apart. I keep my feet on the pedals at all times as I don't trust the footwell – a lace of rust held together by a single, welded plate. A £1 rubber mat from Halfords covers the problem area. I hope the floor stays where it is until I'm in a position to replace the car.

Once I'm on the A10 and have passed the five mile mark, I relax and settle into the journey. Despite my trepidation, I'm loving the freedom as I pootle through the countryside.

I glance now and again at my handwritten directions, instructing me to turn right onto Haywood Lane before I get to Royston, '*BUT DO NOT GO AS FAR AS ROYSTON!!*'

I find the correct turn-off onto Rooks Nest Lane without difficulty. I'm supposed to take the next left into Silver Lane, but miss the sign and end up driving to the end of the road before realising. I do a U-turn in someone's driveway (one thing my Mini excels at), before retracing my route at a crawl. Luckily, the narrow roads are quiet and I find the turn-off the second time, partially covered by sprouting hedgerows.

Turning onto Silver Lane is like stepping back in time. Tarmacked road aside, I could be in medieval England. The oak trees form an imposing archway over each twist and turn, their interlacing branches yet to come into leaf. At the far end of the road, a slice of patchwork countryside splashed with sunshine opens out in the distance, bucolic as a painting by William Holman Hunt.

I pass five-bar gates and fenced paddocks. Driveways bear signs painted on rocks and posts with evocative names - *Avalon* and *The Rookery*. The houses are hidden from view at the end of each private driveway, shielded by shrubs and trees. Every fifty yards or so, passing places have been gouged into the verges - rough cut-outs filled with stones and puddles.

A Land Rover barrels round the next corner and comes straight at me with flashing headlights and horn blaring. Screaming, I yank the wheel to the left. The Mini skids into the verge with a squeal of brakes. I don't have time to yell at the driver as he blasts past. I pull up the handbrake, my heart racing, firing a colourful stream of expletives at the dashboard.

That idiot's driving has dampened my high, and my nerves flare up so much I seriously consider turning round and heading home.

Instead, I pull the finding machine from my rucksack like a reluctant stone, insert the photo of Sputnik and switch it on.

Two solid red LEDs. Three flashing. I give silent thanks to Dad for adding in the extra feature of a proximity indicator. It makes things so much easier.

I wind down my window and listen out for any approaching cars before I put the Mini into first gear and crawl forwards. I take the same corner the Land Rover came round with care, hoping I don't run into any more maniac drivers.

The road straightens and narrows, closed down on both sides by the rampant verges.

Three solid reds.

Seconds later, I pass a muddy turn-off. A barn stands in the distance.

I pull over into the next passing place. Bushes scrape my nearside wingmirror as I park the Mini as far off the road as possible.

Once the ignition's off, I recheck the finding machine. The coordinates are the same as those on my master sheet, a good sign. I'm back to two solid LEDs, but that's because I had to drive past the barn to find somewhere to park.

In the back, I've got a rucksack with a torch, bag, blanket, dog treats and a bottle of water. I gather my stuff and pull on a green waxed jacket I bought in the winter sales at the local garden centre. If anyone spots me wandering around, hopefully, I'll look like I belong here. The jacket sports two cavernous pockets, deep enough to hold a puppy, as long as it's not a Great Dane.

I push the door open against a sudden gust of wind and step straight into a water-filled crater. I didn't think to wear wellies, and my walking boots, while sturdy, aren't waterproof. Now I've got a wet sock. I curse myself for being a typical townie, used to pavements. Out here, mud is your companion all year round.

A crow caws in a tree nearby, as if it's laughing at me. A few sparrows chirp in a nearby hedge. Aside from the birds and sound of rushing wind, nothing else breaks the silence. Above me, a flock of starlings dot the grey clouds.

I stand in the middle of the road, looking both ways. Humanity seems to have vanished. Since my narrow scrape with the Landrover, I haven't seen another car.

I squelch back to the muddy turn-in. At the entrance, a metal gate has been pulled open and lashed to a tree with blue twine. A rust-pitted abandoned fridge lies next to it with the door hanging open. Black bin bags are scattered about. Most have been ripped open and are strewing refuse across the tussocked field.

A bedraggled rooster struts about in the grass. I wonder if it has escaped from the barn.

One of the bin bags sits in the way of a wooden sign staked to the ground. I kick it aside.

The Red Barn. The letters are carved into a slice of an oak stump and painted white, although mould has discoloured the base and the paint is flaking off. I take out my camera and snap the sign, the entrance and the barn.

Impressions of enormous tyres sit in the mud. The tracks lead up the track towards higher ground. At the top, a modern blue tractor is parked outside the barn, its cab empty. The barn is a modern construct with a corrugated roof and red sides. A hole gapes where doors should be. I look round for a house to go with the barn, but there isn't one.

I follow the path of the tractor, aware that I'm on open ground and highly visible. If anyone challenges me, I'll say I'm looking for The Rookery. I got lost, saw the tractor and thought I'd ask directions.

My ears are pricked for yapping or barking, but silence persists. There's nothing except the wind pushing through the branches. I should be glad there are no guard dogs. Yet, something about the quiet gives me the shivers.

The barn seems miles away. I walk and walk but it doesn't seem to get any closer. Why did they build it so far from the road? It's impossible to keep my cool. I speed up to an awkward jog, desperate to get this thing over with.

By the time I reach the barn, I'm breathless.

The barn boasts an immense set of doors that slide back on metal runners. They've been pushed fully open. The barn itself is built on a gigantic scale that could hold a circus of elephants. Inside, wisps of straw drift across the concrete floor. The inner reaches are dark, but I can make out a barrier of hay bales halfway in.

I check the machine. Four red lights and one flashing. Sputnik's here, yet I can't hear anything. I tuck the machine back inside my rucksack and press on.

A harsh wind funnels through the doors, blowing my hair across my eyes. A gust hits me in the back, almost as if it's pushing me across the threshold. My legs carry me inside. After a few steps, the wind dies down, blocked by the sides of the barn.

I stop to let my eyes adjust to the gloom, and the fact I've crossed the Rubicon and am now trespassing on private property.

A hulking piece of farm machinery lurks in the far corner. A long rake attached to the front is the length of a bus. The smell of oil and grease hangs heavy in the air.

I work my way around feed bags and buckets towards the straw barricade. The light level drops with every step I take further into the barn, but I can see enough to make out the bales. They're stacked like bricks to form a holding pen. A gap at the front looks like a missing tooth, blocked by a square of chipboard.

I scrabble in my rucksack for the torch. Switching it on, I peer over the barricade.

I hear a whimper, then something dark emerges from the corner. A brown puppy. I think it's a boxer. More puppies emerge from the dark, three golden labs, really young. One of them is wobbly on its feet. They look lacklustre, the opposite of what you would expect.

Plus, they are filthy. The smell coming from the pen makes my stomach turn.

In one corner is a bowl rimmed with dirt, empty. A few other empty bowls are strewn around.

Shining the torch into the far corner reveals a second pile of puppies curled round each other, an assortment of colours and breeds. At first glance they look like they're sleeping but then I see the white of an eye rolled back and shivering fur. The puppies barely react to my torch or my voice, even when I make encouraging noises. I take out a dog biscuit and break it into small pieces. The boxer comes over and snuffles them up, but I see little enthusiasm from the others.

A tight ball forms in my stomach. How could anyone treat animals this way? Once I get out of here I am definitely calling the RSPCA.

A few more puppies come into the light. Without exception, they are young, pedigree breeds. I spot a couple of terriers tussling amongst themselves. They seem to have some energy. There's a black lab, twice the size of the others. It wags its tail a little but keeps its head down.

Then, I see a dog that looks like Sputnik. He's bigger than the others and still has a spark in his eye.

'Sputnik,' I whisper. 'Sputnik, is it you?'

I fumble in my pocket for the photo, and shine the light on it. Thank God for my torch. It was sheer luck that I brought it - I didn't think I was going to be creeping around in the depths of a pitch-black barn in the middle of the day. I look for Sputnik's markers – white chin, kink in tail, pale spots on tongue.

The lighting isn't good enough to make out the whiteness of his chin against his pale coat, but I can check his tail.

I get my camera and check the flash is on.

'Here, Sputnik, here!' As soon as he looks up at me, I press the button.

The camera emits two flashes, the second to reduce red-eye. I bite the inside of my cheek as I look into the corners of the enclosure for any other Labradoodles. But he's the only one.

I fumble in my backpack for more dog treats and chuck a handful into the pen. I get more of a response this time as a few puppies dive on them. The dog I think is Sputnik turns his back. I see his long tail and there's the kink - halfway down.

A strange kind of madness overtakes me. I don't know where it comes from, but it's a mixture of outrage that galvanises me to action. I throw one leg over the top bale, ready to jump in and get him. I don't care about the legality or danger, all I know is I have to get him out of this awful place.

I'm in the process of swinging my leg over the top when I hear a sound that sends horror through me.

The roar of an industrial engine starting up, just outside the barn.

20

—

The sudden roar of the tractor gives me such a shock, I lose my balance. I make a grab for the hay bales, but my outstretched hand clutches nothing but air. Falling backwards, I land heavily on my backpack. The back of my head smacks against concrete.

The blow to my head stuns me for several, valuable moments.

The impact knocks the torch from my hand. It skitters off somewhere to the side, throwing round wild circles of light. Somehow, I've managed to keep my camera safe by cradling it to my chest. I don't know if the same can be said for the finding machine. The blanket stuffed inside my rucksack might have cushioned its fall.

I have a sick feeling, separate from the stinging blow to my skull, that I might have broken it, but that's not my immediate concern.

A blue tractor is reversing through the double-doors.

I turn on all fours and scrabble towards the torch, grabbing it and switching it off.

A narrow gap runs behind the bales and the far wall of the barn. I slot myself between cold metal and straw and get my panicky breathing under control. Gingerly touching my head, I can feel a lump forming. Luckily, the blow didn't break the skin.

I steel myself and peer round.

The tractor's snorkel-like exhaust sends plumes of noxious fumes up into the roof of the barn. The driver is looking back over his shoulder to perform the manoeuver. He looks to be in his fifties, wearing a brown flat cap. I want to take a picture of him, but first I need to disable the flash, and it's too dark behind the bales to see the switch. I could try and do it by feel, but if I get it wrong I'll blind the driver.

That would be bad for several reasons, not least the fact he's reversing a ten-ton tractor right at me. The huge wheels come closer and closer to the bales. I throw my sleeve across my nose to muffle my splutters as fumes engulf me. The sound is deafening. The puppies must be terrified.

Finally, the diesel engine cuts out with a uneven rattle. I hear the squeak of the door and watch the man get stiffly down from the cab. He looks an outdoor type, with a weather-worn face and deep frown lines. He's wearing a green Barbour jacket and mud-covered wellies.

By the way he grunts and winces as he steps to the ground, he's suffering with back or hip pain.

I tuck myself behind the bales as he approaches the puppy pen. There's a scrape as he removes the wooden board. Fear marches round my belly at his proximity. I breathe slowly through my mouth.

'Not long now, ladies and gentlemen.' He speaks with a rough, grumbling Essex accent.

'Come here, you.' I hear a whimper as he singles out a puppy and grabs it from the pen. 'For God's sake. The state of you.'

A trilling sound breaks out of his pocket.

I'm so wired I nearly jump out of my skin. I clamp my hand over my mouth, determined not to make a sound. Taking a chance the sound of his phone or pager or whatever it is has distracted him, I risk another look round the bales.

The man has ambled back outside, holding a puppy to his chest. In his other hand, he's got what looks like a bulky builder's phone with a long antenna.

'All right, John? I'm at the barn,' he says loudly, holding the handset up to his mouth. It's oversized for a mobile phone, with the large buttons on the side.

I hear a clicking sound and then another man's voice comes back, crackling with static, although I can't make out what he's saying.

'Yeah, they rang earlier. They want the boxer.'

He moves further away. Another *click* and a response. Then it hits me – he's not using a phone. I peer round and take another look at the device in his hand. It's a walkie-talkie.

It makes sense to have one out in the country, far from any phone masts. No need to worry about getting a phone signal. As long as you stay in range and make sure the other person's carrying a second hand-set on the right frequency, you're good to go.

What's the range of those things? I read somewhere it can vary massively, depending on whether you're in a built up area with loads of interference or out in the sticks. But whether his mate John is just round the corner, or ten miles away, he's still too close for comfort.

'That's all very well, mate, but you ain't selling any of them, the state they're in. They look a right sorry bunch. There's no food. There's no water. I ain't doing everything. We're never going to get shot of them looking like this. You need to step up, mate.'

Click. Response.

I hear another click as the man stops talking.

'Look, same as last time,' the man transmits back. 'Clean him up, give him some food. Stick him in the front room with Bella. She looks like she could be his mum and she's friendly enough. Let them see Bella, then get her out of there. We want them in and out quick sharp. Tell them we've got all the papers, the vaccinations, but they're at the vets, they're with the missus, blah, blah. Tell them what you like. This is your end.'

Crackle Click.

'Yes, John. I know you know.'

Crackle Click.

'Three fifty. Nothing less. Look, I'm on my way down. Just be ready.'

He turns and ambles out, releasing a huge gob of spit on the floor.

I fumble for my camera and feel around for the flash switch but I can't find it.

In the short time I'm distracted by the camera, the man grabs the metal handle attached to the outside of the doors. I watch in dismay as it judders, then starts to slide across, cutting the huge rectangle of natural light from the barn's interior.

I use the increasing shadow for cover, fumbling my way towards my only exit. The door rolls across, and daylight shrinks to a narrow bar. Fuming, I watch him pull the other door across.

A dull clunk marks the two doors meeting in the middle.

The only light remaining is a finger-wide sliver beneath the doors.

The metal retaining bar drops into place, followed by the rattle of a chain being drawn through the bar. The *click* of a lock, probably a padlock being secured.

Is this how it's been for the puppies since they were stolen? A couple of hours of grubby daylight and the rest of the day and night in the dark. How they must have suffered.

I'm fearful enough for my own safety. Underneath, anger burgeons within me. I know men like him and his mate exist – I've read the papers, seen the news. But witnessing it first-hand is something else.

The whole thing, from the puppies' suffering to the owners left staring at an empty dogbed and bowl is a web of misery I want to pull to pieces.

Outside, I hear a rough engine starting up, and shuffle over to the beam of light under the barn doors. I lower myself flat to the ground and peer through the narrow gap. Squinting against daylight, I make out the lower half of a white pick-up truck idling outside. It's battered and splashed with mud. The black shape of a trowel is printed on the side of the cab.

It matches the description of the vehicle Maisie saw, making a hasty escape with Sputnik.

A company name: *G M BUILDTEK* appears after the logo. Swiftly, I aim the camera through the gap and take a picture.

The pick-up slowly pulls away, and I get a brief view of the rear of the vehicle. *MITSUBISHI* is emblazoned on the tailgate. I catch the first few letters of the numberplate: YPM 7, and get another photo.

I repeat the details aloud, fumbling round in my rucksack for a pen and pad. Pressing the paper into the line of light, I write everything down, in case the photos don't come out.

With the pickup gone, I get to my feet and give the main doors a try. I grab one of the handles with both hands and yank on it with all my strength. Digging my heels into the concrete, I lean back and heave with everything I've got. The door gives out a low groan. It shifts slightly on the bottom rail, then sinks back into to its original position. I hear the chains on the outside make gentle *chinks* as they settle.

I'm not getting out that way.

Switching the torch on, I head over to the tractor. The step up to the cab door is quite a way off the ground. I haul myself up onto it and try the door. It opens with a squeak and I clamber into the cab. Shining the torch around, I go on a hunt for the ignition switch. I can't find it. Apart from the huge steering wheel, the cab's interior controls are as foreign as an alien spaceship. There are two gear sticks coming out of the floor, one with a red knob, the other one's yellow. God knows what they do. There's a bank of levers to my right hand side set at different angles, and the dashboard's a series of black dials.

Even if I could find the keys in the ignition, I wouldn't know how to put this thing into gear.

What would I do, anyway? Ram the barn doors like I was in the opening credits of the A-Team? Would it even work, a metal leviathan against a metal barn? The barn might come crashing down on my head, and the puppies too.

I'm glad there are no keys in the ignition. I could have been toast.

Clambering down from the tractor, I shine the torch in every direction, into corners, down and then up to the rafters. The modern equivalent in here are metal joists. There's no loft area, no extra level for storing hay with an access window and no ladder with which to get up there. Torchlight reaches the very top of the barn. No windows.

Nevertheless, I must keep trying to find a way out.

I make a slow circuit of the perimeter, checking down by the floor and along the walls for any other means of exit, but the structure is solid. I end up back by the puppies. Looking over, I see they have retreated to the sides of the straw for comfort and are mostly lying down or curled up. They're trying to switch off from their situation.

For lack of any further ideas, I get my bottle of water and fill up their water bowl.

'I'm going to help you,' I whisper.

After twenty minutes, despair begins to bite. I'm out of options. This bloke, John, the tractor driver's mate, could be on his way here to feed and water the puppies.

I've got a chance to do a runner once he opens the doors, but that means leaving the puppies. The first thing he'll do is move them. I wouldn't put it past him to drown them in a sack to get rid of the evidence.

He might do the same to me.

What's worse, he would probably get away with it. No-one's around to witness anything. The roads are deserted. I feel a grudging respect for John and his tractor buddy - they've chosen the perfect spot, far out in the countryside, away from the attention of curious passers-by. Yet, they're close enough to Hertford, St. Albans and London to dip in and out of towns as they please, taking pedigree pups whenever the occasion arises.

A pair of lowlifes.

The thought of getting caught in here makes me sick to my stomach.

I am not a rebel. My greatest misdemeanour is getting a fine for an overdue library book. For most of my life I've run my life straight down the line, yet here I am sticking my head over the parapet.

Naturally, I blame Dad. He seems to have programmed the spirit of adventure into his finding machine.

I sit with my back to the hay bales, pulling the rucksack onto my lap. The machine's bulk chills the fabric. It doesn't feel broken.

Part of me hopes it is. My dad's invention is going to be the death of me. It doesn't seem fair. No, I can't blame a machine. I'm entirely to blame for being stuck in here.

Yet, the facts are grim. No-one knows I'm here. I never told Antony what I was doing. Damn it. I never told anyone what I was doing.

Checking my watch, it's two pm. Antony's not back from the NEC until Wednesday lunchtime at the earliest. The only sign I have been here is my car, sitting in a layby some distance up the road. The sheet with my handwritten directions is still on the passenger seat, but I only started them from the A10, so it's no good to anyone. And my Mini, bless its rusting heart, is in such bad shape that passers-by will assume it's been abandoned.

But not for days.

I can see the scene already - the indignant locals having to wait weeks before the council come and tow it away to the scrapyard, while my corpse slowly disintegrates in the corner.

I play my torchlight on the tractor for the umpteenth time, over the walls, the immense sliding doors, the slim outline of a rectangle set within it.

What is that?

Getting up, I head for the doors again. How could I not have seen this?

A small door is set within the large one. It's built-in for easy access, if you don't want to drag open the huge doors if you need to dash inside and grab a bag of corn or something.

I rest my hand on the latch and, gingerly, depress it with my thumb.

It opens. Dull afternoon light spills into the barn. I stick my head out and have a good look. The driveway leading to the main road looks deserted. I can't hear any cars.

My heart thumps with the thrill of release.

I want to sink to my knees and howl. Instead, I grab Sputnik, tuck him under my jacket and run all the way back to my car with tears running down my cheeks. Luckily for me, no-one's around.

In my rush to unlock the car I fumble the keys and end up dropping them in the puddle by the driver's door. By the time I've fished them out, I've got a wet sleeve to go with my wet sock, but I'm past caring.

After tucking Sputnik in the blanket-lined cardboard box on the rear seat, I get behind the wheel.

My hand goes to the ignition key, then freezes.

Sputnik's whimpers make me think of his companions, stuck inside.

The safest thing would be to drive home and call the RSPCA, the police, anyone. I can say I had a tip off about the place. Work out the details later. I've got part of a number plate, the name John and address of the Red Barn. If I go now, I'm safe. I've done what I set out to do.

With my heart hammering and my tongue stuck to the roof of my mouth, I gulp down the rest of the water from my bottle. Fighting my natural instincts takes everything I've got.

I want to gun the engine and race home to Ware.

Instead, I fire up the engine, perform a sharp U-Turn in the lane and accelerate back up to the barn with my foot pressed to the floor.

21

—
·
—

I leave the Mini running outside the barn. The inset metal door stands open - in my panic to get Sputnik out, I completely forgot to close it.

Really great job covering your tracks, Alex.

I rush inside and grab two puppies, nearly tripping over the high lip of the door on the way out. After unceremoniously depositing the pups in the cardboard box with Sputnik, I go back inside. It takes five nerve-wrangling trips, plus a sweep with my torch before I'm satisfied I've got them all.

Each time I re-emerge into the light, I half-expect to see John and a welcoming committee of Essex bad boys. My luck holds, as I exit the barn for the last time and carefully close the inset door behind me.

Back in the Mini, I floor it down the track to the main road, eyes peeled for approaching cars. I take a sharp right onto Silver Lane without indicating, and change swiftly up the gears to get some speed on the narrow lane.

Just as I'm congratulating myself about my lucky escape, a light blue Ford Astra shoots round the corner. It approaches so fast I have no time to react. I flinch, expecting to lose my wing-mirror and see sparks flying from the bodywork. But the Astra passes without making contact.

I catch a glimpse of the driver; a skinny fellow in his twenties or early thirties wearing a beanie with a cigarette on the go, jaw grey with stubble. He glares at me as he passes.

No! Could that be John?

To my horror, as I watch in my rear view mirror, his brake lights come on.

The Astra stops dead on the road, exhaust fumes pluming.

That freaks me out so much, I put my foot down without any care for the state of the footwell. As I roar off, a little voice tells me I should have waited to see if the driver turned into *The Red Barn*. But it's too late. I keep checking my rear-view mirror for any sight of him until I join the main road, nearly driving into a ditch from nerves.

Surely he can't have sussed me out? He didn't have enough time to make a note of my number plate.

But why did he stop like that? It must be for some other reason, I tell myself. It has to be.

· · • • · • ♦ • • · ·

I've never carried one passenger in the back of my car, and now I've got ten. At least, that's where they start off. Ten minutes into the journey, the scrabbling sounds start. A short time later, the first adventurous pup appears round the edge of the passenger seat with a semi-circle of cardboard between its jaws. I glance at it from the corner of my eye, starting to drift out of lane as the puppy distracts me from the road.

The timing couldn't be worse. I've joined the A10 at rush hour.

A white van flashes its lights as it overtakes, the passenger giving me the middle finger and mouthing obscenities through the glass.

Cursing him, I focus on the road. When a second blighter pushes between the front seats, I realise there'll be carnage if I keep going. I try to hold the puppy back with one hand while looking desperately for a place to stop. He licks my hand and bundles past me, landing on the handbrake.

I grab him up by the scruff of the neck and plonk him on the passenger seat. This can't go on.

A glowing green BP sign is forty yards ahead. A horn blasts behind me as I hit the brakes and yank the wheel hard to the left, pulling off the main road like I'm trying out for a part in The Italian Job.

Squealing sounds are coming from the footwell. I daren't use the brakes or clutch in case I squish a puppy beneath the pedals or, heaven forbid, push one through the floor. A horrible image flashes in my mind, of puppies rolling down the road behind the car.

Aiming for the petrol station forecourt, I let the car coast to a stop with my feet well away from the pedals. I aim for the first spare parking bay, yanking on the handbrake to bring the Mini to an undignified halt.

The engine judders and stalls, leaving the car hanging halfway out of the bay.

Taking a swift look round, it doesn't look like anyone has noticed, but I don't want to hang about just in case.

I grab the puppy in the footwell.

'Naughty!' I admonish it, before giving it a kiss on its head and placing it back in the torn and soggy cardboard box. I manage to restore a semblance of order with a blanket barrier stuffed under the front seats, and my rucksack round the driver's side. I pray it holds, as the only other place I can put the puppies is the boot. There's no way I'm putting them back in the dark. My makeshift barrier will have to do.

I start the engine and pull out of the petrol station. Thankfully, the puppies settle down, soothed by the drone of the engine and the car's motion.

I've done it. We're out.

· · ● ● · ● ● · ·

M aisie lives in a semi-detached house at the end of a cul-de-sac outside Hertford. She waits on the doorstep as I pull up to the kerb, following a swift call I made from a phone box down the road.

She is a portly sixty-something with a grey bob and large blue framed glasses, dressed in black cotton trousers lightly dusted with dog hairs. A knitted purple scarf is looped round her shoulders, woven through with glittery silver thread. Getting out of the car is tricky, involving grabbing a wriggling Sputnik while keeping the rest of the puppies safely inside the car. One of them has gone AWOL. I suspect it's under the passenger seat.

When Maisie sees Sputnik, she claps her hands together as if to thank the Lord, her eyes glistening. Sputnik yips, trying to leap out of my arms and into hers. As soon as I've closed the gap he jumps across, licking her face frantically with his tail wagging. A little stream of wee escapes him in his excitement, but Maisie doesn't give two hoots about that.

Once Sputnik has settled down, I show her what else is in the back of the car. Maisie's tears really begin to flow.

'Oh, the poor, poor things.' She peers through the back window at the wriggling bodies. 'Those little ones should still be with their mum.'

'Maisie, I need you to help me out,' I say. 'I can't look after them at home. I've never even looked after a goldfish.'

'I'll help you, don't worry.' Maisie removes her glasses to wipe her eyes. 'They can go in my dog cage for now.'

She's fizzing with purpose, and after twenty minutes we've successfully installed the puppies in temporary lodgings in the lounge with blankets, toys and plenty of food and water.

'What a great team you must have,' Maisie says, after we've washed our hands thoroughly at the kitchen sink. 'Tell me if I'm wrong, Alex, but do you work with ex-policemen, detectives, those kinds of people? It must be a crack outfit to get results like this.'

Her assumption blindsides me.

'My team?'

'Yes. I'd like to meet them. I'd like to say thank you to each and every one of them.'

As I struggle to come up with a suitable answer, she reaches across to a letter rack by the window and picks out a business card which she hands to me. COBRA SECURITY runs across the front, with a glossy image of a red and black snake rearing up to strike. Below it reads: FOR ALL YOUR PROTECTION NEEDS.

'This is my nephew's firm. He's ex-army,' Maisie says, pushing the card into my hand. 'I always like to put a word in for him. He has experience breaking up criminal gangs.'

'Oh, thank you.' I say, putting it in my pocket.

Maisie's eyeing me curiously, one brow raised over the rim of her glasses.

'So, can I meet them? Say thank you?'

I open my mouth but no words come out.

'I understand if it's not possible.' Maisie puts her hand on my arm, gives it a little squeeze. 'I just want them to know, I'm ever so grateful.'

'Of course I'll pass your thanks on. It's just...my team like to keep their identity top secret. Things work better when we stay off the radar.'

'I get it.' Maisie taps her nose. As I mumble my thanks, hoping this line of conversation will go away, she continues. 'When Nina recommended you, I had a funny feeling you would come through. But, I had no idea you would be *this* successful.'

Neither did I, Maisie.

With afternoon drawing on, I tell Maisie I need to get home to call the RSPCA and maybe the police. I'm worried the gang will do a runner once they've discover the puppies are gone.

'Why don't you use my phone?'

I am never one to say no to a kind offer, especially one that saves me money.

'It's the least I can do,' Maisie says, leading me to the sofa and the button phone set beside it on a little table. 'Those puppies need to get back to their owners.'

116

Foolishly, I thought it would take a single phone call to sort everything out, but I end up spending the rest of the afternoon on Maisie's sofa, being pushed from pillar to post, and having to tell half-truths to the RSPCA without mentioning my 'amazing team' in case Maisie overhears.

Eventually, I reach a senior animal welfare officer who gives the impression I'm causing too much trouble for a Monday afternoon. She takes issue with the fact I was trespassing, and yes, I suppose you could describe what I did as theft, only her tone makes me feel as much of a criminal as the puppy snatchers.

'You should have called us first. Or the police.' She continues to push my buttons.

'I was in the middle of nowhere. There were no phones!' I explode. 'How long would you have taken to get to me, anyway? I couldn't leave them!'

'I understand you're upset, but I can't do any more for you right now. I need to liaise with our legal department, and they've gone home for the day. Can you keep the puppies safe tonight?'

For the first time, a bit of warmth comes down the line.

'My friend Maisie's looking after them, but some of them don't look well.'

The border collie pup lies in the corner of the pen, its tongue pale and lolling.

'Are you able to take the sick ones to the vet?'

I mouth the request to Maisie, at which she nods her head.

'The puppies that are fit and well can go to foster homes in the next few days,' the officer says. 'Then we'll put them up for adoption.'

'What do you mean, put them up for adoption? What about their owners?' As my frustration grows, Maisie moves from her vigil at the dog crate to join me on the sofa with Sputnik cradled in her arms.

'Don't mind me,' she whispers and leans close to the receiver to overhear the conversation.

'I'm pretty sure these dogs are local,' I say. 'One's from Hertford.'

'Even so, I'm afraid we don't have the manpower to follow that up,' says the officer in a cool tone. 'We're stretched enough with the calls we get every day.

Uniting these dogs with their owners is going to be impossible. The best we can do is get them back to full health, then rehome them.'

'It wouldn't take much,' I protest. 'All you need to do, is put an advert in the local paper or on your website with photos of the puppies. Ask people to come forward if they recognise them. They can prove ownership with photos, descriptions.'

'*Give me the phone,*' Maisie mouths, making a beckoning gesture.

I hand over the receiver, relieved to be rid of it.

'My name is Maisie. To whom am I speaking, please?'

She places Sputnik in my lap. Cuddling and tickling the silky ball of fluff makes me feel a bit better.

'Now, *Ms* McDonald, please listen to me. I'm the one who asked Alex to find my puppy. It's what she does, find missing pets. Not only has she done that, bless her soul, but she's also found all these other poor babies. No-one should be able to get away with treating poor, innocent animals like commodities. Do you agree? Good. Then, you'd also agree that the Courier would be *very* interested in this story. I guarantee they'll want to know what *you* are doing about it. Now, how do you spell your surname. Is it M-C or M-A-C?'

Maisie listens for a moment, nodding her head.

'You will? Good. I'm glad to hear it. Yes, we will get a case number as soon as we've contacted the police. Is this your direct line?'

She puts down the receiver and gives me a calm nod.

'Complete jobsworth. We'll show her, Alex. We'll get those puppies back to their owners. I'm contacting the paper first thing tomorrow.'

'Make sure you don't mention me, please.'

'All right. If you don't want me to,' Maisie concedes, although I can tell she's itching to broadcast my deeds far and wide.

'I don't want *any* publicity,' I repeat.

'What should I say if they ask about you?'

118

'Just say you used a specialist pet finding service and you can't say any more because you signed a confidentiality agreement.'

'Could write that down for me?'

After I've jotted the key points down, I go to stand and a wave of exhaustion hits me.

'I don't mind liaising with the RSPCA regarding the puppies,' Maisie offers. 'You look like you could do with a rest and a cup of cocoa. Are you up to visiting the police station to get that case number?'

I give her a weary nod. I'll just have to muster the energy from somewhere.

'Once you've done that, I'll pass it on to Ms Grumpy-Knickers. In the meantime, I'll take the collie down to the vets.'

She gives me a sympathetic look, takes my arm and steers me to the door. There, she hands me a cheque for £350.

'And Alex, no matter what *Ms* McDonald said, you should be proud of yourself. You did brilliantly.'

22

The side office in Hertford police station is hot and stuffy. The culprit is a storage heater under the window, pumping out heat with its dial cranked into the red.

God, I regret wearing thermals. In the heat and quiet of the room, after all the excitement, I'm in danger of falling asleep in the hard, plastic chair. Luckily, one of the overhead panel lights is on the blink, intermittently flickering at the edge of my vision. It's irritating enough to keep me awake.

I tap one foot, waiting for DC Longhurst to go through his notes and give me the reference number I need for the RSPCA. Apart from paperwork, his metal-framed table contains a lamp and push-button phone. There's no computer. The young police officer has slung his uniform jacket over the back of his chair, his short-sleeved shirt revealing muscular forearms and well-manicured hands. As he reviews his notes, I wonder if we might strike up an informal friendship over the table.

But when he looks up at me and gives me a warm smile, I flush and look away, unable to meet his eye. Waiting for DC Longhurst's assessment takes me back to my schooldays and the headmaster's office. I don't know how much trouble I'm in.

To distract myself, I stare at the information posters stuck to the grey walls. Most are boring health and safety instructions on how to lift heavy boxes, or what to do if you haven't got a solicitor.

Two flyers in the middle of the wall catch my eye. '*Police Appeal for Assistance - Murder. Do you recognise this man?*' Beneath the bold heading are two photos of a man's head, sculpted from red clay. The text below states the reconstruction was made from a skull, found in Deptford.

How on earth did they manage to create a likeness of a man from a skull?

The second Crimestoppers poster has a photo of a grungey-looking teen with dirty-blond dreadlocks: *Missing from Hertford since 10th January 1998. 19 year-old Jason Bevin. £10,000 reward for information leading to his return.*

I wonder what has happened to him.

DC Longhurst clears his throat to catch my attention.

'Miss Martin. You have admitted to trespassing on private property by entering a commercial barn without the property owner's permission. You removed ten puppies from the barn that do not belong to you. Is that correct?'

I squirm in the grey, plastic seat. 'Well, I wouldn't put it quite like that, but...'

'And you did this on the basis of a random tip-off?'

'It was a very good tip-off.'

His pale blue eyes assess me. Is that a flicker of humour I see - has he sussed me out already? I manage to hold his gaze this time. He's far easier on the eye than our surroundings. His blond hair is tousled on top, cropped short at the back and sides. The combination of fair hair, blue eyes and prominent cheekbones suggests Nordic heritage. A Viking.

'Who gave you this tip?' DC Longhurst leans over the table.

I reach for an acceptable answer.

'It was anonymous.'

'And on the strength of this anonymous tip, you drove from Ware to Reed End and put yourself in considerable danger, for ten dogs you'd never seen before and have no connection to?'

I bite my lip, uncomfortable under his scrutiny. He's a different kettle of fish to Maisie, who bought everything I told her.

'What I can't help wondering, Miss Martin, is why this person gave the tip to you instead of going straight to the RSPCA or the police?' DC Longhurst's manner is not unkind, despite my evasiveness. However, his perceptive questioning is going to land me in trouble unless I can come up with a convincing story; a version of the truth mixed with harmless misinformation.

It would help if I could keep still, but my foot's tapping away of its own accord and I'm tweaking my lower lip like plasticine. Aren't those 'tells?' Whatever I say next had better sound believable.

'OK. This is what happened,' I go for it. 'I was looking to buy a puppy. Then I saw a flyer advertising pedigree puppies and rang up the number. A man at the other end gave me an address and time to meet. I arrived at the barn early. When I saw the state the puppies were in, I panicked and hid before John's mate arrived on the tractor. I heard him on his walkie-talkie lining up the next sale and knew I had to do something. I never meant to cause any trouble.'

The last bit, at least, is true.

'Have you got the number, or the flyer?'

I shake my head.

'If you find that flyer or any other information, let me know for the crime report.' DC Longhurst makes a note. 'We don't have you on record, Miss Martin, do we?'

'I'm a law-abiding citizen.' I pause, then add. 'Squeaky clean, officer.'

'Up until now.' He points his biro at me. 'You had a lucky escape, getting away from the barn.'

As if I need reminding.

'You should leave these things to us.'

'Absolutely.' I nod like the dog in that car insurance advert, demonstrating humility and absolute understanding. I want nothing more than the police to take over so I can slide back into my nice, safe, mediocre life.

'The man I described,' I say. 'Do you have any idea who he is?'

DC Longhurst shakes his head. 'It's possible he and his mate John could be part of something bigger. Organised crime has grown massively in Hertfordshire, and a lot of the networks are run by Eastern Europeans. They use locals as front men to avoid arousing suspicion. But my guess is they're working alone. It wasn't exactly a sophisticated operation.'

He chucks his pen on the table.

'We'll look into the barn and the two culprits you mentioned, but the vehicle is the best lead so far. You need to get me the photos you took as soon as possible,' DC Longhurst makes a note on a pad. 'We'll try and trace the owner of the barn, although we'll be lucky to get anything connecting the land owner or holding company with the two men.'

'So, I'm not in trouble for trespassing then?'

'Trespass is a civil matter. Not a criminal one.'

'Am I going to get a caution?' I feel sick at the thought and my heart starts pounding. I hate having my knuckles rapped.

'You sound like you *want* me to stick something on you.' DC Longhurst stretches back in his chair with an amused smile.

'God, no, that's not what I meant!'

'Relax, Miss Martin.' He raises an eyebrow. 'I'm pulling your leg.'

His joke lands on stony ground.

'What happens now?' I eye the slip of paper in his hand.

'To be honest, I'm not sure how far we're going to get with this. Tying John and his mate to the dogs is going to be impossible now you've removed the evidence. If they're no longer in possession of the stolen goods...' He shrugs.

'Dogs are more than stolen goods, surely?'

'Afraid not. The law treats pet theft the same as loss of property.'

'That's ridiculous.'

'That's the way it is. Look, you got the dogs out and they're safe.' He hands me the slip of paper along with his card. 'That's your crime reference number. You can pass it on to the RSPCA. In the meantime, send me the photos. If we can track the van down, it might give us some leads. Give me a ring if you think of anything else.'

As I get up to leave, he says, 'Miss Martin? Stay away from any more 'tip-offs,' would you?'

'Don't worry,' I assure him. 'You won't see or hear from me again.'

23

— ∘ —

That night, I have a nightmare where I'm trapped in the dark with a gang of thugs closing in on me. I wake up with a massive yell, my sheets tangled round my legs. My eyes have been opened to the miserable underbelly of the pet trade and I can't unsee it. I wish I could wind back the clock.

I lie awake in the dark with my mind racing until the doorbell goes off just before eight am. Despite the early hour, I'm glad to hear a fellow human outside the door. Glad, too for the excuse to get out of bed and break my monotonous, dark thoughts.

The postman appears surprised when I answer the door so promptly. When he greets me with a smile, I have to stop myself putting my arms out for a hug.

'Miss Martin? Special Delivery.' I sign where he points and he passes me a white envelope with my agency's name and address on the back flap.

'Thank you!' I wave him off with a smile.

On the way to the kitchen, I stop short at my reflection in the hall mirror. The postman did well not to scream and run off. I look half-deranged with straggly, unkempt hair, grey-tinged complexion and puffy eyes.

The house seems colder than usual without Antony around. After throwing on a dressing gown, I make coffee and porridge and eat breakfast at the table, staring like a zombie at the unopened letter.

Yesterday's fiasco has cemented my decision to put the finding machine away for good. The machine survived my crash-landing on top of it and appears to be in full working order. Once again, I've wrapped it up and hidden it in my bottom drawer.

No more finding lost animals.

I must have been crazy to think it was going to be as simple as finding Sputnik, rescuing him, getting the reward and back home for tea, like the girls and boys in an Enid Blyton story.

The machine brought joy to Nina and Maisie, Sebastian and Sputnik. But it hasn't brought joy to me. There is something compelling about its power, its promise of finding things, but I can't help feeling it has a darker side as well.

I slip my finger beneath the flap of the envelope and tear it open. The letter's contents are short and to the point.

Dear Agency Worker,

With regret, we are writing to inform you that WRITE ON! formally ceased trading on 28th February 1998. A combination of factors including the downturn in the transcription and typing market and the widespread increase of home PCs means we are no longer able to continue operating profitably.

Our legal firm, Parker, Chatman, and Ness are overseeing the process as we go into administration.

We enclose a cheque covering your outstanding invoices. Thank you for all your hard work.

Any queries should be directed to Parker, Chatman, and Ness [details enclosed].

Yours faithfully,

The team at WRITE ON!

All the years I worked for them, they couldn't be bothered to put in my name. I expected they'd at least do that. And it would have been nice to have more warning. This bolt from the blue leaves me completely high and dry.

The cheque is for £832.67. After rent, bills and food, it's not going to keep me going very long.

Agency work was the one thing I could rely on. I thought of it as a partnership, but it seems I was nothing more than a disposable temp. A nobody.

I wrap up warm and take a slow walk into town to pay in the cheque at the bank. Once that's done, I wander aimlessly by the river before returning to my empty in-tray. I tuck my headset away in my desk drawer, unplug my transcription machine and log onto my emails.

No new emails.

•••••••••••

Т he best remedy for worries and woes is keeping busy. Despite having no paid work, I fill my hours with painting, jogging and spring-cleaning the house before Antony gets back on Wednesday. I've had my Kodak film developed at Boots (again) and emailed the photos of the barn and the dognapper's pick-up truck to DC Longhurst.

Evern now and then, I get a cold flash of fear that John and his mate are coming to get me. Hopefully, my worries will fade in time.

Finding work can wait until I'm in a better frame of mind. I prime a new canvas and apply a base wash to the shattered oak tree and try not to think about the finding machine or lost cats and dogs.

Out of curiosity, I take the business card Maisie gave me and ring the company: Cobra Security. The receptionist tells me about the different kinds of personal protection services on offer. It sounds fantastic to take a bodyguard round with you for the day, but when she tells me how much it costs, I cut short the call and throw the card in the recycling bin.

I work on updating my CV and email it to a couple of London agencies I worked for before, plus one in Hertford. I have no burning desire to re-enter the world of touch-typing speeds and whether I have Advanced or Intermediate skills on Excel, but I have to do something.

Wednesday lunchtime, I stand at the window like Miss Havisham, watching for Antony to arrive. When he eventually pulls onto the drive at quarter past two, I stop myself racing down the stairs and throwing myself in a blubbering heap on top of him. Despite my desperation to divulge everything that's happened since he left, I play it cool and stay in my room, resolved to give him time to settle back into Ware life before I hit him with my epic tale.

He knocks on my door less than fifteen minutes later, and pokes his head into the room.

'Hey. Miss me?'

A beaming grin spreads across my face. It is so good to see him, my spirits sing. I run across the room and throw my arms round his neck. He leans over to reciprocate and we have a proper hug. I could stay that way for the rest of the afternoon, but there's too much to catch up on.

'Here, I brought you this.' Antony hands me a plastic bag with *INTEL PENTIUM III* on it. The bag's stuffed with pens, notepads and keyrings, each one emblazoned with company logos. 'You can never have enough pens. There's some chocolate in there as well. Pentium chocolate. How awesome is that?'

We grab a coffee and sit at the kitchen table and I ask how he got on at the NEC.

'It was great.' Antony's eyes sparkle. He tells me about the scale of the exhibition, how he gave out loads of business cards, met amazing contacts.

He adjusts his glasses. 'I've had a couple of job offers. You know, permanent employment, not self-employed. One company's from London and the other one's up in Birmingham.'

My mug stops halfway to my mouth. Is this the moment he tells me he's leaving?

Considering the week I've had, it would be the final straw. I swallow back disappointment. I've been expecting it for months, but it still hurts. The Midlands is a long way away. If Antony moved to London that wouldn't be as bad, but I'd rather he didn't move at all.

128

My future's looking bleak. My car's on its last legs. I don't have a job. If Antony goes to Birmingham, I'll never see him again. And if he goes, I'll have to move because no way am I sharing my house with a stranger.

Finding someone to replace him would be impossible. No-one else would buy me little treats, or demonstrate the patience of a saint indulging my weird ideas. Antony makes me breakfast, fixes my technical issues, laughs at my terrible jokes and puts up with my 1980s music. Plus, he's never fazed when I get grumpy and he gives me great advice, despite the fact I rarely take it.

'Have you decided what you're going to do?' I ask, dreading the answer.

'Nope. I'm not one hundred percent sure I want to work for an employer.'

My heart lightens.

'I like choosing my own hours, being my own boss. But change is good, yeah?'

Sinks again.

'I'll really miss you if you go,' the words blurt out.

'I'll miss you, too, you fool,' Antony says, putting his hand over mine across the table. 'Never a dull moment with you around, that's for sure. I don't know, maybe you could come up to Birmingham with me, if I decide to go. You can work from anywhere, right? It's just a thought. You want to stay here, that's cool.'

'I don't know.' I sound pathetic.

'Think about it. There's time.'

Stay here, I try to transmit the words to him.

'That's enough about me. What about you?' Antony looks over his glasses at me. 'Anything happen while I was away?'

24

‘What were you thinking, Alex?’ Antony gives me a pained look. ‘You could have been hurt.’

I lean my elbows on the table, weighed down by exhaustion and shame. Telling Antony was supposed to lighten my burden. Instead, it's done the opposite.

‘Something came over me. I didn't stop to think. Don't worry, I've learnt my lesson.’

‘And to think I gave you props for being Peter Parker.’ Antony leans back in his chair, assessing me. ‘You just about got away with it. By the skin of your teeth.’

I stare at the grain of the wood. As if I need reminding.

‘You needn't worry about me using the finding machine again.’ I meet Antony's eyes. ‘This is the second time it's got me into trouble. There won't be a third.’

‘You can't blame the machine. All it does is point to stuff.’ Antony rubs his forehead, wincing slightly, as if I've given him a headache.

I push back from the table, my cheeks burning from his insinuation I only have myself to blame. ‘I know I acted rashly. But for your information, there *is* something weird about the finding machine. You know there is. Don't you remember, you were the one who made a song and dance about it in the first place? You told me you were worried it was nuclear, or made in Russia, or whatever.’

'That's because I don't know what's in it,' Antony replies. 'It's too cold. It's too heavy. It could be pouring out illegal CFCs or Freon or a ton of radioactivity. Until we take it to pieces we won't know. But it's not influencing the outcome of the stuff it finds like something in the X-Files. It's not changing destiny or fate. No way.'

I stare at him with my arms crossed.

'Can't we agree there's something creepy about it? Neither of us can shake that feeling. Remember what you told me about the Russians?'

Antony stretches back and looks up at the ceiling. With his arms hanging down, he appears to have given up on me.

'Forget I said that. I was being paranoid. I've watched too many films, read too many books. We need to chill out.'

· · · ●·● ● ·· ·

I didn't tell Antony I lost my job. He's coasting high on success following the exhibition and it would be wrong of me to put a downer on that.

On Friday, one of the London agencies asks me to go in for an interview. Instead of putting on my smart suit and getting the train in to see them, I tell them I've got work and will be in touch soon. I'm such a sap.

Monday morning, after a weekend solidly painting, I check my emails. Since work died, I've been receiving one or two a day.

My inbox shows fifty-four new messages.

My first thought – it must be spam. Antony's continually warned me about clicking on links, but he's installed decent anti-virus software with a spam filter on my PC. Always security conscious, he made me create a new email for business: *martinadmin@tiscali.co.uk*. You can read it as a man's name, surname, or it could be a company. It gives nothing away.

Something strange must be going on.

I hesitate for a minute, my mouse hovering over the first new message from *adriana@aol.com*, before I click on it.

To The Finder, I have lost my King Charles Spaniel Gus on a walk down the river please can you find him I will pay you twenty pounds I know its not much, but I am on benefits. He has brown eyebrows and dark brown splotches. He ran off on the Basingstoke Canal near Ash Vale on March 21ˢᵗ and I put posters up but no-one can find him. If you find him I will be forever greatful, Adriana.

I stare at the screen in puzzlement. Where has this come from? I've never even heard of Ash Vale. I take a minute to look it up in my AA Big Road Atlas and discover it's a small place on the border between Surrey and Hampshire, about seventy miles away. Well, that's not local. I wonder how Adriana heard about me. She hasn't sent me a picture of Gus, so I can't help her.

With a growing sense of confusion, I open the next email from *spiderboy@tiscali.co.uk*

Mr Simons kept me company. Since my wife died, he kept me occupied. He was a little devil. He was into everything. You wouldn't believe it when you looked at the size of him. He shredded my carpets, chewed my slippers and you should of seen the state of my sofa, but I miss the little bugger to death. Can you find him? His favourite food is Sheba.

Just as I'm trying to put a lid on my growing confusion, I open the next email. A giant eye with stars arranged round it, stares back.

When will you find love? What opportunities are round the corner for you? Regular readings lead to better lives. Check out our testimonials at psychicsinsideyourhead.com

What the...? I click down the list with growing confusion. For every three or four emails regarding lost pets I get another one from a psychic, medium or spiritualist.

Miriam, Spirit Reader, available for all messages from the nether to the NOW! Have you lost someone you want to contact, was there something important you needed to say? Do you need to know if someone has passed over peacefully? Miriam can help you, email me a photograph miriamskydiamond@tiscali.co.uk. Call me: 07700-900365. I can do your reading from a photo!

I read Miriam's message twice. The bit about doing readings from a photo has an eerie echo of my dad's machine. Has she got another finding machine? *Course not.* I print her message off and put it to one side.

There are more requests for help to find lost cats and dogs, even a horse. Then:

Astral Jayne - The work you are involved with has put you in great danger. It will bring you sorrow. You have brought into action sinister forces that govern the placement of elements in the astral plane. Your interference with the spiritual dimension has created instability in the ether. I urge you to stop what you are doing. Contact me to find out more. 0909-879666

The hairs at the nape of my neck prickle.

Has some essence of my dad crossed over the spirit realm when I put his photograph in his machine? Or does the machine reach out to unknown dimensions every time I switch it on? Is it cold because it's channelling the realms of the dead?

It seems as though anyone with a spirit eye has locked onto me, like the Eye of Sauron. From the messages I've received (by email, I reassure myself, not by ethereal transfer) I appear to have ripped a hole in the firmament, allowing the living and the dead to cross paths. Or something. The messages from the mystics seem to imply that something bad could come through this portal, and it would be my fault.

Perhaps I need to put the finding machine in a lead-lined box. Or bury it a hundred feet underground.

The emails go on and on, a litany of desperate requests to find dogs and cats and the horse, of course. Some people have sent photos, most haven't. How do pet owners and psychics go together? How did they get my email address in the first place?

A few of the pets went missing around here, but most are from further afield. One man has contacted me from Glasgow, over five hundred miles away. He must be desperate to think I can help him. The same goes for the rest.

Everything is spiralling out of control. It's too much. I slump forward on my desk.

I only wanted to help a few pets to check the machine worked. What am I supposed to do now? I don't want to let these people down. But the long and short of it is – I'm not finding any more animals.

Only with the last email, do I get an inkling of how they found me.

Dear Finder, Brandy was a replacement for our last dog, Schnapps, who died of a tumour just before Christmas. I cannot tell you how much joy she brought us for the few weeks that we had her. When she looked at me, love shone out of her eyes. She was taken from the back of our car when we popped in to see a friend. Please can you help us find her? We will pay your fee.

P.S. I got your details from the Courier.

25

I heard the Courier land on the mat sometime this week, but with everything that happened, I didn't have time to glance at it. Next time I looked, it had gone.

Antony has probably chucked it in with the recycling. He's not a fan of small town news, whereas I like to know what's going on locally. I pop downstairs to check, hoping he hasn't been a dutiful eco-warrior and taken everything to the communal recycling bins down Bowling Road.

Thankfully, the recycling box beside the kitchen bin is full of pizza boxes, flyers, bottles and cans. I find the Courier wedged down one side, grease-stained and soggy in places, but still in one piece.

After blotting the newspaper with kitchen roll, I read it on the floor.

HOUSE FIRE IN HODDESDON – LUCKY SURVIVORS.

A dramatic photo captures the fire brigade bringing a blaze under control. Black smoke billows from a first floor window above a row of shops. The occupants escaped unhurt, but lost everything.

Below is an article on Hertford Toy Library, which is to close due to a lack of volunteers: FUN WILL BE THIN ON THE GROUND.

Maybe I got away with it.

I turn the page. The headline hits me like a smack between the eyes. I lean back with my hands tightening into fists, squeezing my eyes shut. It's no good, I have to look.

HERTFORDSHIRE DOGNAPPING RING BROKEN.

135

Half the page is taken up with a whacking great colour photograph of Maisie in her lounge, smiling broadly as she cuddles Sputnik. The other puppies gambol behind her. The collie that was sickly when I last saw it is up on its back legs, pawing at her. She must have got him sorted at the vets.

Despite the happy photo, my spirits take a dive as I read the article. I should feel proud, but I can't muster any enthusiasm.

Maisie has given an imaginative account of 'my team's' raid on the barn that reads like one of Andy McNab's military memoirs. She says the team staked out the barn and then silently infiltrated it to extract the puppies, using the latest surveillance and tracking technologies. I'll say this - it's a definite change from the usual council notices and charity galas. Maisie rounds up her madcap version of events with, 'The rest is top secret.'

I suppose I should give her props for remembering that part of the script.

Reading on, the police are investigating the tractor driver and his colleague, John. They are asking the public to come forward if they know the owner of the Mitsubishi pick-up or the company, G M BUILDTEK, as it's not a registered company. They've printed the first part of the number plate.

The puppies' photos fill the next page with an RSPCA hotline number for anyone who recognises their pet. Seeing the faces of the pups again forces me to acknowledge my achievement.

I did really well.

And Maisie hasn't mentioned me by name. She says she employed 'a Finding Agency' to return Sputnik to her and all had come good. So far, she's kept her side of the bargain.

The kicker comes at the bottom of the page, in a line added by a staffer: *If you would like The Finder to locate your missing pet, email martinadmin@tiscali.co.uk with details and a photograph.*

Oh, Maisie, my soul sinks. *How could you! I told you to keep me out of it!*

My email address links me directly to the missing dogs, and the people who stole them in the first place. Maisie meant well, but I could strangle her! I grab the paper and leap the stairs three at a time and am on the phone to her within seconds, fighting down bubbling rage.

'Maisie, you put my email in the paper!' The words explode from me as soon as she answers.

'Who is this?'

'It's Alex. The one who found Sputnik.' My tone is barely civil. 'I specifically asked you not to mention me, and you gave them my email!'

'Oh, Alex, I am so sorry to hear that. But I genuinely never gave the paper those details, my dear. I did as you asked.'

'Doesn't look like it to me.' I pull at the phone cord, twisting it round my fingers.

'I give you my word.' Maisie remains calm despite my onslaught. 'I'm so sorry, Alex. I don't know where they got it from. I don't understand.'

I take a deep breath. Maisie wouldn't lie to me.

'Well, who else would have told them?'

'Let me think,' Maisie says, followed by a long pause. 'Oh, dear. I don't like to point the finger, but I'm afraid it could be Nina.'

'Nina?'

'I told the journalist you'd found her cat, Sebastian. He seemed very interested in the story. It sounds as though he went to talk to her, and she gave him your email. I really am sorry. Is there anything I can do to make things better?'

'You can't do anything now. I have to go.' I hang up on her and let off steam by swearing out of the window.

I rattle off two emails at lightning speed, one to Nina and one to The Courier. I tell Nina not to pass my details on to anyone else as I'm not finding pets any more. Although I'm tempted to give her a piece of my mind, rationale tells me to wait until I've calmed down. I'm starting to feel guilty about the way I spoke to Maisie.

My third email is to The Courier with the same request. Hitting 'Send' makes me feel marginally better.

'Heard you shouting down the phone.' Antony's in the doorway. 'Can I come in?'

At my tight nod he walks over. He glances at the newspaper clenched so tight in my fist, it's concertinaed in the middle.

'What's going on?' He peers over his glasses. 'Are you going to tell me, or what?'

His concern takes the edge off my anger. I let my shoulders drop and loosen my grip on the paper, opening it at the relevant page.

'Ahh.' Antony moves closer, scanning the article. 'So, you're famous. That the dog you found? Cute.'

'Yeah, and now the whole of Hertfordshire knows my email address.'

'I'm sure it's not as bad as you think.' Taking the paper from me, he sits at my desk and reads through the article.

'It's probably worse.' I pound the floor in a circle, throwing my hands in the air. 'Why didn't Nina ask if I was OK with it before she gave out my email?'

'She's over the moon to have Sebastian back,' Antony says without looking up. 'Forgot herself.'

'It's her fault I've got all these emails.'

'What emails?' Antony looks up from the article.

'I've had fifty-four come in this morning. People wanting me to find their pets. And psychics. Have a look for yourself.'

Antony takes the mouse and goes to my inbox. As he clicks through the messages, I fill him in on the warnings I've received about meddling in the spiritual world.

He barks with laughter.

'It's not funny!' I snap.

'I'm sorry.' He points at the screen, one hand covering his smile. 'It's this guy from Glasgow. What's he thinking, that you've got a nationwide web of spies, or something? And the one who lost a horse. How do you lose a horse?'

'Have you seen the psychic ones?' I ask. 'They don't like what I'm doing, Antony.' I pace a tight circle on the carpet. 'They want me to stop using the finding machine. They've told me as much. They want me to ring them to find out more.'

'Where does it say that?' Antony returns his attention to the screen. 'Show me where it says, '*stop using the finding machine*.'

'The messages imply it. They don't need to say it specifically. I know what they mean.'

I let out a groan and throw myself onto the bed.

'Are you for real? That's what they do, Alex. These people just chuck out Barnum statements for people to latch onto and then they make them fit. That's how they hook you. They're chancers. All they want is for you to ring them at 60p a minute.'

I'm not so sure, and I'm still worried about the Courier having my email address. The whole fiasco has raised my stress to astonomical levels.

'Hey, you. You need to get a grip.' Antony rattles the newspaper at me. 'None of this mentions you specifically. That's good. We can always change your email address, so we've got that in our back pocket. Anyway, it's pretty hard to trace someone from their IP address without permission from their ISP. That rarely happens, definitely not with low grade scumbags like the ones who stole the puppies. They don't know your full name or location. You're safe. And anyway, you've got a boy's name. They don't know who you are.'

'Maisie knows me. What if they go after her?'

'With all this heat in the paper, they'll vanish and move on. Or, they'll get caught. Don't sweat it.'

'I hope you're right,' I say disconsolately, rolling over to face the wall.

I hear Antony clicking at my keyboard and more rustling as he goes back to the paper.

'Did you read the whole paper, Alex?' he eventually says.

I struggle to sit up. He's holding the Courier open at a different page. I rush over to see the image he's pointing at. A photo of a rusty shed surrounded by weeds and police tape.

I clap my hands over my eyes.

'Put it away,' I say. 'Don't read it.'

So he does.

A GRANDFATHER who was convicted of possessing indecent images of children, hid them for years in a shed on an allotment in Ware. Terrence Harber, 74, stored images of ~~various forms of sexual activity involving~~ children under the age of twelve, on video cassettes and recordable compact discs. The contents of Harber's shed came to police attention after the Green Lane Allotment Society raised concerns about the condition of his plot and undertook an inspection.

Harber told Hertford County Court magistrates he was storing the images for a friend alongside his family's photo collection, but the content did not match the assertion. Harber, of The Roundway, Ware, was put on probation for the maximum three years. He will remain on the sex offenders register for five years. An ongoing investigation continues into any contact he may have had with children during his time as Group Scout Leader in Harlow during the 1970s.

'That's just great.' I lie back down and put my head under the pillow.

Antony slumps back in my office chair.

'You told me about this bloke Terry. I didn't know he lived on our doorstep. The Roundway is less than five minutes away. Are these kids local too?'

I don't have an answer. It's too depressing to contemplate. I wonder how Geoff, Green Lane Allotments' secretary, is dealing with the awful publicity. For the forseeable future, Terrence Harber is the only thing the allotments will be remembered for.

'Does the article mention me anywhere?' I ask Antony.

'No. I don't think so.'

Geoff hasn't mentioned me. That's something.

· · · ● ●· ● ● · · ·

A fter pinging Maisie an apology for being short with her on the phone, I spend the rest of the day sorting through the missing pet emails.

While I can't go round the UK finding the lost animals, I can do the next best thing.

Ten more enquiries have arrived during the last hour - I email them straight back with an apology, saying I am no longer in business.

The hardest bit is retrieving the finding machine. I stare long and hard at it. Somehow, it doesn't seem as cold or heavy as before. Antony refuses to engage with my fears regarding its stranger aspects. It's just a machine. It doesn't alter fate or change destiny. I'm not in an Arthur C. Clarke Unsolved Mystery.

It's just a machine.

'I control you,' I say aloud. 'Do you hear me? You're just a machine. You are going to help find these pets.'

One last time.

After resizing and printing out all the pet photos, I feed them one by one into the finding machine and make a note of the locations. I leave it a couple of hours and recheck the readings to see if the animals have changed position.

Six cats haven't moved in the intervening time. They are in various places - in the middle of woodland, on the margins of main roads or developed areas, and two are inside buildings. The same goes for three of the dogs.

I respond to each owner in turn, from the man living in Glasgow to the widow on the Isle of Arran. Even the owner of the horse. After stating I am no longer accepting new cases, I say 'my team' has ascertained the last known locations of their pets, and wish them the best of luck in finding them.

Whether they succeed or not, they won't be able to contact me on my old email address. Antony has closed down the account, leaving my personal email, known only by close friends and family.

No more pet-rescues for me. Ever.

26

*D*ear Alexandra, this is my first email to you! Your Uncle Fintan taught me
how to send attachments. Here is one.

It is the Youth for Mary flyer!

*When will we see you across the water? I thought I'd invite you again as I know
how lonely it can be living on your own. Don't be a stranger now,*

Love, Mammy x

Yet another communication from Mum that leaves me grinding my teeth.

I have repeatedly told her I'm house-sharing with Antony, even shown her
pictures, but she insists on referring to me as 'living on my own.' I wonder if it's
because she considers every woman who is not married 'alone.' Madness, in this
day and age. Or she's choosing to ignore Antony's existence because she doesn't
like the fact he's black.

For some reason, she can't handle the idea of me and Antony becoming an
item. Maybe it's the idea of him standing out in family photographs. What the
neighbours might say. It may be 1998, but my mum's views are stuck in 1940s
rural Ireland.

Mum goes down a set route if she doesn't like something. She starts off with
a glib remark or excuse and then changes the subject.

I asked her to check for any old photos of Dad's family or diagrams or plans
relating to his finding machine. I wanted to know more about Uncle Stanley
and his shop as well as anything about Lilian. Nothing. I've had enough toing

and froing with Mum regarding Dad's machine. She's very much 'do as I say, not as I do,' which is rich considering the way she's always banging on about family values.

She's ignored my request for Margaret Long's phone number. Clearly, she doesn't think it's important. I'm starting to think she's hiding something.

The one thing she remembered is the church youth group. So, we have both succeeded in annoying each other as much as possible.

I click on the flyer with low expectations. It's a Word template with her church's logo plonked on top, and a load of shamrocks added round the banner. I skim-read it with exasperation. A disco for young parishioners 18+ starting at 6.30pm and ending at 9pm. Sounds banging! Oh, and no alcohol as most of the Irish youth have taken the pledge.

When it comes to Mum, I'm living a lie. I don't know the name of the Catholic church in Ware. I've walked past it often enough, but the name just won't stick. It's probably something like Our Lady of Supplications and Interventions. It may as well be Our Lady of I Told You So.

I suppose I could find out and do a bit of research as protection against Mum's questions. But if the priest challenged me, I'd have to pretend to be interested in joining the church. That's a venial sin right there.

Besides, I can't forgive her for leaving out Margaret's details. It's like Mum's sticking two fingers up at me. She's made it crystal clear - if I want to find out anything, I'm on my own.

What Mum doesn't realise, is that I've got a few tricks up my sleeve. I suspected she'd leave me high and dry, which is why I went to Ware library yesterday, to flick through the phone book. I was counting on Margaret still being listed, like a lot of her generation. My hunch paid off when I found her under '*Long, M.*'

On the off-chance, I looked for Uncle Stanley. Of the eight Martins in the phone book, none of them started with S and four were women. Maybe Margaret can shed some light on what happened to him.

Margaret and I had a lovely catch-up conversation, ending in an invitation to come and see her.

Plus, if anyone can tell me more about Lilian, it's her.

· · · ●·●·● · · ·

W are to Sudbury is a fifty mile journey. I set off early on a fresh April morning with the sun burning through a cloudless sky, promising a first taste of proper warmth.

Lilian Martin has to have a history. The best place to start is the churchyard where my father's buried. Lilian was his sister; they must have records ●

After crossing the county border into Suffolk, I wind my driver's window down to let warm air flood through the car. Why is it I remember the summer holidays of my childhood more than school and the rain? All those sunny days, when we were free after lunch to take our bikes and go off wherever we liked. Our only instruction - to be home by five o'clock without fail, or else.

I spent twenty-two years in and around Sudbury. Nostalgia hits me as I reach the outskirts of town. The surrounding hamlets and villages around the River Stour boast scenery that inspired Constable and Gainsborough. And me.

My first stop is St Gregory's C of E. In his will, Dad stipulated he wanted to be laid to rest here. It must have meant a great deal to decide not to be buried next to Mum. She was shocked, and rarely came here after the funeral, to my knowledge. If Dad had ended up in the Catholic graveyard, she would have visited every week without fail. But Church of England wasn't worth the bother.

Mum has always been supremely confident her place 'up there' is guaranteed, like a celebrity who regularly waltzes past the queue outside The Ivy, to find their regular table waiting in the best location by the window. She gave me the impression, Dad's destination was less assured. He'd be lucky to get the table outside the toilets.

St Gregory's church is Anglican, old, stone built. It sits near the centre of town on a spacious plot with plenty of greenery and a large car park. I think its origins are Norman, yet its stones gleam following a restoration. The care and investment continues throughout the well-tended grounds.

The church would look good in an episode of Midsomer Murders or an Agatha Christie dramatisation. Its squared-off tower with battlements instead of a steeple, makes it look like a castle. Whenever I came here as a youngster, I imagined running around those battlements with a sword to fight off the invading hoardes.

My route from the carpark to the graveyard takes me past a modern addition attached to the back of the church - a vaulted, glass fronted hall. Inside, toddlers run around while mums and dads sit by the wall in small groups, chatting away.

The path meanders through the graveyard. Many of the oldest graves nearest the church are crumbling and leaning over as the ground has shifts over time. Beneath layers of moss, many of the inscriptions have worn away to nothing.

Lots of people visit their loved ones gravesides regularly, but I've been here once in the last two years. It sounds terrible to say it, but I don't tie my memories of someone to a plot of land with a headstone, although I like to believe we have a soul. As to what form it takes, that's another question. Perhaps we come back as bumble bees. Or we're recycled into a hundred thousand atoms of soil. When my time is up, I'd like my ashes scattered across the countryside. Or have a tree planted on me.

Further out, where the oak trees spread across the railings that demarcate church land, the gravestones stand at perfect right-angles to the ground, their edges sharp, cut by machine.

Dad's grave is here, in the Martin family plot. The black slab next to theirs is filled with green stone chips and looks like a miniature driveway. The flowers are artificial, gaudy.

My father's side of the family were traditional, Church of England all the way through. I don't know what they felt about him marrying a Catholic because no-one told me anything, but Dad's heart was here. I'm happy he got his choice of final resting place.

I stand before the grave. Although his bones are under there, I get more sense of him from the photo on my desk at home. The headstone for all three Martins is a simple dark grey slab, with a pale cross engraved in the centre, leaving plenty of space for the inscriptions below.

IN LOVING MEMORY
Vera Anne Martin (neè Gardiner) 1898–1971. 73 Years.
With love we remember a Loving Wife, Mother, Nan.
'Sleep on now, and take your rest': Matthew 26: 45
***
Jack Frederick Martin 1895-1986. 91 Years.
Beloved Husband and Father. Now safe in God's care. 'Be Faithful unto Death,
and I will give you the Crown of Life': Ephesians 2:10
***
Richard Anthony Martin 1919-1993. 74 years.
Forever Missed. 'You will seek me and find me, when you seek me with all your
heart.' Jeremiah 20:13

I take out my Kodak and snap the headstone. Then, I retrieve the black and white photo of Vera holding baby Lilian and wander round the surrounding graves, looking for a little girl born in the mid 1920s.

Nothing jumps out. The dates in the vicinity are wrong and I can't spot her name.

'Hello there,' a soft voice comes behind my shoulder. Turning, a middle-aged woman with an auburn bob gives me a warm smile. Her eyes sparkle behind snazzy thin-framed glasses with chunky, purple arms.

'Reverend Cheryl, isn't it?' I say.

She took the service at Dad's funeral, and made an exceptional tribute to him that was both celebratory and informative. It was clear she'd known him, or at least done her research. By the end of the service, I was left with the feeling everything would be OK in the end.

She sports the clerical collar and black clergy shirt. Instead of robes, she wears a fuschia jersey over her shirt. Where the sunlight hits her hair, the orange tints turn fiery.

'Just call me Cheryl.' She shakes my hand and indicates the graves. 'Visiting family?'

'Something like that.'

Cheryl goes on. 'I like to pay a visit to old friends in between all the desk work. It keeps me grounded.'

I glance up at the battlements. 'I've always loved this church. The tower.'

Cheryl removes her glasses and points them towards the church. 'Our records show there has been a place of worhip here since the year 1000, so there are a lot of old bones beneath our feet.'

She looks round at the trees. 'I sometimes think of the oak trees growing as the centuries pass, as we grow and then die. The things they must have seen.'

In my mind's eye, I conjure the scene - oak trees sprouting from acorns. I see the shadows of cowled monks filing out of the apse. I wonder what they would make of life in the twentieth century: church services in English, women in trousers, women running things, even women vicars. They'd probably have everyone tied to stakes before you could say, 'Heretics, Brother Cuthbert!' After they'd burned the women, they'd have to deal with hoodies and atheists. And science.

Maybe I'm wrong. The monks might relish our new world once they got over the initial shock, and would appreciate our rationale and logic, the equality of the sexes, secular law, takeaway pizza, duvets and fridges. I like to think so, anyway.

'Did you know Dad, his family?' I ask.

'I remember Richard,' Cheryl says. 'He used to come to Sunday service about once a month. His parents died before I came here, I'm afraid. I understand from a few of the older parishioners that they were a lovely family. Very close.'

I show her the photo of Lilian.

'This is Lilian Martin, Dad's sister,' I explain. 'She disappeared when she was a child, but nobody knows what happened to her. I'm looking for evidence she existed. Can you help?'

The Reverend Cheryl replaces her glasses. Sunlight reflects off the lenses. 'What is it you want to know?'

27

—— · ——

I grab the opportunity to ask Cheryl the questions that have burdened me since February.

'I'm looking for information on Lilian Martin and Stanley Martin, who was Dad's uncle,' I say. 'Birth certificates, records of their deaths, anything like that.'

'Well, I do like a mystery.' A glint appears in Cheryl's eye. 'There are several routes open to you. Our Parish Records would be my first suggestion. There are a few gaps between the wars, and we had a flood back in the 1930s and one terrible administrator, but I'll do my best. If we can't find anything, your next port of call should be the General Register Office in Southport. After that, there's St Catherine's House in London. They have records of all births and deaths from the nineteenth century onwards.'

I scrabble round in my bag for my notepad and pen and jot down some notes.

'First things first, we'll check the Parish Register,' Cheryl says. 'Your grandparents worshipped here, so they should have left a paper trail.'

Her positive attitude lifts my spirits. Finally, I'm on the way to solid answers.

'Dad was baptised here,' I add. 'Which means Lilian would have been as well. I think she was born between 1920 and 1925. She was a few years younger than Dad.'

'I'll check those dates,' she says. 'You'll have to give me a few days, as our archives have been stored in the basement during the church refurbishment. Just email me what you need. My details are on the website.' She checks her watch. 'I've got a meeting in fifteen minutes. Is there any other way I can help you? We can walk and talk.'

Cheryl starts walking back to church, beckoning me to join her.

I gather the courage to confront something that's been on my mind since I unwrapped the finding machine. Antony's made his feelings crystal clear on the matter, but my doubts won't go away; I have to talk to someone.

'Do you mind if I ask you something completely unrelated?' I say as we walk side-by-side. 'It might sound a bit strange.'

The vicar follows a wide trail between the graves, wrapping her arms around her jersey as though bracing herself for what's coming.

'My dad made a machine. He built it back in the 1970s, but it does things that are technologically way ahead of its time, like communicating with satellites. I don't know how it works, and I'm worried using it comes at a cost.'

'What do you mean?' Cheryl looks at me as a bank of clouds rolls overhead. The light levels drop like someone's flicked a switch. Where before the graveyard was streaked with golden light, it now looks flat and dark.

'Alex?' Cheryl stops walking and touches my elbow. 'Are you OK?'

I nod, crossing my arms against a sudden breeze. 'It's just...I've been getting warnings from psychics. Actually, it's a mixture of psychics, mediums and spiritualists. This probably sounds completely crazy, but they say they know what I'm doing. One of them said I'm meddling in dangerous realms. I must stop at once or sinister forces will come and get me. They make it sound like something terrible's going to happen.' I pause, gathering my thoughts. 'My housemate says psychics are fraudsters, but I'm starting to feel there's *something* in what they're saying.' I look Cheryl in the eye. 'What do you think?'

'I suppose there are two answers.' Cheryl considers her words. 'The church's view and my view. Of course, there's your view, but you sound conflicted. It doesn't sound like the machine was built to cause harm, like a gun or poison. It's neutral, like a kitchen knife.' She peers at me over her glasses. 'You can use that knife to prepare a fantastic dinner, or you can stab someone. It's not a very good analogy, but do you see what I mean?'

'I think so. You're saying my dad's device is neutral. But what about when I'm using it?'

'Well, that depends on what it does. I can see you're reluctant to tell me.'

Troubled thoughts turn in my mind - Terry's shed full of videos. Puppies kept in the dark. Finding animals was supposed to be the best thing ever. Instead, it's brought a mixture of joy, sadness and danger. More than I bargained for.

'What bothers me is I don't know *how* Dad's machine works,' I say. 'My housemate's worried it could contain nuclear material, or spill out chemicals when I turn it on.'

'It sounds like you should be worried about contamination, rather than spirits and demons.' Cheryl smiles, her eyes crinkling at the edges. 'Maybe an engineer could check it out? That might help put your mind at rest.'

Her practical response comes as a surprise. I was expecting a theological spiel.

I give her a quizzical look. 'I thought you were going to offer me prayers and a bit of scripture to read.'

'Well, I can certainly do that if you like!' Cheryl lets out a laugh. 'If you want the church's response, I would say that as a Christian, it's my responsibility to listen to God. When I listen to spiritualists and fortune tellers, I am removing myself from that conversation.'

She comes closer and places her hand on my shoulder.

'And if I was speaking to someone who doesn't believe in God, I would say they need to listen to their inner voice. We all have one of those.'

She looks kindly at me. 'Practically, my advice would be to take care when dealing with psychics and people who say they can see into the future. You look like you're still hurting after the death of your father. This makes you vulnerable.' Cheryl looks at the grass, her lips pressed together. 'Some years back, there was a gentleman in the parish who lost his wife to cancer. He almost bankrupted himself with tarot readings and psychic hotlines. A year or so later, a friend of mine lost her son in a car accident. He died very young. She went to spiritualist assemblies trying to contact him, to the point where she fell out with her family. It took a long time to patch things up.'

'So, are you saying all psychics are frauds?'

'I can't answer that, but for myself, I wouldn't like the idea of taking direction from a stranger on a premium rate number. And what if you don't agree with what they say? That creates a new dilemma - one you've paid for. I think there are some very rich psychics driving round in Ferraris.'

'You've given me a lot to think about.' I close my notebook. 'Thank you.'

Cheryl checks her watch. 'I'm going to be late for my meeting. It was nice to meet you, Alex. Remember to send me that email!'

She walks off, throwing a wave as she goes.

28

— · —

Margaret Long lives in a 1950s semi in Leavenheath, a village about seven miles outside Sudbury. An empty driveway sits one side of the house. It would be a shame not to take advantage of it.

After parking on the concrete strip, I lock up the Mini and have a quick look around. A padlocked, rusty side-gate leads to the back garden. The lawn has been invaded by clumps of dandelions and daisies and needs a mow. In the borders, an overgrown tangle of rose bushes, weeds and shrubs fight it out.

Margaret loved gardening. The deterioration saddens me.

I go to the front porch and press the bell. Nothing happens for ages, and I'm about to press it again when I see a shape slowly approaching through the obscure glass. When the door opens, my eyes go to Margaret's gnarled hands, one of which grips a walking stick. Her grey hair is elegantly curled and set. She is immaculately turned out in a cashmere cardigan buttoned over a floral house dress. On her feet, smart black patent shoes with a low-heel.

The shoes catch my attention because she is so obviously frail. Surely she'd be safer in a pair of trainers? I suspect she has always dressed up for visitors, just like my grandmother, Vera.

Margaret squints at me through thick-lensed glasses.

'Alexandra?'

I smile and say hello.

Her face brightens and the years fall away, making the resemblance to her photograph clear. She even stands straighter.

'Richard's lovely daughter! We met at the funeral, didn't we? My eyesight is not so good these days but I can still see you have his look about you. I suppose you've been told that before.'

'A few times,' I say with a smile.

Margaret ushers me across the threshold onto orange, swirly carpet. The longer I stare at it, the more the pattern appears to be moving. I look away as my eyes start crossing, worried for Margaret in her heels, having to judge her step. I suppose, after all these years she must be used to it.

A beige rotary phone sits on the hall table, next to the telephone directory, a flip top address book and a red emergency button. The house has a fusty smell. There's nothing modern here except for the paraphernalia that comes with old age and infirmity – a walking frame, hand rails and a stair lift. A wave of sadness hits me. No-one thinks about this when they're young.

I take baby steps behind her as she shuffles along with her stick.

'It's lovely to see you,' she says as we finally enter the lounge. 'Please, take Bernard's old chair in front of the TV. I'll get us a cup of tea.'

I tell her I'd love to take the chair. First of all, I will make the tea. I dare not let her do it – apart from worrying about scalding herself, it would take up most of the afternoon. I hover over her as she sinks down into her chair. To my relief, she still has a level of confidence with her mobility and controls her descent with a firm grip on the pine arms.

The adjoining kitchen is neat and tidy. The fridge is stocked with essentials and smells fresh. The milk is in date. I'm guessing Margaret gets help with her shopping.

Once we're settled with our floral china cups of tea, Margaret takes a sip and smiles.

'You could have had a glass of sherry, you know.' She nods to a decanter set in the centre of the sideboard. 'Bernard was partial to a tipple when the rugby was on. That was before his stroke.'

I remember Bernard sitting in this chair whenever I visited, back when they lived next door to Granny Vera. Whenever I popped round, Margaret had something fun for us to do. She found joy in gardening, baking cakes or sorting out old books for charity.

By contrast, my life at home was routine. Most things were bland or a chore. Dad wasn't green fingered, and Mum would never dream of 'growing your own' because it brought back memories of her impoverished upbringing in Ireland, subsisting on a diet consisting almost entirely of vegetables. Besides, British potatoes would never taste the same.

Margaret and I raise our teacups to each other. I grin. She's still got that spark.

'Bernard enjoyed your visits,' she says. 'We had many happy years before he became ill, but I have to say, we got used to our own way of life afterwards even if it was different. I still miss him. The man he was. On Sunday afternoons, I look across to where you are, Alexandra. Do you know, I still expect him to be sitting there, watching the rugby.

'They're a strange thing, memories. Nothing has faded at all. Like getting old. You don't notice it. I mean, it's a shock when you look in the mirror, but when you're getting on with things, you're still twenty-five at heart.' She smiles. 'I was sorry to hear about your dad. How long has it been?'

'Five years. But some things still set me off and I don't know why.' My lower lip starts to wobble, and I put my cup down on a side table before I cry into it. 'I wish he was here. I've got so many questions about his past and his family. I should have asked him before, but he went so suddenly.'

Margaret's cup rattles as she sets it down. We have a good chat about the funeral, which makes me feel better. Then, she asks after Mum and Matthew and how they've both settled outside the UK.

'I suppose, in a way, Mum's gone home,' I say. 'But Dad was born and bred in Suffolk. He loved it here.'

'My eldest is the same,' Margaret says. 'He lives only a few miles from here. The other one lives in New Zealand. They're not so little now.'

She casts her gaze up to the TV. Three framed family photos sit on top. There's one of Bernard standing beside an old car, another of the two of them beaming outside church on their wedding day, and the last shows two portly older men standing in a car park with their arms around Margaret. One is bald with a a cheeky grin, the other has a ruddy complexion and wisps of white hair.

I have to say, Margaret looks better than they do in the picture, and she's got over twenty years on them.

'Christopher is seventy-nine years old, and Alan's two years younger,' she tells me.

'So, your boys were around the same age as Dad?' I struggle to work it out in my head.

'Well, I think your dad was born in 1919, the same as Christopher.' Margaret recalls dates and perform feats of mental arithmetic effortlessly.

'That sounds about right,' I reply, ashamed I can't work it out.

'The time has flown,' Margaret adds. 'Can you believe that I'm going to be a hundred next February?'

'That's incredible. Are you looking forward to getting a telegram from the Queen?'

'Well, let's see if I get there first!'

One hundred years old. I try to imagine myself the same age as Margaret, which will be in 2069, but fail miserably.

'When Bernard and I married, I was only twenty-two years old. That's considered young now, but back then you were considered no spring chicken. My mother used to tell me I was late to the feast. She thought I should have been married by eighteen.'

And here I am, still single at twenty-nine. Margaret's mum would have been horrified.

'We lived next door to your grandparents for over forty years,' Margaret says. 'Good times, for the most part.'

I remember the house from my childhood. Although it was small and narrow, it felt warm and welcoming.

Margaret's glasses catch the afternoon sun as she shifts in her chair. 'Something clicked the moment I first met Vera. In no time, we were thick as thieves. I copied the way she styled her hair. It was *immaculately coiffeured*. We learnt that expression from the Paris fashion magazines in the newsagents. Vera had a bit of Joan Fonteyn about her, as I recall.

'She was a good friend. You have to remember, I was recently married and in charge of the home for the first time. I felt thrown in at the deep end. Bernard was away in London working as a railway manager. He'd leave at seven in the morning and be back by six-thirty. I would have been terribly lonely if it hadn't been for Vera.'

'I have a picture of the two of you together,' I say, digging around in my bag. I pass her the VE Day photograph. Her face brightens when she takes it in her hand.

'There I am!' She taps the picture with a yellowed fingernail. 'I look terrible, don't I? I never had any screen magic, though we all wanted to look like film stars in photographs. Look at me, eyes closed, when everyone else is picture perfect. Vera and Jack look happy. We all were. You wouldn't believe the celebrating once the war was over. Someone rolled a piano onto the street and we were all singing and dancing round it! I don't suppose you have a photo of that?'

I regret I don't, handing her the next picture of Dad outside the shop.

'Ah, yes. That's Stanley's shop.' My heart leaps to have it confirmed.

'Can you see him, inside the window?'

Margaret peers closely at the image. 'I'm sorry, Alexandra. I can't make him out. Is that him, that blur?'

'I think it must be. Can you remember anything about him?'

'Stanley Victor Martin, his name was. I always thought it sounded rather posh, even though he was a down-to-earth chap. Ever so fond of your father, he was. I doubt he would be alive now.' Margaret looks up to the ceiling, blinking.

'He was a confirmed bachelor. You don't see too many of them these days. He devoted six days a week to his shop, and did well from it. Sunday afternoons, he visited Jack, Vera and the family. They'd walk by the river or he'd take your father for an ice-cream, or back to his workshop to show him his latest invention.'

'Invention?' I break in. 'What do you mean?'

'The men on your side of the family were always fiddling with something. Jack was mad about radios. Your dad loved TVs. Stanley was the same, always reading up on the latest technology. It ran in the family.'

'Do you remember Stanley and Dad making anything together?'

'Yes, your dad was always round his house, tinkering with radios or electrical bits and pieces. As far as I know, they were close.' I make a mental note before passing over the photo of Jack, Vera and Dad in the lounge.

'I remember this like it was yesterday.' Margaret beams. 'Jack and his pipe. Half the time he would chew on the stem without lighting it. He was precious about his tobacco.' She points at the radio. 'That old monster. The two of them were always fiddling with it and reading *'How To'* magazines while Vera got on with running the house.

'Doesn't she look elegant? She never wore a housecoat or apron or anything, yet she baked her own bread and cooked a proper dinner every night for Jack and your dad. She was wasted as a housewife. I always thought she would have made an excellent secretary or a telephone operator, but times were different back then.'

She peers closer at Dad. A wistful look appears in her eye.

'It was lovely and warm that day. The fire was off and the back door was open.'

'You were there?' I ask in surprise.

'Who do you think took the photo?' Margaret gives me a mischievous look. 'Jack had a little box camera. He was always up with the latest things. I'd never used one before, but I followed his instructions. I was no good with it, really. You can see Vera's not really looking at the camera.'

I rummage around in my bag for the last photo of Vera holding the baby, wondering if Margaret took it. It would explain why the photo is terrible, with the baby looking away from the camera.

Margaret takes a close look at it, then puts her hand to her mouth.

'I haven't seen this for a long, long time.'

'Do you know who she is?' I prompt gently.

And then Margaret does something that astonishes me. She sinks back into her chair with her head tipped back. She pulls a tissue from her sleeve and removes her glasses to dab at her eyes.

'We never talked about it,' she said, her voice wavering. 'Certain things were not mentioned. By the time the story was out of the papers, people had forgotten about her.'

'In the papers?' I'm shaking my head, at a loss for words.

'Poor thing,' Margaret whispers. 'Poor little mite.'

29

— • —

'Lilian Anne Martin. Richard was four when she was born. Everyone adored her. She was such a chubby, cheeky little thing.'

Margaret takes an unsteady breath. She gulps the last of her tea, placing the cup down with a shaking hand. She starts rubbing small circles over her chest, and I fear she's about to have a heart attack or collapse from shock. The thing about spending time with someone nearly a century old, you can't stop thinking of their health.

'My mouth went dry, excuse me,' Margaret continues, her eyes red-rimmed. Although she's tearful, her voice remains strong. 'I never thought I'd be talking about her after all these years. When you put something behind you...well, you think that's it. I remember her face so clearly. She had dimples and golden curls. She was a delight.'

If only I had a proper photograph of Lilian, I could see this for myself.

'Is this the only picture?' I ask. 'Dad never mentioned her.'

'There may be other photos.' Margaret waggles her forefinger. 'I remember your grandfather had a box camera.'

'I've already asked Mum. She's gone through everything Dad left behind, and there's nothing else.'

Margaret's eyebrows rise. 'I think I've got a box of old photos somewhere. Sylvia, my carer, could help me go through them. I need her help as my eyesight's not very good these days. I can't say for sure there are any of Lilian. But we'll have a look.'

'Do you have any photos of Uncle Stanley?'

Margaret shakes her head. 'We were never close. Besides, he was funny about having his picture taken.'

She stares at the photo of Lilian. Her grip is so tight, the blue veins on the back of her hand stand out.

I sit forwards in the armchair, willing her to go on.

'Bernard and I were there when this photo was taken. Lilian would have been around two or three months old. My boys ran round the garden in circles all afternoon with your dad, even though it was very warm.' She pauses. 'Happy times.'

'What do you remember about Lilian?' I ask.

'Lilian was a ray of sunshine.' Margaret gives a sad smile. 'She was obedient and well-mannered. I wished my two were the same. They were such a handful. I don't think I had a decent night's sleep from the day they were born to the day they left for school.

'Maybe that's me, I was probably a terrible mother. I don't think I was strict enough. But that's in the past, now, and I can't complain. The years go by so fast and I still have my boys, which is more than can be said for Vera. Oh, here I go again.'

I offer to get more tea. Seeing Margaret upset is giving me a lump in my throat. By the time I return with refreshed cups, she's gathered herself together.

'I'm not much use, am I?' She smiles up at me.

'Oh, no, please,' I hand her tea over. 'You're being brilliant. Please take your time. We've got all afternoon.'

Margaret sips her tea. The familiar action appears to calm her.

She settles back in her chair. 'It was the last day of term. December 1928. I remember it well because Christmas was ruined, not just for them but for all of us.

'Vera and I walked to school after lunchtime, to collect the children. We lived in a little terrace off New Street which was convenient for everything, and it was an easy walk. Lilian had started to act very grown up now she was in big school. She loved the uniform and the little satchel she carried with her sandwiches and stationery tin.

'Vera was suffering with a migraine. She used to get them whenever it turned cold. She looked exhausted that day. I would have taken Richard and Lilian off her hands, but my boys were coming down with colds.' Margaret shakes her head. 'A decision I will forever regret. I told Vera to take her pills when she got home, and have a nap.

'I went inside to get dinner on. I heard nothing out of the ordinary. Alan and Christopher wanted to go for a kickabout with Richard before tea, but as they were sniffing and sneezing I kept them in. I must have dozed off by the fire. The next thing I knew, it was dark outside and Vera was at the door. The pills had knocked her out, and she'd woken up to an empty house. She asked if I'd seen Lilian or Richard.

'At first, I wasn't overly concerned. I went round to Vera's with the boys and searched for them. We thought Lilian might have been playing hide-and-seek in the house. The back door was unlocked, but that was nothing out of the ordinary. Our boys were used to going in and out as they pleased.

'I went out the back to the lane that ran behind the houses, but couldn't see her. Soon after, Richard came home from playing football. He told us, when he left for the park Lilian had been in the house.

'Vera started to panic. I told her not to worry, but I can remember thinking something was wrong. I instructed her to stay in the house in case Lilian turned up. The boys got their coats and the four of us went outside to look. We went round the block. The boys ran ahead calling out for Lilian. They knew all the places she could be hiding, but she wasn't anywhere.

'By the time I got back, Vera had called Jack at work. He told her to phone the police. That made it very real, I can tell you. I waited with Vera. The constable who interviewed her was very thorough, and within a few hours they had patrols going round the town, knocking on doors. I was in a bit of a state by then. God knows what it was like for Vera.

'I didn't for one moment think Lilian had been abducted. She'd most likely run off to explore, or followed a cat. I was worried she would get run over or find her way down to the river. The thought of that made my blood run cold.

'When Bernard got back from work, I gave him his tea and made extra for Vera and Jack. Jack ate his, he was always an-old fashioned stick like that, but Vera wouldn't touch a thing. She must have paced around the house all night. When I saw her the next morning, she was in tears. Jack had torn a strip off her for not keeping an eye on Lilian. I thought that was cruel. She was suffering enough.'

Margaret stops to wipe her eyes again. I offer her a glass of water, but she waves it away.

'What about Uncle Stanley?' I ask. 'You said he was close to Jack and Richard. How did he take the news?'

'Very badly,' Margaret says. 'He'd been away on business, and came to see how the search was going a few days later. He had a right go at Vera for leaving the children unsupervised. Neither he nor Jack took into account the affect the migraines had on her. Children those days were left to their own devices. It was the way it was back then, but Stanley and Jack weren't having it. Stanley was so upset about the whole business, he refused to speak to Vera after. The whole thing turned sour, and he moved away to Leeds.'

I look out of the window, shocked by the men's callous attitude to Vera. Especially Stanley, who had no right to judge, as he was a bachelor. The fact he abandoned his family when they were at their lowest ebb doesn't sit right with me.

For the first time, I wonder if he had anything to do with Lilian's disappearance. Sometimes, you think you know someone, and it turns out you don't know them at all. Like that paedo Terrence Harber. He was doing dodgy things in his shed for years without anyone having a clue.

164

'Where did Stanley go?' I ask. Even if Stanley wasn't involved with Lilian's disappearance, he could still be a shortcut to finding her.

'I don't know.' Margaret shrugs. 'Neither did Vera. She wanted to make amends. Richard wanted to write and visit. But Stanley sold his business in Sudbury and disappeared. Richard was upset over Lilian and when Stanley left, it was a double-blow. It took him ages to recover.'

'What happened with the search?' I gently prompt Margaret, wondering how anyone could recover from such a terrible event.

'Oh, it was awful.' She looks on the verge of tears. 'Jack had to take leave. That was no small thing in those days. He told Vera to stay at home in case the police had news, but she wasn't having it. The two of us went round town. We knocked on every door we could and looked everywhere. We walked down the river. There was nothing.

'The police searched the lock-ups at the back of the lane. They searched our houses. It was at this point, I began to wonder if someone had taken her. After all, how could a little girl disappear like that, in school uniform, without anyone noticing her?'

Margaret stares down at the tissue clutched in her hands.

'I wish I could give you a happy ending. Lilian was never seen again. The whole town knew the story, it was in all the papers. The days came and went. The police stopped coming round. Jack went back to work. Everyone went on with their lives.'

A sigh escapes her. 'You never forget the sadnesses in your life. It's like my Bernard. I have good days. Then, there are the bad days when it's such a struggle, I wish I was with him.' She gazes over my shoulder with a faint, thoughtful smile. 'I suppose we'll be together soon enough.'

I go over and give her a hug.

'You've helped me so much. Thank you.'

'That's all right.' Margaret grips my arm. 'It's lovely to spend time with someone who isn't here just to help me get up the stairs or down them! You're always welcome.'

I say my goodbyes and remind her to look in her old box of photos. I write down my phone number and address in big letters on a page from my notepad. I cannot see a computer in the house, so don't bother with an email address. It's the phone, a letter, or nothing.

'Please can I drop by again?' I ask. 'I'd love to talk more about your childhood and hear some stories about Dad when he was younger. When you talk about my old photos, it's like you're bringing them back to life.'

She gifts me with a warm smile. 'Drop by any time.'

30

By the time I return from my trip to Suffolk, I muster every bit of remaining energy to bung two bits of bread in the toaster and whack the kettle on. After my meagre tea, I roll into bed with the latest *Peter James* novel. The last thing I hear, before falling asleep with the light on, is a *thunk* as the book hits the floor.

Upon waking, it's past ten o'clock. I must have fallen into some kind of coma from information overload.

I need time to process everything I heard yesterday. I have a new aunt. It feels strange to be the only person in the world who wants to know what happened to her. Uncovering Lilian Martin's fate is down to me. If I don't do it, she'll disappear into the ether of history. Forever lost without a trace.

After breakfast, I boot up my PC and check my emails. Three responses have arrived regarding temp work. The first is from Brook Street in Holborn. They want me to interview for a job covering six months' maternity leave for the 'fast-paced' position of PA to the Director of a Japanese Bank. Already, I'm shuddering. I don't need to speak Japanese, but the strict dress code insists upon a skirt suit and the company cravat. Long hair must be worn up in a chignon or bun. I'm never at my best at six in the morning, and I can imagine my attempts to achieve this will leave me looking like a dog had an accident on top of my head.

I politely decline, citing other work. The second agency wants me in for a battery of tests including Word, Excel and mail-merge documents as well as the obligatory touch-typing speed test. I can't face that, either. Lastly, the agency just down the road in Hertford has two week's admin work for a cable company. The pay isn't great but it's the best out of the three.

After an hour of hedging, I turn that down too. How can I face it with everything that's happened?

Instead, I lose myself painting the shattered oak and eventually find my happy space. Antony's told me he thinks it's 'really spooky.' I've decided my next painting will be based on a misty photo of the marshlands near Hertford. The heavy atmosphere, threatening sky and approaching band of rain strikes a chord with me.

I dig out the card Antony picked up from the gallery in St Albans and give them a ring. The gallery owner is happy for me to pop down this afternoon with my portfolio, so I decide to take my newly-framed 'Cow by the Noisy Bridge.' It's amazing what you can squeeze in the back of a Mini with the seats down.

The Gallery is a smart Georgian building close to St Albans Cathedral. Inside, the space is contemporary with white walls. Anne, the gallery owner, looks extremely chic in a white trouser suit with red silk blouse. Her black, glossy hair is cut, Cleopatra style, with a heavy fringe. She's got panache.

To my surprise, she appears to like my work and makes the right noises. She steps back to assess the cow painting with her chin cupped between her thumb and forefinger.

'Yes, I can see your theme, the way you weave the modern into the traditional. It's a good twist. There's broodiness. Soul. I think we could definitely do something with this.' She consults her diary and runs her finger down the upcoming weeks. 'I'm afraid we're full up until October. The earliest slot I could give you would be later on that month.' She looks up from the diary. 'We would need at least five pieces. Do you have five?'

'Yes, I do!'

'All right, then. I'll put you down for October 20th. In the meantime, we have an exhibition travelling around Hertfordhire. At the moment, we're at Van Hages Garden Centre. Would you like to exhibit a painting there?'

'Van Hages in Ware?'

Anne nods. She hands me a flyer with the heading 'Our Green and Pleasant Land,' showcasing a painting of a heron standing at the edge of a lake, poised to strike. The dramatic yellow beak and black slash above the eye gives it a Japanese flavour. It really packs a punch in heavy oils and a thrill goes through me at the idea of exhibiting alongside work of this quality.

'I'd love to exhibit!' I press the flyer to my chest, giving Anne a heart-felt grin.

'Take your painting there and mention my name. They'll find space for you. We manage to sell quite a few of our artists' work by bringing the paintings to the people. And Van Hages's clientele are our type of people.' She tilts her head on one side. 'Have you given any thought about how much you want to charge for your work? Our commission is forty percent.'

I hesitate, taken aback. Forty percent's a lot! Ten percent more than *Write On!* My mind races as I try and come up with a price that makes it worth my while but doesn't sound cheeky. I chew the inside of my mouth, at a loss. My problem is, my heart and soul have gone into my paintings. Part of me wants to keep them.

Eventually, I shrug and shake my head.

'I'm really sorry. I'm afraid this is new to me.'

'Well, if I could make a suggestion? Let's start at £1,950 and see what interest we get.'

I stare at her, thinking that's way above what I would have asked.

'Oh, we get London buyers here,' Anne smiles, seeing my surprise.

· · · • · • · • · ·

B ack home, I log onto my personal emails. I've kept my old, business email on archive for reference, as all my agency communication is there.

Another six emails managed to slip in before Antony shut everything down for the last time.

Four are requests to find lost pets, inspired by the article in The Courier. The fifth email is impossible to ignore.

TO THE FINDER

Beware your ignorance. YOU meddle in realms of which you know NOTHING! Every time you reach into the blackness, the blackness reaches BACK. Only a fool invites the darkness. Bailey the Seer divines to Protect, call 0908 SEERS for life changing advice.

Is it just me, or are the messages getting darker?

Despite the advice Cheryl gave me regarding mediums and their ilk and Antony's no-nonsense bluntness about where they can shove their auras, I worry that the finding machine has opened a door into a different, darker world. However crazy it sounds, there is an undeniable mystery to the way it works. I'm no scientist, but I'm pretty sure there isn't a branch of physics that can explain how it locates the living and the dead from photographs. Cheryl suggested I get an engineer to take a look at it, but who on earth would I ask? Where would I find someone suitably qualified?

Antony thinks it could be military. But it's not like I can walk up to my local military base and say, *'Hi! My name's Alex. Have you got a scientist in there who can have a look at this for me and tell me how it works? My dad made it years ago using bits of an old TV. It can find anyone in the world, whether they're living or dead. Be careful though, it might be nuclear. Oh, and can I have it back when you're finished ~~with it~~?'*

It's bad enough using something I don't understand, without feeling like other people have a window into my soul. Bailey the Seer, Mystic Miriam, Psychics Inside Your Head – they're desperate for me to contact them.

Should I ring one of them? I go back and forth between yes and no like a pendulum. Eventually, I delay resolving my dilemma by opening my final email.

To The Finder,

My name is Mr Bevin. I saw your article in the Courier.

My teenage son has been missing since January. Jason has suffered from panic-attacks and delusions since his early teens. His condition took a definite turn for the worse at Christmas, when he stopped taking his medication without telling me. He locked himself in his room with the internet, listening and watching I know not what. His paranoia grew to such an extent that he started treating me with extreme suspicion. He thought I was part of a strange government conspiracy.

He ran away early in the New Year. If I was in better health, I would be out on the streets searching for him, but I have a lung-condition that prevents me walking without assistance. My wife, God bless her, passed away recently from cancer, which I fear may have triggered Jason's decline.

The police have put out posters and nationwide bulletins. They've tried to reach out to the general public for help, but the tip-offs they received led nowhere. They were probably fraudsters, after the reward.

I understand you used a 'specialist team' to locate and rescue the stolen puppies. With this in mind, I am writing in the sincerest hope that what works for dogs can work for people, too. I am offering £10,000 to whoever finds him.

I worry what Jason might do without his medication. It could be dangerous for him and for others if he has one of his episodes.

I enclose the police poster.

Yours faithfully, Mr Bevin.

I read the email twice, taken aback at the depths of Mr Bevin's hope. He's pinning everything on me, on the basis of one unverified report in the local rag.

He must be desperate. His son's one of many missing people who fall through the cracks. Unlike murders, terrorist attacks or child abductions, they don't hit the headlines. Apart from his dad, nobody seems to care. I guess he's at the bottom of the pile where the police are concerned as he's old enough to have left home of his own accord.

I've been here before. Part of me says this is third time lucky. The other says I'll be blown up or suffer some other gruesome fate, because I couldn't say no.

The reward money. It's tempting. Ten thousand pounds - enough for a new car. Enough to buy me time to plan my future.

There must be *something* I can do.

I open the attachment. The poster is the same one I saw in the police station. Jason is a pale, gangly teenager with shaggy corn coloured hair. He wears a black T-shirt with DWEEB on it. He looks grungy, but his eyes are bright, his smile genuine. I guess it was taken before he came off his meds.

Out of curiosity, I resize the picture for the finding machine and switch it on.

51.5196751, -0.1103715

An internet search reveals the co-ordinates are in London - the City of London, to be precise. I decide to track his movements, checking his photo over the next 24 hours.

Jason spends most of his time in a building down an old market street in Farringdon called Leather Lane. He leaves his place around 11.30am (he's alive!) and goes for a wander round Old Street and The Barbican. He doesn't go far afield or stay out for long.

My geospatial website isn't very sophisticated, and the white finger pointer is large in comparison to the map no matter how far I zoom in, but it looks like he's at 23 Leather Lane.

Confident I have solved the mystery of Jason Bevin at absolutely no risk to myself, I email his father and give him the good news, using my personal email address. Antony wouldn't approve, but I don't care.

I suggest he rings the police so they can recover his son.

'Ten grand, in the bag,' I congratulate myself, high-fiving no-one.

W ednesday lunchtime, I find Antony at the kitchen table, a single place setting neatly laid before him with a platter of sushi, chopsticks, teapot and cup of green tea. It's the middle of the week and already the gourmet lunches are coming out. A computing magazine is open beside him. The pages show a baffling array of PC parts like circuit boards and fans. Knowing Antony, he's plodding methodically through the boring bits, saving the gaming section for last.

What's all this, then?' I say in my best PC Plod accent.

'Say it with me, Alex. Su-shi.' Antony looks up, chewing. 'Not to be confused with sash-imi.'

'I know what sushi is,' I say, indignant. 'I'm not a complete Philistine.'

My housemate picks up a salmon maki roll with chopsticks and proffers it to me.

'Open up and say...Ahh!'

'That sounds dodgy, Antony.'

'I was going for sexy,' he smiles, raising his chopsticks higher. 'OK, here comes the choo-choo train, heading for the tunnel. Show me the tunnel, Alex.'

'That's sounds even dodgier!'

I make a moue of disgust at the dark green Nori seaweed wrapped round the rice Antony's proferring.

'You don't see people running into the sea at Brighton to grab mouthfuls of kelp, do you?' I say. 'And as for the fish, that's raw, isn't it? I've had food poisoning once from scampi. Never again.'

'Durr, Alex. This is fresh. They wouldn't be in business very long if it was off. Come on, just try it.'

I take a deep breath for luck, lean over and pop the piece in my mouth, chewing quickly. To my surprise, it's not overly fishy, the rice and creamy avocado complement the seaweed, and the saltiness of the soy sauce makes it a perfect mouthful.

'Told you, didn't I?' My eyes must have widened in surprise because Antony gives himself a congratulatory smile. 'Learn from the master.'

'Don't push it.' I flick the kettle on and rummage through my bare cupboards for something normal to eat.

'So, what are you having?'

'Looks like it's Pot Noodle, Chow Mein,' I reply, peeling the lid off the pot. 'You're having Japanese, I'm having Chinese.'

'Pot Noodle!' he laughs. 'The slag of all snacks.'

I pour boiling water up to the fill-line inside the pot, trying to ignore him.

'Do you know how much salt is in one of those?' he asks.

'We can't all afford to eat restaurant food for lunch,' I protest. 'This was 99p. How much was yours?'

'Four pounds fifty.'

'Four pounds fifty! How the other half live.'

Antony flicks the page of his magazine. I'm disappointed to see more computer bits. Not a monster or blood covered marine in sight.

'I'm going to build myself a mega-PC,' he says, seeing my interest as I sit opposite him. 'I've gotta have the best if I'm thinking of joining the big league.'

I say nothing, twiddling noodles round my fork. What does he mean by 'big league'? Has he decided to take a job in Birmingham or London, after all? I'm too much of a coward to ask.

I bring up a forkful of steaming noodles. The first mouthful burns my mouth, and I end up blowing through my mouth like an expectant woman sucking on gas and air.

'Hey, this is going to be good for you. You know why?' Antony reaches over and taps my hand. He's searching for signs of enthusiasm, but I'm in pain from the hot noodles and my eyes are watering. I wave my hand in front of my mouth.

'Tell me,' I manage to say.

'I know things are a bit tight for you at the moment because you're saving for a new car,' Antony says diplomatically. He squeezes my palm before sitting back. 'How about you have my computer when I've built the new one? Yours was all right five years ago, but the newer Pentium chips are ten times better.'

'You'd give it to me?' I look at him, my mouth dropping open. 'For nothing?'

'Technology's changing so quickly, it's hardly worth anything, compared to what I paid for it. Giving it to you is like keeping it in the family.'

With my family, that's not necessarily a good thing.

'You'll get Quake. Half-Life.' Antony looks baffled at my lacklustre response. 'All your favourites. What's not to like?'

I nod at him, but my mind's on other things.

'All right.' Antony pauses. 'What's going on?'

'I'm sorry. Your offer's amazing. It's just that I'm finding it really hard to concentrate with everything Margaret told me.'

'I guess you'd better tell me about it.'

Over a long lunch, I relate my journey to Sudbury and the conversations I had with Rev. Cheryl and Margaret Long.

Antony listens patiently, dipping his salmon rolls in a tiny dish of soy sauce before devouring them. He pours me a cup of green tea.

'I can't think about anything else,' I almost wail. 'I have to find out what happened to her.'

'Actually, you don't.' Antony wipes his mouth on a serviette. 'This isn't down to you. And, whatever you decide to do probably won't change a thing.'

'I know that.' I point my fork at him. 'But this is the reason Dad made the machine. To find Lilian.'

'I'm not saying you're wrong.' Antony pours the last of the tea. 'But digging up the past? Sounds to me like everyone hid Lilian's story away because it was bad. They wanted to forget it and move on. Maybe you should, too. It was a long time ago, Alex. Around seventy years.'

I rake my fingers through my hair, scrunching big handfuls. Unless I can find some way of extracting everything I've learnt about Lilian from my mind, I can't let her go.

'Do you have a plan?' Antony asks. 'What are your next steps?'

I stare into the dregs of my Pot Noodle. 'I'm not sure. I've hit a brick wall.'

'Then, promise me something.' Antony's gaze bores into my skull. 'Before you decide to go off and do anything rash, tell me what you're doing and where you're going. Deal?'

I reach out and give him a fist-bump.

'Deal.'

31

'Enjoying the ride?' I snatch a glance at Antony in the passenger seat beside me. He's squeezed into the Mini with the window rolled down and his elbow sticking out. Cool air streams through the car. I'm glad I've got my snood on. Every morning, I think it's time to ditch it, but the weather has yet to make the big spring turn.

We're heading for the art exhibition at Van Hage's. Anne from The Gallery reserved a space for me and now we're on the road, my painting wedged behind us on the backseat, swaddled in bubble-wrap.

'Now I know what a sardine feels like,' Antony mutters.

'Thanks for coming.' I beam at him, proud that for the first time in our relationship, he'll be sharing my moment of glory.

'No problem.' Antony says. 'Though you should have let me drive.'

'Ah ah.' I shake my head. 'This time, I'm chauffeuring you. My treat.'

The seat-springs creak loudly as we go over a speed bump. Antony's head squashes into the roof lining.

'Some treat.' He tenses every time we hit a pothole or go over a ridge, no doubt longing for his Audi's cushioned suspension and padded, leather seats.

The sun's shining. I'm taking my first step towards becoming a bona-fide artist. Were it not for one persistent niggle, I would be over the moon.

Antony has two job offers still on the table. I've got a suspicion he's taken one and not told me. But surely he'd have said something by now if he was leaving? The issue keeps popping up in my head and it's driving me crazy.

I grip the steering wheel tightly, my nerves jangling.

'I've been meaning to ask.' I try for a casual tone, but my voice comes out unnaturally high. 'You know what you said yesterday about joining the big league? Does that mean you've taken one of those jobs?'

Antony is staring at the trees and at first I don't think he heard me. But then he turns to meet my eye.

'Yeah. I took the Birmingham one.'

I swallow hard. Even though I half-expected the answer, it hurts.

'When do you start?' I stare fixedly out of the windscreen. My former excitement drains from my body. My voice sounds flat. Emotionless.

'Four weeks.'

'Four weeks!' I shoot him a vicious look. 'That's hardly any time! Were you going to tell me before you left, or just leave me a note?'

'I'm sorry, Alex. I was afraid to tell you, coz I was afraid you'd react like this. I didn't have the balls. Imagine that, me not having the balls.' He lets out an explosive sigh, clamps his hands on his thighs. 'They wanted me up there quicker but I told them I couldn't do it.'

'Nice of you.' My voice drops, bitter. What am I supposed to do now? How will I pay the bills? I suppose I'll have to get another tenant in. That means interviewing total strangers.

We drive along the windy country roads in uncomfortable silence. I wish I'd kept my mouth shut.

'Look, I promise we'll sort out the details.' Antony's voice is warm, but I feel like ice inside. 'Don't worry about the bills or any of that. I'll cover everything for six months. I know this is rubbish. I'm sorry.'

A car zooms up behind me. Staring in the rear-view mirror, I see the front half of the bonnet swiftly disappear as the driver closes the gap.

I don't normally let other drivers pressure me, but this guy's coming for me in a really aggressive way. I floor it to put some distance between us.

The Mini lurches forwards, its engine screaming in protest.

'Look, there's no need to act like this! Calm down!' Antony shoots me a glare. 'You're over-reacting. Just chill out. When we get to Van Hages we'll sit down and talk it through properly.'

'It's not that!' I eye the rear-view mirror as the car which had fallen back, zooms closer until he's centimetres from my bumper. 'Someone's right up my backside. I think he's going to ram me!'

'What?' Antony grabs the plastic strap on the inside of the door, turning in his seat to look.

I ram my foot down on the accelarator, thrashing the Mini to within an inch of its life. The engine roars as the revs climb but we're not gaining speed. I drop down to third gear to get more acceleration. The needles on the rev. counter swing into the red. I look at my driver's wing-mirror to see who's in the car, but the uneven road surface makes the glass judder.

The rear-view mirror's vibrating less. The reflections shows one man wearing a beanie, the other one with a flat cap. I peer closer, trying to make out their faces.

Before I get a proper look, Antony shouts out.

'Keep your eyes on the road!'

The wheels on Antony's side slide onto the verge. The Mini skids over grass and leaves, sending gobbets of mud flying. I pull on the wheel, hauling us back onto the tarmac.

Antony swivels round.

'Oy! Pillocks!' He yells out of the passenger window and flicks them the finger.

'Why did you do that?' I shout. 'Now they're going to ram me, for sure!'

'Just stay on the road. Don't look at them. Look at the road.'

'Who are they? Boy racers?'

'Nah, older. Rough types. They look like gypos.'

Antony swears out the window again, calling them every name under the sun.

'Thought they'd overtake,' he says, looping one arm round the back of the seat, still gripping the strap with the other. 'I don't suppose this heap of crap's got any airbags?'

'Just your body,' I give him the bad news.

Up ahead, a miniature windmill marks the entrance to Van Hage's garden centre.

'We're nearly there,' I say. 'Hold on!'

I wait until the last possible moment before yanking the steering wheel hard to the right. With a squeal of tyres, the Mini executes a sharp turn into the garden centre. We go up on two wheels for a heart-stopping moment before falling back to earth.

A group of customers with trolleys full of garden stuff stop to stare.

'They've driven past,' Antony tells me, keeping an eye on the cars behind us. 'Yeah, they've gone.'

I drive into the car park at a sedate pace and find us a space large enough for my shaking hands to steer us into.

· · • • • • • • · ·

'You all right?' Antony pushes back in the car seat, taking deep breaths.

'Give me a second.' I throw my door open and get out, filling my lungs with fresh, country air. The garden centre is surrounded by paddocks and woods. I go over to the fence and watch a couple of fat ponies grazing in a lush field.

Every time a car enters the carpark, I turn to look. The first car's a dusty people-carrier, driven by a mum with her toddler strapped in a carseat in the back. A Rover containing an older couple follows her in.

As more cars arrive and leave, I tell myself there doesn't seem to be any harm done. We must have been in the wrong place at the wrong time. As the shock fades, it puts my other worries into perspective. The fact that Antony is leaving seems less important. We're in one piece, about to deliver my first commercial artwork. I want to celebrate it.

Antony sits on the bonnet, keeping an eye out for me. I go over and sit next to him. Heat from the ticking engine warms my legs through my jeans.

'We good?'

I nod and let him put his arm round me until I feel things are back to normal.

The art exhibition is at the Victorian orangery, at the back of the café. A pair of orange trees flank the entrance. They're a snip at £200 each. The label says they're for ornamental purposes only, and I wonder what the point is of having an orange tree with oranges you can't eat. Inside the café, customers sip cappuccinos and tuck into toasted paninis at small tables under large windows.

The exhibition hangs on rustic brickwork on the left-hand wall, linking the shop to the café.

'Very nice.' Antony nods as he studies the paintings. Some of them have little red dots on, to show they've sold. The quality of art is several steps above what I've seen at the local library or at summer fairs. There are a few paintings that catch my eye. In particular, the heron on the lake looks better in real life than on the front of the flyer. It's large, about six feet square, and could do with a wall to itself.

The Van Hages team makes short work of hanging my painting. Seeing the results of all my hard work is intoxicating and I have to stop myself from jumping up and down and squealing with joy.

Finally, I'm up there, amongst other artists. I put my hands to my mouth, trying and failing to compress my grin. My smile gets wider.

'Well done, you.' Antony puts his arm round me and gives a squeeze. 'Why don't you grab a table? I'll get a couple of cappuccinos so we can savour the moment.'

A cappuccino and a gloat? Antony knows all my weaknesses.

We grab a table by the window and I finally allow myself to relax. The orangery looks onto a small animal park where families with babies and buggies move at a snail's pace round the winding, woodchip paths. The children dictate the pace, stopping to stare into aviaries containing love birds and parakeets. By the paddocks, a little girl catches my eye. She's up on tiptoes, watching a black and white goat nimbly skipping up a barricade of branches to a little platform at the top, loaded with hay.

She looks the same age as Lilian Martin was when she went missing. At that age where life is magical.

I follow her progress as she skips like the goat past the peacocks and pot-bellied pigs. I imagine what I'd do, if by some miracle of time-travel, Lilian were here now. I'd buy her an icecream and after we'd seen all the animals, I'd take her on the little train. The miniature track runs in loops at the other end of the centre. It goes through tunnels and across a bridge, and all the children wave madly at the little gnome families that live in groups around the track.

I have to admit, I always wave at the gnome families, too.

'I'm sorry I didn't tell you about the job, earlier.' Antony interrupts my musings, setting down two frothy cappuccinos, dusted with cocoa. 'I didn't want to upset you. I'm upset about it myself, if I'm honest. Leaving you. And Ware.'

'I've often wondered if Ware was really you,' I admit, putting thoughts of Lilian aside. 'I always imagined you living in an apartment by the Thames. Or some trendy house in Zone Two.' I look back out of the window, but the girl has gone.

Antony sips his coffee. 'Let's face it. We're the wrong demographic for this place. If we were about to have a family or retire it'd be perfect.'

He's got a point. It doesn't look like I belong here, either.

'Plus, you're the only black guy in town,' I say, dabbing foam from my lip.

'I'm not the *only* one, Alex. You're forgetting the bloke who pulls pints down The Bull.' He smiles to himself. 'But I get what you mean. This place isn't exactly diverse, if you know what I'm saying.'

Outside the window, a chubby toddler has tripped over on the lawn by the *Keep off the Grass* sign, followed by mum, pushing a three-wheeled buggy. I watch her pick up the writhing bundle and land kisses on the red cheeks and crying eyes, getting mud smears across her camel coat from the toddler's wellington boots.

'Why don't you come with me to Birmingham?' Antony says.

'What?' I shake my head. 'Where did that come from?'

'I mentioned it before. Don't you remember? It makes sense. I'll be renting until I get to know the area. Then the plan is to buy somewhere. The city's got canals like Ware and art-galleries. I think you'd like it.' He pauses. 'I hear the libraries are great.'

'Oh, well now I'm sold.' I sip my coffee. 'Look, I'm sure Birmingham's the bomb, but I can't just follow you around the country like a lost dog because you feel sorry for me.'

'I don't feel sorry for you.' Antony puts down his cup. 'We get on great, don't we? I'm going to have to share a place at the start. May as well be with the devil I know.'

'I'll have to think about it,' I say.

Truly, I don't want to be a hanger-on. It would probably start out great, but then Antony would find a glamorous girlfriend and they'd want to move in together, maybe get married. Where would that leave me? I'd end up a spinster aunt figure, resigned to the box room, wearing all-grey and a haunted look.

'If nothing else, Birmingham's a city on the up,' Antony says. 'Being there will throw you in the way of jobs, galleries, books. Exciting stuff.'

My favourite. Exciting stuff.

'Just think about it.' Antony drains his cappuccino and slings on his jacket. 'Drink up. I want to get you a present.'

I throw him a worried look. 'Not a goat, I hope?'

'Far better than a goat.' He grins. 'Come with me, and I'll show you.'

· · · · · · · · · ·

'*Dracaena Marginata*. Common name, dragon tree.' I read the label. 'This is your answer to life's problems? A house plant?'

I touch the brown scales overlapping the stem. It looks like it would be at home on a tropical beach somewhere, with its palm-like trunk and spiky, red edged leaves.

'This is no ordinary house plant,' Antony informs me. 'It's nature's air purifier. Dragon trees remove all kinds of nasties from the environment. They make the world a better place.'

'It doesn't look much like a dragon.'

'I know, but you can't have everything. It's a really good plant for a beginner. It can take a ton of neglect.'

I arch a brow. 'Don't you trust me to water a plant?'

'Small steps, Alex. Small steps.'

'Well, thanks. I'd love one.' I give him a warm smile.

It comes in a nice, white pot with a woven, rattan band running around it. I carry it over to the tills.

'Think of it as a reciprocal arrangement.' Antony won't stop with the new age advice. 'Look after the plant and it will look after you.'

Watching the dragon tree travelling down the moving belt to the till, I struggle to imagine it looking after me. Unless it comes alive like one of those brooms in Fantasia. Still, it will be something to remember Antony by once he's gone. A twinge of sadness hits me, but I turn my mind to better things, like my painting hanging up for all to see.

Once Antony has paid the cashier we walk out of the main doors into the car park.

I spot the black plumes of smoke first. The acrid stench of petrol follows an instant after.

Then I see flames where I left the car and I'm running over, barging past a security man in a fluorescent jacket and a small crowd of gawping spectators.

'Wait, Alex!' Antony yells behind me, but I ignore him.

Heat sears my cheeks. I put my hand up to shield my eyes, running forwards.

Amidst the snapping and cracking and choking smoke I see my yellow Mini burning away and red letters daubed across the blistering, sizzling bonnet.

THIEVING BITCH

'Stay back, madam.' The security guard takes my arm and drags me away from my car to where a mum is watching with her toddler. In the distance, I can hear sirens.

'He said, stay back!' Antony steps up behind me, slipping his arm round my waist and holding me tight.

'It hot and on fire!' the toddler adds helpfully, before popping her dummy in her mouth. Her mother hefts her onto her hip and takes her away.

I stand stock-still in shock, my heart accelerating at the message I read. The stuff left in my boot, the library books that need to be returned, my sunglasses, all that inconsequential stuff. My life is in danger. They're coming for me.

'It's OK,' Antony says. 'I'm here.'

The security guard puts out his arms, herding us a few more steps back.

'Keep your distance. The fire brigade are on the way.'

The flames are spewing black bits as the smell of oil and petrol intensifies. The interior of the car where we were sitting not an hour before is burning furiously. I watch the mustard paint blister and turn black.

BANG!

The shocking sound resounds somewhere beneath the car. The Mini jumps off the ground.

Gouts of fire spout around the bonnet along with black, oily smoke. Metal particles stick to my face and eyelashes. Choking and waving away the fumes, the spectators retreat to the glass porch by the main entrance.

I lean over, hacking and spluttering. Antony turns to one side and spits into the grass.

'It was them, wasn't it?' My voice is rasping.

'Who?'

'The guys who tried to run us off the road.' I wipe my face and my hands come away black. I must look like a chimneysweep.

'What do you mean? You know them?'

'Now I do.' I remember the gruff, older man with the walkie-talkie from the red barn and his mate who clocked me outside in the road. 'It's the dognappers. It's got to be. They've targeted me. And now they've found me.'

Two fire-engines gun it into the car park with their alarms and blue lights blaring. They stop a safe distance from the disaster area, blocking our view.

Moments later, a couple of police cars turn up.

'I suppose they're going to want to talk to me,' I groan, handing the dragon plant back to Antony. 'This is just great. Really great.'

32

The side enquiry room at Hertford police station looks the same as last time. The same posters on the wall, the same table bolted to the floor and the same Viking sitting behind it with his jacket off because the heater's too hot. It's Groundhog Day, with one small change - a packet of John Player Special cigarettes on the table.

I used to smoke at art college but kicked the habit years ago. Now, looking at the gold-lined packet, I feel the urge to grab it, light up and start chain-smoking. God knows, I need something to calm my nerves after seeing my car blow up.

Antony wanted to stay with me, for moral support, but I couldn't see the point of him hanging around while I gave my statement. I told him to go home after dropping me off. I can get the bus back.

When I waved goodbye, instead of waving back, he gave me a searching look and slowly shook his head.

'I'll wait outside.'

He's worried for my safety. I guess that means he'll be accompanying me everywhere like my personal bodyguard until he leaves for Birmingham. Idly, I wonder if he'd agree to remain in Ware, to be chivalrous. After all, I'm going to need a chauffeur for the forseeable future. It makes perfect sense for him to do both jobs at the same time.

DC Longhurst follows my gaze to the cigarettes.

'You can take the packet. They're not mine.' I wait for him to add, '*filthy habit.*' Instead, he adds, 'The last person in here must have left them.'

'Actually, I don't smoke,' I blurt. 'It's just...I've not had the best day and cigarettes are supposed to be a stress reliever, aren't they?'

DC Longhurst pauses from flicking through my statement.

'The tobacco companies would love you.'

He points to the bottom of each page of my hand-written statement, hands me a fancy rollerball pen.

'Sign here and here.'

I scribble my name with an sooty hand and slide the papers back to him, aware I'm not looking my best. Strands of hair have stuck to my face. When I try and unstick them, greasy residue comes off on my fingers. I grimace in distaste at the smell of engine oil mixed with petrol. I probably look like I've surfaced from a mine.

I pull my sleeves over my hands and tuck them in my lap as DC Longhurst puts my statement on top of a neat pile of paperwork. He leans back in his chair, turning the pen in his hand.

'If I remember rightly, you told me I wouldn't hear from you again.'

'That was before those dognappers decided to come after me.'

I've been thinking about my escape from the red barn with the puppies. At the time, I had a weird feeling about the Astra that passed me on the road when I was making my escape. I remember the driver hitting his brakes as soon as I drove past. The way he just sat there.

I thought I'd got away with it. Stupid of me.

'John must have memorised my numberplate,' I tell the officer.

'He might have. But he didn't need to.' DC Longhurst stretches his arms behind his head. Watching his shirt pull tight across his pecs is diverting for a few seconds. Then the reality of my situation comes rushing back.

'What do you mean, he didn't need to?'

'Your Mini's the only mustard yellow Mark Three in Hertfordshire. If it was John and his mate who firebombed your car, they got lucky. Simple as that. Right time, right place.'

'But at Van Hages?' I think of the windmill, the animal park, my art up in the gallery. 'What were they doing there?'

'Sorry to burst your bubble, Miss Martin, but criminals don't just stick to sink estates. Places like Hertford and Ware are full of opportunities, things to steal, dogs to nick.' He shrugs. 'There is one bit of good news. A shopper saw the culprits leaving after setting fire to your car. It wasn't a great description – one man in a black beanie and donkey jacket, the other in flat cap and jeans. But the car's a blue Vauxhall Astra, like the one you previously reported. We've got a partial plate. Hopefully, we'll get the rest from CCTV.'

'I hope so.' I tug my snood further down over my shoulders and hug my arms round myself, feeling cold despite the heat. 'They're coming after me, aren't they?'

DC Longhurst gives me a sympathetic look. 'Try not to worry. It's more likely they got lucky when they spotted your car. They drove off to get a can of petrol, then returned to finish the job.' His tone softens. 'If they were serious about targeting you, they would have taken more care. They were making a point, that's all. I doubt you'll see them again.'

'How can you be so sure?'

'They set fire to your car in broad daylight with witnesses present. Unless they're thick as two short planks, they would have known security cameras cover the car park. Think of it as a parting shot from them. They don't know you from Adam, or should I say Eve? They only know your car.'

'Well, they killed the car. Well done them.'

DC Longhurst writes down my case reference number.

'For your insurance company.'

I take the slip without enthusiasm. The payout for my Mini will probably be 20p. Less than the price of a Starbar.

DC Longhurst slips a sheaf of paperwork into a manilla cardboard folder.

In a casual tone, he says, 'By the way, I saw the article about you in the Courier.'

189

'What article?' The words blurt out.

'All those dogs you rescued. Impressive, Alexandra.' DC Longhurst carries on. 'I understand quite a few of those dogs are now back with their owners.'

My ears prick up. Since that fiasco, I've avoided reading the local paper. Now, I wonder if I shouldn't have paid more attention. Some good news for a change, but I daren't show it.

Instead, I tuck my arms by my sides and sit very still, hoping he'll stop talking about it.

'I'm not saying I agree with your choices, or the risk you took. Officially, I can't approve of members of the public going vigilante. But off the record, good for you.' DC Longhurst leans across the table with his hands linked together, armed with a secret smile. 'I liked the bit in the paper about your surveillance team and their latest tracking technologies.'

'How do you know it was me?' I say. My cheeks are starting to burn.

'Trust me. I know.'

I look up to the ceiling. 'Am I in trouble?'

'Maybe, if you'd written the article. But it was -' he consults a slip of paper - a woman called Maisie. Seems like she got a bit carried away once she got Sputnik back.'

'You're telling me!' I blurt out.

'One thing I'm curious about.' DC Longhurst cocks one brow. 'This team of yours. Is it real?'

'Uh-uh. It's just me.' Despite everything, I shake my head and can't stop from smiling.

'You seem to have quite the talent for it, don't you?' He raises an eyebrow. 'The dogs weren't the only thing you found. Correct me if I'm wrong, but wasn't there a cat called Sebastian, too?'

My heart gives a huge thump. 'How do you know about that?'

'I interviewed the allotment secretary. Geoff something-or-other. About that stash of illegal videos. He mentioned you in his statement. He didn't have your name but he gave a good enough description. Long, chestnut hair. Tartan snood. Sounds a lot like you, doesn't it?'

Touching my snood self-consciously, I give a resigned nod.

'Did you have a tip-off about the cat, too?' DC Longhurst asks.

'Something like that,' I mumble.

'I have to say, your lucky tip-line is far better than ours.' He gives a knowing smile. 'Perhaps you might consider joining the police and helping us out?'

As I look away, flaming with embarrassment, my gaze lands on the poster of Jason Bevin, still stuck up on the wall.

I gave Jason's address to Mr Bevin days ago - he must be home by now. Jason's hopeful expression makes me worry. Surely Mr Bevin rang the police as soon as he got my email? He only needed to make one phone call. Why haven't they taken the poster down? Have the staff been too busy?

'You were staring at that poster the last time you were here,' DC Longhurst says.

'I was just wondering if you were still looking for him. Jason.' I meet the officer's steady gaze. 'He's been up there a while.'

'A lot of people go missing for a long time. Sometimes, they're never found.'

'It's just -' I twist my hands together, unable to say what I want without giving too much away.

'Is there a particular reason you're interested in Jason?' DC Longhurst scrutinises me. 'You're not thinking of finding him too, are you?'

'God, no!' I bluster. *I've already done that!*

'I just wonder if you could check whether there's been an update. If he's been found.'

'Not as far as I know.' His blue eyes bore into me. 'Unless you know something I don't.'

'I don't know anything,' I say in a rush. 'That's why I'm asking.'

'Going from the morning bulletin, Jason's still out there somewhere.'

'Is there any more you can do to find him?'

'Hopefully, he'll come back on his own. There was a campaign in the papers, but it didn't generate any leads.'

'Can't you try again?' I say lamely, realising I'm sounding far too interested in this random stranger.

'He's one of sixty thousand young people reported missing each year.' DC Longhurst stares at the poster. 'We don't have the resources to find everyone, so we prioritise missing minors, suspected abductions, known criminals and violent offenders. Plus, Jason's at that age when teenagers decide to do it. Lots of them come back of their own accord. Add the fact he's hit eighteen and legally an adult...'

'You're saying he's at the bottom of the pile.'

DC Longhurst shrugs.

'It's the way it is. We've passed his details to the National Missing Persons Helpline. They have a network of volunteers. Maybe they'll have better luck.' He sighs. 'But the fact is, some of these kids don't *want* to come back. Others just don't come back.'

Silence stretches between us.

DC Longhurst jots down something on his notebook.

'Maybe you should consider helping the NMPH? It sounds like you're interested in the work they do.'

My mind's all over the place. I can barely concentrate on what happened an hour ago, let alone the direction my career might take me. My mind swirls with thoughts of Jason.

Why hasn't he been found? The thought occurs to me that maybe, for the first time, the finding machine has failed.

'Take my card.' DC Longhurst pushes it over. 'I've put my mobile number on there. Call me any time.'

I glance down at the card. *Henry.* His first name is Henry. And there I was, expecting Wotan or Ragnor.

I stand up. I can't wait to leave this barren room and go home to wash the grime away.

'I promise, this time I'm not coming back.'

Henry Longhurst rises to shake my hand, a twinkle in his eye.

'Well, when you do, I'll be here.'

33

— • —

*G*ood morning, Alexandra.

It's Rev. Cheryl Storey. It was lovely to meet you in the churchyard the other week. I've been looking into your request regarding your aunt Lilian Martin and your great-uncle Stanley Martin. I can confirm we have a record of Lilian's baptism here at St Gregory's. I have attached a copy of the Baptismal certificate which I hope will be of some help to you.

Stanley drew a blank, I'm afraid. I did check thoroughly, but he was never registered with the parish. Might he have worshipped elsewhere or been brought up in a different faith?

There is no death certficate for Lilian. I checked our records to the present day but there is no further mention of her following the baptism.

From looking at the government's website, I see that after a person has been missing for seven years, a relative can apply for a Declaration of Presumed Death. There is a process to be followed and a fee to pay, but this route may bring you comfort and closure regarding your aunt. If you go down this route, you would be issued with a Death Certificate which would enable you to have a funeral or other farewell ceremony for Lilian. Please contact me if you would like me to help you make arrangements.

I am sorry if this is not the news you were hoping for, but be assured that I will be including you, Aunt Lilian and your family in my daily prayers throughout next week. The congregation will also pray for you on Sunday. I have enclosed a Prayer for Comfort that may be useful to you in the meantime.

Wishing you blessings and peace,
Cheryl.

A lump comes to my throat. I had hoped for more. Cheryl's suggestion of having Lilian declared dead feels like a physical blow. I've only started to get to know my aunt and now I've hit a full stop.

As for Stanley, he's the ultimate mystery man. I don't know how I'm going to track him down.

I click on the attachment to open Lilian's birth certificate. Her date of birth is 11 May 1923. Jack and Vera Martin are named as her parents.

While it's nice to have it, there's nothing new here.

Dad must have hoped for more in his lifetime. I suspected he built the finding machine as a labour of love with the sole purpose of finding her. It must have eaten away at him as the years went by, without further news.

Now the burden has passed to me. I'm facing the same problem that stumped him. Without a photo of Lilian, there's no way to find her. I will never know if Lilian is alive or dead. How can I have her declared dead if I don't know for sure?

One thing's for sure, I don't want to spend the rest of my life with the same uncertainty as my father.

· · · ● · ● · · ·

That afternoon, I email Mr Bevin. I hope a gentle nudge will get him to tell me what's happened with Jason. The following morning, I haven't heard back. To prevent myself emailing him again, I switch off my computer and pace the room, restless at the lack of closure.

Why hasn't Jason been found? What am I going to do when Antony leaves for Birmingham? Where's Lilian Martin? All I've got is half-finished stories.

A knock comes at the door.

'It's open.'

Antony steps in, looking uber-cool in a black T-shirt, with a dark canvas man-bag slung over one shoulder. His shades are in one hand. He taps them against his leg.

'You up to anything?' he asks.

'Can't you see how busy I am?' I put my arms out to my silent, dark room.

'Just wanted to say, I'm popping into town to get a SIM for your phone. Should finish setting it up today or tomorrow. Want anything while I'm there?'

After the fiasco at Van Hage's, Antony gave me the expected 'lone-female in peril' conversation and made me promise to stay out of trouble. Out of concern, he's decided to give me his old mobile phone, a chunky Nokia with a green screen. All I have to do is keep it topped up.

He's given me strict instructions once I've got the phone, to put five pounds credit on it, never leave home without it and ensure it's always charged. Then I can call the police wherever I am. No more getting stuck inside barns, worrying I might die without anyone knowing where I am.

I suppose this is my life now, constantly looking over my shoulder, the days of peace and quiet gone forever.

'So,' Antony prompts me. 'Why don't you come with me? It's quite safe.'

'I know that.' I roll my eyes. I've seen nothing out of the ordinary the few times I've ventured on foot into town, yet I've lost something of my former, carefree self.

'Hey, listen.' Antony comes closer with a knowing smile. 'Tomorrow morning, I'm off to Bury St Edmunds to pick up a new PC case. Why don't you come along and we can go shopping together?'

'Bury St Edmunds? Isn't that past Sudbury?'

'Kind of.' Antony eyes me with suspicion. 'What are you up to, Alex? I hope you're not having one of your ideas.'

I have indeed sniffed an opportunity and it's not for shopping. If I want to find out more about Lilian, I reckon I can get some answers in the newspaper archives.

'Could you drop me off tomorrow?' I cling to his arm and give him a beseeching look. 'I don't mind how long you take, as long as you don't forget to pick me up on the way back.'

I'm depending on his goodwill. The money I was saving for a new car has turned into my survival fund until I go back to work. The insurance company gave me fifty quid for the Mini in the end. Fifty quid!

I suppose it should have come as a pleasant surprise, as I'd only been expecting 20p.

'All right, I'll take you.' Antony's posture slumps. 'As long as I'm not going out of my way to drop you at a library.'

34

S udbury Library is a classy building in the middle of the high street. The exterior boasts curves, balustrades, columns and flourishes. Ornate enough to be a church or the home of a Marqués, the building looks like a folly, squeezed between rows of traditional Georgian buildings.

Inside, its glory has faded. The original floor is hidden under grey carpet tiles. Several storage heaters pump out heat, yet a musty smell lingers in the air. A large bucket sits beneath stained ceiling tiles, a temporary solution for a permanent leak.

The librarian behind the reception desk is an elegant lady in her sixties. Tortoiseshell-framed glasses hang on a silver chain round her neck. She's smartly dressed in a twinset, but no pearls, inputting information from a Rolodex into her computer.

I introduce myself and ask if she has records for the Mercury.

'All this year's editions are available,' she says. 'The past five years are in our archives. If you want to go back further, you'll need to book a slot on the microfiche machines. What year were you after?'

'Well, it is quite far back. I want to start at December 1928 and go through the next few years.' I explain that I want to follow a news trail.

The receptionist taps through a few menus.

'You're in luck,' she says, raising a silver brow. 'Our papers from the late 19th century onwards are available on microfilm. We had a major leak a few years ago which damaged a lot of the older publications in our storeroom, but the newspapers survived because they were stored in metal boxes. May I ask what you're researching?'

'A child who went missing in Sudbury,' I explain. 'She was never found, to my knowledge.'

'That's so sad. What was the name of the child?'

'Lilian Martin.'

'The name doesn't ring any bells, but then it was a long time ago.' She taps her fingers on the desk. 'You know, if this was a major incident you might find reference to it in the national newspapers as well as the locals. The British Library holds those.'

'I could pay them a visit if I don't find anything here.'

She peers over her glasses. 'Oh, you can't go there now. Not for a few months, at least.'

'Why not?' I ask, wondering if you have to be a member or book ahead.

'They're in the process of moving to new premises. You can imagine, with millions of documents and books, this is going to take some time, but it will be well worth the wait. The new British Library will be state-of-the-art, with robots looking after the books, ~~and each room will be atmospherically control~~led.' *Had a billy, won't*

That's not much help to me. I'll have to hope I can find what I need here. The librarian makes a list of my requirements and disappears into the archives. After fifteen minutes she returns with a batch of microfilm.

I really hope Antony's enjoying Bury St. Edmunds, because I've been here half an hour and I haven't started my research.

'The microfiche readers are upstairs in the far right corner. No-one's booked a slot today so please take as long as you like. There are instructions next to each machine. They are easy to operate, but do let me know if you have any problems.'

I follow her directions up an elegantly curved staircase and cross to the back of the building. The Computing section consists of a single rack of dated books. Two microfiche readers sit next to the rack, by the back wall. They look like extra-large computer terminals, mounted together on a sturdy metal table. Despite their bulk, they're dwarfed by an industrial printer that takes up the right hand corner of the room. It looks heavy enough to go through the floor.

It's been quite a while since I've used a microfiche machine, but the sheet of A4 instructions taped to the side of the screen is straightforward enough. I turn on the light, load the microfiche film with the white strip facing up and at the top. There are directional knobs and zoom buttons so you can focus in on articles. There's even a print button. It's not cheap at 40p per print, but in this instance the more articles I print out, the better.

I spend five minutes getting the hang of the machine, ensuring the films are in focus and putting them in order. You need twenty-twenty vision to read the small, dense script covering the old broadsheets, and I'll be relying on the magnifier. The text is broken up by a few adverts - Johnson's Paste-Liquid-Powdered Polishing Wax, the new Standard 9 saloon car and The Burberry, 'The World's Best Weatherproof.' They used to fit a heck of a lot on the page.

It takes me ten minutes to get my first hit in the evening edition of the Mercury, printed the day after Lilian's disappearance. There is no picture.

SUDBURY CHILD GOES MISSING – DID YOU SEE HER? *Five year old Lilian Martin went missing from her home in New Street on 14th December, at approximately four thirty in the afternoon. Lilian has blonde hair and was wearing her school uniform. It is thought she may have gone outside to play and got lost. Sudbury police have performed a thorough search of the area and are undertaking door-to-door enquiries. A resident of Cross Street spotted a blue Austin van driving slowly past the terrace that afternoon. Did you see this van? The police need to speak to the driver to eliminate him from their enquiries. They are continuing their search through Sudbury and towards the Stour. Anyone with information should contact Sudbury Police.*

The story correlated with what Margaret told me, although the details of the van are new. Was it something, or nothing? It sounds significant to me. I can't begin to imagine how Vera must have felt, hearing about the van and the possibility Lilian may have been abducted.

She must have blamed herself for going to bed that afternoon, despite the fact she lived in a safe area of Sudbury with neighbours who kept an eye out for each other.

I print out the article and continue my search. An article printed a week later says an initial search of the river threw up nothing.

The next article appears in the New Year.

MISSING LILIAN MARTIN CASE - BLUE VAN DISCOUNTED.
Following the questioning of a series of local blue Austin van owners, this line of enquiry has now been dropped by the police. Did you see anything on 14th December last year? The police have drafted the underwater search unit to search the Stour further downstream from Sudbury. There are no further developments in this case but Sudbury Police are still appealing for information and urge the public to remain vigilant.

Vera and Jack must have been in pieces at the lack of information. What a horrible Christmas for them. They would have wanted any news, however dreadful, rather than be held in suspense with the days and months ticking by.

I slide through page after page of microfilm until my eyes start to blur. 1929 goes by with nothing until December.

LILIAN MARTIN. A YEAR MISSING AND STILL NO NEWS. It is a year to the day since five-year old Lilian disappeared from her back garden in Sudbury. Despite river searches, enquiries and tips from the general public, the police are no closer to finding out what happened. Her mother, Vera Martin, has issued a plea for anyone who has information but did not come forward for any *reason, to call the police now. The family will be holding a vigil for Lilian at St. Gregory's Church on 23rd December. All are welcome.*

The story of Lilian Martin has turned into a cold case.

'Yo!'

Antony's voice next to my ear makes me jump in my skin. I accidentally hit the focus knob and the viewing screen goes blurry.

'*Shush!* You're in a library!'

'*Yo,*' he whispers, plonking two bags on the table. One's branded Diesel, the other Reebok.

'How are you getting on?' He stares at the microfiches. 'Having fun?'

'Good. You?' I'm happy to give my eyes a break from the screen.

'I got some trainers, a T and chinos. And that coffee you like.'

'Thanks!' I lean over to the Whittard's brown paper bag he's holding up and breathe in the delicious aroma of pure, ground arabica. As I close my eyes I wish I had a giant mug of it right now. I should really treat Antony to something by way of thanks for his driving, but everything he likes is frighteningly expensive.

'Did you get what you needed?' he asks, leaning on the edge of the table.

'I think so. I've got one more microfilm to check through.'

'This place gives me the creeps,' Antony says, taking in the yellowed paint and the atmosphere of age and decline. 'It's completely dead. There's nobody here except us.'

'There's a librarian downstairs.'

'I didn't see anyone. Must have been a ghost.' He shoots to his feet, paces across to the staircase to have a look over the railing before returning. 'This place is empty, I swear. Finish up, would you? I don't want to get locked in and have to spend the night here. Especially not with a ghost.'

'Chill out, Antony. It's a library. You know, like the one you used at Uni.'

'That was modern, not like this place.' He stalks across to the rack of computing books and pulls one out.

'Jeez,' he says under his breath, holding the book up to me. 'Check out this nerd.'

Applications in Computer Science, the cover reads, the background an unpleasant shade of mustard. Below the heading is a blurry photo of a guy in his thirties sitting at a huge computer terminal, wearing enormous glasses above a thick moustache. His shirt is chocolate brown, with a collar long and pointed like party bunting.

I can't help snorting with laughter. 'That's my type of guy!'

Antony flicks through more of the titles. He holds a couple of books up. 'How's this for cutting edge?'

Ticker Tape Trading. Reel-to-Reel Storage for Beginners.

'They've got to be kidding.' He throws the books back on the shelves any old how. 'This stuff's twenty years out of date. What they should do is chuck out all these books and turn the place into a night-club. Up here could be the chill-out zone.'

I pass him the printouts. 'Here, read these while I finish up.'

He reads standing up as I swiftly check through the last microfilm.

1930 goes by without any word of Lilian. The next year passes in the same manner. Eventually, I stop at 20th January, 1936 on the announcement of the death of King George V.

OUR KING IS DEAD. THE WHOLE NATION MOURNS.

'That's it,' I sigh, pulling out the film and switching the microfiche off. My head feels fuzzy. 'I haven't found out much more, except there was a blue van. No other leads.'

Antony returns the print-outs and picks up his bags, eager to get going.

'Things would have been different if Lilian disappeared today,' I say, following him down the stairs.

'Yep.' Antony agrees. 'We've got forensic testing. We've got CCTV on high streets. We can track phone calls and cars. And people are less trusting now, they don't leave their children outside to play unsupervised.'

It's sad, but he's right. Whatever happened to poor Lilian, it seems she was unlucky enough to be in the wrong place at the wrong time. Unless I come up with something completely out of left field, I'm not going to find any further leads.

35

My in-tray's been empty for two weeks. The temp agencies in London and Hertford stopped contacting me about jobs last Friday - hardly a surprise after I failed to respond or offer any sort of excuse. My attitude to work has turned to apathy. I'm off the grid and I don't care.

My 'working' day consists of lying in bed reading trash fiction, walking along the river and browsing the world wide web, ignoring the fact I have no income and no future. For the first time, painting has lost its allure. Whenever I sit down at my easel, I cannot find the motivation to mix colours and end up staring out the window.

I shouldn't be acting this way. The weather is finally warm - spring has sprung. I have every reason for optimism with my first painting in an exhibition and a gallery show planned for a few months' time.

But inside, I'm flat.

The previous weeks spent dashing round Hertfordshire rescuing animals and looking for lost aunts seem surreal. Now I've taken a step back, my previous adventures have taken on the quality of a really weird dream - one where I step into one of Antony's Marvel comic strips as a dark shadow with a tartan snood, the only part of me in colour.

I can't go an hour without thinking of Lilian. I wish I'd known her as a real person instead of a victim or a mystery to be solved. Would she have shared Dad's facial characteristics or his mannerisms and sense of humour? Would she have teased him, loved me?

I owe it to Dad to give her one more shot before I give up. Even though I don't have a photo of Lilian, there *must* be another avenue of investigation I've missed, some way of coming at the problem obliquely.

There is one thing left to try. Antony wouldn't approve.

It goes against the advice Rev. Cheryl gave me, as well as my own good sense. Yet, something inside urges me to go for it. After all, what have I got to lose?

· • • • • • • • • ·

Antony's view on psychics is they're fraudsters. Once they've lured you into their web, they string you out with the promise of answers, so you can't escape.

Keeping this in mind, I re-read the email I printed out from Miriam, Spirit Medium. Of all the mystic people who messaged me, I keep coming back to her.

Miriam, Spirit Reader, available for all messages from the nether to the NOW! Have you lost someone you want to contact, was there something important you needed to say? Do you need to know if someone has passed over peacefully? Miriam can help you, email me a photograph miriamskydiamond@tiscali.co.uk. Call me: 07700-900365

Yes, I can do your reading from a photo!

The last line hooks me. I wonder if she can gain insights into Lilian from the one photograph I have of her.

I dither about putting my money where my mouth is. Am I being gullible? Everyone knows the premium rate industry is full of scammers, and yet people call them in droves. Considering Antony's view - I may as well take my money and flush it down the toilet - it's better if he doesn't know what I'm up to.

Mum used to tut-tut about anything New Age. She said people who hung up dreamcatchers and balanced crystals along their chakras were looking for any old thing to fill the space where God should be. Then again, she said the same thing about anyone who had different views from her. You'll find her in the dictionary, under *narrow-mindedness [see Martin, Brigid]*.

It's hard not to be cynical the way I was brought up. I was taught absolutes. You sin, you get judged. You get married, you die, you get judged. You go up or down. The idea of communication between the living and the dead and lost people inside spirit realms is way outside my comfort zone.

I go on with my internal wrangling for so long that when Antony brings me up a mug of chamomile tea, his brow creases at my doleful expression.

'You OK?' He touches my shoulder. 'You look like you've got the weight of the world on your shoulders.'

'I'm fine!' I force a smile, take the tea and take a sample sip, nearly gagging at the taste. 'Just thinking about where I'm going with my painting.'

'You're doing that by reading an email?' Antony peers over my shoulder at Miriam's message.

'This? This is nothing!' I screw the print-out into a ball and chuck it over my shoulder.

I go to my easel and pretend to study the unfinished canvas.

'Give me a shout if you need a refill or anything,' Antony gives a half-hearted wave as he leaves. Moments later, I hear music blasting out of his room. Public Enemy, of course.

I set the tea down by my dragon tree to go cold. I'll feed it to the tree later - it will appreciate the anti-oxidants more than me. Then, I email Miriam the photo of Vera holding Lilian as well as Stanley standing in his shop window. I give her the bare minimum of information.

The next morning, with Antony safely away at the gym, I receive an email asking me to call her. The number's premium rate at forty-five pence a minute. I get my trusty kitchen timer and set it to count up from zero. She gets ten minutes before I brand her a total fraud.

I dial the number. The voice that answers is warm and motherly with a Cornish twang. It conjures up the image of a plump granny sitting on the sofa watching Gems TV through a pair of 1950s cat eye glasses. She'll have a floral cup of tea beside her and a psychic ticklist resting on a copy of *Knitting Today*.

'Hello, Alex. This is Miriam.'

She's not getting points for knowing my name.

'Hi.' I fall into silence, waiting for her to make the next move.

'Thank you for calling. Before we start, let's make sure we are relaxed. Take several deep breaths, close your eyes, and let me know what you want help with.'

I try and do as she asks, but I'm too on edge to breathe slow and easy. Instead, my exhalations come out ragged. Suspicion rises at her instructions. What if she's telling me to relax to use up my money? If she makes me do breathing exercises for five minutes, that's over two quid for nothing.

'I sense tension in you,' Miriam says, cool and calm. 'Please try not to worry. I'm here to help you find your aunt.'

She said 'Aunt'.

My heartrate picks up. A strange sound escapes me.

I never mentioned anything about Lilian being my aunt on the form. All I said was that I wanted to know more about the baby in the photo.

Could she have struck it lucky first go? Antony said psychics throw out statements hoping one catches. Even if they get ten things wrong, it's the one they get right that sticks in the caller's mind. The caller's left thinking the reading was an unqualified success, even if ninety percent of the information was bullshit.

Back when I was at art college, one of my housemates had a battered Witches Tarot wrapped up in a silk scarf. The rest of us would ask her to do regular tarot readings to foretell our love lives. It was the only thing we wanted to hear about. You'd have thought we would be desperate to know about our future careers as bright young things on the contemporary art scene. That was what our bank accounts were going overdrawn for. But no, our only concern was whether

Elliott or Karl or Jamie fancied us. The tarot cards always showed 'a mysterious man on the horizon,' however they were dealt.

I think my mystery man got lost somewhere.

'I feel you are distracted by something,' Miriam says. 'Your focus is elsewhere.'

Her words shake me back to the present. I can't believe I'm wasting my own money after all my concerns about Miriam being a scammer.

'Sorry,' I say.

'I'm holding both photos,' Miriam goes on. 'You want to know more about the baby?'

'Absolutely.'

I take a deep breath and take a leap of faith. I have to trust Miriam to find truth within the psychic realm. After all, the finding machine picks up signals from people who've died. If a machine can have a type of spiritual inner eye, the idea of Miriam owning one sounds less wierd.

'Something's coming through,' Miriam says slowly. 'I can sense -'

'What is it?'

'Alex, it is important as I do the reading that we go with the flow, or the spirits will be disturbed and won't settle.'

A metaphysical rap on the knuckles. I check my timer. Seven minutes have passed.

'A man is appearing. He is on the borderlines of the spirit world. His name begins with the letter 'V'. He looks very presentable, dark-haired with an old-fashioned pencil moustache. I sense this is how he looked in the past, how he best remembers himself. The rest of his body is out of focus. Do you have any idea who this man could be?'

I rack my brains, but I don't know any deceased men in my family with a name beginning with 'V'. I tell Miriam as much.

'This man is closely connected to the baby.' She pauses. 'Ah, now it's clearer. He says he was very fond of her.'

'Could it be a woman's name instead?' I ask, as something occurs to me. 'Could it be Vera?'

Oops. That just slipped out. I shouldn't have handed her the clue. I want her to work for it.

'As I said, it is a man. His name begins with 'V.' He is sad about what happened. Does this make sense to you?'

It doesn't. I was so sure the man in the shop was Stanley, I didn't consider it might be anyone else.

'What did this man do, Miriam?'

'I will ask, but the spirit world isn't a place where a direct question always gets a direct answer. The spirits tell us what they want us to know, and sometimes it doesn't make sense until later on.'

She goes silent down the line, and I keep quiet too. I don't want to break her flow.

'It is getting very hot. There is a circle of fire, like the sun. But it is something different.'

'What did the man do?' I push her. 'Ask him.'

'He says he is together with your aunt in the house upon the hill.'

'Does he mean Lilian's alive?'

'I can't sense your aunt right now,' Miriam says. 'I cannot say if she is alive. Spirits can hover close to the boundary for a while before moving onto their final destination. Equally, if she crossed over a long time ago, she may be too far away to contact. Hold on...the man is going.'

'You have to get him back. Try!'

'That's not how it works, Alex. I cannot control the spirits. I can only invite them to come.'

She pauses.

'Wait...someone new is coming into view. I see a pale shape, but no detail. This sometimes happens when spirits have just crossed over, or when they are hovering between our world and theirs. Now I can hear her. She says your father would be proud of you.'

I listen hard, wondering who it could be.

'She says not to worry. She is with her husband now, and he is right as rain. That's what she says, *right as rain*. I think that's everything, dear.' Miriam sounds tired. 'It's rare to have two spirits appear in one session. I know you wanted to know more about your aunt and the other man, but let me assure you, things will become clearer to you in the week ahead. That's all I have for you now, but call me again in a week or so and I will search for new messages.'

After thanking her and hanging up, a strange kind of buzz goes through me.

I feel as though my mind is expanding, without any need for an acid tab. The world that Mystic Miriam communicates is utterly alien to me, but I get that it doesn't run like ours. If she's right, the rules are different. Time and space work differently there.

I go back over what she told me. A man called 'V' with a pencil moustache. A circle of fire like the sun. Together in a house on a hill. A woman recently passed over, reunited with her husband who is now as right as rain.

She says that my father would be proud of me.

I am so preocuupied by Miriam's reading that it takes me a while to realise I've left the timer running. My hand shoots out to stop it.

Twenty-eight minutes. I wish it had gone on for longer.

36

— • —

In the middle of the night, I shoot up in bed. *Margaret!*

Oh my God! Is she the woman Mystic Miriam was referring to? Her husband Bernard spent the last quarter of his life unable to speak after his stroke. He could be the husband who is now right as rain, if she were to meet him on the other side.

I toss and turn for the rest of the night, eventually falling asleep with unsettling dreams of strange voices in the distance. A sense of hollow loss consumes me.

The next morning, I wake exhausted and force down some porridge, counting the hours until I can check on Margaret. I know her carer gets her up each day which probably takes a while, so I leave it until ten o'clock before I call her.

The phone rings on and on until my mouth goes dry.

Please pick up. I don't care how long you take, please pick up.

After an eternity, I hear a click as the answer machine kicks in.

'Hello. This is the Long household. Please leave a message after the beep.'

'Margaret, it's Alex Martin. I wanted to catch up with you and check you're OK. I will call again in -'

'Hello?' Margaret's voice cuts in. 'Alex, is that you?'

The sense of relief that runs through me is overwhelming, like a giant plug has been pulled, allowing my anxiety to drain away. I blink back tears at the sound of her voice.

'Margaret! Is everything all right?'

'Same as ever,' she replies with a little laugh. 'The usual aches and pains. But I can't complain.'

'I'm so pleased to hear that!' I let out a hysterical laugh. Mystic Miriam was wrong. She didn't see Margaret. Maybe she didn't see anyone at all. In fact, everything she told me could have been a load of rubbish.

'Are you all right?' Margaret asks.

'Yes, I'm great. Everything is fine. I'd love to come up and see you again. I just need a car. Mine died.' I wince as I say the last word.

'I remember your little Mini. Well, you know where to find me when you get a new one. I haven't forgotten about the photos. Sylvia is going to sit down with me later this afternoon and we'll go through them. I should really try and put them in some kind of order, but I'm not sure I've got the patience for that.'

'Good luck, and let me know if you find anything. You can ring me on the number I left you. Do you still have it?'

'Yes, it's beside the phone. It is lovely to talk to you, Alex. You are a breath of fresh air.'

I smile at her words. The feeling is mutual. Margaret is a goldmine of information about my family and has a keen memory. Little seems to escape her.

I tell her I'll be in touch soon, at which she thanks me again.

'You know, your father would be proud of you.'

Her words send a jolt through me. My smile freezes at hearing the exact words Miriam relayed to me from the lady she saw in the spirit world. The exact same.

I struggle for something to say, but Margaret has already put the phone down.

· · · ● · ● · · ·

I receive news regarding Jason Bevin the next morning via email:

Dear Finder, thank you for your tip. I passed it to the police who duly attended the address in London yesterday morning. Unfortunately, 23 Leather

213

Lane has been subdivided into various flats and businesses and some of the occupants were not in when the police called round.

It is possible that Jason was in one of those flats, but the police don't have authority to take things further with an authorised search on the basis of a tip. They followed up several earlier tips to no avail. They told me they will try the address again if they are in the area, but as far as they're concerned, they've done their bit.

Is there anything further you can do? I am at my wits end regarding Jason's welfare.

Kind regards,
Mr Bevin

A bitter pill for Mr Bevin to swallow. If the police had been more persistent, they would have found Jason. I check his photo in the finding machine for my peace of mind. He's still inside the address.

In all likelihood, Jason was in when the police called round but refused to answer the door. If that's the case, it doesn't matter if I go up to London myself. He won't open the door to me either.

Surely the police will go back? It would be crap if they didn't.

DC Longhurst mentioned priority lists, stretched budgets and reliance on charity volunteers. The police are too busy with serious crime to spend time on low-priority cases such as Jason's.

I wonder if there's another way to help his dad.

My meandering thoughts take me to Antony's room. The door is ajar. Antony's at his Mac, working on a Star Wars layout. The images up on his display show TIE fighters and X-Wings fighting a laser battle somewhere far, far away.

A fragrant breeze, carrying scent from the lilac trees next door, circulates through the open sash window, sending the linen curtains swaying.

'Help me, Obi-Wan Kenobi,' I say in my best Princess Leia voice. 'You're my only hope.'

Antony swivels his chair round.

'Aren't you a little short for a Storm Trooper?' he returns, grinning.

I laugh. 'What are you working on? Looks impressive.'

He explains he's creating a website to promote The Star Wars Fact Files, a series of collectible folders, and shows me an example - a glossy printed insert filled with illustrations, photographs and diagrams.

'There's gonna be a hundred and forty of these to collect. If I was a kid, I'd be spending my pocket money on them, for real.'

'Did you get pocket money, back in the '70s?'

He looks at me as though I needed to ask. 'I got zilch. I was being hypothetical.' He turns his attention back to the folders. 'Look at this index. A lot of this art is brand new. They're going to cover every character, every planet, every weapon, and that's just for starters.'

'Nice.'

I take a closer look at the material. The page is open, showing an illustration of a fat green pig guy in a flight suit.

'Wow. Pigs will fly.'

'That's Voort saBingring.' Antony is looking at me as if this should ring a bell.

'My knowledge of Star Wars is basic,' I tell him. 'Luke and Leia basic. The only minor character I remember is Boba Fett, and that's because I used to fancy him.'

'Yeah, OK, Voort is pretty minor. But there's no way Piggy would be able to get into an X-Wing cockpit without a bucket of grease and a ton of artistic licence.'

'That actually bothers you?'

He raises his arms in protest.

'Yeah! Course it does! The Star Wars nerds won't buy into this unless everything's spot on, from Voort's eating habits to the story of how he was dragged into the Galactic War.'

'I'm sure you'll work it out.' I pat him on the shoulder. 'Maybe I could distract you with something else.'

'What are you after?' His eyes narrow. 'Hold on. I have a bad feeling about this.'

'There's nothing to worry about. It's just...a job's come up. A finding job.' I tell him Jason's story before handing over a print-out of the missing poster. I point to the reward money.

'Ten thousand pounds!' I enthuse.

'You know what I think?' Antony pushes back in his chair, stretching. 'No. No. And no.'

'So, I'll take that as a maybe?'

Antony lets out an exasperated sigh. 'I know you need the money, but you said you were knocking it on the head. Putting the finding machine away.'

'I did say that, but I know where Jason is. All I have to do is locate him and ring the police. They'll do the rest. I don't have to bring him back or anything.'

'How are you going to locate him if he won't answer the door?' Antony scrutinises me with a frown. 'Or, what if he does answer the door and turns out to be a psycho nutcase with a knife? Did you think about that?'

'I could ring Cobra Security and hire one of their guys to protect me. They can shoulder the risk.'

'But not shoulder the door in.' Antony gives me a warning look. 'You don't want to end up back at the police station again, Alex. You'll end up on file.' He pushes Jason's poster back into my hands. 'Don't you think it's time to drop the whole finding machine thing? You never seem happy when you use it, and the rewards aren't worth the risks you've taken. Look, if you were giving advice to me, you'd say the same thing. You're trying to find someone who doesn't want to be found. My advice to you, as your best and most loyal friend - say no.'

I turn and leave, disconsolate.

· • • • • • • • • ·

L ater that evening, I cross the hallway to Antony's room. I hesitate before knocking on the door.

'Antony, is the Nokia set up, yet?'

There is a long pause before the door swings open. Antony leans on the doorframe, blocking my way into his room. He gives me a suspicious glare.

'Why do you need it?'

'You said you'd have it ready for me, that's all.'

'You're going after Jason, aren't you?' His tone is sharp and hurts.

I put my arms out. 'I'd be mad not to. Bevin's offering ten thousand pounds. Ten thousand pounds! Or do you want to be driving me around like Parker in Thunderbirds until the day you leave for Birmingham?'

Antony frowns. 'Don't put this on me, Alex. After your recent escapades, you can't blame me for thinking about your safety.'

'I'll be safe. I've decided to do the job and now I need the phone. Are you going to let me have it or not?' I stand there with one hand on my hip, a ridiculous pose that I fail to carry off, so I let my arm fall against my side.

'When were you planning to go?' He's still glaring.

'Tomorrow, first thing. Get the first train down, find Jason, call the police, wait for them to collect him. Bob's your uncle, back before teatime.'

'Yeah, right. And what if Jason's lying low in some drug den with a load of unsavoury characters? What if -'

'Antony, that's not helping! I was thinking you could give me updated location information from your computer on the morning, in case he goes out for a walk. When I get to London I'll ring you. If I've got the Nokia, I won't have to waste time looking for a phonebox.'

'Let me get this straight. You want me to stay here while you go poking around dodgy parts of London? I'm tempted to say no. No to the Nokia. No to updating Jason's location. I want you safe.'

'Fine, then,' I return, petulant now. 'I'll just take a reading before I go and manage somehow on my own.'

He gives me a long, measured look before he turns his back on me and heads to his desk. At first I think he's blanking me, but then I see him lean over to slide open the middle drawer.

'Come here,' he says, taking out the Nokia. It's a sleek looking thing with a silver body that fits comfortably in his hand. A stubby aerial protrudes from one corner.

He passes me a piece of paper with the new phone number written on it. 'You press this button to make or answer a call. This one to end it. Got it?'

I nod, whisper my thanks.

Antony continues to give me instructions. 'I've programmed the home phone and my mobile into the address book. You can add others if you want. The battery's fully charged, but don't go playing Snake on it or it'll run it down quickly.'

'I'm not going to be playing any games,' I assure him.

He pushes the Nokia into my hand.

'Call me as soon as you find him, wherever you are.'

Then he grabs my wrist and gives me a stern look.

'Promise me, Alex. Be careful.'

37

— • —

The following morning, I set out early for Ware station. My aim was to be on the platform by 7.30 for the 7.45 to London Liverpool Street, but I've been out of the commuting game so long that I forgot how difficult it is to get out of bed when your alarm goes off at stupid o'clock.

I march down to Station Road, already running late. The queue snaking from the ticket office sends my stress levels spiking. By the time I've got my travelcard, the train is lumbering into view. Luckily, it's going about four miles per hour, so I have plenty of time to meet it.

Unfortunately, so has everyone else. Hoards of commuters start galloping down from both ends of the platform. I guess they were expecting a much longer train. This one has four carriages crammed with everyone who got on at Hertford. By the blank resignation on the faces of my fellow travellers, this kind of thing must happen regularly.

I spend the next forty-minutes rammed against a door, straining my neck to catch the trickle of fresh air coming from an open window further down. I've paid to be shoehorned into a train. Passengers try to disassociate themselves from each other by finding something else to look at. They hold books at weird angles and one-handedly manipulate broadsheet newspapers with dexterity The Magic Circle would be proud of.

I keep my back to the train door to protect my shoulder bag, containing the finding machine, my Kodak and the Nokia.

As the train rattles along, those of us standing are forced to adopt stress positions as the train shrieks to a stop several times for no apparent reason. The Daily Telegraph is two inches from my nose. By jerking my head back, I read on the letters page the brand-new currency, the Euro, is dividing opinion, with Mr Benington-White from Bristol declaring, '*Giving up the pound would be worse than giving back India!*'

At Liverpool Street, we explode from the train like strings from a party popper. I go with the flow, heading for the underground like a fish at the edge of a shoal, when a large, dark hand grasps my forearm. I'm about to scream when I recognise Antony.

He ushers me to an oasis of benches in the centre of the platform.

I blink at him, grab his forearms, and squeeze hard. 'What are you doing here?'

'I didn't sleep well last night, thinking of you going it alone. Reckoned you could do with my help.'

He doesn't look his usual chipper self. His eyes are red and bleary and his glasses have smudges. Mind you, he's been squished like a sandwich inside a train for nearly an hour. But the worst thing is, he's wearing a blue T-shirt with blue jeans. An absolute no-no, as far as he's concerned. Even his brown suede Chelsea boots can't save him from the disastrous combination.

'I was relying on you to stay home so you could check my readings on your computer,' I protest.

He gives me a glare. 'Thanks for coming, Antony. Love you too, Antony.'

I run my hands up his forearms, a conciliatory gesture. 'I'm sorry. You know I'm no good early in the morning. Let's start again.' I smile up him and give him a hug, buoyed by his presence.

'Anyway, I was curious about Dope Boy.' Antony pulls me close and squeezes me back.

'It's brilliant you're here,' I beam at him. 'We can get it all done in double-quick time. As long as Jason doesn't move off before we get there.'

'We can still track him if he goes on the move,' Antony says. 'There's an Internet Café down the market. We can use it to check the GPS website.'

He unslings a single-strap rucksack. 'Give me the Nokia, and your dad's machine. It will free you up.' He catches my look of uncertainty and shows me the inside of his bag, lined with towels. 'To stop any of that cold, nuclear stuff touching me,' he explains as we make the transfer. And there I was, thinking he'd done it to keep the finding machine safe.

We head to the underground. Thankfully, it's only three stops on the Metropolitan Line to Farringdon and the tube isn't as crowded as the train. Once we exit the tube at Farringdon, Antony pulls me to one side.

'Can we just run through this.'

'Sure.'

'You know it never goes down the way you think it will. Let's grab a coffee and go through a few scenarios. Just in case it all goes tits up.'

'That's not very positive! I've given this a lot of thought,' I reply somewhat defensively. 'It's low risk.'

'Says you.'

I consult my London A-Z, bookmarked at the relevant pages with post-it notes. 'We need to take a right here, past The Bleeding Heart.' I slowly turn a full 360 degrees before I spy the distinctive red pub on the corner of Greville Street. Apart from the modern light fittings inside, the pub doesn't look like it's changed one iota since Victorian times.

'Coffee, Alex. I need caffeine. Maybe a dirty bacon roll. You said this guy doesn't move until after lunch.'

'All right,' I relent, seeing it's not yet nine o'clock. 'Let's get breakfast down the market. It's this way.'

We wander up a gradual incline towards London's diamond quarter, Hatton Garden. History oozes from the narrow streets, the shops with Dickensian bullseye glass, the cobbles underfoot and the lanes too narrow for buses and lorries. The pubs have peculiar names like The Jerusalem Tavern and Ye Olde

Mitre. A massive, brass-banded barrel squats outside the door of The One Tun. I run my fingers along the ancient-grain wood as we pass by.

Winter must be magical here, especially when there's snow on the ground - walking through the frosted streets must be as close as you can get to stepping back in time.

Two Orthodox Jews exit a jewellers, stopping to talk in low voices in the doorway before walking up the hill. One of them carries a soft, velvet bag under his arm. His colleague clutches a slim, leather briefcase and I wonder if they contain diamonds or gold. The shop displays are stunning, with prices to match. Antony points to a Rolex he likes the look of. It's three grand. Not to be outdone, I point to a platinum, princess cut ring set with a solitaire diamond. 0.5 carat, reads the little sign in italics. £3,850.

'That'd look good on you.' Antony puts his arm around me. 'A woman like you deserves nothing less.'

'Shut up!' I give him a playful shove, but he pulls me closer. 'I wouldn't feel comfortable wearing a fortune like that. A mugger might come and chop off my finger.'

Antony smiles, shakes his head. He directs my gaze to well-dressed men and women in business suits ogling the wares in various jewellery shop windows.

'Take a look around, Alex. Half the guys round here are wearing Rolexes. The women are blinged up with diamond studs, solitaires, the lot. You're too used to living like a student.' He points through the glass. 'You deserve that ring. I bet you, once it was on, you'd get used to it soon enough.'

'Maybe I would. All I need is a fiancé with deep pockets.'

Antony strikes a thoughtful pose by cupping his chin and gazing into the distance. 'I might know someone. He's standing not a million miles from you.'

'That's lovely, Antony,' I dismiss him. 'I know you like to show off a bit of bling, but that's taking it a bit far.'

'I like you.' Antony shrugs, seemingly lost for words. I've never seen him like this before.

'I like you, too.'

'No, Alex.' He looks down on me. 'I ~~really~~ like you.' A lot

I'm utterly confused. And slightly infuriated. *Where has this come from?*
I arch a brow, waiting for him to explain himself. Instead, he turns and walks backwards up the hill, beckoning me to follow.

'Come on, let's do what we came here for.'

An overwhelming temptation comes over me to say, *'Come back here, Antony Eastwood, and explain yourself this second!'*

Instead, I revert to our usual banter. 'But you don't like me like that.'

He gives a broad grin. 'Is that right?'

'Stop teasing me!' I follow the maddening man up the hill onto Greville Street, crossing a main square flanked with Georgian buildings and past more jewellery shops to reach Leather Lane market.

We go from diamond shops to market bargains in under fifty metres. Clothes stalls and market traders stand behind their stands, drinking hot tea and coffee out of polystyrene cups. The sound of the crowd mixes with traders calling out for custom.

'Look at these 'ardy chrysanths! I'll do three bunches for a fiver. They was four pound a bunch!' The flower seller catches my eye and grins. 'How about you then, darling?' As I walk past, he calls out, 'Please yourself, love.'

'Original magnetic bracelet! Rheumatism! Arthritis! The best you'll ever try. No more pills!'

It's been so long since I've been into London, I'd forgotten how exciting it was.

''Ave a look at these strawberries. I'm practically giving them away! Big punnet for one-fifty. One-fifty a punnet!'

Rows of coats sway on hangers from the top bar of one stall. A red, felt coat catches my eye. The beauty of the market lies in its prices. The coat is only £25, and I'm tempted to try it on, but Antony's already heading for a shop called *Department of Coffee*. He stands in the doorway and waves me over. The aroma of freshly-ground beans hits me the instant I duck under his arm. The warm atmosphere and sight of customers chatting away is welcome after the stressful journey.

We order two cappuccinos and a couple of bacon butties and take them to a table in the far corner.

'So, all the green tea and sushi's just a cover,' I comment as Antony devours his breakfast. 'The reality is, you like slumming it just as much as me.'

'Cheeky mare,' Antony wipes ketchup from round his mouth. 'A job like this calls for a bacon butty.'

'Well, it's good to know you're human.'

After he's polished off his roll, Antony watches me finish my breakfast.

'Don't give me the doggy eyes,' I laugh at him. 'I'll get you another one. We've got time.'

I stand up, reaching into my pocket for change.

'No, I'm eating light, just in case it all kicks off,' Antony says, lifting his bag onto the table. 'Let's check up on Jason.'

He retrieves the finding machine, still wrapped in its towel, using the bag to shield it from view of curious onlookers. Two older ladies drinking tea on the next table glance over. I shoot them a friendly smile and they swiftly return to their conversation. Together, we check the reading on Jason's photograph.

'It's the same as before,' I confirm, having compared the display against a previous reading I took first thing this morning, jotted down on a post-it note.

One of the five lights is red.

'He's in a building half-way down Leather Lane. Number 23. I made a note of it on the map. It's only a few minutes away.'

Antony checks his watch. 'Let's go catch Jason in bed.'

'Are you sure?'

'Yeah. We can catch him off his game.'

'Antony, I know you want to help me,' I say, clasping my hands together like I'm beseeching him. 'But this is my job, my find. It's important you let me go first on this one. Mr Bevin asked me to approach Jason and I've spent so long thinking about how it'll go, I'd be really disapp—'

'It's cool. I get it,' Antony breaks in. 'It's your gig. I'll just hang around in the background.'

We finish our coffee and leave the café. I carry the finding machine so that I can check the LED lights, heading a short distance down the market to number twenty-three, in the centre of a Victorian brick-built block. On the ground floor is a takeaway, Star Kebabs. A further two floors are above it. Craning my head, I spot a window set up in the eaves, so that's three.

To the left of Star Kebabs, a staircase leads up a short flight of concrete steps to a chipped, blue door. I glance up, looking for cameras, but apart from an overhead light covered in cobwebs, there are no visible security devices. The finding machine shows two solid red LEDs with the last three flashing. I hand it back to Antony.

My nerves kick in the instant I set foot on the first step. It's hard to convince yourself everything is going to be OK when you are already panicking.

A steel intercom hangs on the left-hand wall by the door. A column of six plastic buttons sit next to the speaker.

1. Green Arrow Recruitment
2. Fellowes
3. A&B Language Course
4. China Clothing Industries
5. Sam and Farouk
6. L Finney

How are all these people crammed inside a single, narrow building? Inside, I reckon it's one of two extremes: either Dr Who's Tardis or Dickens' blacking factory.

225

Jason's holed up somewhere inside, either staying with a friend, in the back room of one of the businesses or squatting under the eaves. I've got six chances to find him.

The top button lights up with a loud buzz when I press it.

'Hello!' I speak loudly.

A woman's voice comes through the intercom, distorted by crackles.

'Green Arrow Recruitment.'

'Hello, can I speak with Jason Bevin.'

'*crackle...hiss...*repeat that?'

'I'm looking for Jason Bevin. He's staying here.'

'*hiss...* This is an agency. Do you have an appointment?'

As I struggle to come up with a reply, I hear more crackling followed by a clunk as the receptionist breaks the connection.

Now I've started, I suppose I'd better keep going. I look back at Antony. He's leaning against the wall, super-casual, watching the market crowds.

I press twice on Fellowes but there's no answer. On punching number three A&B Language Course, I hear the familiar crackle of the intercom.

'Nǐ hǎo, A, B?' The voice is deep and male.

'Hello, do you speak English?'

'Qǐng wèn nǐ zhǎo shuí?'

'I'm looking for Jason Bevin. Ja-son-Be-vin.'

'Bào qiàn, nǐ dà cuò hào mǎ le. Zhè lǐ měi yǒu zhè gè rén.' A long pause follows. 'No Ja-son-Bee-vin here!'

I throw a look back at Antony. He flashes a smile, the cheeky sod.

'Need any help?'

'No,' I hiss back. Now I know why the police had so much trouble finding Jason.

I lean down and peer through the letterbox. Inside, I catch a glimpse of a dark and narrow hall with a staircase leading up from the left wall and a door at the end of the corridor.

My hopes of finding Jason at China Clothing Industries are low. I ring the bell but no-one answers.

That leaves two buttons.

'Hello?' a female voice calls out when I press the buzzer for Sam and Farouk.

'Hi, is Jason there with you? I'm looking for Jason.'

'Sorry, there's no Jason here. You've pressed the wrong button.'

Despondent, I gather my resolve for the last button. Just as my finger goes to press it, Antony gets in first, slamming his hand down on the first button for Green Arrow Recruitment. As it crackles into life, he leans his head close to the intercom and in a gruff voice says:

'DHL. Delivery.'

There's a loud buzz and the door clicks open.

I refuse to meet Antony's eyes, but I can feel his smugness as I push through the door into a hallway. The door closes behind us, shutting off the market's clamour. In the relative quiet, the muffled sounds of phones ringing, conversations and creaking boards reach us from the upper floors and rooms across the hall.

A large plastic capped utility light is set into the stippled ceiling. The floor is beige vinyl. The place has zero atmosphere. There are six numbered pigeon-holes on the left-hand wall along with a sign that says, 'Green Arrow Recruitment 1st Floor, Red Door'.

I rifle through the post. It's mostly pizza and kebab flyers with a few official letters from DVLC and HMRC, some white window envelopes that look like bank statements, but nothing with Jason's name on.

Antony shows me the finding machine. Three solid reds, two flashing.

'The signal's stronger here. Still not the best, though,' he says.

He continues to the door at the end of the corridor, then lifts the finding machine up and waves it about, giving me palpitations.

He looks up the stairs and gives me a nod. Together, we climb the staircase to the first floor, and round again to the second. A tiny staircase winds all the way to a tiny landing with a door at the top. Number 6.

I look at the machine. Five solid reds.

38

I pack the machine safely away in my rucksack, before readying myself in front of Jason's door.

Anthony catches my eye. 'You ready?'

I nod gamely, raising my fist. I rap on Jason's door.

No response. I try again. Nothing.

'He must be lying low,' I whisper.

Antony nudges me out of the way and pummels on the wood like he's part of a SWAT team.

'Delivery!' he yells through the keyhole. He continues banging until the door cracks open.

A wave of stale fags and cannabis wafts from the apartment. I just about recognise Jason Bevin from his photo. An assortment of stains cover his Pearl Jam T-shirt and grey jogging bottoms. God knows how long he's been wearing them.

'You got a package, or something?' Jason peers out with barely open, red-rimmed eyes, a shadow of his former self. There's no sign of the smiling, clear-eyed teenager in the poster.

He puts one hand up to shield his view, as though he's looking at the sun instead of into a dingy hall.

'Jason, I'm Alex.' I give him a friendly smile. 'Your dad sent us to find you. He just wants to know if you're OK. May we come in and have a quick chat?'

'If that's OK,' Antony adds over my shoulder.

'My dad?' Jason's face screws up. 'How did you know where to find me?'

I give a pathetic shrug, caught out by his question. I can't think of anything to explain our arrival.

'We've got our ways,' Antony jumps in. 'We're professionals.'

'Right.' Jason's shoulders slump. 'I should have known you were coming. I've been getting signs for days.'

'We need to check you're all right. Can we come in?' I ask.

Jason looks blank. I'm unsure whether he's taken in a word of what I said. I put my foot over the door in case he tries to close it in our faces. But then he shrugs, takes a step back.

'You may as well, now you've found me.'

'Do you mind if I go first?' Antony waits for my nod before he crosses the threshold.

Jason holds up his fist for a bump, but Antony simply says, 'Yeah, hi mate.'

I follow him in, and the door clicks shut behind us. I turn and eye the latch — a simple Yale lock, easy to open in a hurry. The short hallway opens into a single reception room. Antony moves to the centre, his eyes following Jason, who sinks on the sofa and starts making a roll-up with shaking hands.

I follow Antony into a fug of smoke. There doesn't seem to be anyone else here.

The apartment looks like it should be in the basement rather than up in the eaves. The only illumination is provided by a single pendant lightbulb. It can't be more than forty watts. The dim light reveals a small kitchenette down the far end.

'This place gives me the creeps,' Antony mutters.

'Sudbury Library gave you the creeps,' I whisper back. 'Let's get on with it.'

Plastic packs of Evian mineral water are stacked on the floor by the cupboards. I wonder if Jason's water supply has been cut off. But one of the taps is dripping, and I remember reading somewhere that the water board wasn't allowed to do that.

Besides, the lights are working, so someone must be paying the bills.

The worksurface and backsplash round the sink are covered in tin foil. An untidy pile of plates and mugs fills the sink. Even though my vision is hampered by the dim light, I can make out reflections from standing water half-way up the sink. Scum floats on top, company for the smears of stale food clinging to the crockery.

I hope Antony doesn't notice. He's very sensitive about that sort of thing.

'Do you want a cup of tea, or something?' Jason asks.

'We've just had one, thanks,' I say quickly, shuddering.

A strange noise is coming from nearby; a low thrumming muted behind a door. It's coming from one of the rooms leading off the lounge.

The whole set-up seems wrong somehow; the lighting, the water bottles, the foil and the fact that Jason appears sublimely unconcerned about how this looks to outside eyes.

I look round for any other surprises and spot the reason for the lack of natural light. I hadn't noticed the window before. Now I see why. It is covered in foil. The shapes of the individual glass panes are pressed into relief beneath it, but no light can get through.

Antony notices my interest. 'Do you mind if I open the window, mate?' he asks Jason. 'I'm not a smoker, and I could do with some fresh air.'

'Three inches, no more.' Jason fumbles around in his pocket, eventually producing a tape measure. 'Use this.'

'Look, Jase, can I just open the window?'

Jason sinks back into the sofa. 'Sure, I guess it doesn't make any difference, now.'

Antony pulls the sash window up. Light streams in along with a welcome blast of fresh air.

Below the window is a flat section of roof. We must be at the back of the building. Down on ground level is a small parking area, crammed with vehicles, bicycles and overflowing bins. An extraction fan mounted to the flat roof makes a *chug chug* sound, sending the aroma of kebabs through the open window. It's not often I welcome the smell of greasy lamb, but it's better than stale fags mixed with unwashed teen.

Antony stays by the window, watching Jason reach into his pocket again. This time, he pulls out an orange, disposable lighter.

'I knew it was going down today.' He lights his roll-up. His eyes flutter closed as he takes a deep drag. 'As soon as I opened the door, I knew.'

Antony and I exchange a loaded glance.

'Time to call the police,' I mouth.

Antony reaches into his pocket and pulls out his Nokia. He checks the screen, wiggles the phone at me.

'No signal.'

'Whose place is this?' I direct Jason's attention away from Antony who is now pacing round the room, checking the number of bars on his display.

'It belongs to the uncle of a mate of mine. He's living in New York. He's cool.'

I'm not so sure his mate's Dad will be cool when he returns and sees the state of the place.

'How are you managing for food?' Jason doesn't look like he has two pennies to rub together.

'I get by. I get cash in hand work down the market. I help them pack up their stalls at the end of the day, do the odd job. They often throw in a box of fruit or veg. I can make a mean veggie stew.' He shrugs. 'And I live above a kebab shop.'

He seems harmless, yet utterly distanced from normal life. He keeps throwing nervous glances towards the open window as he smokes his roll-up. White plumes escape his nose and mouth. From the funny smell of the tobacco, I realise if I want any sense from him, I need to do it quickly before he gets high.

'Your dad's really worried. He couldn't get hold of you.'

'I panicked,' Jason admits. 'Ditched my email address soon as I got here. Pulled the landline. I'm living off-grid as much as I can, using a back way into the internet, but I'm not safe here. None of us is while we're hooked up to DS surveillance.'

I don't know what DS is, and not sure I want to know.

Antony rolls his eyes. He extends his arm holding the Nokia out of the window and moves it around, checking the bars on the display. 'Dammit,' he says in a low voice.

I guess there's no signal there, either. I return my attention to Jason.

'Look, Jason, your dad's got your best interests at heart. He wants you back home, safe.'

'I'm never going to be safe.' Jason sits forward and taps the ash from his roll-up into an empty take-away carton. 'Nowhere's safe, while they're out there looking for me.'

'Well, we found you first. And we know what we're doing. We will keep you safe, I promise.'

'You think you can do that? Seriously?' Jason's mouth widens in a grin. His teeth are stained yellow. 'I came here to find out the truth. Get to the bottom of things. I'm making progress, but it's going to take time.' He taps his forehead. 'It's a full-time job, finding them.'

'*Them?*' The question comes out before I can stop it. 'Who do you mean?'

'I told you. Deep State.'

I have no idea what he is talking about.

'Deep State's a conspiracy theory,' Antony returns my questioning look from the window.

'That's what they want you to think!' Jason jabs a nicotine-stained finger at him. 'You're living in ignorance like the rest of the masses. Deep State's beyond anything you can imagine.'

'Hyped rumours from a bunch of conspiracy nuts,' Antony snaps. 'None of those crazy theories are true.'

'This isn't helping, Antony!' I hiss. 'Pipe down!'

Jason shakes his head. 'You're the one who needs a reality check. There's a hidden organisation within the US federal government, running everything. The elected officials are nothing more than puppets on show.' He fumbles around the magazines on the table as if he's looking for something.

I catch Antony's eye and jab my finger at the front door.

'*Police! Call them now!*'

I'm desperate for him to get on with it. It could take ages for the police to get here and I don't know how I'm going to keep Jason occupied while we're waiting.

Antony gives me the nod.

'I guess both of you think the moon landings were real? Huh? What about Y2K? That's gonna be a disaster for everyone.'

'Y2K. You mean, the Millennium Bug?' Finally, I'm able to contribute something to this conversation. 'But that's just a glitch in the way computers process the year 2000. There'll be a hardware update or something way before then. No-one's really worried about it.'

Jason's laugh is an unpleasant high-pitched wheeze that deteriorates into a hacking cough. I find it hard to believe that he is only eighteen. He sounds about eighty.

He takes a swig of something from a mug.

'Tiny glitch!' he smirks. 'When the clock turns midnight on December 31st 1999, you and the rest of the human population are going to find yourselves back in the stone age. All the computers will think it's 1900 all over again. They never considered this stuff back in the '70s, but now it's coming back to bite you - and everyone else.' He puffs furiously on his roll-up.

'When the computers crash, everything we rely on them for is going down. Stock exchanges, air traffic control, your hospital records, even your age on your driving license. Everything. You need to open your eyes. It's happening.'

The thought crosses my mind that if he's right, the finding machine might stop working, too.

Antony opens the front door and drops the rucksack in the gap to stop it closing.

'*You gonna be all right? I can't get a signal in here.*' He mouths the words, waggling the phone. '*He's harmless. Just keep him talking.*'

'I will.' I shoo him out.

He gives me the thumbs up and heads downstairs.

Jason doesn't notice our interchange. He's transfixed by the swirling smoke in front of his face.

'Y2K is *nothing* compared to Deep State.' He's off again. 'Your mate's wrong when he says they're not real. That's what they want you to think. They use that as cover while they target individuals through the dark web. Track them. Experiment on them. Deep State's responsible for injecting viruses into the brains of test subjects. They use remote viewing platforms, back tracing, truth serums. Once DS finds you, you've had it.' He runs his hand through his hair, coughing. 'They're watching all the time. They targeted me. I see them in the street...things people say. They send me messages.'

'I'm here to help,' I try and reassure him. 'You can trust me.'

Jason flings himself back on the sofa.

'It's so deep I can't think straight.'

'Just relax, Jason. Let's have a proper chat and you can tell me everything that's on your mind.' I reckon I can keep him talking until Antony gets back. 'I'm a really good listener.'

His eyes crack open. 'You're really interested in Deep State?'

'Absolutely.'

Jason stares at me, lips pressed together. His fingers tremble as he grinds out his roll-up in the ashtray. Several expressions cross his face, as if he's going through an internal struggle.

Then he hoists himself from the sofa and heads for a door leading off the lounge, the one with the strange sound coming from behind it.

'Come on.' He beckons me over. 'You've got to see this.'

39

I throw a desperate glance to the front door but Antony's nowhere to be seen. I listen out for approaching footsteps or sirens, but apart from the continuous chug of the extractor fan and voices of the street-traders outside, the top floor lies quiet.

Antony told me Jason was harmless. He'd better be right.

A cold stone settles in my stomach. I should have been the one to call the police. Now, I'm stuck with a delusional teenager who may be suffering from psychosis.

Antony, come on. Hurry up!

Jason cracks open his bedroom door and pushes through the narrow gap. The industrial noise I heard earlier gets louder, like a jet engine warming up. Strange light flickers inside, casting a green haze below the threshold.

I follow Jason to the door with reluctance; things are weird enough already. Sounds of rummaging come from inside, but when I try to push the door open, something's blocking the other side. I use my shoulder to shove it open, dislodging a pile of bedding and magazines. Light falling through from the lounge enables me to make out a few titles: NEXUS, Excluded Middle, Red Lobster.

The room is a gargantuan mess. This must be where Jason sleeps, although I cannot see a proper bed. A darkroom light shines from the pendant light fitting. The eerie, red glow illuminates next to nothing.

The place smells damp and earthy. God knows what spores and organisms are thriving in here.

Jason sits at his PC - a tower computer like mine, only twice the size. Two armoured cables snake into a reinforced metal box on the wall.

He moves the mouse, and the monitor wakes up, throwing light onto his face and across the rest of the room. The artificial light reveals a black-out blind covering the window and a huge metal block sitting next to the computer, generating the noise. Green lights strobe from the box vents.

'What is that thing?' I say loudly, strangely captivated by the lights. I start to feel light-headed, which I put down to inhaling too much second-hand smoke from Jason's wacky baccy.

'Jason taps his mouse. 'It's a signal disruptor, a jammer. You wouldn't have found me if I'd been able to use it properly, but the poxy fuse box blows every time I set the frequency blockers to max. I've tried reconfiguring the setup, but the wiring in this place is seriously dodgy and it keeps killing the power.' He chews on one fingernail, waiting for his PC to boot up. 'They got upset with me downstairs and I'm pretty sure it was Mr Zhang from Flat 4 who left a dead cat on my doorstep as a warning. I tried to explain what I was doing but he didn't get it. No-one understands.'

And no-one ever will.

The logo of a man wearing a red hat appears on the screen.

'That doesn't look like Windows,' I comment, chewing on a fingernail.

'Its Linux. You can't trust Windows. It's not secure.' Jason's hands fly over the keyboard. 'I don't want Microsoft getting hold of my data. Linux is better for everything.'

I thought I was pretty fast with touch-typing, but Jason leaves me for dust. Not bad for a dope-head.

'Are you a professional coder?'

'Nah, I'm rubbish compared to some of the guys on here.' Jason continues hammering at the keyboard.

I hear the shrill machine-code sound of his computer connecting to the internet.

'I thought you said you were off-grid?' I ask, feeling uneasy all of a sudden.

'I am. This is ultra-secure. Decentralised.'

Everything is happening so fast, and although I want to believe that he's connecting to the world-wide web with the intentions of a normal person, I start to have my doubts when the light from his disruptor box suddenly changes from green to orange.

I step out into the hall to look for Antony, but there's no sign of him. When I check back on Jason, he's double-clicking an icon at the bottom of the screen.

A large, black window opens with the following words in bright green:

HELLO JASON. I AM READY. ARE YOU?

'Yeah, I'm ready!' He claps his hands and grins at the screen.

A new sound joins the cacophony along with the orange light. The thrumming music roots me to the spot. I recognise the song instantly. The Beloved, that's it - *The Sun Rising*. It was massive at house parties back in my student days, a mellow background tune, but Jason's playing it so loud it's splitting my head open.

'Please, turn it down!' I say from the doorway, hugging my arms around myself.

'Just until we're through the rabbit hole.' Jason looks round at me, his eyes wild like he's having the time of his life. His expression sends a cold spike through my guts. I venture closer to the monitor, nearly slipping on a magazine.

On the monitor, lines of green code start scrolling inside the black box, a load of technical gobbledygook. A flashing block cursor sits at the end.

'Jason! What are you doing?'

The music suddenly cuts out, leaving my ears ringing.

Numerous windows appear on the screen, stacked up behind each other. One of them has the image of a Bedouin on a camel in the corner and the words

Silk Road. There are various images of pills and bottles. *Oxycodone, Diazepam, Tramadol, Cocaine, White Frost* with prices in US dollars.

What else is he taking, apart from the cannabis? In the background, green text scrolls. Jason merrily types, strands of greasy hair hanging across his face. He dismisses the page and another comes up with a red banner stating *Internet Explorer is Evil!* Alongside is a window headed *Arson Attacks for Animal Rights Activists.*

'Isn't this stuff illegal?' The messages and images up on the screen are unsettling, but I force myself to look.

'Not all of it. Lots of people use the dark web as a private space to talk about stuff. It's somewhere they can connect to like-minded individuals without being judged.' Jason turns to me, taking his hands off the keyboard. 'The dark web is apolitical. It accepts everyone, the opposite of what's happening in so-called 'normal society.'' He forms air-quotes.

'How do people find others like them?'

Jason stares at me intently. 'There's loads of ways. Search engines. Links on websites. Or they can use specialist forums. Hey, you want to see Deep State at work? The mind injections?' He opens a website before I can protest. A dense mass of white text on black fills the screen. Images flicker of needles piercing skin. I look away.

'This has been going on for years. Some of the stuff they've been doing, you won't believe it until you see it. It's totally sick.'

'What about these forums?' I'm desperate for him to change the subject and get away from the needles.

'Oh, yeah, there's tons of them.' He leans back in his chair. 'They talk about everything. What kind of stuff are you after? Deep State radiowaves? Thought experiments? Tell me and I'll find it for you.'

'Find it for me?'

An inspired idea occurs to me. Once it pops into my head, it won't go away.

'There is something, Jason. It's top secret. If you could find out anything about it, that would be awesome.'

'About what?' He looks at me with suspicion. 'Is it dangerous?'

'No way. The opposite. It's what helped us to find you.' My mouth has gone dry. 'Wait here a sec.'

I dash out to retrieve the rucksack from the front door, leaving a magazine wedged in its place and have a quick look out into the hall.

Before, I was desperate for Antony to hurry up. Now I want him to take his time. For the first time since meeting Jason, I feel in control of the situation. I've got this.

Returning to the room, I unzip the bag and take out the finding machine. My hands are shaking so badly I nearly drop it.

'What's that?' Jason's eyes narrow as I place it on the desk.

'It's a finding machine. It finds people, Jason. This is how we found you. My dad made it back in the 1970s. You said the dark web has everything on it. Can you find out anything about this machine?'

'Wow.' He picks it up in a surprisingly gentle grip and looks it over, runs his fingers down the side of the machine. 'What's this cold stuff coming out of the vents?'

'I have no idea.'

He leans over and gives it a sniff. He's certainly braver than me.

'My dad made it,' I tell him. 'He was an electronics engineer. He built our TV back in the '70s and made this from the components left over.'

'Clever. Looks like he repurposed a case from an accounting calculator.' Jason examines the electronics and on/off switch.

I lean over and turn it on for him, triggering the display.

'It shows the co-ordinates of the person you're looking for in longitude and latitude,' I tell him.

'You mean, like GPS?'

'Yes.' I marvel at his perspicacity. Underneath the haze of cannabis and mental issues, Jason is clearly a clever dude.

'So, who was your dad working for? CIA? M15? Or maybe he was hooked up to NASA scientists.' He grins. 'This is crazy. I love it!'

'He wasn't working for anyone. He just liked making stuff. This really appealed to him, the idea of finding someone from a photograph.' I talk him through what I know and how it works with the computer thrumming beside us.

'Epic!' Jason takes in every word. 'Bet it's classified.'

'This has to remain top secret, you understand?' I'm keen to impress on him. 'You cannot tell anyone about it.'

He taps his nose. 'Got it.'

'Jason, there must be some plans somewhere or some bloke who came up with this technology who knows how it works. It goes back to the 1960s or earlier.'

I cast a glance back to the door. *Take your time, Antony.*

'This is time-critical, Jason. How quickly can you get something for me?'

'I'm on it.' He straightens at the keyboard and for a moment I see a bright, young boy with a future, instead of a drug-addled, paranoid teen.

I say nothing more as he gets to work.

40

— . —

Turns out, there's more than one Finding Machine. Jason gets his first result in five minutes. I spend the intervening time in a semi-doped-out state, staring wide-eyed at the green light pulsing from his disruptor box, while he types multiple commands and clicks his mouse like a rapid-firing gun.

Out of the corner of my eye, black boxes filled with green text stack up against the bright, back-lit monitor.

I snap to attention when a large image fills the screen - an intricate, engineer's diagram of an intimidating contraption standing over fifteen feet tall (assuming the two Victorian gentlemen standing out front with waxed moustaches and pocket watches have been drawn to scale). The machine looks like an industrial loom combined with a swarm of locusts. Spindly, metal legs run along the top in rows, coupled to multiple gears and rollers by a confusing array of belts.

'The blurb says it's a 'Living Soul Engine.'' Jason's eyes dart from one part of the diagram to another. 'It's a prototype dating back to 1848, but it was never built.'

The news doesn't surprise me. Who on earth would want to build something like that?

'It doesn't look anything like my dad's machine,' I point out.

'No, but it means we're in the right area,' Jason says. 'The Living Soul Engine is listed under the *finding machine* category.'

My mouth drops open. 'The finding machine has its own category on the dark web?'

'Sure.' Jason seems unfazed. 'I told you, everything's on here.'

Before my belief in reality fractures, and the enormity of the portal into which Jason is drawing me melds my brain, I shake out my crazy thoughts and take a closer look at the picture.

'How was it supposed to work?'

Jason points to a podium at the front, with an open frame at head-height. 'Someone stands there and puts their head through.'

'What's the point of that, if you're already there? It's not finding you.'

'Maybe it finds your relatives, or something. Maybe it draws a picture of your soul.' Jason shrugs. 'Let me keep searching. I reckon I can do better.'

I give him the nod, dismissing the machine as one of those weird inventions the Victorians were famous for. I used to look them up in old journals for a laugh – things like the 'Niagara' rocking bath, designed to give you the full sea experience without any splashes (guaranteed!). And the Multi-Purpose Cane – apart from aiding walking, it could be played as a flute, used to measure a horse or to smoke opium, though not all at the same time.

'OK, look at this.' Jason draws my attention to a black and white photo from the 1940s. A man in a white shirt with heavy rimmed dark glasses is leaning forward over a wooden framed console of lights and switches. The model of a human head, its scalp covered with a wired cap, sits on a table alongside it. Multiple wires run from the cap to the machine.

'This is a 'Positionsrechner für Menschen,'' Jason says, followed by the English translation. 'A Positional Human Calculator. It was made in Germany in 1943 by Konrad Zuse. He was a legend in computing.'

'Does it work?' I ask, my eyes straining against the contrast of dark room and bright screen. As I'm still coming down off Jason's fumes, the whole scenario feels surreal, like I'm not really there.

'It doesn't say.' Jason shoots me an apologetic look. 'I'd need more time to look into it.'

As he starts clicking away, I hear sirens in the distance. My time with Jason may be running out.

'Don't worry about that Konrad machine. Can you find out anything about my dad's machine?'

'That's what I was doing,' Jason assures me. After a nail-biting wait where nothing comes up on his screen but more boxes of code, an image appears of a black wedge with two antennae poking out of the top.

'There!' I shout, making Jason jump in his seat. 'That's the Finding Machine!'

'It's not called that.' Jason peers forward.

This one's got a real ring to it: The Turing-Tesla League Human Drive.

The sirens are getting louder. I pop my head out of the hallway. Footsteps are coming up the stairs.

'You've got one minute to find out everything,' I urge Jason.

· · · ● · ● ● ● · ·

A ntony and I descend the short flight of concrete steps to street level, following the two Met police officers escorting Jason to a waiting squad car. After being stuck inside the stuffy dark of Jason's flat, the bright sunlight, fresh air and noise of Leather Lane comes as a shock.

God knows how Jason's coping with the sensory overload.

An eastern-Asian man stands behind us on the top step, watching proceedings with a mobile phone pressed to his ear. I wonder if this is Mr Zhang of dead cat fame.

The flashing blue lights have drawn a crowd in the tight, market street. Jason keeps his head down, shuffling like a zombie.

'Mind your head, Jason.'

The female police officer protects his head as he gets into the back seat, while her colleague radios an update to HQ. I smile at Jason through the window, but he doesn't notice. He looks ahead with a fixed stare, in some kind of self-imposed trance.

'What happens now?' I ask the police officer. Antony and I have given our personal details and a short statement. Now Jason is safe, that seems to be the end of the matter.

'We're taking him to the Royal London Hospital for assessment and observation. All being well, his dad can see him there.'

'How long before he's released, do you think?'

'I couldn't say,' she shrugs, glancing back at Jason. 'He looks like he needs a stint in rehab to get his medication sorted. But that's for the doctors to decide. You did well calling us in.'

A big, tattooed stallholder comes over. 'What's up with him? He don't look too clever.'

'Please step back from the car,' the officer instructs as she gets into the passenger seat.

A guy in a donkey jacket pipes up. 'Oy, that's Jason. Where they going with him? Is he 'urt?'

He shoots a glare at Antony.

'He's been missing,' Antony says. 'His dad wants him back.'

'He looks like a junkie,' shouts a woman, looking pointedly at me. To be fair, the distinctive smell of cannabis that follows Jason hangs like a cloud over the police car and is stuck to my hair.

'Oy, you!' The guy leans down and raps on the window. 'Sort your life out!'

The police officer puts the window down. 'Stay back from the car, please.'

Antony stands with me. We watch the car reversing slowly down the centre of the market, blue lights flashing, after which the stall holders quickly lose interest and get back to business.

'Well done, you.' Antony smiles. 'You got the job done.'

'*We* got the job done! Team effort!' I give him a fist-bump. 'Do you think Jason will be OK?'

'Sure, now he's getting proper medical attention. His dad will be over the moon.' He puts his arm round me and gives me a squeeze. 'I thought you might be mad at me, for leaving you alone with Jase. Did he do anything weird while I was gone?'

'The whole thing was weird,' I say. 'But Jason? He's harmless.'

'That's what I reckoned.' Antony nods. 'As threatening as a stick-insect.'

'I did wonder why you went outside to call the police, instead of me,' I say, as we walk back through the market.

'There's no way I could have stayed with him.' Antony steps back and raises his hands. 'No way! All that stuff about Deep State. I'd have decked him after five minutes.'

'Ah, so *that's* why you were so keen to leave.' I thrust my hands in my pockets as we descend the hill through the diamond quarter. 'The phone signal gave you the perfect excuse.'

'Sorry. Come on.'

We head back towards Farringdon tube station.

'As it happens, you did me a favour,' I say, adjusting the rucksack on my shoulder. 'Jason found out something about Dad's machine.'

'How did he do that?' Antony's brow shoots up. 'Did he plug his butt into the Stargate portal, or something?'

My laughter is short-lived. We approach the entrance to the tube just as a London Underground employee pulls a concertina security grill across the entrance, leaving a small exit gap. The staff inside the station usher several frustrated-looking passengers back onto the street before drawing the grill shut and securing it with a padlock.

A whiteboard outside on the tiles carries a message in thick, black marker:

Farringdon Tube Closed due to Signal Failure

'Typical.' I give an exaggerated sigh.

'It's London, baby.' Antony shrugs. 'Tell you what. I'll buy you lunch, and you can tell me what I missed.'

·········

'Very nice Pooey Fuses.' I raise my glass of white wine to toast Antony. \
'It's Pouilly-Fuissé.' Antony sighs.

We're in the Royal Spice off St John's Street, surrounded by the Clerkenwell lunch crowd. There can't be many people eating at their desks as they're all in here. Still, the atmosphere is warm and friendly, and my rice forms a perfect dome on my plate, surrounded by spiced partridge and dhal. It's a step-up from my usual Tikka Masala.

Antony slathers a poppadom in red chilli chutney.

'Jason took a real shine to you,' he says. 'He was eating out of your hand by the time I got back.'

I dollop mint yoghurt dip on my poppadom, with a drizzle of mango chutney. Between bites, I say, 'I don't think anyone's paid him attention or shown any interest in him since he ran away from home, that's all.'

Jason's self-imposed isolation has probably been going on for years. He seemed desperate to share his world with someone, which made him extremely receptive to my questions about the finding machine. For a guy who lived his life by conspiracies, hidden plots and top-secret technology, my little problem was right up his street.

'I just hope he doesn't tell anyone about it.'

'Doesn't matter if he does.' Antony spoons more dahl onto his plate, breaks up a poppadom and digs in. 'Once the men in white coats hear him going on about microwaved brains and laser targeting from outer space, they won't take any notice of a finding machine.'

'I hope you're right.' I take a cool sip of fine wine, content that Jason is in safe hands and will be back home with his dad. For once, I didn't put myself in danger. Dare I consider it a job well done?

'So, what did he find out, then?' Antony's eyes are bright with anticipation. 'Blueprints? Detailed plans?'

'I wish.' I give him an awkward grin. 'My dad's machine was an experimental prototype. It doesn't look like it ever went into production. Jason said the finding machine in the photo was probably an empty shell. The rest is snippets and rumours, because we ran out of time.' I break up my poppadom into pieces. 'Shame.'

Antony's face falls. 'If I'd known you were getting somewhere with Jason, I'd have given you more time.'

'I'm not blaming you.' I reach over the table and grab his hand. 'Sorry, it was a stupid thing to say. You did the right thing, calling the police and getting back as soon as possible. The dark web's not somewhere I want to go again.'

Appeased, Antony pours the last of the wine into my glass. 'Are you going to show me what you've got?'

I rummage in my pocket for a sheet of notepaper covered in scribbles. I turn the paper this way and that, trying to make sense of my frantic note-taking.

Antony eyes my leftovers. 'You going to eat that?'

'What, my notes?' I look up, astonished. 'Oh, sure, have what you want.'

After swapping plates, I go on. 'The Turing angle. Jason found a chat on a forum about a place called Bletchley Park. Do you know anything about it?'

Antony chews and nods. 'Alan Turing worked there during the second world war. He was instrumental in cracking the German's Enigma code with a special computer.'

'That's right. There were a lot of experimental computing technologies developed by the team working with Turing. But it was a bit of a mystery what happened with the team after the war. The Turing-Tesla League was made up of research fellows and clever bods who wanted to follow up on the work of these two scientists, using original plans and notes. How they got hold of them, we don't know, as a lot of this stuff is still classified by their respective governments.'

'Yeah, and if this all started in 1945, the original members are probably dead by now,' Antony adds.

'You'll have to do the maths. But the posts Jason found were put up there by people who still worshipped Tesla and Turing. A member of the League must have come up with this machine for finding people using photographs and radiowaves, and somehow my dad got wind of it.'

'Do you think your dad was a member?'

'Jason searched for the Turing-Tesla League, but he couldn't find anything. Surprisingly, considering Jason said you can find *everything* on the dark web, their secret society drew a blank.' I brush a few grains of rice from my notes before putting them back in my pocket. I think of the words Jason used to describe the dark web. 'This is just another rabbit hole, Antony. I don't want to get dragged into it. I know what the Finding Machine does. That's all that matters.'

Antony nods. 'Good for you, Alex. I've thought that for ages. When you mentioned this Turing-Tesla League, I started to worry you were going to drag me to another library.'

I reach over the table and grab his hand.

'You've been brilliant, putting up with me.' I smile, feeling a surge of happiness. 'The Turing-Tesla League isn't active anymore. Or they're so far underground, no-one can find them. I don't care, to be honest. I don't need to know everything my dad did. That was his life, not mine.'

'Well, your research tells us one thing, at least. Your finding machine isn't Russian.'

'I thought Tesla was Russian.'

Antony splutters wine on the table.

'Don't ever say that again in public! He was Serbian, but he spent most of his life in America.'

'Fine. So Serbian American then.'

'Whatever. But I don't buy that your machine is based on plans made fifty years ago or more. It uses satellite technology and there weren't any satellites orbiting earth then.'

'Ah!' I throw my hand up in the air like I'm asking teacher to answer a question. 'But it was *you* who told me Tesla invented stuff ahead of time, like lasers and microwaves. Haven't scientists looked at them and said they would work?'

'Sorry, she's talking to me, not signalling you.' Antony dismisses the waiter who has suddenly appeared at our table.

Then he leans forward, lowering his voice. 'Look, I meant what I said...in theory. I suppose you could argue they had radio waves back then, just like satellites use now. But it's still a massive leap to imagine satellites flying round the earth in 1920 when Tesla was around.'

'Unless Tesla knew what technologies were in the pipeline.' I cock an eyebrow. 'Turing must have done, getting all the latest at Bletchley Park. They were alive the same time, you know.'

'Well, now you're getting into X-files territory,' Antony wipes his mouth with his napkin. 'At least we know it's not nuclear as it's not Russian. And frankly, after everything we've gone through with the finding machine, I'll take that.'

41

—— • ——

We leave the restaurant in that lovely, drunken haze you get after a boozy lunch. Antony suggests we walk back to Liverpool Street to avoid the problems on the tube. It's no hardship, being outdoors on a lovely, spring day.

Antony hooks my arm through his and leads me up several flights of stairs to a walkway high above ground level. The walkway takes us through the Barbican - a 1960s Brutalist complex at odds with its historic surroundings. We pass a large courtyard garden overlooked by flats with grey, block balconies. To my surprise, the area is lush with shrubs and trees planted round a large, rectangular wildlife pond.

As we stroll through the raised gardens, I hear buzzing in my coat pocket, accompanied by repeating vibrations. It takes a moment for me to realise it's not some weird hip condition, but my Nokia phone.

I stare at the green-lit screen with slight temporal confusion. Then I remember - yesterday evening, I spent an hour programming the Nokia's directory with my contacts and sending my new number out.

ANNEGALLERY

My heart picks up pace and I sober up. I make a nervous face at Antony before pressing the green button.

'Hello. Is that Alex?' Anne's refined voice sounds faint.

'Speaking.' I cover my other ear to block out the traffic noise and turn my back to the road.

'It's Anne from the gallery in St Albans. Are you free to chat?'

251

'Yes, sure. I'm sorry about the noise.'

'I can hear you just fine. I've got some good news. Your painting at Van Hages sold yesterday. The buyer is a collector of contemporary art and wants to see more. And on the strength of that, I'd like to bring forward your exhibition date to the end of July. I was thinking of an open evening to kick everything off. What do you think?'

My mouth opens and closes. I cover the phone with my hand and give Antony a wide-eyed grin, mouthing, *I sold my painting!*

'Can you hear me, Alex?'

'Sorry! Yes, I'd love that,' I say. 'It sounds fantastic!'

'Good. I'll get on it. I'll send through your payment on Friday, when our accountant's in.' Anne wishes me the best and rings off. She probably does deals like this every day, whereas it's such a phenomenal occasion for me, I want to run along the concrete parapets, screaming my news to everyone on the streets below.

I beam at Antony, my arms wide.

'Well done, you.' Antony wraps his arm round me, ostensibly to keep me steady, but I rather like it. I give him a squeeze.

'I can't believe it!'

'Well, I can. You're going places, now.'

We walk to a parapet that overlooks a medieval church on the level below, in a brick courtyard. The church looks out of place, with its stained-glass windows and Gothic tower hemmed in by modern concrete. Whoever decided it was a good idea to plonk the Barbican round it, needs their head examined.

I stop walking and lean back against the concrete parapet, facing Antony.

'I lost my job.' Finally, I admit it. 'My agency went bust weeks ago, and I haven't lifted a finger to find work since.'

Antony frowns. 'Why didn't you tell me? I could have helped.'

'It's complicated.' I look down at my hands. 'When you came back from the NEC, you were so happy with how everything went, I didn't want to put a downer on you. I *know* I could have told you, but to be honest I was fed up. I couldn't face more administration work.'

I tell him about DC Longhurst's suggestion of a career with the police service.

'I'd like to do something like that. I still want to paint, especially now I've had the best news from Anne.' I bite the inside of my cheek. 'I'm not sure I can make a living at it, though.'

'Won't know 'till you try. I love your painting. Try it and see how you get on,' Antony advises me. 'But I also know you're really good with people. Don't want to see you on the beat, though, with all the morons out there.'

'I wouldn't have to chase drug dealers. Or be on the front line.'

'There's something else you should consider.' Antony moves closer. He takes my hands in his and gives them a squeeze. 'You know what I said about coming to Birmingham?'

How can I forget? The day my car blew up.

'Come with me.' He gives a sheepish grin. 'It could be a new start. For both of us.'

I look off into the distance, feeling torn.

'I don't know. My art exhibition's down here. Anne said July.'

'You can be in Birmingham and have a show in St. Albans. The two places aren't a million miles apart. Besides, it's not like you have to stand next to your paintings the whole time,' Antony points out. 'Sometimes, you have to just go for it.'

He's right. I know he's right. I think back to the day the finding machine arrived on my doorstep. The subsequent adventures, the highs and lows that led me to today — one of the best days of my life.

'All right, I will come to Birmingham.' A stupid grin spreads across my face and electricity zaps round my stomach. 'I will!'

'I'm really glad you said that.' Antony closes in, his arms circling my waist, pulling me close.

253

A voice somewhere in the back of my mind is yelling that we are holding each other and that this is dangerous. But it feels right. Antony's arms and chest are softer than I imagined, he's not all unyielding muscles. I fit really well against him and he smells good which makes me snuggle closer.

It doesn't occur to me to break away. In fact, I think that would be a bad thing.

Then his mouth is on mine and we're kissing and it's the most natural thing in the world, better than finding Jason, better than selling my painting. His kiss is courteous but its gentle insistence soon turns passionate. When we finally pull apart, he's smiling.

'I've been wanting to do that for ages,' he says.

My mouth tingles from the kiss. My jaw, too, from where his stubble's grazed my skin. My emotions are all over the place. Since this morning, I've been shocked, scared and excited. Now, I'm running hot with a heart that could use a defibrillator to stabilise its erratic beats.

'I...I...'

'Come here.'

We kiss again, for longer this time. I'm determined to work on perfecting it for the rest of the afternoon.

· · · · ● · ● · · ·

I'm in the engine room of a submarine. Red lights are flashing in the dark, and an emergency alarm is blaring close-by. Crewmen race past, but I can't move. A heavy coil of rope is tied round my waist, binding me to thick pipes. And my arm won't work.

The shrill warning echoes throughout the vessel.

'Just ignore it,' Antony says in my ear.

I jar awake to his voice and the sound of the shrilling doorbell. I pry my eyes apart to look at the display on my alarm clock but find I'm facing the wall.

Antony's arms are wrapped round me. Joyous fact. *Antony is in bed with me!*

My arm's gone to sleep from where I was lying on it. I flex my fingers to get the blood flowing again, sending pins-and-needles along my hand.

'Good morning.' I raise my voice to be heard over the sound of the bell.

Antony leans over, presses his leg between my thighs, and nuzzles into my neck.

'Morning.'

Memories from last night flash in my mind. A flush spreads across my chest and through my face. I should feel shocked about the speed with which everything happened last night, but it hadn't felt sudden to me. It felt natural.

Yesterday, after we returned to Ware, events took a magical turn. We went on a slow walk by the river. Somewhere past the swans and the gazebos, Antony took my hand. I thrilled at the simple pleasure of walking with my fingers interlaced with his as we chatted about everything. It was like being on a first date, without any of the usual fears about being rejected or disappointed.

We walked into a little Italian bistro off the high street and ate rustic stone-baked pizzas with a bottle of red. On the walk home, Antony skimmed stones across the river, making the reflections of streetlights ripple. I was buzzing from the combination of good food, alcohol and the anticipation of what might happen next.

A haze of satisfaction settles on me at the memory, despite the doorbell going on in the background.

'What's the time?' I ask.

'7.48.'

'What is wrong with that guy?' I moan. 'Was he a milkman before he was a postman or something? Or has he got OCD?'

'I'll get it.' Antony puts his glasses on and gets out of bed, despite my best protests. His physique makes me shiver. I can't help thinking I've been to bed with someone who should be on the front cover of a magazine. Clad only in his boxers, he considers himself appropriately dressed. The next moment he's out the door and heading downstairs.

Sometime later, the bell stops. I snuggle under the covers, wallowing in X-rated memories of last night. Things are starting to come back. Like the fact I'm wearing Antony's T-shirt. His sexy scent is all over it. I might keep it and never wash it. My clothes are nowhere to be seen. I'm pretty sure some of them are strewn on the stairs. The rest must be down the side of the bed or lost under the duvet.

Antony flings back the duvet to rejoin me and starts doing wonderful things with his hands.

'What was it, then?' I can't help asking.

'Stop spoiling the moment,' Antony silences me with a finger to my lips. He lifts my T-shirt and starts tracing kisses down my collarbone.

I tense up.

Antony sighs, sending a stream of warm breath across my skin. 'All right, I give in. It's a letter for you. I left it in the kitchen, coz I didn't want you opening it and reading it straightway. It's nothing vitally important.'

'You're right.' Of course, he's right.

Antony presses the length of his body to mine and all thoughts of postmen and letters disappear.

42

I awake later on, to the sound of chirping sparrows. Sunshine falls in a gold rectangle across the carpet. There's a warm dent in the mattress beside me. I glance at my alarm clock. ~~Be mindful and live in the moment. What will be, will be.~~

Half eleven! I haven't had a lie-in like that since I was a student.

Finding my discarded clothes is a partial success; my jeans are on my keyboard and my jumper's down the side of the bed. God knows where my underwear ended up. Little thrills zip through me as I throw on a fresh change of clothes. Plus, a huge weight's gone, simply from finding Jason.

The shower's going across the hall, and I briefly wonder if I should get undressed again and join Antony. But I'm enjoying my indulgent, romantic thoughts too much, and besides, I don't want to get my hair wet.

With the sash window open to let in fragrant, spring air, I assess my latest misty landscape canvas. Anne's given me a July deadline for the show, so painting is my number one priority.

The finding machine is tucked away in my drawer. I've put the theories about who built it and Lilian's whereabouts to bed. Maybe for good. I need to concentrate on the real world.

I examine my background oil washes, building up heavy clouds and streaks of descending rain. In the top corner, I've left the canvas bare so it looks like light is breaking through. I want the viewer to decide if the storm is over, or just beginning.

The band of rain lends an ominous air to the composition. It's sombre, every bit as dark as the shattered oak painting, but the mood feels right. The February gloom I've portrayed is a world away from my current mood and the sunshine outside my window.

I'm pondering if my current loved-up mindset is the right one for a dark painting, when my landline rings.

'Hello, Alexandra. DC Longhurst here. How are you?'

'DC Longhurst?' My voice comes out unnaturally high.

'Is it a good time to talk?'

Numerous excuses spring to mind - I don't want his news to erode my newfound joy.

'I'm in the middle of painting.'

'Oh yes, you're an up and coming artist. I saw your picture at Van Hages when I went to check the CCTV footage. I thought it was very good!' The warmth in his voice and honest praise ease my worries somewhat. Maybe his call won't be bad.

'I don't know how you manage to bring your ideas to life like that,' he goes on. 'I can just about manage stick men and women.' He chuckles, deep and friendly. 'I don't think I'll give up my day job.'

The comment feels like a nudge in the ribs. I can't rely on my art to make a living. The money from the sale of my painting will only keep me going so long.

DC Longhurst clears his throat, a sign he's about to hit me with something. 'Anyway, I had a very interesting conversation with Sergeant Price from the Met yesterday. He told me you found Jason Bevin.' He pauses. 'Correct me if I'm wrong, but didn't you tell me you had no interest in finding him?'

An awkward silence hangs between us. My mind races to come up with something to throw him off the scent.

'Actually, I didn't find him,' I say. 'Mr Bevin did.'

'Oh, really?' His credulity sounds paper thin.

'Mr Bevin contacted me after I found the puppies.' My explanation's off-the-cuff. I hope he buys it. 'He had a tip-off about Jason's location, but when the police went to check it out, they found the building was sub-divided into flats. Some of the occupants weren't answering their buzzers, and they couldn't force their way in to check. Mr Bevin has mobility issues, so I offered to go to London with my housemate to take another look. And, hey presto, there was Jason!'

'Just like that, eh?' DC Longhurst sounds sceptical. 'Well, I'm glad you've cleared that up, Alexandra, because my boss is becoming very interested in you.'

'Oh, it's all just a fluke!' I gush, pacing as wide a circle as the phone cord allows. 'A blip in the temporal distortion of the fabric of reality.' I bite my tongue, realising I sound like Jason. 'How is Jason's doing?'

'He's still at the Royal London. I'm going to see him and his Dad later on, as a matter of fact. I'll make sure to pass on your regards.'

'Thanks.'

I silently pray DC Longhurst doesn't dig further. My account won't stand up against Mr Bevin's. I could email Mr Bevin to explain my side of things. At the same time, I could gently remind him about the reward money. But that sounds awfully mercenary, with Jason still in hospital.

'I've got some other news for you, and then you can get back to your painting,' DC Longhurst says. 'This should set your mind at rest.'

'What is it?' I twiddle with the telephone cord, bracing myself.

'We got John Kitching and Keith Crouch, the two you suspected of dognapping.'

My breath catches in my throat. 'That's great news!'

'It gets better,' says DC Longhurst. 'We've got CCTV footage of them torching your car. The cameras also captured their vehicle's number plate which we traced back to John. Both of them are on file with long rap sheets. They're a couple of secondary school dropouts who became career criminals the moment they got expelled.'

Relief surges through me. 'So, what happens now?'

'We're still questioning them. I can't go into details, but the pair have been linked to a string of serious offences by the Fraud Squad. You'll be asked to come to court in a few months, regarding the charges of torching your car and dognapping.'

'Oh, right.' I'd been naive to think their arrests would be the end of it. 'I'll have to see them again.'

'It'll be all right, Alexandra. I'll be there to look after you. We've got a chance to put them away for a long time.'

'That's the main thing,' I say, without conviction.

'I'll keep you informed of any further developments. Good luck with your painting.' Just as I think he's going to put the phone down, he adds, 'Let me know when your next exhibition is. I'd like to come along. Maybe we can have more of a chat about your special talents that have got us flummoxed?'

'Sure!' I put the receiver down. *No chance!*

'Who was that?' Antony enters the room, fresh from his shower and dressed in Nike jogging bottoms and vest top. He pulls on a matching sweatshirt before giving me a hug, pressing the length of my body to his, before kissing the top of my nose.

'DC Longhurst,' I tell him. 'They've got the crims who torched my car. Same guys who stole the puppies.'

'That's great.' Antony lifts me from my feet and squeezes me so hard I squeak. 'We should go out for dinner to celebrate. That French Bistro behind Tesco's looks good.'

'I'd love that!' I fling my arms round him and give him a big hug. Looking up at my new boyfriend I smile broadly. 'Today I'm going to paint like crazy, thinking about you!'

Antony gives me a brilliant smile.

'I'd better get down the gym, then, make sure I keep in good shape for you. Too many bacon butties and meals out with wine, and I'll end up looking like The Nutty Professor.'

'Hardly!' I think of my own desultory fitness regime. For once, I don't care. I'm going to stick to the advice I gave myself back in February.

43

A fter a swift catlick at the bathroom sink, I head downstairs for a brunchy breakfast. Antony's left a dark-crust artisan loaf on a wooden board with a bread-knife neatly alongside. I forgo my usual porridge, cut a thick slice and pop it in the toaster with my stomach rumbling. While it's toasting, I have a mellow stretch in the band of warm sunshine flooding through the back door.

Something on the kitchen table catches my eye - the letter that arrived earlier, propped up against the salt and pepper mills.

Curious, I take a closer look. A Royal Mail 'Special Delivery' sticker covers the top right corner. The envelope is A5, bogstandard manilla, with my name and address scrawled in block caps. The hand is rough but economic. I'm almost certain it's a man.

I put the kettle on and fetch my letter opener.

Inside the envelope is a folded page of A4 lined paper and a second, smaller white envelope carrying the faint scent of rose perfume. I put the fragrant envelope to one side, and read the note.

To Alexandra, my name's Christopher. I'm Margaret Long's eldest son.

My mind skips back to the afternoon I spent with Margaret. I remember the photo of her two sons on top of the TV. I can't recall which one was which, although one son was red and one was bald.

Mum left a letter for you but hadn't filled in the address. I only just found your post-it note with your details.

I'm sorry to tell you that Mum took a turn for the worse last week. It happened while her carer was there, thank God. Sylvia called an ambulance right away. The paramedics did everything they could, but it was just her time. They said the cause of death was a heart attack. Mum was taking heart tablets and blood pressure tablets and all kinds of painkillers. She'd been in poor health for years. By the end, she could barely get about the house and needed help to do almost everything.

My brother Alan flew over from New Zealand for the funeral, so the arrangements had to be done in a rush. Sorry you couldn't be there.

We had the service at her local church in Sudbury - St Gregory's. It's only now that I've had a chance to go through her things. I'm spending a lot of time clearing the house out. It's going on the market next week and that's another thing ticked off the list.

Mum spoke fondly of your visit. Thank you for spending time with her.

Regards, Christopher Long

The toast pops up, but my appetite's vanished. My lower jaw starts trembling and I reach for a sheet of kitchen roll to wipe my eyes. I can't believe Margaret's gone. When I spoke to her a week ago, after I had consulted Mystic Miriam, she sounded fine.

Miriam said she'd seen a woman on the other side who was now with her husband. Had she been referring to Margaret and Bernard, after all? I scrunch my hands on the table, trying to get my head round the incredible idea that Miriam sensed Margaret hovering between worlds, about to die.

If that's true, does it mean inexplicable forces are hovering around all of us? Forces we can't see, but are always there? I never understood how the finding machine could find dead people from photographs. Maybe Dad's machine picks up on these spiritual, otherworldly energies.

Margaret was a wonderful person. She was a rock to my grandparents, Vera and Jack, at the most difficult time of their lives. Even at the grand old age of ninety-nine, there was a light in her eyes that could not be diminished. Despite the fact her body was failing, she stayed young inside.

Tears fall as I remember her voice, her perfectly set hair, the veins on the backs of her hands. I think of her old, swirly carpet and the sherry decanter on the mahogany sideboard. I'll never see those things again.

After I've had a good cry, I re-read Christopher's letter. His tone is pretty much emotionless. Then again, maybe I'm being too harsh. He is in his seventies, after all, born in an era when men kept it all inside. Christopher's given me blunt facts: this has been done, that's to be got on with, as though his mum's death and funeral were a duty and nothing more.

Christopher's brother, Alan, doesn't sound like he doted on his mum, either. He booked his flight for a quick in-and-out no frills funeral before returning to his life on the other side of the world.

Who else will remember Margaret? She never mentioned any other family, neighbours or friends from church.

At least Margaret's together with Bernard. She'll be keeping good company with her best friend Vera, Dad and Jack close-by. As soon as I have a car, I'll go and pay my respects. Reverend Cheryl will wonder why I'm such a regular visitor to St Gregory's. Searching for graves, looking at graves, it hardly bears thinking about.

I force myself to make tea and sit at the table with my hands round the mug to catch the heat. The upset has made me cold and shivery. I remember the Prayer of Comfort Rev. Cheryl emailed for Lilian. I will say it for Margaret later. She deserves someone to be thinking of her.

My gaze lands on the white envelope. I prise open the flap and extract a sheet of cream bond paper, written in Margaret's elegant hand.

Dear Alexandra,

Thank you for dropping in. I don't get to see many people these days except those who are not strictly friends, but here to do tasks for me. Although I am lucky to have a few good neighbours, it is very lonely being so old. All the people I knew and loved have gone. You know, sometimes I sit by the window for an hour and nobody goes past. When we moved here in the 1950s we were pleased to be on such a quiet road, as I am a poor sleeper, but now it only adds to my isolation.

But you really mustn't worry about me. I am fine much of the time and when things get a bit too much, I simply take a glass or two of sherry.

I spent an enjoyable afternoon with my carer, Sylvia, yesterday, going through my old photos. Thank you for the suggestion, Alexandra. It brought back wonderful memories of our wedding and the boys. We found a shoebox with all the older photographs, thrown in willy-nilly.

You will be pleased, I hope, that we found one of Lilian. Her story is very sad, but we can still hold those who are lost to us close to our hearts. I certainly think that way about Bernard, and he has been gone a long time, now.

I won't go on. I hope the photo is helpful.

With love from Margaret.

P.S. Please do call again if you are in the area. No need to plan ahead, just drop in.

By the end of the letter, I'm sobbing again. Christopher's letter shocked and saddened me, but Margaret sounds like she's in the room, talking to me. Eventually, I go out into the back garden and stare up at the clouds to get some perspective. At least she's free of pain and loneliness.

When I've pulled myself together, I look inside the envelope and retrieve a single, square photograph.

My hand shakes as I look at it.

Finally.

Even though it's black and white, I can tell it was a lovely sunny day. Lilian stands by the river, holding an icecream cone. A blob of it is stuck to her nose. A few people are strolling across a bridge behind her. She looks around four years old with lovely chubby arms and legs. That would have been sometime in the mid to late 1920s, if my memory serves me correctly.

Lilian's a gorgeous little thing with curly fair hair, lighter than mine. She poses for the camera with her tummy pushed forwards, her free hand holding her skirt to one side.

Auntie Lilian has my eyes. My smile. Even the quirky rise of her eyebrows, one slightly higher than the other.

It makes me want to rummage through my photo albums to compare pictures of myself at the same age.

I flick the photo over to see if anything is written on the back, maybe a date or place.

There is something there, but it's not what I expected.

44

A ntony gets back from the gym to find me slumped at the kitchen table with my head on my arms. Margaret's letter is clasped in one hand, the photograph of Lilian in the other. My cold mug of tea sits on the table. I don't look up, even when I hear him pull a chair next to me.

He takes my arm and raises me to face him. I wipe my eyes with my sleeve, thinking I must look a mess. I've been crying so hard, I can barely make him out. He pulls me close so my wet face mashes into the angle of his shoulder.

'What happened?' His voice comes close to my ear, the frames of his glasses pressing against my temple. 'Alex?'

'Margaret died.' My words come out in stutters. 'It's not fair. Why did she have to die?'

'I'm sorry.'

He surveys the table, slides the photo towards him.

'Is this Margaret when she was young?'

I shake my head. 'That's Lilian. My aunt.'

Antony takes a moment to absorb what I'm saying. He takes a closer look.

'My dad looked for her his whole life. He should have found her, Antony. He should have found her.'

'She looks a bit like you. Something in the eyes.'

'You can see it, too?' My tears have leaked into Antony's hair. I need to get a grip. I push myself up and blot my eyes on a scrunched-up tissue.

'Look at the back.'

He flips the picture over and reads the words aloud.

'*To Margaret, I thought you would like this photo of Lilian. From your friend, Brigid Martin.*'

His hand goes to his forehead, his thumb rubs at his temple as if the news has given him a headache. 'That's your mum, right?'

'I can hardly bear to call her that.' I blot my eyes as the tears keep coming. 'How dare she!'

I look beyond his shoulder, into the garden. The sun is blazing across the lawn, but I feel cold to my core.

'I've been chasing ghosts the whole time.' Small tremors go through my jaw, making my voice shake. 'I've only had glimpses of Lilian's life second-hand through other people's eyes, through newspaper reports. Dad knew more than anyone, but he's gone. And now Margaret's gone. The only person left alive who knows anything has to be my mother.'

I haul in a shuddering breath.

'She lied to me. I asked her specifically if she had any photos of Lilian. She knew about this photo, but for some reason decided not to tell me about it. Where did she get it from? Why did she send it to Margaret? Why did she keep it from Dad?'

The corners of my mouth tug down again. I lean my elbows on the table, covering my eyes with my hands.

'I wish she'd never sent me Dad's machine. It should be called the misery machine. Please, fetch the cooking rum. I need a drink. I need something.'

'I'll go out later and get you some decent brandy. In the meantime, what you need is a fresh cup of tea.' He pushes the box of tissues closer to me. 'With sugar, yeah?'

I wipe my eyes with the heels of my hands as Antony puts the kettle on.

'I *knew* there was something dodgy going on with Mum,' I say. 'If Dad had known about the picture, he would have used his machine to find her. It would have given him closure.'

'How do you know he didn't?' Antony replies, pouring boiling water into my favourite mug.

'For a start, he would have put Lilian's photo in a frame and told us about her. He wouldn't have let her be forgotten. Fade into nothing.'

'There's a lot you don't know.' He places a cup of tea in front of me, stirs in a teaspoon of sugar before I can protest. 'This is raw. You need time to process it. But don't do anything rash with your mum, OK? There might be another side to this. I know what you're like when you get an idea in your head but this is something you need to weigh up. The pros and cons.'

'How could Mum keep it from me?' I stare at the swirling tea. 'Lilian's probably dead. What difference does it make if I have her photo or not?'

'You'll have to ask her.' Antony squeezes my arm. 'But not now.'

I sip tea, wipe my eyes on my sleeve as my tears peter out. I think of all the times I've dragged Antony into my mess, forced him to drive me round on wild goose chases. Watched my car blow up.

'Thanks for putting up with me.'

'Yeah, there must be something wrong with me.' He sits next to me again, smiles. 'I think the world of you, Alex. I'm here if you need me.'

I manage a steady breath, feeling stronger for Antony's unquestioning support and loyalty. It seems unthinkable that I was going to let him leave for Birmingham without a fight. He would have taken a massive part of me with him. And I would have been left with an Antony-shaped hole in my heart.

'Come here,' he beckons and I lean across to hug him.

After a few more minutes my sniffles have stopped. My breath catches every now and again like a toddler recovering from a tantrum. At least, that's how it sounds to me.

'Thank you,' I mutter.

'It's OK.' He checks his pockets for his keys. 'How about we get out of here? Let me grab my wallet. We can go for a drive, walk down the river. Whatever you want.'

His eyes fall to Lilian's photo.

'You need some headspace before you make a decision.'

· · · ● · ● · ● · ·

B ack home that afternoon, I spend a long time looking at Lilian's photo. I've placed her next to the photo of Dad in his orange cardigan. I want to put them both in one frame so they can be together. It's the only way I can make it happen in this life.

When I'm ready, I reach for the phone and dial Ireland.

'Mum, it's me.'

'Alexandra! I wondered where you'd got to. Did you not get my email?'

'I can't recall.' My voice is world-weary.

'Did you see the photos I sent you of the new patio?'

I did get her pictures. But the only thing on my mind is the one photo that really matters.

'Looks handy for summer,' I mutter.

I let her ramble on about the news in Ireland. Something about an influx of tourists driving up the prices of groceries at McColls, something else about the big shop and the 462 bus to Sligo.

'Mum, I've got to ask you something really important.' Before I can back out, I start telling her about Margaret Long and the photograph of Lilian.

'Poor Margaret. God rest her soul,' my mum replies, all sympathy. 'But I can't remember any photo for the life of me. Who did you say the little girl was?'

You know who she was. I close my eyes. Take a deep breath.

'Dad's sister. Lilian.' Somehow, I keep my tone civil. 'Remember, I asked you to look for photos of her. You said you didn't have any. At first, you told me Dad never had a sister. Then you changed your story. But you must have known about her all along, because you wrote her name on the back.'

It is the closest thing to calling her a bare-faced liar.

270

'Oh. That photo.' Mum's voice drops. It goes quiet at the end of the line.

'Mum, I want to know. You have to tell me.'

'Lilian was your father's obsession.' Her tone is flat. 'Once he was on the subject, it was impossible to get him off it. Even on our wedding day, of all days! I remember him going on about how he wished she could have been there. The whole family together.'

I press the receiver to my ear, stunned at what I'm hearing.

'There I was on the biggest day of my life, feeling like a ghost was following us down the aisle. It was dreadful, Alexandra. If I'd had some salt, I'd have thrown it over my shoulder. He was like that throughout the early years of our marriage. I can't tell you how I wished to be free of her.'

'But Dad was only trying to find her,' I say, hesitant. 'That's to be expected with what happened.'

'No, it was more than that. The way he went on, it gave me the shivers. Richard would have set a place at the table for Lilian if I'd allowed it. And he kept up with this notion of finding her. Every year on the anniversary of her disappearance, he would walk down to the river and around town as if she was suddenly going to pop up and surprise him.

'He would sit by the fire, reading the old journals from December 1928. God knows, that's a date I'll never forget. He bothered the police every year for updates until they told him to stop as there were no ongoing lines of enquiry and the case was all but closed. I told him to stop as well but he wouldn't listen to me. I obviously didn't know anything.'

A sick feeling rises in me. Dad sounded tormented. Yet, I never saw any of it in him. I think of the love he showed me growing up, the conventional childhood I shared with Matthew. Was he hiding his trauma the whole time? Why hadn't Mum supported him, loved him?

'Vera had a notion, though. So did Jack. As did I.' Mum goes on blithely. 'It was obvious to all three of us. Lilian was dead. No doubt, she died shortly after she disappeared. It's a horrible thing to say, but that's the truth.'

'But you had her photo!' I blurt. 'Why didn't you give it to Dad? It would have meant the world to him. It would have given him something to remember her by.'

All those years he spent researching and building the finding machine for nothing. With the photo, he could have got to the truth. And I would never have inherited this mess. But no, Mum kept it from him because she knew best.

'There's no need to get yourself worked up over it.' Mum goes on in the same matter-of-fact tone she uses to describe the weather. 'That photo of Lilian turned up after Richard's mum died in 1970 or thereabouts. I was up in the attic going through her things, and that's when I found it, in a box with an old ragdoll and a few children's books. I thought, what good is that now? If I give it to Richard, it'll only reignite his mania. No, better to put it out of sight, out of mind.

'Margaret had moved by then to the other side of Sudbury. Your dad sent her a Christmas card, but they didn't correspond or see each other anymore. They'd gone over the old ground so many times in the past, there was nothing new to say. So, I sent it to her, told her we had a copy.'

'If you felt like that, why did you even bother?' I demand. 'Why didn't you bin it or tear it up?'

'Well, now, my Mammy was always superstitious about photographs. She believed a bit of your soul was captured inside the picture and a little bit of that must have brushed off on me. I didn't want any harm to come to poor Lilian, only to see your father move on.'

The photo could have changed everything and ended Dad's torment. But Mum never thought of that. I can't bear the way she thinks she's right.

Something occurs to me. 'Did Dad tell you anything about the machine you sent to me?'

'You mean, that cold block of a thing?' Mum pauses. 'No, I'd never seen it before. What does it do?'

'Nothing,' I say firmly. 'It does nothing.'

As I thought, Dad must have continued his search for Lilian in secret without Mum knowing he'd made the finding machine in his workshop at the end of the garden.

'Alexandra, there comes a time when you have to leave the past behind. Your father spent far too long in his foolish belief that finding Lilian would make everything right again.' My gall rises as she pours fuel onto the fire. 'If you were to put yourself in my shoes you would have done the same. Anyone would. I saved him from himself, and I stand by that decision.'

'But, who were you to decide?' I splutter. 'It was none of your business what you thought best! You did nothing to try and help him. You should have given him the photo. It was his sister, not yours! You should have helped him get counselling. It's obvious he needed someone to listen to him, to show him compassion. You did the opposite!'

What follows is the single longest pause I've ever heard from my mum. For a few moments I think the line's gone dead.

'Would you mind your tone, Alexandra.'

'No. I won't mind my tone.' My reply is brusque. 'What if I was the one who'd been abducted at the age of five? Would you have said the same things then? *Oh yes, we used to have a daughter, but she went missing. That's life. Move on.* Why are you so cold?'

'How dare you?' Mum gasps.

'Answer me. What would you do if it had been me?'

'Y...you're talking about two completely different situations.' Mum stumbles over her words. 'Richard barely knew his sister. He was only a child when she disappeared.'

'It haunted him his whole life!' My voice shakes with barely concealed rage. 'Margaret told me Vera and Jack were devastated. They never got over it. Can't you understand? It split the family. Uncle Stanley was so upset, he left Sudbury and no-one ever saw him again. The repercussions affected Dad for life. If you can't see that, you must be immune to normal feelings.'

'Alexandra, you weren't there, so you don't know the facts, ' Mum says. 'Everything I did was for the best. You'll understand when you have a family. Richard had me and the two of you. That should have been enough. All this wallowing in the past. What good can it do?'

'It made it worse! Dad never stopped searching for Lilian until the day he died.' I'm so angry, I can't help twisting the knife. 'That's why he asked to be buried with his parents at St Gregory's. It was in case they found Lilian, so she could be laid to rest alongside him.'

'Think that if it gives you comfort.' A hard-edge creeps into Mum's voice. 'But that was to do with the family plot. Richard's parents were very specific about that from the get-go. His mother, God rest her soul, could be overbearing in these matters.'

Vera? Overbearing? If I wasn't so annoyed, I would laugh down the line. My nan was the sweetest of women, always ready with a pot of tea and a freshly baked scone. Margaret thought the world of her. Yet now, Mum sees fit to blame Vera for Dad's handwritten, final wishes.

I am going to have to spell it out.

'What you did was wrong. You hurt Dad. You hurt me.'

'Is that how you see it?' The Irish twang cannot soften the steel in her tone. 'You know, your father would be disappointed in *ye*.'

That's low. Using *ye*. God help me. She reserves that for the greatest sinners.

'Disappointed in me? How's that?'

'The way you're living your life over there,' she comes back at me. 'Like one of those new women. Those career women.'

Her tone says *prostitute* or *atheist*.

'I see how you're enjoying the easy life over in Hertfordshire. With your *friend* Antony. God knows what the two of you get up to in that house on your own. Maybe you don't understand what you're throwing away. There are no second chances, Alexandra. We are judged constantly, and I may be guilty of some things but one thing I do know. Your duty to God is not to take the easy path.'

The battle lines are drawn. It has always been Mum's way or the highway. No-one is allowed an opinion if it doesn't chime with hers. All pretense at niceties have gone.

As I suspected, she hates the idea of me and Antony together. I guess she's finally twigged that I'm not a good Catholic and no longer go to church. Hardly a surprise considering the sterling job she's done - using religion to make me feel crap about myself.

'You remember my Mammy?' she says.

'Yes, I've heard it before,' I protest.

'And you'll hear it again. There were the twelve of us and how she brought us up, I don't know. We were three to a bed with no central heating or anything like that, and yet Mammy managed to feed us all on whatever my father didn't drink away down the pub. She was a saint. She taught at the local school and still attended Mass every morning at six. And never once did I hear her complain.'

'She was a great woman,' I say. 'But she's not me. And I'm definitely not you. This is my life and I'm living it my way.'

During the long pause that follows, my mouth goes dry. Standing up to my mother likes this makes me feel sick.

'Your way?' Mum says. 'There's only one way and that's the Lord's way. Remember that.'

Click.

She's put the phone down on me.

I pause and take a deep, shuddering breath and sit shaking in my chair with the receiver still clutched in my hand as the emotional fall-out from our exchange rips through me.

45

— • —

5 **2.040265, 0.738481**

My breath catches in my throat. It's taken over twenty years for the finding machine to fulfil its purpose. For most of that time, it has sat in a suitcase in a cold attic before being sent across the Irish Sea in a shoebox. Its dated electronics and circuit boards, gradually accumulating dust over the decades, have stood up to years of neglect, damp, cold and being moved around.

It's a miracle it still works.

'That thing's like Big Brother.' Antony puts his hands on his hips, staring at the machine on my desk. 'It's always watching, wherever you are. Even when you're dead, it watches.'

'Stop creeping me out.' I scribble down the co-ordinates on a post-it. 'I'm pretty sure these co-ordinates are for Sudbury, or somewhere really close. Let me plug them into the internet.'

I establish a connection via my modem and wait for the website to load.

Antony catches my eye. 'You ready?'

How can I be? But I have to know Lilian's fate - where she ended up. My mind has an inexhaustible encyclopaedia of dreadful scenarios to throw at me, none of which bring me joy.

I lean against Antony. 'The main thing is, I'm doing this for Dad. Not to get back at Mum.'

'I know.' Antony gives me a reassuring squeeze. 'Have faith in yourself.'

My disastrous conversation with Mum hit me hard. I didn't get through to her in any way, shape, or form. She used all her favoured tactics - changing the subject or putting the blame on someone else. It made her impossible to reason with.

'You're righting a wrong. That's how I see it.' Antony takes a wander round my room while my PC grinds through the co-ordinates. He pauses by my easel and looks the canvas over - the calm after the storm.

'Every time I look at your painting, I see something new.'

'I worked through my terror over the dognappers on that one,' I say. 'I don't know how I'm going to replicate that once my life's all peaceful and boring again.'

Antony cocks an eyebrow. 'Are you saying I'm boring?'

'Not you! I mean - '

'I'm joking.' Antony swipes his hand, dismissing my concern. 'But you're crazy to think you need to be stressed out to paint.'

I stretch back in my chair, letting out a sigh. 'I don't want to lose my inspiration.'

Antony shakes his head. 'I'm not buying the tortured artist narrative. Unless you're Caravaggio.' He shrugs. 'My stuff's creative, but it's still work. My clients expect me to deliver even if I'm sick with 'flu or I've got water coming through the roof.' He rubs his nose, gives me a cheeky grin. 'If you need me to wind you up before starting your next painting, I can arrange it. I'll hide your phone cable, nick your Simple Minds CDs and replace all your Pot Noodles with beetroot and goats cheese salad.'

'That won't inspire me!' I screw up my face. 'It'll make me projectile vomit!'

He comes over, leaning on the back of my chair. The map has appeared on screen.

13 Grosvenor Hill, Sudbury CO10 2HH.

'That's to the east of town.' I peer closer at the map, just as my phone starts ringing. 'It's close to where Dad's parents, Vera and Jack, lived.'

I reach for the receiver.

'Sudbury's an hour away.' Antony heads for the door, giving me privacy. 'Let me know when you're ready. We need to get on the road.'

• • • • • • • • • •

'Well, if it isn't the persona non-grata herself!' My brother, Matt, has put on the most terrible Irish accent. He always uses it when he does an impression of Mum. He sounds annoyingly upbeat at the other end of the line, calling all the way from Seattle.

'News of your transgressions has crossed the pond, to be sure. Prepare to repent, ye sinner!'

'Ha, ha. Very funny.' Just thinking about that phone call to end all phone calls gives me mild nausea. In the aftermath, a load of childhood memories have resurfaced relating to Mum's one-dimensional views.

'I knew something was up when Mum rang me earlier,' Matt says. 'She only ever rings once a month, but this is the second call I've had from her this week. She told me you'd had words.'

'It was awful,' I gasp. 'I'm off the Christmas list forever. I think she might disown me.'

'She was doing her best to get me on side but I promise you, I stayed absolutely neutral.'

'Couldn't you have stood up for me? You are my brother.'

'Nah. I'm like Switzerland. Not getting involved.'

'That's a shame,' I say dryly. 'Especially since I told Mum you like to celebrate Beltane on May first with your local druid circle. And you go skyclad.'

'Ha! You didn't!' He pauses, a note of uncertainty creeping in. 'Did you?'

'I should have done! It's all right for you, Matt! You're the golden child. Mum never expects a thing from you, and you get bonus points for being married with a respectable job and a kid.'

'Look, I may be neutral but I won't lie to her,' Matt says. 'Mum knows I'm an atheist. Oscar isn't baptised. I usually get a 'quiet word' about that every time she rings. I reminded her we're free to believe or not, but it didn't have much effect.'

'Her laser sights are still on me,' I say with a sigh.

'She'll come round, sis, give it time.'

'How much time? Ten years? Twenty?'

'Sooner,' Matt assures me. 'She's running scared. She kept going on about a lost aunt called Lilian and how none of it was her fault. What was that about?'

I take in a deep breath. 'I'll tell you, Matthew, but you'll need to keep an open mind. And you can't tell anyone else. Not even Kate. I mean it.'

'O...K.'

Matt is good to his word, and listens patiently for the next fifteen minutes, interrupting only to ask me to clarify something. I briefly explain how I got Dad's machine working, and describe the four photos hidden inside. A weight lifts from my shoulders as I recount my conversation with Margaret, leading to the discovery of Lilian's photo and the epic fight with Mum.

'It's incredible,' my brother says. 'When you first told me about it, I thought it was one of Dad's unfinished projects. But it actually works.'

'You need to see it first-hand. I've found loads of stuff with it. Pets. People.'

'Now I understand why Dad kept mentioning how lucky I was to have a sister.' Matt's previous joviality disappears. 'What I don't get is why Mum deliberately hid the photo from him. It's like she was trying to hide the fact Lilian ever existed. Erase her from history. If the same thing had happened to you, I'd never get over it.'

I wait for him to make a sarcastic comment, like how good that would have been or something in that vein, but it doesn't come.

'Poor Dad,' Matt says with rare sentiment. 'He must have felt so alone, wondering what happened to Lilian. No-one seemed to care much, did they? Seems like after a few years everyone forgot about her, or died.' He adds, 'I heard about Margaret. I was sorry to hear she passed away. I remember her at the funeral, a really lovely lady.'

'I'm the only one left to carry the baton for Lilian,' I say. 'That's why I'm so angry at Mum.'

'Don't beat yourself up about it,' Matt tries to reassure me. 'We're both sinners in her eyes. She's probably worried everyone in Ireland will find out. To my mind, she's got two choices - stop contacting us or come to some sort of acceptance of us as adults. Once she's decided, we'll all be a lot happier.'

'I've got too much on my mind to waste time worrying about it,' I say. 'I'm going to find Lilian.'

'For real?' Matt's voice rises. 'Wow. That's incredible. Just stay safe, OK?'

'Don't worry. Antony will be with me the whole time.'

'You will let me know, won't you?' Matt asks. 'If you find her? What you find?'

'Of course,' I say straightaway. 'We're family.'

46

From the comfort of Antony's passenger seat, I watch the Suffolk countryside whizz past the window. He's doing over ninety on the A131 with plenty more in reserve.

I never dared push my Mini above sixty. The Audi's in a different league - power, comfort, styling, everything. Warm air rushes through the open sunroof, mixing with the smell of high-end leather. On any other day I would love being chauffeured in style, but my frayed nerves have put paid to that.

Antony tried to get me to relax by playing my favourite CDs. When that didn't work, he turned the stereo off and made small talk.

But I can't settle. I look at the post-it in my hand.

13 Grosvenor Hill.

The location's less than a mile away from Lilian's childhood home. Whoever took her must have known her. And maybe, she knew them.

I sink into the sculpted seat and look through the sunroof at the picture-perfect fluffy clouds and blue sky. A plane flies overhead. Sunlight glints off its body as it powers through the atmosphere. I lose myself in my thoughts, staring at vapour trails criss-crossing the sky.

After a few miles, I break the silence.

'Soon we'll know what happened to Lilian.'

'You'll know where she is. Not necessarily what happened.' Antony looks at me briefly. 'Expect the unexpected. Remember Leather Lane? That went nuts.'

'This is completely different.'

'We'll see.' He shrugs. 'Can you check the map? I think we're coming off at the next junction.'

Antony slows down as we enter the outskirts of Sudbury, passing a grassy common bordered by woodland. Half a mile further, we drive past a modern secondary school. An ex-council estate and shabby row of shops flash past before the houses become smarter. As we get closer to the town centre, Victorian and Georgian buildings predominate.

Antony drops down the gears as traffic starts to build up.

'This road takes us all the way into town.' I consult my A-Z of the Home Counties. 'We go left by St Gregory's Church, where Dad's buried.'

Almost like it's meant to be.

I clench my hands in my lap as Antony takes the turn, staring at St Gregory's tower standing proud above the trees. My mouth goes dry as we drive past. I wish I'd brought a bottle of water.

'We go round clockwise and then it's a left into East Street,' I say through my parched throat. 'Grosvenor Hill is on the right, past The Horse and Groom pub.'

Antony follows my instructions, and we turn into Grosvenor Hill. The road rises past a mix of modern bungalows and Victorian houses. Number ~~forty-two~~ **13** is at the end of the road - a detached ~~Victorian~~ villa with wisteria running rampant across the front aspect. A tall hedge screens the driveway.

As we creep past, I notice a 'For Sale' sign out front. The front door is open. A young man in a smart, dark suit and bright red tie stands on the porch, holding a bundle of leaflets.

Antony parks further down the road and turns to face me.

'So, what's your plan? How're you going to finagle your way in?'

I grab my rucksack containing the finding machine and the photo of Lilian.

'Leave it to me.'

· · · ● · ● · · · ·

W e walk up the drive. The estate agent is engaged in sales-talk with a retired couple on the porch step. The husband's sparse grey hair is swept over his bald patch. He rocks back on his heels, the property details in one hand. His wife clutches the strap of a mustard-coloured handbag, her fuschia lipstick matching her nails.

'What do you think? A real gem, right?' The estate agent flashes a plastic smile. With his dark-hair and good looks, he reminds me a bit of Tom Cruise, only he's trying too hard.

'A gem in the rough, maybe.' The husband eyes the flaking windowsills and the out-of-control wisteria. 'It needs a lot of work. And it's already at the top end of our budget.'

'We've had an enormous amount of interest,' the estate agent barrels on. 'This is what buyers are after, original houses in desirable roads, especially where there's scope to add value.' He points to the ground floor plan. 'I'd think about sticking a rear extension on the back and putting in a kitchen diner. With the size of the garden, you're not going to lose out there. In fact, Mr Knight, the world's your oyster with this place.'

'Those high ceilings.' The wife squeezes her husband's arm. 'I know they're fashionable, but at my age I feel the cold.'

'A nice log burner would keep you nice and toasty.' The estate agent has an answer for everything. 'Bit of secondary glazing! Chuck down some rugs and Bob's your uncle!'

'We're going to think about it.' The husband gives a farewell nod and ushers his wife past the agent.

'I wouldn't leave it too long,' the estate agent calls after them. 'This place isn't going to hang around!'

'Excuse me, can we go and have a look?' I take Antony's hand, glancing towards the open door.

The estate agent's expression brightens the moment he claps eyes on Antony's Breitling and his buffed, Armani shoes.

'Welcome to Morgan & Seymour's open house by appointment! I'm Shaun.' He shakes our hands and thrusts a sheet at us containing the house specs. 'It's madness today. Absolute chaos.'

Preliminaries over, he whips a clipboard out and looks down a list of names with phone numbers beside them. Most of them are ticked off.

'And you are?' he prompts.

'Mr and Mrs Martin,' I say, unable to come up with an alias on the spot. 'We love the look of this place. Really looking forward to seeing inside.'

Shaun frowns, running his fingers down the list.

'I don't seem to have you down here. I'm sorry.'

'Really?' I try to look astonished. 'But I did ring up. I hope it's not going to be a problem. We've driven up from London.'

Antony leans forward and adds, 'We're cash buyers.'

Shaun nods, giving him a conspiratorial grin. 'Who did you speak to, do you remember?'

I pretend not to hear. 'God, I love Victorian houses!' I move closer to the front door. 'This one looks jam-packed with character. Has it got original features?'

'It's got them by the bucketload.' Shaun counts them off on his fingers. 'Original fireplaces. High ceilings. Pantry. This place is a golden opportunity for the right person.' He scribbles our names down. 'I'll give the guys in the office a ring, find out which berk forgot to add you to the list.'

He pulls out a smart black clamshell Motorola.

'Go and have a look around. Give me a shout if you've got any questions.'

One immediately springs to mind. 'Do you know who's selling the house? Are they still living here?'

'Nah.' Shaun's finger hovers over the dial button. 'It's an estate sale for some old geezer.'

'Estate sale? So, the previous occupant has died?'

'I'll check when I ring the office.' He gives me a curious stare.

'I've heard estate sales can be tricky,' I blag. 'Relatives fighting over the price. It can turn into a nightmare.'

'We're used to sorting stuff like that. Morgan & Seymour are experts.' Shaun starts pressing buttons. 'Let me ring the office, Mrs Martin, and I'll get back to you.'

Hearing him call me that sounds weird. It makes me think of my mother. I don't like it.

I'm hit by a fusty smell the moment I step into the hallway, and into the first room on the left. The front parlour is decorated with floral wallpaper that has faded with age and is coming away from the wall. An original, cast-iron fireplace strung with cobwebs forms the focal point. An old, misted mirror hangs above it.

Quickly, I get the finding machine out of my rucksack and set it on a dark wooden desk sitting by the bay window. Two solid reds, three flashing.

'Must be upstairs,' Antony suggests, staring at the cobwebs and the yellowing paint over the cornicing. 'This place hasn't been touched for years.'

I look up. 'I suppose we'd better go and have a look.'

The stairs creak as I climb up to the wide, galleried landing. Antony follows a few steps behind. A middle-aged man in a business suit passes us the other way. At the end of the first-floor hallway, a young couple have formed a huddle in the bathroom, squeezed between the apricot three-piece suite as they discuss the pros and cons of the house. The new dad carries their baby in a sling, which is occupying itself by waving a bar of pink soap around.

I hold the finding machine in front of me and move from room to room, checking the display. Each of the four bedrooms is a study of a house stuck in time. Frilled lampshades hang from pendant fittings next to the windows, instead of where you would expect them - at the centre of the ceiling. The beds are made-up with faux-silk bedspreads and faded blankets. Lace curtains hang grey and dusty above the scattered husks of dead flies. A musty smell hangs over everything.

Antony has a good look into corners, under beds and behind furniture. I wonder what he's expecting to find - a skeleton tucked alongside a pile of old jigsaw puzzles?

'What have you got?'

I show Antony. Three solid reds.

'It's the same in every room. Worse at the front of the house. We're not in the right area.'

'Let me try something,' Antony puts his hands out and I give him the machine. He's found a small step-up ladder from somewhere, which he sets beneath the loft hatch.

The couple with the baby emerges from the bathroom. The soap is nowhere to be seen.

'We never thought to look up there,' the dad says, taking the baby's hands and jiggling it in the sling. Do you think it's got space for a loft conversion?'

'That'd be a bonus wouldn't it, pushkums?' The mum tickles the baby's cheeks, eliciting a squeal of excitement and a flurry of kicks.

Antony pushes the loft hatch up and slides it back, revealing a pitch-black hole.

'Anyone got a torch?' he asks the couple.

The mum rummages round in her baby bag and comes up with a penlight. She twists the dial round the narrow lens until a white beam of light shines round the hall.

'Cheers.' Antony shines the torch around. I catch glimpses of the eaves but nothing else.

Antony puts the torch between his teeth and holds the finding machine up until its body is lost in the dark. Two solid reds. We're further away than we were before.

'What's that for?' the dad watches Antony move the machine around and gives a nervous laugh. He steps back with the baby. 'Not radiation, I hope?'

'Nah, just checking for gas leaks,' Antony replies smoothly. 'You can never be too careful. Looks good, though.'

'How high is the roof?' the mum asks, trying to peer past him.

'Can't see much, to be honest.' Antony clambers down and hands her back the torch. 'Come and take a look for yourself. Or even better, ask Shaun to find out if there's a light switch up there. It'd give him something to do.'

Antony comes up to me, huddles close.

'You know what this means, don't you?' he whispers once we're out of earshot of the couple.

My mouth has gone so dry I can barely answer.

'I need some water.'

·········

I stand at the kitchen sink and run the tap, scooping handfuls of water into my mouth. The window above the sink looks out onto a large back garden. To the right, a long garage with wooden doors sits at the end of the driveway. A small orchard flourishes amidst the overgrown wilderness at the end of a large lawn. Closer to, a basic, concrete patio joins up to the back of the house.

There are many places where Lilian could be.

Wiping my mouth on my sleeve, I force my shaking legs to take me outside. The garden is lush, and the borders are full of daffodils and grape hyacinths. The smell of apple blossom drifts on the breeze, birdsong reaches us from all directions. Such a glorious day, but I feel hollow inside.

I take the finding machine from Antony and start walking down the garden.

Three solids with one flashing.

Instinct tells me to head for the garage.

Four solids.

I go up to the green, wooden doors and depress the iron latch. The left-hand door swings open. Light filters through the dusty windows, casting yellow bands across the floor. The cavernous floor-space is empty. A long, wooden workbench runs along one wall, cluttered with G-clamps, soldering irons, and boxes full of screws. Socket sets, saws, and other tools hang from the wall on nails. Various electrical and mechanical items sit on the bench, stripped down to their composite parts.

It reminds me of Dad's workshed, but on a grander scale.

Stepping into the middle of the shed, I check the finding machine.

Five solid reds.

My hands shake and Antony takes the finding machine out of my hands. I swallow hard and step away from the spot, my eyes blearing. Beneath my feet, concrete.

My voice comes out in a whisper. 'My God, she's under here.'

We stand together in silence, looking down.

What happens now? I don't know exactly what or why, but this is not a fitting end to my journey. I can't take Lilian with me. I'm going to have to walk away and leave her under this burial place. I shudder at the thought of her bones under the earth, trapped beneath concrete. Darkness and rock.

'We found her.' Antony says, working his shoe over the floor. 'At least we know.'

I wipe tears from my cheeks.

'We have to find out who lived here.' I look back at the house. 'We have to.'

'Do you think that's going to do any good?' Antony asks.

'How can I leave her here?'

'I don't see what else you can do, Alex.'

'I could call DC Longhurst. Tell him everything I know. Show him how the finding machine works. Tell him a murderer lived here,' I say with a shudder. 'Lilian might not be the only one under the floor.'

'We don't know that.'

'Well, I do know little girls don't find themselves dead and buried beneath concrete, a few roads away from home, unless something absolutely terrible happened.'

'If they dig up these foundations, it's going to be front-page news. Is that what you want, for Lilian's remains to be plastered all over the TV and the tabloids with sleazy headlines? It was so long ago. It's too late for anything to matter now. Whoever did this to her is probably dead.'

'You can't let people get away with things because they're old,' I sniff. 'You see it on the news with the SS camp guards. They're still bringing them to trial fifty years after the end of the war.'

'Yeah, but they were active perpetrators of mass murder and they left behind a ton of documents and evidence. You can say that for the Third Reich. They knew how to file.'

'How are you two getting on?' Shaun appears in the doorway, his city-boy image at odds with the overgrown garden and the dated house. He clocks my tear-stained face and Antony's glumness. 'Is there a problem?'

'Just not a good time, mate,' Antony says.

'Sure, sure, I get it.' Shaun backs away, pauses on the threshold. 'Just one thing. I spoke to the guys in the office but no-one put their hand up to taking your call, Mrs Martin.'

Shaun shoots me a curious look, at which I shrug in response.

'We reckon it was probably Bradley, our new intern.' Shaun adds a rueful shake of his head. 'His head's all over the place. My colleagues would definitely have remembered you, as you've got the same surname as the owner of this place. The old bloke you were asking about.'

'The old bloke?' I stare at Shaun in shock, my mouth going slack.

'Yeah. The man who lived here. I just found out he's gone into a home. His name's Martin too. Victor Martin.'

47

I huddle up to Antony in the phone box, with one hand tucked deep inside my pocket to stop myself touching anything. The other clings onto the belt loops of his jeans. The cramped, grimy space is covered in graffiti and cards advertising all kinds of massages and kinky services. The body of the phone looks like it's been at the blunt end of a few Friday night drunken rages.

The phone box is the fourth we've visited in town, and the first to contain a complete, unvandalized telephone directory. It's a recent edition, chained to a bare metal ledge.

Antony flicks to the Business and Service section near the back, looking for care homes and retirement villages.

Shaun, the estate agent, refused to tell us where Victor was living, 'for data protection reasons.'

'Don't worry, Mrs Martin. It's not one of those tricky estate sales,' Shaun had assured me. 'We're experts at pushing things through quickly. Victor Martin's living close-by if we need his signature on anything.'

'How close?' I pushed him.

'Only a few miles away.'

We couldn't get more out of him and left Shaun rubbing his hands in anticipation of our offer. Rather, I stormed off, leaving Antony to follow in my angry wake.

A line of fire courses through me, a toxic mix of fury and grief at Lilian's fate, rage at Victor and a sense of impotence we're so close, yet so far.

I peer over Antony's shoulder at the directory. 'How many old-people places are there?'

'Enough.' He starts jotting down details on my notepad.

I can't keep still. As I shift weight from one leg to another, the floor sticks to the soles of my boots. Victor's so near, I can feel him. I clench my left hand as violent thoughts consume me, involving baseball bats, guns, and my great-uncle's head.

Dad must have put the photo of Victor inside the finding machine because he suspected him. The fact Dad never got the proof he needed makes me madder. A lump sits under my ribs as I think of the photo - Victor's sinister dark dots for eyes, staring through the shop window.

'Great family I've got,' I say through my clenched jaw.

Everything's falling into place, including Mystic Miriam's psychic reading. She saw a man whose name began with 'V' and Lilian, together at the house upon the hill. Grosvenor Hill. The last thing she saw was something glowing like the sun.

'Mystic Miriam was right about everything,' I say. 'The only thing I haven't worked out is the sun reference.'

'She got lucky, that's all.' The directory's flimsy pages crinkle as Antony flicks over. 'She could've given you any letter of the alphabet and you'd have come up with a name eventually.'

'No, Antony. She saw Victor. 'V' isn't a common first letter.'

'Whatever.'

'Stanley Victor Martin,' I sound out the name. 'I've only ever heard him called Stanley. He must have swapped round his middle name after he killed Lilian.'

'We don't know if he killed her,' Antony gives me a warning look.

'She didn't end up under the garage by accident! He lived alone in that house, as far as I know. He had every opportunity. And then, he had the audacity to blame Vera for Lilian going missing!'

'You're saying it was a smokescreen?' Antony's pen pauses on the notepad.

'To cover up his guilt.' I nod. 'He acted angry at Vera to shift the blame onto her. I've seen it loads on TV.'

'You mean, crims fronting it?'

'Exactly. Afterwards, Stanley, sorry *Victor*, moved away from Sudbury and disappeared.' I look off into the distance. 'I wonder why he didn't sell the house.'

Antony scribbles down details. 'We'll find him.'

We both jump at a loud rap on the glass. A middle-aged woman is peering through the door. Despite the sunny weather, she's dressed for rain in a beige raincoat with a yellow scarf tied around her hair. Two bulging shopping bags sit on the ground beside her.

'Are you two going to be long?' She calls through the glass. 'I need to call a taxi.'

'We're busy,' Antony calls back, scribbling away. 'There's another phone box round the corner.'

'But you're not using the phone.' She eyes us with suspicion. 'That's what it's for.'

Antony rolls his eyes.

'Oh, come on,' I say, reaching across and ripping the care home pages out of the directory. Antony looks up at me with astonishment.

I raise my eyebrow. 'Can't believe you didn't think of that yourself.'

I push the door of the phone booth open and head past the woman who tuts loudly at the sheaf of pages in my hand.

· · · • • • • · · ·

Antony drives past a solid bank of white hoarding that forms a privacy screen round a construction site. The words '*Invicta Heights*' are emblazoned across a large billboard staked into the grass verge. '*Next Right, 200 yards.*'

'Independent Senior Living Your Way. All the comforts of home. Assisted living, dementia care and on-call nurses. Brochures and tours on request.'

We struck it lucky on the third phone call. Victor Martin is a resident in the completed First Phase, in a place called St. Andrew's Wing.

The hoardings are covered in heart-warming pictures of older people having the time of their lives in sunlit, modern apartments. Without exception, all of them look pleased as punch to be there. The care staff handing them cups of tea and chatting in beams of sunlight do everything with a smile. They look very smart in their rose-coloured uniforms, clearly not to be confused with bog-standard NHS nurses.

'He must be selling the house to fund his care.' Antony breaks into my thoughts. 'This place is top end.'

I concentrate on spotting signs to St. Andrew's Wing, not wanting to miss a turn.

'It's the next right.'

Antony flicks on his indicator and turns onto a narrower, unmarked road. The hoardings run out and we see the full scale of the development. Workmen and site managers wearing hi-viz jackets look as small as Lego figures against a backdrop of giant concrete silos and aggregate mountains. A haze of dust hangs in the air, kicked up by earth-moving vehicles.

We slow to a crawl as the car tyres judder over pits and ridges. Deep ditches run along either side of us, filled with huge yellow pipes. The sounds of construction invade the Audi's cockpit - the pneumatic drill is deafening, even with the windows up.

Antony swears as stones ping off the bodywork. He smacks his hands on the top of the wheel, glares at the ditches to either side.

'The things I do for you.'

A hundred metres further on, I spot a yellow sign with a red arrow.

St. Andrew's Wing. Visitors Car Park.

'This is it. We're here.'

We turn into a half-empty carpark, split by an ornamental island covered in trees and shrubs. Rose bushes are blooming alongside giant purple alliums. Silver birches with brilliant white trunks form a light canopy with their bright green leaves. Two Mediterranean cypresses sway in the breeze, reminding me of a Monet landscape.

Antony parks up and turns off the engine.

'That was fun,' he says.

We sit in silence against a backdrop of distant machinery noise, staring through the screen of foliage at a Victorian church with crisp-edged sandstone lintels. A large sign reads *Welcome to Invicta Heights Senior Care.*

St. Andrew's has undergone a complete restoration, from the wooden sash windows to the slate roof tiles. The lawn has been recently laid, with visible lines between the turf.

Victor is inside. This is the end of the line. I leave my rucksack in the car.

I've brought a smart suit jacket with large pockets. I slip my phone and the black and white photos inside and check I've got everything ready.

'I want to do this on my own,' I say quickly, seeing Antony unbuckling his seatbelt.

'Are you sure?' Antony's brow creases. 'I don't like the idea of you confronting Victor by yourself.'

'Victor's about ninety,' I point out. 'If it all goes wrong, I'll just run away. What's the worst that can happen?'

Antony looks at the sunroof, lets out a breath.

'All right, I'll wait here.' He pushes back his driver's seat to stretch out his legs. 'I suppose it's not like Victor's gonna take me for a relative.'

'Thanks, Antony.' I reach out for his hand.

'Be careful,' he says softly. 'I'm here if you need me. You've got my number on speed dial. Call, and I'll come running.'

'I will.' I take a deep, fortifying breath. 'You know the plan.'

I came prepared this morning; on the off chance I got this far. There are no guarantees my plan will work, but it's worth a shot. Antony agrees...in principle.

He gives me a warning look. 'I get that you want to know what happened. But once Victor tells you, it's out of the box and you're never going to be able to put it back.'

'I know.'

'All right then.' Antony pulls me over for a quick kiss. 'For luck.'

As I step out of the car, he presses a button to recline his driver's seat and plays some hip-hop at low volume.

I close the car door and rest my hand on the roof, the metal warm against my skin. Then, armed with five old photos, I head for the main entrance.

The doors to St Andrew's Wing open into a vaulted, airy reception area that smells of fresh paint. The room retains its original church architecture. It looks uber-modern, all white, with framed prints showing macro photographs of leaves and flowers.

My lips have stuck together. A water dispenser is on the far side of the room, past the blue velveteen sofa and glass coffee table stacked with glossy brochures. I scoot over to get a drink. The chilled water gives me brain-freeze as I gulp two cups down. An unpleasant twinge lingers in both temples as I scrunch my cup into the bin and approach reception.

The receptionist is in her twenties, heavily made-up. With her red jacket paired with a mulberry cravat, she looks like an air-hostess. The badge pinned to her jacket reads - *Jessica Sanders, Team Facilitator.*

Jessica looks up with a quick smile. 'Be with you in a minute.'

Her computer is set at an angle on the desk's curve with an Excel spreadsheet visible. I scan her desk, but apart from the pile of correspondence she's working from, her work-surface is clear of clutter. Her in-tray's empty.

I shift my gaze to the set of glazed, wooden double doors just beyond the reception desk. Through the glass, a corridor leads down to a further set of double-doors where it takes a sharp right and continues out of sight.

Jessica finishes typing with an emphatic click.

'Can I help you?'

'I've come to see my great-uncle. I only found out he was a resident here today. His name's Victor Martin.'

'Oh, you're the one who rang up earlier.' One of Jessica's drawn-on eyebrows rises to a perfect arch. 'You should really make an appointment. Visiting times are ten until eleven and two until four.'

She glances pointedly at the clock, which reads 11.30.

'I'm sorry. But when I found out Victor was here, I had to come straightaway. He's very old, and I'm his only surviving relative.'

Jessica nods. 'Victor hasn't had many visitors since he arrived.'

'Has he had any?' I ask.

Jessica sighs and pushes the visitor's book over. 'Fill out your details and put down the time.' She pins me in place with a look. 'Sign out before you leave.'

I hesitate with my hand over the book. Something tells me to cover my tracks, in case things don't go well. I write down the first name that comes to me, an old friend from school: RACHEL WALSH.

Once Jessica's issued me a visitor's pass, she leads me to the double-doors, pressing her lanyard to a panel on the wall. A light turns green, and she pushes through, past a Fire Safety notice and a framed poster headed *Daily Activities* with a list of events.

Lunch is at 1.30 followed by bingo.

I have time.

Our progress is silent on the carpet tiles. At the end of the corridor, Jessica peers through a long rectangular window into a large, airy dining room with the tables set out for lunch. The sounds of cutlery, banging pans and lunch preparations are coming through a large serving hatch.

'We'll check the activities room,' Jessica says.

Next door is a comfortable communal area with armchairs and tables stacked with magazines and jigsaw puzzles. Inside, an elderly man in a three-piece suit is reading the newspaper by a picture window, looking out onto the gardens. A spindly woman wearing a large pair of glasses is crocheting a jumper.

Jessica continues down the corridor. A nurse wearing the rose-coloured uniform I saw on the hoardings passes us, throwing Jessica a smile. The doors to left and right are numbered, with brass nameplates.

Jessica stops outside number four.

Victor Martin, reads the nameplate.

She knocks briskly. 'Victor, it's Jessica,' she calls through the door. 'I've got a visitor for you. It's your great-niece. Are you up for visitors today?'

A long pause. Then, a man's voice calls back.

'Tell her she can come in. I'm decent.'

Jessica pushes open the door and ushers me in with a smile.

'I'll let you two get on with it! I'm sure you've got lots to catch up on.'

48

'**C**ome in.' Victor has a gravelly voice like an ex-smoker's. 'I don't bite.'

I enter a spacious, bright room that smells of fresh paint.

Victor scrutinises me from an armchair, a large-print *John Grisham* novel on his lap. Sunken skin clings to his cheekbones. Strands of grey hair hover above a pink scalp. I can see my grandfather Jack in his long, rectangular face and the pattern of deep creases between his eyebrows. Thankfully, he doesn't look anything like me.

Victor is deep into the winter of his life. Maybe ninety. Or even a hundred.

His right leg is propped on a footrest with a pink foam bandage wrapped round the ankle and foot. The tips of his toes with their gnarly nails are visible. His left foot rests on the floor, cosy in a beige fleece slipper. The other one sits alongside it.

With his blue, round-necked jumper paired with grey trousers, Victor looks unremarkable. He stares at me through clear-framed bifocals.

The fire door closes behind me with a loud sucking sound.

The bed is at the far end of the room, beneath an open window framed by rose curtains the same colour as the nurses' uniforms. I could squeeze out of the window, at a push. Beside me, a propped-open door leads to an ensuite bathroom. Opposite, a compact study area comprises a straight-backed chair pushed under a desk.

Amongst the books and other nick-nacks, two black and white photos catch my eye. The first shows an RAF crew posing in front of a fighter plane, the second is a portrait of an Edwardian couple – my great grandparents, perhaps?

'So, you must be Richard's girl. Alexandra.' Victor breaks the silence. His tone is blunt but not unfriendly.

'Everyone calls me Alex.'

'You look like your dad.' Victor taps his age-spotted temple. 'Around the eyes.'

'It has been said before.'

He reaches out a shaky hand. I take it without thinking. His grip is dry and firm and I'm surprised at his strength. The back of his hand bears white, raised burn scars.

'I didn't think you knew about me,' I say.

'Course I do. Vera kept writing to my old house, even after I moved away. She sent me news about your christening, first communion, all that religious stuff.' His tone is matter-of-fact. 'She kept on writing, though I never wrote back.'

'Why not?'

'That's complicated. Best not to rake up the past.'

Victor's reticence tells me he's going to be a tough nut to crack. I need to tread softly.

'What happened to your leg?'

Victor stares at his encased foot. 'Stupid of me. I came down the stairs too fast and twisted my ankle. Luckily, it's not broken. Just a bad sprain. I can hobble around on my sticks.' He nods at a pair of crutches propped up in the corner, next to a large red call button set on the wall. 'That was the final straw, what with the cost of heating the house through winter and all the work that needs doing. I decided, if nothing else, I wanted to be somewhere warm. Here, you get a proper cooked lunch and tea. Though you have to watch you don't end up as big as Billy Bunter.' He points to the door. 'Fred across the hall is going that way.'

Taking a slow, deep breath, I pull the desk chair over and sit so we're eye-to-eye.

'What brought you back to Sudbury?' I ask.

Victor links his hands in his lap. 'When you get to a certain age, you want to be where you feel at home, and that house was my pride and joy.'

'So...you never sold it?'

'I rented it out over the years.' He pulls at the corners of his mouth. 'It's not good for a house to lie empty.'

But the house isn't empty, is it? An unsettling thought comes to mind. Did Victor rent out the house so he could control any repairs or changes made in his absence? Without his permission, no-one could demolish the garage or dig up the concrete floor. I am almost impressed by Victor's ingenuity - his scheme kept the evidence safe while he stayed miles away.

And now he's come back because he thinks he's safe!

I squeeze my lips together to stop myself saying something I'll regret.

'So, why are you here, young lady? I'm sure it's not for my charm.' Victor assesses me. 'I've spent most of my life on my own and I'm stuck in my ways. There's nothing interesting about me.'

'You'd be surprised,' I squeeze the words out with a sensation like a fist clenching in my gut. 'Everyone has something interesting about them.'

'Not me.' Victor's eyes harden. 'How did you find me, Alexandra?'

'I'm house hunting, looking to buy a place in Sudbury.' I meet his eyes, setting the first part of my plan into action. 'I just came from your old house. As soon as I found out you owned it, I had to come and pay a visit to my long-lost great-uncle.'

'I'll be having a word with that Shaun. Him and his big mouth. Giving my name out like that.' Victor shows his teeth without smiling, revealing artificially white dentures with shiny, plastic gums. 'And here I was, wondering why you were bothering with an old fogey like me. You should know, young lady, I've spent all my money. There's nothing left for any relatives.'

His assumption that I'm sniffing round for an inheritance raises my hackles. I suppress a retort.

'I'm here because you're part of the family.' I pick my words carefully. 'I knew very little about you until today. My parents always referred to you as Stanley. I didn't know you'd changed your name to Victor.'

Boom! The first challenge has been delivered.

'I didn't change it. I swapped it.' Victor says nothing for a long moment, absent-mindedly scrunching the material of his trousers above his knees. 'I never liked the name Stanley, but my parents wouldn't let me use my middle name. So, I decided to swap it. Simple as that.'

On the day you killed Lilian.

'You're called Alex as well as Alexandra.' Victor challenges me with his stare.

'They're still the same name.'

'Well.' He presses his lips together.

I take a deep breath. 'I've brought some old photos.' Rummaging in my jacket pocket, I pull out the four pictures that started my search plus the one of Lilian, and hand them to Victor.

'Haven't seen these for a very long, time.' Victor starts flicking through them. His eyes widen slightly as he looks at the ones of Dad and Jack and the VE day celebrations. 'There they are, the fellas.'

He brings the photo closer to his glasses. 'I liked your dad. Clever chap. He loved coming over and helping me with my radio and fixing electrical things. A chip off the old block, he was.'

I stir the pot. 'Vera's there, too.'

The creases between Victor's eyes deepen.

I pass over the one of Vera holding the baby, and the portrait of Lilian by the river, watching him closely to see if the image jolts anything free.

Victor looks at the pictures. Licks his lips.

'You remember Lilian? Your niece?'

'It was a shame.' His dark eyes glint. He hands back the photos. 'What happened.'

'What did happen?' I take the pictures and slip them inside my pocket.

'She went missing from her house while Vera took a nap.' Victor inhales sharply. 'Shirking her duties.'

I take a deep breath, concentrate on speaking calmly.

'My dad spent most of his life looking for Lilian,' I say. 'You've no idea how hard it hit him, losing his sister.'

Victor shakes his head emphatically. 'He was only a boy. They get over things like that. I lived through the Great War. People went missing, dads, sons and brothers. Families had to get on with it, put on a brave face. That's the British spirit. You keep it in and forge on.'

My irritation rises several notches. This man has no compassion.

'War's different,' I say, my tone short. 'You know your enemy. When Lilian disappeared, nobody knew anything. The family never got closure, Victor. They lived their lives in limbo, especially Dad.' I pause to gather myself for the next step. 'He tried to find her every single day of his life.'

'What are you on about?' Victor shakes his head, his lips tight as though he's trying not to hear. 'Richard wasn't like that.'

'How would you know? You never saw him past the age of nine!'

'He was like me and Jack. A chip off the old block.'

'Dad was nothing like you. He loved his sister. He would have done anything for her.' My voice falters. I gather my courage. 'When Lilian was five years old, she went missing. The date was 14th December 1928. On that day, your old life as Stanley stopped and your new one as Victor began.'

'What are you saying?' Victor glares at me, his jaw working. A trickle of fear runs through me despite the fact I'm sitting opposite a man approaching a hundred years old who only has the use of one leg. 'Are you accusing me of something? I didn't invite you in to give me jip. I'm not having it. I think you should leave.'

'I told you, I came from your house.' I raise my voice. 'But I didn't get to view it. The estate agent told me there was a problem with the drains. When I got there, the drain company was digging under the foundations of your garage to get to the blockage.' I pause. 'Can you guess what they found, Victor?'

Victor blanches, shakes his head. 'They wouldn't do that without telling me. Shaun would have phoned.'

'Shaun didn't call you because of what they found.' I fix him with a glare. 'Bones, Victor. Little girl's bones.'

Victor's mouth falls open and his jaw trembles. A sheen of sweat rising on his bald brow.

'No.' He shakes his head, staring at the floor. 'No. No.'

The details of the story I worked out earlier comes together. 'The police are there, Victor. Their investigative team is setting up one of those white domes by the garage.' I leave a nice, dramatic pause. 'It's only a matter of time before they pay you a visit. I reckon they'll be here later today. Tomorrow, at the latest.'

'I don't believe you.' Victor's face is ashen. His hands grip his knees. 'You're lying!'

He casts a nervous glance to the door and the red call button set beside it, and I worry he'll keel over with a heart-attack before I get the truth out of him.

'Shall I describe the exact location?' I ignore the emphatic shake of his head. 'Inside the garage. Three paces down and one to the left. That's where you buried Lilian. And covered her with a load of concrete.' I keep my tone level but it's hard. The urge to yell and scream in his face is overwhelming - how could he do such a callous, cold-hearted thing?

'You know it's the truth. Admit it.'

Victor's jaw works, saliva glistens in a crease running to his jaw, but still no words come out.

I link my hands loosely together and soften my tone, despite wanting to lean over and slap him.

'I'm your only family, Victor. Right now, I'm the one person who can vouch for you. If you want any chance of avoiding the grisly details splashed across the front pages and spending your last days in prison, you need to tell me exactly what happened to Lilian.' My voice shakes uncontrollably. 'I want to know.'

Victor closes his eyes for a long moment. His shoulders slump and his fingers release their grip on his trousers. He shrinks in his armchair, all bravado gone.

'All right.' He swallows hard.

I lean forwards to catch every word.

'It was one unfortunate turn after another, what with Vera, Richard and Margaret.' His eyes meet mine, shining with fear. 'But you will stand up for me, won't you? When you see how it went, well, you'll understand why I did it.'

49

14TH DECEMBER 1928

'I ate all my sandwiches, Mummy!' Lilian Martin took her mother's hand and skipped along the road. The school day had ended early after lunch and the Christmas break stretched invitingly before her. 'They were egg, but I ate them!'

She beamed up at her mother, hoping for praise, but the smile Vera gave in return was thin and didn't reach her eyes.

'You're a good girl.' Vera huddled deeper into her camel coat. 'Shall I carry your satchel for you?'

Lilian shook her head and kept a good grip on the handle, keen to show she was a big girl and could be trusted. Margaret walked alongside them, carrying her two sons' schoolbags.

All three boys were in high jinks - Lilian's brother Richard let out a yell and ran down the street. Margaret's two, Christopher and Alan, set off after him in hot pursuit. Half-way down the road, Christopher stopped to let out a giant sneeze.

Vera winced.

'Rowdy lot, aren't they?' Lilian put on a deep voice, doing an impression of her father. A joke should get her mother smiling again.

'They certainly are!' Margaret laughed, before looking over at Vera. She touched her arm. 'Are you all right, Vera? You've gone awfully pale.'

'One of my headaches.' Vera rubbed at her temple, displacing a few curls peeking from under her cloche hat. 'They get worse when the weather turns bitter.'

'When you get home, take your pills and have a little nap,' Margaret advised. 'You know I'd have Lilian and Richard over at mine, but my two are coming down with colds and I'll more than likely be joining them, knowing my luck.'

'Maybe I will have a lie-down,' Vera said. 'Richard will be out playing football, and Lilian knows how to amuse herself until Jack gets back from work.' She gave Lilian's hand a reassuring squeeze. 'I'm sure I'll feel better once I'm back in the warm.'

Lilian, overhearing the conversation, knew that if Mummy had one of her headaches, tea would be late, and she was looking forward to a hot dinner after her sandwiches. She would ask Richard to make her a hot drink and cut her a slice of teacake, and make sure he spread it with lots of butter.

The three boys pounded down the street, and Lilian was tempted to run after them. The journey wasn't far, but she tugged on her mother's hand the whole way, keen to get out of the cold.

Once Vera and Margaret reached their respective front doors, Margaret waved goodbye and ushered her boys across the threshold. Lilian hopped impatiently from foot to foot until she could rush through to the kitchen and warm her hands by the stove.

'You'll feel warmer if you take your coat off.' Vera followed her in, putting her hat on the rack. 'Richard, make your sister a cocoa and then you can take yourself outside.' She fixed the boy with a stare. 'Make sure to be back before dark.'

'Yes, Mother,' Richard nodded, and went to get the milk from the pantry.

By the time Lilian had eaten her cake and drunk her cocoa, Vera had taken her pills and gone upstairs. Richard wolfed down a slab of cake and went to meet his friends in the park for a kick-about. He left by the back door.

Lilian wandered from the kitchen to the front room. She knew she had to be quiet and shouldn't sing or tap-dance in the kitchen while her mother was resting. She took her old ragdoll, Betty, wrapped her up in a crocheted blanket and put her to bed in Father's armchair. Hopefully he would see the funny side of it, although he was often short-tempered with everyone when he came in after a day's work. On second thoughts, she placed Betty in Mummy's chair.

Her soft toys kept her amused for a short while, before boredom set in.

She went to stare out of the front window. A few women were coming and going with bags of shopping. From time to time, a car drove down the street. The rag-and-bone man drove his horse and cart past, ringing his bell. The sound of hooves clopped on the cobbles.

Lilian hoped the noise did not wake her mother. She went to the bottom of the stairs to have a listen but heard nothing from her parents' bedroom. As she stood there, the clanging bell faded down the road, replaced by a different sound.

Tap. Tap. Tap.

Lilian followed the sound through to the kitchen and paused by the back door.

Tap. Tap.

'Hello? Is anyone home?'

Lilian recognised her uncle's voice and unlatched the door. Uncle Stanley stood on the step, his eyes widening in pleasure when he saw her. He was dressed in a work suit and tie and wore his usual flat cap. His pencil moustache looked very smart.

'Hello, young lady. Just the person I was looking for. Is Richard around? And your mother?'

'Mummy's in bed with one of her my grains.' Lilian shivered from the cold air coming through the back door. 'I'm in charge until Father gets back.'

'And a fine job you're doing, too.' Stanley added a little bow, which made Lilian laugh. Then she remembered her mother was sleeping and clapped her hand over her mouth.

'Where's Richard?'

'He's out playing football.'

For a second, Stanley's face fell, before his usual brightness returned.

'I've parked my van in the back lane. We can collect him on the way. We should have enough time, if we get a move on.'

'Time for what, Uncle Stanley?'

'My latest project. It's very exciting. You don't want to miss it, do you?'

'Of course not!' Lilian jumped on the spot. Her uncle was always building things that made sounds or had flashing lights. He let her play with the radio in his lounge, tuning in to all the different stations. Father got angry whenever she moved the dial away from the BBC National Programme, but Uncle Stanley was happy to listen to anything.

'What about Mummy?' Lilian asked, chewing her lip. She threw a glance back to the hall. 'I'm supposed to stay here until Father gets home.'

Stanley checked his watch, his other hand deep in his pocket against the chill.

'I'll have you back before anyone knows you've gone. Leave the back door on the latch, so you can let yourself in afterwards. I promise, your mother will be none the wiser. It will be an adventure.'

'I love adventures!' Lilian grinned, thinking of the escapades Richard read to her at bedtime, from *Winnie the Pooh* to *Just William*. She clenched one hand and punched to the side, a gesture her brother made when he was determined to do something. 'Let's get a move on!'

'Fetch your coat,' Stanley urged.

Wrapped up warm in her coat and scarf, Lilian took care to close the back door quietly and skipped down the path after her uncle under fading daylight, to the green door set in the back wall.

Outside in the lane, a smart blue van was parked under the orange streetlamp. Faint shadow words down the side read: 'Bradley & Sons'. The word - AUSTIN - ran diagonally across the enormous front grill.

Stanley opened the passenger door and gestured Lilian towards the vehicle, like a chauffeur.

'Madam?'

Lilian could barely contain her excitement at the prospect of a ride in a motor car.

'Is this yours, Uncle Stanley?' Lilian asked as she hopped into the passenger seat and ran her hands along the shiny vinyl.

'It's my new work van. I've just been up to Leeds to get it. The old one was on its last legs.' He pushed the start button. The chassis shuddered as the motor caught and fired into life. 'You're my first passenger.'

He opened the vents to let air from the warm engine circulate round the cabin.

'I'm going to get my company name painted on the side, so that everyone will know who I am when I drive past.'

'What will the name say?' Lilian asked, sitting on her hands to stop herself bouncing up and down on the springy seats.

'It will say, 'S. V. Martin. Tea Dealers and Provisions.'

Lilian remembered the shadow words. 'Why's there a different name on the side, Uncle?'

'That's the name of the previous owner,' Stanley patiently explained. 'It won't be there for long.'

Lilian stretched in her seat to see out of the window as Stanley let out the clutch and the van moved off.

'Right, where does Richard play football?' Stanley asked at the end of the lane.

• • • • • • • • • •

T he ride in the Austin van was a real thrill, and Uncle Stanley made the return journey to his house in Grosvenor Hill in next to no time.

Unfortunately, they hadn't managed to spot Richard in the park, and Stanley repeated the importance of getting back in time for the main event, whatever that was.

Uncle Stanley's house was grand compared to Lilian's. Whenever she drew a house, it looked like his, with a central front door and large sash windows. The gnarled branches of wisteria twisted across the front, attached by wires to the brickwork. In spring, large, lilac flowerheads covered the front facade. In the middle of winter, it looked dead.

Stanley steered the van along the narrow drive down the side of the house and stopped in front of a large garage. He got out to open the wooden double doors and switched on the light before parking the van inside on the boarded floor.

Lilian stared out of the passenger window at a long workbench that ran down one side of the outbuilding, containing various contraptions and tools.

Once the light was switched off and the garage doors closed, Stanley ushered Lilian into the house via the back door. They crossed the chilly kitchen and hallway and entered the parlour at the front of the house. Lilian hugged her arms round herself as she looked at the fireplace which sat black and empty. She would have to keep her coat on.

'Don't worry,' Stanley said, seeing her shiver. 'We'll soon have you warm as toast.'

He went over to a portable, circular electrical heater with a grey wire snaking out behind and plugged it into a wall socket. In an instant, a burning orange glow filled the circle and threw out a welcome wave of heat.

Lilian stepped closer, putting her hands out.

'Careful,' Uncle Stanley warned. 'It's as dangerous as a real fire.'

He beckoned her over to a desk by the bay window, upon which sat a curious wooden box. The box was crafted from dark wood, forming a case around a small, convex screen.

'What is it?' Lilian peered closer at the device, wondering if it was another radio.

'This is a Baird television, the very first of its kind. I went to see Mr Baird demonstrate it at Selfridges. Baird's a Scot. A stern-looking chap. Once you get past that, he's a man who knows what he's about.' A smile crossed Stanley's lips. 'His television is a modern marvel. As soon as he turned it on, I knew I had to have one. It cost a pretty penny, but I think of it as a worthwhile investment.'

Stanley went round to the back of the device and fiddled with some wires. He flicked a switch and the curved, glass screen flickered and came to life.

'Wow!' Lilian clapped her hands, leaning over to see better. 'Richard will be mad he missed this!'

'He will.' Stanley stepped back and checked his watch. 'Just in time.'

He folded his arms, shaking his head in wonder as a shady image appeared on the screen.

'See that, Lilian?'

Lilian peered closer, trying to make out the moving forms and shapes. Dark, flickering lines ran down the screen, followed by a moving blur. She screwed her face up as shapes wavered in and out of focus.

'This is a moving picture broadcast,' Stanley explained, staring hard at the screen. 'What you see on the screen is happening right at this moment, even though it's miles away. It's marvellous, isn't it?'

Moving closer to the set, he drew Lilian's attention to a pattern at the bottom left corner of the screen. It looked like a chequerboard, with only the black squares visible. The white ones were lost in the fuzzy, shifting background. It amused Lilian to see her uncle transfixed by the shifting patterns of light and dark.

It interested him so much that he suddenly stopped blinking.

Lilian watched her uncle's pupils dilate. His breath caught in his throat; a sound Lilian took for wonder. Uncle Stanley's eyes were glued to the images. His hands formed tight fists by his side, and a small muscle in his jaw started jumping.

When Lilian looked back to the television, the patterns on the screen flashed and whirled faster.

'I see a man, Uncle Stanley!' Lilian squinted at the screen as a head came into focus, with a moustache and dark smudges for eyes. The mouth moved. It was an exciting puzzle, trying to make out what was in the picture. 'Look, the man's talking but no words are coming out.'

She looked round at her uncle to share this exciting moment, but Stanley was frozen to the spot with his eyes wide open. He stood still and unblinking like the shop dummies in the high street windows. Then, her uncle's lower jaw dropped open and a great shudder travelled along his body.

'Th...th..th,' he stuttered. He gripped his arms so tightly, his knuckles turned white.

'What is it, Uncle Stanley?' Lilian gave her uncle's arm a little shake, but it was too stiff to move.

Stanley's eyes rolled back in his head until only the whites were visible. Lines of saliva ran from the side of his mouth as his teeth clacked together.

Lilian whimpered.

'Uncle, what's wrong?' she forced her words out in a shuddering whisper, her lower lip wobbling. 'Is it the television set? Is it hurting you?'

For the second time, she caught hold of Stanley's sleeve and pulled on it, but he continued to convulse. Froth spilled from the corner of his mouth and dripped onto the table.

'TH...TH...TH.' Stanley stammered and drooled as Lilian watched on in horror.

She started to cry.

Stanley stopped making noises. He toppled over like an old chimney she'd once seen demolished, falling heavily on his side. As he fell, he struck the portable heater and knocked it over.

He continued to convulse in silence, lying crossways with his body blocking the door, one arm flung out in front of him.

The heater landed on its side with a loud *clang*, casting an orange cone of brilliant light and heat across the rug.

Stanley fell facing the lamp. His hair illuminated bright orange.

Moments later, the old woollen fibres started to sizzle, along with the hairs on the back of Stanley's outstretched hand. The concentrated force of the glowing tube sent tendrils of smoke rising from the rug, along with the smell of burnt dust and faint aroma of scorched flesh.

Lilian cried out as the heat raised a red blister on the back of Stanley's hand.

'No no no!' she cried and got down on her hands and knees to pull his arm away.

The heat was scorching. Lilian raised an arm to shield her face.

Tremors continued running along Stanley's limbs, forcing jerky movements in his hands and his feet. His teeth clattered together, his jaw relaxing and clamping tight as he suffered in the grip of a never-ending fit.

Lilian took her uncle's arm and hauled on it with all her strength, trying to roll him away from the heater. After several attempts she gave up, panting from the effort. Tears streamed down her stricken face.

Beneath the furious halo of light, the rug sent up a thickening stream of smoke, obscuring the images on the television screen.

Lilian grimaced at the bitter smell of burning wool and cried on her knees.

'Help!' she wailed into her hands. 'Help me!'

Where were the adults to help and take charge of the situation? Richard would know what to do, even though he was only nine. He was clever. Strong. He had a sharp mind, like all the men in the Martin family. Her father said the Martins could work through any problem.

Lilian looked in desperation at the heater and the cable winding away to the wall. She knew that electrical things needed to be plugged into the wall to make them work. Her uncle had warned her not to touch the heater, but touching the cable was different and it wouldn't take much strength to cut out the electricity.

She hopped over Stanley's shaking hand and followed the cable to the electrical outlet. From watching her dad and her uncle, she knew the plug pulled out, so she grabbed the cable beneath the plug and gave it a pull. Nothing happened, so she adjusted her grip on the exposed wires below the plug and pulled hard.

One final pull.

In the distance she heard a flash and felt something seize her insides. A huge fizzing feeling travelled through her, accompanied by painful pins and needles.

The heater's orange light went out.

Then, the world went white.

50

‘When I came round, Lilian was lying next to me.' Victor stares at the burn scars on the back of his hand. 'She pulled on the cable instead of the plug and exposed the wires. She must have touched them and electrocuted herself. Poor thing.'

'She saved your life.' My voice breaks up. I clutch the fabric of my T-shirt over my heart and take long, ragged breaths to hold myself together. 'If it hadn't been for her, the house would have burned down with you in it.'

'She would have died either way,' Victor says stubbornly.

'But not you, Victor.' I bite down my anger. 'You wouldn't have survived if it hadn't been for her.'

Victor sighs and looks down at his knees, blinking rapidly. I can't tell if he's fighting back tears over Lilian or thanking his lucky stars he didn't burn alive that day.

'It doesn't bear thinking about,' he says.

'Yes, it does.' I push him. 'Tell me what happened when you came round.'

Victor closes his eyes and falls silent. I hope to God he doesn't decide to clam up. When he takes up the story once more, I let out a pent-up breath.

'I didn't feel right, so I went away for a while,' Victor continues with the story. 'That's what I call it when I get one of my turns. The second time I woke up I was still lying on the floor. It was dark, past five o'clock. My mind was fuzzy, but I managed to put two and two together. Vera would be up and getting the tea.

Richard would be back from playing football. Jack would be on his way home from work.'

Victor runs a hand over his sweating scalp. His mouth forms shapes but nothing comes out. For a moment he looks like he's about to have another seizure. The way I'm feeling right now, I'll happily leave him to it.

'I panicked.' His glance is sheepish, but if he's looking for sympathy, he's out of luck. All I've got for him is a cold, hard stare.

'I couldn't face telling my own brother what happened.' He clears his throat. 'It was a freak accident. My epilepsy came and went, but I never had a seizure like that. It must have been the flashing lights and patterns on the television that set me off.'

He pats the breast pocket of his shirt, beneath his jumper.

'These pills they've put me on are marvellous. I haven't had any turns like that for over twenty years.'

Much as I want to tell Victor I don't care about his pills, I'm impatient to get to the end of his tawdry tale.

'How did you know for sure Lilian was dead?' I ask. 'Why didn't you try and resuscitate her?'

Victor shakes his head. 'I was out for ages. The room was cold, and so was Lilian's skin.' He hesitates. 'I checked for a pulse. Nothing.'

'So when did you decide a fitting end for Lilian's sacrifice was to bury her under the garage floor?'

'It wasn't like that!' Victor snaps. 'I wasn't acting rationally, but I couldn't go to Jack and tell him the truth. There was no explanation I could give that would sound palatable.'

'Death isn't palatable!' I bite back another retort. 'You should have called an ambulance, the police, Jack, everyone and told the truth!'

'I know that now.' Victor gasps, clutching the armchair with shaking hands. 'But by the time I'd set things in motion, it was too late.'

'Did you do it straightaway?' I ask.

316

'I couldn't stare at her on the floor any longer.' Following his initial reluctance, Victor seems keen to get it out. 'The garage was boarded out with an inspection pit under a trap door.' He lets out a ragged breath. 'It was easy, after a few swigs of whiskey. I put her in the pit, wrapped in the old rug. I had several bags of sand and cement, enough to cover her. I mixed it up with water and poured it into the pit. I knew I'd have to pull up the rest of the boards and concrete the garage floor to finish the job, but that would have to wait.'

He must be telling the truth. Anyone else would try to soften the details, but not Victor. The only thing I don't buy is his assertion that he was confused following his epileptic fit. Nothing about his cold and clinical actions sounds confused.

'What about the blue Austin? Witnesses saw your van that night, but it was never traced.'

'I was lucky there.' A self-congratulatory tone creeps into Victor's voice and I sit on my hands to stop myself smacking him. 'A few people saw me driving the van round Sudbury, but the old lettering on the side, Bradley & Sons, couldn't be traced to me, and Lilian was the only person who knew the van was mine. No-one knew I'd got back from Leeds. As far as work and Jack's family were concerned, I was still away on business.'

He links his fingers on his lap.

'I knew I had to get rid of the Austin, so I drove it back to Leeds that night after the business with Lilian was done and dusted. I booked myself into a small guesthouse under a false name and sold the van at the auction-house the next day. Bought another one, a red Ford, and returned a few days later, once the initial fuss had died down. I'd never been in Sudbury, you see. I'd been up north.

'Jack took to my story straightaway. He never suspected me. And I had a red van, not a blue one. The police visited to find out when I'd last seen Lilian, but they stayed on the doorstep. Got rid of them sharpish once I'd told my version of the story and showed them paperwork from Leeds with the date on. Once they saw my red van on the drive, that was the end of it. Never looked back.'

If I'd been feeling better, I would have reached for Victor's throat; his self-congratulatory manner sickens me. But my head is whirling like a merry-go-round. I stagger to the bed and sit on the edge with my head between my knees to get the blood flowing, battling faintness. Black spots dot my vision, accompanied by a dull buzzing sound. I really don't need this. I close my eyes with my head thumping and a high-pitched noise ringing in my ears.

Victor's revelations have hit me harder than I thought possible.

The warm breeze coming through the open window caresses my face, soothing me. I haul in great breaths and manage to sit up, willing the grey patches at the edge of my vision to go away.

What was I thinking? That this would have a happy ending, and Lilian would thank me for exposing her gruesome, terrible end? How naïve was I, to think Victor would show remorse!

The truth hasn't made it better. Vera, Jack, my dad and Lilian are dead. There is nothing to be gained for anyone, least of all me.

Victor lets out a grunt and manages to swing his bad leg off the footstool. He grips the armrest and starts pushing himself up from the chair, eyes flicking to the red button on the wall.

A decent person would see the state I was in and call a nurse to check me over. But Victor is not a decent person. He'll make something up to get rid of me, anything to paint me in a bad light. I wouldn't put it past him to call me a thief, a scammer or a bare-faced liar, anything to deflect attention away from him.

Blinking back stars, I force myself up and lurch across the room with my centre of gravity all over the place. I stumble into the desk, knocking over the black and white photo of my great-grandparents. A final push gets me past Victor who tries to grab my arm.

I move out of reach, haul open the door and lean against the frame, staring back at this horrible, old man.

'Off to call the police, are you?' Victor bares his teeth in a menacing grin. 'You won't have any luck with that, not this late in the day. They need DNA evidence. I'm just a confused old man. No-one can tie me to the house that day.'

Victor stands on his good leg, no doubt wishing he had his walking stick to smack me with.

'What are you going to do, Alexandra? After everything I've told you, you owe me that much.'

'I owe you nothing.' Rubbing my aching forehead, feeling a cold sweat breaking out, I glare at him. 'I'm not telling you what I'm going to do. You can stay here and sweat.'

I drag myself into the corridor and head for the fire exit at the far end, bracing myself against the wall the whole way.

Beep! Beep! Victor's red button alarm goes off.

Still feeling at sixes and sevens, I reach the fire-exit and throw down the bar, expecting a fire alarm to start blaring out. But the only sounds I hear as I stumble into the light, are birdsong and the distant rumble of machinery.

I want Victor to dread each knock on the door. I want him to wake up each morning not knowing if this is the day his crime will catch up with him. It's a tiny taste of what my dad went through.

Reaching into my jacket pocket, I press the *Stop* button on my micro-cassette recorder.

I've got everything.

· · · ● · ● · · · ·

I emerge from the back of the building and follow a short service path to the main carpark, taking deep breaths of spring air tainted by acrid base-notes of tarmac.

Antony's leaning against his Audi, watching the main reception doors.

319

When I call out his name and wave, he runs to close the gap. His eyes narrow as he pulls me in for a hug.

'You've really pale. What happened in there?' He kisses my forehead. 'I should have come in to get you. I'm sorry.'

'No, I had to do it alone.' I sag into his arms. 'Victor would have clammed up if you'd been there.'

'Did you get it?' he asks.

'I got it. Please, can we get out of here?'

The next moment, I'm sobbing into his T-shirt. The tears are for my dad. For what might have been.

Waves of sadness hit me as Antony guides me back to the Audi. He holds open the passenger door and helps me into my seat, crossing the seatbelt over my shoulder before rushing round to the driver's side.

He fires up the Audi and we drive off.

'I'm glad we're not hanging about.' Antony shoots a glare at the main entrance. 'The receptionist's been out twice to stare at me like I was some drug dealer. I was waiting for blue lights and sirens.'

We retrace our route back through the building site.

'Do you want to tell me?' Antony prompts.

'Give me a moment.'

I sink into the seat, sniffing into a tissue. As my thoughts whirl, I barely notice the sounds of diggers and pneumatic drills. We pass the last of the hoardings, travelling in silence until we rejoin the main road back around Sudbury. I stare blankly at the secondary school and large common we passed on the way here.

After a mile of driving in silence, we reach the slip road leading back to the motorway and Antony puts his foot down. Watching the lines of the motorway whizz past, I start to tell Lilian's story.

'Jeez,' Antony whispers when I reach the end. 'You say Victor was a bachelor who lived alone?'

'Yep. He was more interested in his Baird TV and his garage workshop than his niece.'

'There were a lot of men like that, back in the day,' Antony says. 'I've got three uncles who still live together in a house in Hackney. All confirmed bachelors. They don't know how to relate to women or people in general. Victor sounds like that.'

'I doubt your uncles would do what Victor did to Lilian.'

'No, that takes a special type of monster.' Antony shrugs. 'And it goes to show, family doesn't mean much to some people.'

I put my hand to my mouth, fresh tears blurring my vision.

'Sorry, sorry.' Antony reaches over with his left hand and gives my arm a reassuring squeeze. Come on babe, it's OK. Your dad would be proud of you. You've completed his work with the finding machine.'

'I know. I got what I wanted.' I say with a sniff.

After a long silence, he asks if I want some music.

'No, this is nice. Let's just drive.'

51

— : —

FOUR WEEKS LATER

The doorbell rings just before eight o'clock, Friday morning. I'm in the kitchen, setting the table for a French style breakfast. Croissants are artfully arranged in my favourite rustic bowl. I inhale the rich aromas of arabica coffee brewing in the cafetière and the buttery smell of croissants warm from the oven.

Early morning sun falls through the open back door. The clear skies herald a sizzler of a day. I'm dressed in jeans and T-shirt and have finally ditched my slippers for flip-flops, showing off my fire-red toenails. The run of beautiful mornings and lengthening days have had a miraculous effect on my spirits.

Antony's hired a van for the weekend. Tomorrow, we move to a rented apartment in Digbeth, in Birmingham's creative quarter. We went up and stayed two weekends in a row, the first to get the feel of the place, the second to search for somewhere to live. I would have preferred a house with a garden, but Antony's persuaded me it's better to be in the middle of things until we find our feet.

He's happy for me to stay with him rent-free, but I insist on paying my way just in case things go wrong and he ends up kicking me out for being a freeloader. Despite my inherent pessimism, a little bird tells me that's not going to happen. We're in it for keeps.

'Are you getting that?' Antony yells. He thunders downstairs in a vest-top and shorts with his gym bag slung over one shoulder and flings open the door.

Looking down the hall, I catch a glimpse of DC Longhurst wearing a short-sleeved shirt, no jacket. His impressive frame stands up well to Antony's statuesque buffness. Each time I see the officer, I think of a Viking who's been transported into the 20th century.

My stomach flips in anticipation of the news he's brought with him.

'DC Longhurst,' the officer introduces himself, extending his hand to Antony. 'You must be the Antony who helped find Jason Bevin. Part of Alexandra's *team*.'

Eavesdropping from the kitchen, DC Longhurst's tone is blatantly tongue-in-cheek.

'Yeah, that's me.' Antony shakes his hand. 'Good to meet you.'

Antony looks back at me and raises his hand in farewell, blowing me a quick kiss.

'Running late. I'll see you later.'

Antony knows how pivotal this meeting is and doesn't want to impinge. He wants to go the gym and return to find everything sorted. I'm with him on that one—both of us need to move on.

I hover on the kitchen threshold, as DC Longhurst steps back to let Antony out. Brown packing boxes labelled in thick marker pen are stacked both sides of the hall, making it impractical to go out to greet my guest.

'Come through,' I wave the officer through to the kitchen. 'Mind the boxes.'

Somewhere in that nondescript pile is my mum's old Scholl shoebox, the contents encased in bubble-wrap. I removed the 9-volt battery from the finding machine before I sealed it up for good. Antony suspects the machine emits silent, powerful energy waves that only rats can sense. Without the battery, hopefully it will return to being a nondescript and inexplicably cold lump of out-of-date electronics.

When I labelled the box, I couldn't stop thinking of the final scene in Raiders of the Lost Ark – the bit where the warehouse guy pushes the box containing the Ark into a top-secret storage facility. I'm doing the same thing, only on a smaller scale.

DC Longhurst treads a careful path along the narrow corridor. At the kitchen door, he grasps my hand and we shake like old friends.

'Thanks for coming, DC Longhurst,' I say.

'Please, call me Henry.' He glances at the boxes. 'When are you moving?'

'Tomorrow.'

'Birmingham, wasn't it?' He meets my eyes.

'Yes.' I gesture to the table. 'Coffee?'

'Thanks. Milk and sugar.'

Henry places a stack of paperwork beside his plate. I stop pouring coffee for a second, eyeing the police forms and leaflets.

His amiable expression puts me at ease. We sip our coffee and chat about the good weather and if it will continue. Then, he passes over the leaflets.

'Let's start with the easy stuff. This is everything I could find on careers in the police, volunteering as a Special Constable or for Crimestoppers. There's a leaflet in there about the National Missing Persons Helpline. You were interested in them, weren't you?'

I nod. 'I'll give everything a good read.' I've had ample time to consider my future career while I complete my paintings. I like the idea of combining my art with part-time work. The finer details can come later.

'Next item on the agenda.' Henry pushes a sealed envelope over with a police receipt. 'Sign here and it's yours. The timing is fortuitous, as it turns out. Kind of like a going-away present.'

I write my signature and open the envelope. Inside, is a bankers draft for £10,000. The reward for finding Jason Bevin.

'Wow!' I exclaim with immoderate enthusiasm. 'He paid!'

'Mr Bevin asked me to apologise for taking so long to pay up. He's had a lot on his mind,' Henry says. 'He's eternally grateful for the trouble you went to, finding Jason.'

'It was nothing,' I wave my hand, dismissing the hurdles Antony and I had to leap over to make it happen. 'How is Jason doing?'

Henry reclines back in his chair, sunlight falling in a band across his chest.

'We talked for about five minutes before he started dozing off. He spends a lot of time sleeping, due to his medication. And of course, he's going through withdrawal. There's a long way to go, but Jason's on the right track. He's lucid for the most part, although he did start rambling on about some conspiracy theory until I changed tack.'

I remember sitting through Jason's crazy rants about Y2K and Deep State in his dingy apartment. Yet, as soon as I tasked him with researching the finding machine, it was like a switch flipped. He blew me away with his ability.

'Once he's sorted, maybe he can go back to college,' I say. I like to think Jason's got a good future ahead of him.

'Mr Bevin mentioned the possibility he could go back in September to study Computer Science.' Henry says.

'And once Jason's done a degree, he can run the world!' I add. 'It's unbelievable, the things he can do with computers.'

'It's interesting you say that.' Henry finishes his coffee. 'Because I don't know anyone like *you* when it comes to finding people. I can see a career in that, if you'd care to follow it up.'

I give an emphatic shake of the head, my cheeks burning. 'Let's just say I was lucky before. I'm not going to push it.'

Henry levels me with an icy blue stare.

'I think I deserve *some* kind of explanation.' He presses his lips together. 'You're not much cop at lying.'

'I'm trying to get better at it.'

He ignores my attempt at a joke. 'So, are you going to tell me how you found him, or what? I knew it wasn't a fluke after you found the puppies. My guess is you work with a team of ex-police and military who have access to our systems. Illegal, by the way. Or you work for MI5.'

'As if!' I give a short laugh. 'I wish it was exciting as that, but it was Mr Bevin who tipped me off.' I give him the spiel. 'He gave me the address of one of Jason's mates — a flat in Leather Lane. The police had already tried the address but got no response, so Antony and I went up to London to see for ourselves. Lucky us. Jason answered the door.'

Little creases appear between Henry's brows as he pours himself more coffee and offers the cafetière to me. I put my hand out to refuse – I'm wired enough under his obvious suspicion without more caffeine.

'There's just one small problem with your story.' Henry tears off the end of a croissant, takes his time eating it. 'Mr Bevin said you gave him Jason's address *without* any input from him.'

'He must be confused.' I cradle my face in my hands. My excuses have dried up. 'Look, can we just agree I was lucky? Really lucky? The fact is, finding Jason was one of the best days of my life. I did something good. Made a difference.' I pick at my croissant, breaking flakes of pastry onto the plate. 'That's what made me consider joining the police.'

'Yeah, but the difference between us in the Hertfordshire Constabulary and you, is we don't find people magically.' Henry leans his elbows on the table and gives me an intimidating stare. 'We've got a pool going at the station. Most of the officers think you're using an insider. Whereas I quite like the idea of magic.'

'You're right. It was magic,' I say. 'I used a magical finding machine.'

The way Henry links his hands and scrutinises me across the table gives me flashbacks to the interview room at Hertford police station.

'Why won't you tell me the truth?'

The intensity of his gaze makes me flush.

'That is the truth!'

'What if I were to suggest you have a method of finding people that no-one else has. Would that be right?'

'Yes,' I finally concede.

Henry demolishes the rest of his croissant. 'So, theoretically, I could ring you regarding any of our ongoing cases involving missing individuals?'

'In theory,' I say cautiously. 'But I'm not saying I'll be able to help you.' I don't particularly want to use the finding machine again.

His eyes glint. 'No harm in asking, right?'

'No, I suppose not.'

Henry checks his watch. He sits back with his arms folded, the humour fading from his expression.

'We'd better get to the main reason for my visit.' He hesitates. 'I wasn't able to tell you anything before.'

'I understand.' My hands shake round my coffee mug. I passed the tape of Victor's confession to Henry a month ago. I was interviewed by investigating officers three times. The overwhelming sense of relief I felt at passing the burden on is still with me. It was the right decision.

'We found Lilian,' Henry says simply. 'We've got her.'

I press my lips together and blink my tears away. I'm determined not to cry. I've cried enough.

'We've done our best to be discreet, but I'd steer clear of the news for a while.' Henry pauses. 'It's probably best you're moving. You don't want the press doorstepping you. We'll be in touch if we need anything else.' He pauses. 'Are you all right, Alex?'

'Yes.' I force a nod and tiny smile. I've been avoiding the news headlines and broadsheets recently, dreading seeing the case come up. It's one to capture the public imagination, and I've had a taste of what happens when you end up in the paper. I wouldn't get any peace if I stayed.

'Do you know how she died?' I ask.

'The coroner's report was inconclusive, due to the deterioration of Lilian's body.' Henry shakes his head. 'If Lilian was electrocuted, it could have caused cardiac failure. But there was no way to confirm it ~~with the state she was in~~. I suspect it'll be an open verdict.'

'Do you know if she suffered?'

'I think it would have been quick,' Henry says. 'She wouldn't have known anything.'

My gaze locks with Henry. 'This open verdict. Does it mean Victor's going to get away with it?'

'Not at all. The circumstances of Lilian's death are suspicious, and preventing lawful burial is a crime with an unlimited sentence attached to it.'

'You mean, Victor could go to prison for the rest of his life?'

'In theory, but Victor won't be going to prison.' Henry sighs. 'He suffered a massive stroke a few days after his arrest, Alexandra. He's in intensive care, and his prognosis is poor. I'm sorry.'

I can't work out if he's sorry Victor will escape jail, or if he's simply being polite.

The news means little to me. I'm past caring about Victor. If he dies, the state can bury him. He won't be missed. His death marks the end of the whole, sorry saga, that's all.

The only thing that matters is Lilian.

'I'll keep you updated on everything, of course.' DC Longhurst gathers his paperwork and gets up.

For a moment I sit, staring towards the garden, gathering my thoughts.

'Are you sure you're all right?' Henry puts a hand on my shoulder. 'Can I get you anything?'

I put my hand on his. 'I'm fine. Just coming to terms with the fact it's over.' I force a smile, and remember something.

'This is for you.' I slide an envelope across the table.

Henry opens the flap and pulls out a glossy card.

'You are cordially invited to the launch event of 'Hertfordshire Landscapes, the Old and the New,' by Alex Martin,' he reads aloud, smiling warmly. 'Thank you! I would be honoured to attend.'

He tucks the invitation carefully into his pocket.

'You deserve every success.'

'The invitation is to say thank you,' I explain. 'For being so understanding.' And accepting what I said, even though you didn't believe a word of it. — *tol*

52

— • —

I lean into Antony under the ancient oak trees of St. Gregory's churchyard, as Reverend Cheryl prays over the Martin family grave.

'We commend Lilian to the eternal care of God, as we meet in the faith that death is not the end, and may be faced without fear, bitterness or guilt.'

All around, a summer breeze rustles the leaves. Cheryl is in full regalia for the occasion, wearing a white alb with a bright orange stole draped around her neck. Her auburn hair and purple-rimmed glasses lend a modern twist to the centuries-old ceremony she's conducting within St Gregory's ancient churchyard.

My worry that I would fall to pieces during the ceremony has proven unfounded, and this is down to The Rev. Instead of treating it as a downbeat or sombre occasion, Cheryl conducts the service with a sparkle in her eyes and a warm smile on her lips. She's celebrating a life.

It feels right and just.

Antony puts an arm around me and gives me a squeeze, but I don't feel sad. Cheryl's confident, empathic delivery is uplifting. As she comes to the end of her concluding prayer, as though she has a hotline to a greater power in the sky, the sun bursts through the fluffy clouds and casts a golden band of light across the crisp, new engraving on the granite headstone, underneath those for Dad, Jack and Vera.

IN LOVING MEMORY
Lilian Anne Martin 1923-1928. 5 years.
Taken Away Far Too Soon.
'I once was lost but now am found.' John Newton

Lilian has been found. She lives on in my heart, the same as Dad.

For a fleeting moment, I regret the fact Mum isn't here. I did invite her, but she made some excuse about the plane times being wrong. She told me she would go to Knock instead, and say the rosary in Lillian's memory. I guess she's still coming to terms with everything, and that's fine by me. It's up to Mum to make the first move. I've got enough to be getting on with.

The Rev sprinkles holy water onto the gravestone. 'Comfort all who loved Lilian on earth, through Jesus Christ our Lord. Amen.'

'Amen,' I repeat automatically. Antony remains silent, a fish out of water where religion is concerned. I told him it was an informal ceremony and not to worry about it, yet he insisted on wearing his Armani suit and tie for the short service, despite the fact I'm in jeans and a T-shirt. I bet he's stifling under that collar.

'You all right?' he mouths the words when I give him a swift smile, his focus wholly on me.

I nod and squeeze his hand before returning my attention to the Martin family headstone. Every time I re-read the inscription I chose so carefully, something inside me releases. At long last, Lilian is back with her family. She is remembered, respected.

Before the service started, I took Antony to visit Margaret. She now lies alongside her husband, Bernard. Their headstone dates back to the 1980s - square and traditional. Although Margaret knew her time was coming, and wanted to be together with Bernard, I miss her terribly. She was a truly remarkable lady and Vera's greatest friend.

As for Victor, DC Longhurst called me with the news he died last week. I thanked him and quickly changed the subject. Some things are not worth dwelling on. Not when there are so many others worth celebrating.

The cost of exhuming Lilian was high, with the press furore and police interviews, but it was worth it. Others have labelled her a tragic victim, but I will never see her that way.

Whenever I think of Lilian she's smiling, like in the photo taken down by the river. I picture her as a happy, inquisitive girl who liked skipping home from school holding her mother's hand, looking forward to a slice of cake and cocoa.

She is not the sum of her mortal remains. The finding machine dutifully pointed to her final location, but Lilian's spirit was no longer there.

It's time to let her go.

Cheryl raises her hands over the granite stone and closes her eyes.

'Neither death, nor life, nor things present, nor things to come, nor powers, nor height, nor depth, nor anything else in all creation, will be able to separate us from the love of God.'

The Reverend closes her prayer book and spends a moment in silent contemplation.

'Lilian is in good hands,' she tells us. 'It will be a pleasure to pray for her, and I will make sure to visit her often. She's not just part of your family, she's part of our church family, too.'

I nod my thanks, wiping back a last rogue tear, and tell myself to stop crying.

'Good luck to both of you in Birmingham.'

'Cheers,' says Antony, one hand going to undo the top button and loosen his tie. He casts a glance at me, kisses the top of my head. 'I'll see you back at the car. Take your time.'

He leaves with a wave to Cheryl, stripping off his jacket and throwing it across his shoulder as he crosses the grass.

Cheryl and I walk together back to the church through shifting, dappled sunlight. Birdsong rings out as we travel in companiable silence. An overwhelming sensation of well-being settles on me.

'I can't thank you enough,' I say. Cheryl helped me with every aspect of today, from arranging the inscription on the gravestone to choosing suitable prayers for the service.

'It was my pleasure.' The Rev tilts her head to one side. 'I remember when we first met, you were at sixes and sevens. You seem happier, now. At peace, and in love.'

'Everything's better,' I admit with a smile. 'Everything.'

'If you don't mind me asking, I have a question. It's been on my mind since we last spoke.'

'Ask away,' I prompt.

'When we met in this very spot back in the spring, you told me about a machine your dad left you. You were worried that it had strange powers and abilities. Have you managed to get to the bottom of that?'

I nod, thrust my hands into my pockets, feeling a familiar trickle of fear mingled with excitement.

'That's all sorted. I've decided to put my dad's machine away for good. No more adventures for me.'

I doubt I'll use the finding machine again. It's tucked inside a box under three layers of bubble-wrap, bound up in sticky-tape with sheets of kitchen foil on top of that, at Antony's insistence. Getting the machine out and operational again isn't going to be a casual decision.

I look up at the trees, sunlight on my face.

'I'm here if you need to talk about it, or anything else for that matter,' the Rev says in parting. 'But something tells me you don't need my help. You're going to be just fine, Alexandra.'

Cheryl heads back to the church. The sun is warm on my back.

The Rev is right. I'm going to be fine.

Thank you for reading! Please leave a review - it's so helpful for other readers. To keep in the loop about my latest projects, exclusive content, sneak peeks and other random cool stuff, sign up for my newsletter on my website and receive a FREE book. Come find me at: https://lucylyonswrites.com

ACKNOWLEDGEMENTS

A book is not written alone. It is a collaborative effort involving many generous people, who I do not have space to list on one page. Thank you to my husband, Carl, and all those who read a disjointed first draft and praised it enough to make me think I had something. Thank you to the ladies and gents at Any1CanRun who read and supported me (often while running!) For technical support on GPS, thank you Larry. Thanks goes to my international critiquers at Scribophile, who took a rough and ready book and helped turn it into a polished, finished novel. Special mention must go to Robert Parker, Sonny Kohet and Max Snowden. Lastly, thank you Henry Longhurst and Alex Martin for having enough belief in me to let me borrow your names (you can have them back now!) If I have missed anyone out, forgive me. This book is, in part, yours.

Printed in Great Britain
by Amazon

18300092R00195